KILL DECISION

ALSO BY DANIEL SUAREZ

Daemon

Freedom™

KILL DECISION

Daniel Suarez

DUTTON

DUTTON
Published by Penguin Group (USA) Inc.
375 Hudson Street, New York, New York 10014, U.S.A.
Penguin Group (Canada), 90 Eglinton Avenue East, Suite 700, Toronto, Ontario M4P 2Y3, Canada (a division of Pearson Penguin Canada Inc.); Penguin Books Ltd, 80 Strand, London WC2R 0RL, England; Penguin Ireland, 25 St Stephen's Green, Dublin 2, Ireland (a division of Penguin Books Ltd); Penguin Group (Australia), 250 Camberwell Road, Camberwell, Victoria 3124, Australia (a division of Pearson Australia Group Pty Ltd); Penguin Books India Pvt Ltd, 11 Community Centre, Panchsheel Park, New Delhi—110 017, India; Penguin Group (NZ), 67 Apollo Drive, Rosedale, Auckland 0632, New Zealand (a division of Pearson New Zealand Ltd); Penguin Books (South Africa) (Pty) Ltd, 24 Sturdee Avenue, Rosebank, Johannesburg 2196, South Africa

Penguin Books Ltd, Registered Offices: 80 Strand, London WC2R 0RL, England

Published by Dutton, a member of Penguin Group (USA) Inc.

First printing, July 2012
10 9 8 7 6 5 4 3 2 1

Ⓐ REGISTERED TRADEMARK—MARCA REGISTRADA

LIBRARY OF CONGRESS CATALOGING-IN-PUBLICATION DATA
Suarez, Daniel, 1964–
  Kill decision / Daniel Suarez.
    p. cm.
  ISBN 978-0-525-95261-9 (hardcover)
  1. United States. Army. Special Forces—Fiction. 2. Women scientists—Fiction. 3. Drone aircraft—Fiction. 4. Artificial intelligence—Fiction. I. Title.
  PS3619.U327K55 2012
  813'.6—dc23
  2011052061

Printed in the United States of America
Set in Electra LT Std
Designed by Eve L. Kirch

PUBLISHER'S NOTE
This book is a work of fiction. Names, characters, places, and incidents either are the product of the author's imagination or are used fictitiously, and any resemblance to actual persons, living or dead, business establishments, events, or locales is entirely coincidental.

- The First Truth -
Humans are more important than hardware.

KILL DECISION

CHAPTER 1

Boomerang

From eight thousand feet the rescue workers looked like agitated ants as they scurried around the wreckage of a car bomb. An MQ-1B Predator drone zoomed its cameras in for a close-up. Debris and body parts littered a marketplace. Scorched dirt slick with blood filled the frame. The dying and wounded groped silently for help.

The techs called it "Death TV"—the live video feed from America's fleet of unmanned Predator, Global Hawk, and Reaper drones. The images poured in via satellite onto ten large HD screens suspended at intervals from the rafters of the U.S. Air Force's dimly lit cubicle farm in Hampton, Virginia. Officially known as Distributed Common Ground System-1, it was half a world away from the daytime on most of those screens. The local time was two A.M.

Monitoring the feeds and clattering at keyboards in response to what they saw were scores of young airmen first class arrayed in groups of six before banks of flat-panel computer monitors, watched over by technical sergeants pacing behind them. And watched in turn by their officers, like pit bosses and floor managers in some macabre casino.

At his workstation in the semidarkness, twenty-six-year-old First Lieutenant Anthony Jordan glanced up occasionally to gauge the mood of the world. From the look of things it was shaping up to be a pretty typical day: scattered violence.

Between glances Jordan typed chat messages to an army civil affairs team at the U.S. embassy in Baghdad's Green Zone, just a few miles down the road from the car bomb blast on-screen. He simultaneously monitored chat threads from two other operations in theater and satellite radio chatter in his headset, all while his desk phone lit up at intervals. He sensed a presence behind him, and a sheet of paper slid into view from his left. He spoke without looking up. "Lazzo, goddammit, IM me. You're messing with my work flow."

Technical Sergeant Albert Lazzo leaned in from the right, his jowls hanging to the side like a plumb line. "Urgent, sir."

"Well . . ." Jordan gestured up to the carnage on the big screen above them. "There's your benchmark. Start talking."

Lazzo smacked the sheet of paper. "AWACS is tracking a gopher south of Karbala. They want us to get eyes on."

Jordan's fingers clattered over his keyboard. "Send the bogey dope, and I'll see what I can do."

"It's the Day of Ashura, Lieutenant."

"Is that supposed to mean something to me?"

Lazzo sighed the sigh of the knowledgeable underling. "A million Shiite pilgrims on foot commemorating the martyrdom of Husayn ibn Ali, the grandson of Muhammad, at the Battle of Karbala. The pilgrimage has been attacked by Sunni militants in the past, and we've got an unidentified aircraft inbound."

"Ah . . . right . . ." Jordan frowned as he finished typing a reply to a military intelligence unit. "What are we looking at?"

"First showed up three clicks west of Al Hiyadha. Altitude two zero, speed two hundred knots. Heading three-five-zero." Lazzo studied the printout. "A single-engine plane, maybe. Smugglers or local VIPs. But then again . . ."

The civil affairs folks had briefed Jordan on the sensitivities of his sector. He recalled that the shrines of Imam Husayn and Al Abbas at Karbala were among the holiest sites to the Shia Islamic faith—that is, to about a quarter billion people.

Lazzo offered the printed report again. "According to Geeks, you've got the closest tail, sir."

"Okay, I got it. I got it." Jordan grabbed the printout and clicked on one of the three LCD monitors on his desk. He brought up GCCS, the Global Command and Control System that tracked the real-time location of all friendly forces in the field.

He scrolled the map view of his sector and noted the tail number of his Predator drone nearest the radar contact. He then clicked through another screen to establish an encrypted satellite radio link to the drone operators in Nevada. "Kodar Tree, Kodar Tree. We are tracking a gopher, slow and in the weeds. I need tail one-zero-seven to come off current target and move south. Check your feed. MCR. Out." He typed the AWACS info and destination MGRS coordinates into a chat window directed to the pilot's handle. He waited several moments.

"Copy that, MCR. Proceeding to grid tree-eight, sierra, mike, bravo, one-two-tree-niner-zero-eight-zero-eight."

Jordan and Lazzo looked up at the large screen above them as the image switched from the car bombing to another scene entirely—a tan, flat horizon. It was eight hours later in Iraq, midmorning, and the horizon leaned right as tail one-zero-seven yawed over the brown, ancient city of Karbala at an altitude of nine thousand feet. At that height the drone would be inaudible and all but invisible to casual observers on the ground.

Each Predator system consisted of a pilot, his sensor operator, and a set of four separate Predator drones that they controlled from inside an air-conditioned military shipping container—in this case at Creech Air Force Base, near Las Vegas, Nevada. They pulled twelve-hour shifts there in what were called "reachback" operations, and then went home for breakfast in the suburbs. Jordan sometimes suffered the same disorienting effects the Predator teams reported from remote operations. It made it hard to keep up a battle rhythm when you found yourself in a convenience store buying a Slurpee an hour after ordering the deaths of five insurgents half a world away. It was easy to forget this was all very real somewhere and not just a super-high-res game. There was counseling for that, but he didn't think it was a good career move to take advantage of it.

Jordan continued to monitor the contents of several screens at once. "SO, *we've got forty degrees more of heading.*"

"*Sensor copies.*"

A voice from higher up the command chain suddenly broke in on the radio. "*Kodar Tree, this is Sentinel. Request weapons load-out.*"

Others were listening in, then. It underscored to Jordan the sensitivities of operations above the masses of Shia pilgrims moving through Karbala. U.S. combat forces had officially left the country—a pronouncement that seriously pissed off the U.S. troops who were still there. These drone flights were overhead to look for trouble and pass intelligence to the Iraqi army. And Lazzo was right; the Ashura festivities had been attacked by militant Sunnis before.

"*Sentinel, we are Winchester.*"

Unarmed. This close to the shrines, he damned well better be Winchester.

"*Kodar Tree, you may proceed. Sentinel out.*"

"*Copy that, Sentinel. MCR, we are on-station, heading one-seven-eight. Pilot out.*"

They watched for several moments as the optics package zoomed in along Route 9, the wide, gritty boulevard stretching cracked, sun-blasted, and arrow-straight south through the city. Lined with run-down housing blocks, the road was packed with tens of thousands of pilgrims moving on foot. Jordan whistled. "That's quite a crowd." He keyed his mic. "Pilot, keep tracking south, and you should intercept that gopher momentarily."

"*Wilco.*"

"There." Sergeant Lazzo pointed up at the screen with a pocket laser pointer, but it was already obvious to them all.

"*MCR, we've got a visual on that gopher. It is a cyclops—repeat, cyclops—heading tree-fife-eight. Probably has a bent parrot.*"

Jordan saw the unmistakable outline of an American drone as it motored north at barely two thousand feet altitude. *What the hell?* "Kodar Tree, copy that cyclops. Designate cyclops Target One. Shadow Target One, and get me its tail number."

Lazzo raised his eyebrows.

"*Pilot copies.*"

"*Sensor copies.*"

Lazzo shrugged. "One of our drones with a malfunctioning transponder, then."

Jordan studied the screen. "But how the hell did it get there? And why isn't there a record in Blue Force Tracker? I mean, that's a Reaper." Jordan stared at the high-def video of a gray American MQ-9 Reaper drone, still tracking north above the highway. Visually similar to the smaller propeller-driven MQ-1 Predator, the Reaper was half again as large, and capable of carrying far more weaponry. This one was flying lower than any drone—especially a Reaper—should. Was it having engine trouble?

"*MCR, Target One has stars-and-bars, but no visible tail number. Repeat, no visible tail number.*"

"Copy that, Kodar Tree." Jordan changed radio channels. "Sentinel, MCR, heads up. We have a visual on MQ-9 cyclops with bent parrot and no visible tail number over Karbala, slow and in the weeds, heading tree-fife-fife. No record of this flight. Please advise."

Radio and instant message chatter swelled in response, and Jordan muttered to Lazzo as he dialed an extension on his phone. "I thought CIA had stopped this cowboy shit."

Lazzo was still squinting at the screen. "But AWACS would have checked with JSOC before calling us."

Jordan held a finger to his headset switch, waiting for an answer. "Well, it's somebody's goddamned drone, and it couldn't just wander into the neighborhood without anyone knowing about it."

"That thing's loaded for bear."

As the optics zoomed in on the Reaper, Jordan could see the hardpoints on the wings bearing a full complement of fourteen AGM Hellfire missiles. In the background below it, thousands of black- and white-robed pilgrims pointed up as the shadow of its wings passed over them.

"This is one hell of a Charlie Foxtrot." He could see pilgrims in the crowd filming the drone with video cameras and cell phones. "You watch, that'll show up on Al Jazeera later."

Just then a tall, stern-looking air force colonel wearing ABUs marched into Jordan's workspace. "What the hell's going on, Lieutenant?"

Jordan stood and saluted along with Sergeant Lazzo. "Colonel, sir. Unidentified Reaper above Karbala. No IFF. No tail number. We're still trying to ID it."

The colonel pointed at Lazzo. "Get CIA on the line, and find out why the hell I didn't know about this." He then gazed up at the screen as several other techs were now doing. "Christ on a cracker, this breaks half a dozen airspace restrictions, and I'm not about to take the heat for it. Where is it now?"

"Roughly three clicks south of the Imam Husayn and Al Abbas shrines."

"How did it get this far undetected?"

"No idea, sir. AWACS only alerted us a few minutes ago."

"Find out who's controlling that drone."

Jordan grabbed a phone and glanced at Lazzo, who simply shrugged in confusion as he manned a phone as well.

As the colonel and other nearby airmen watched the screen, the view rotated. Their Predator was falling behind the faster, more powerful unidentified Reaper drone. Up ahead, they could see the golden domes of the twin shrines gleaming in the sunlight. Hundreds of thousands of pilgrims filled the open squares around them. The Reaper was silhouetted, coming in low, like a spiked hornet against the city.

The Predator pilot's voice came over the intercom. "MCR, *heads up. Target One appears engaged offensive. It's sparkling the shrine. Repeat, cyclops is sparkling the shrine.*"

Now everyone was standing up, gazing at the overhead screen. Jordan lowered his phone receiver. "Which shrine is it lasing?"

"It could be prepping for a missile launch." The colonel turned on Jordan and Lazzo. "Give me that goddamned phone!"

Lazzo shook his head. "CIA says it's not their drone, Colonel."

"Bullshit!"

Just then a Hellfire missile burst forth from the left wing of the Reaper in a puff of smoke, screaming skyward in an arc. A whole section of DCGS-1 staff gasped as the missile continued its trajectory, rising, and then suddenly arced straight down above the Imam Husayn shrine. By then two more missiles had launched and were beginning their upward arcs as well.

"MCR, *heads up. Ripple!*"

Lazzo called it out. "We've got multiple missile launches."

Jordan was stunned by the magnitude of what he was watching. As his eyes went wide, the Predator's optics focused in on the packed crowd in the square. The first missile impacted, spreading a visible shock wave through the air—quickly followed by a sustained fireball that in turn sent an even more powerful shock wave through the crowd—disintegrating them. Pieces of human beings flew in all directions.

"Lieutenant!" The colonel turned to Jordan. "New picture. Shoot that drone down! Take it down!"

Jordan came back to his senses and immediately got AWACS on the line. "Bandsaw-one-six. Bandsaw-one-six Sprint! Sprint! Sprint!"

As he spoke, he could see the remaining missiles roaring forward from the hard-points on the Reaper wings, raining down in a broad pattern among the pilgrims.

The colonel and most of the staff stared in disbelief. They had seen horrible sights on "Death TV" before, but this one was off the chart.

Lazzo stared at the explosions silently blasting holes into the dense crowds. "The bastards are using thermobarics. How could they just . . ." His voice trailed off as several technicians around him covered their mouths in horror.

The Predator's optics played across the huge crowds roiling like ocean waves as they fled from the gore in the square between shrines, trampling each other in terror. Some of the DCGS staff actually howled in outrage.

"MCR, *recommend Target One be destroyed immediately.*"

The colonel looked truly livid—his face red, his eyes blazing.

"Sir, we have Falcons inbound. ETA three minutes."

"Well, the damage is goddamn done already, son! I want that drone tracked, and I want to know who's operating it! Get me some goddamned ELINT, and find out where it's being controlled from."

As the smoke and flames rose above the city, they could see the Reaper banking away and descending even farther—having let loose every missile it had.

"MCR, *Target One turning to new heading . . . two-one.*"

"Kodar Tree, MCR copies."

They could now see the silent flash of small-arms fire from the crowds below. Their vantage point was still over a mile above the mystery Reaper—most likely their own Predator was still unseen by the crowd below, but the Reaper was in full view of hundreds of thousands of people.

"MCR, *I'm seeing SAF from the ground. Looks like IA is having a go.*"

Suddenly, above the narrow streets of Karbala's old quarter, the Reaper exploded—blasting into fiery pieces that spun downward across a dozen city blocks, trailing streamers of smoke into the narrow-alley neighborhoods around the shrines.

The colonel turned to face Jordan. "What the hell just happened?"

Jordan shook his head. "It wasn't us, Colonel. The F-16s are still inbound."

The colonel kicked a chair, sending it spinning away. "Goddammit!" He turned quickly. "Call off the jets. The last thing we need is more armed aircraft over this disaster."

Jordan called off the strike and hung up the phone. He then gazed up at the screen like everyone else in the place—staring in mute shock at the magnitude of the carnage.

The Predator's optics panned across the thousands of wounded and dead, pilgrims in bloody clothing, Iraqi soldiers rushing forward to carry away wounded. People weeping and tearing at their clothes and hair as dead or dying relatives were pulled from their arms.

Jordan sat back down. Numb. "There'll be hell to pay for this. . . ."

Henry Clarke awoke facedown and still dressed in a black Castangia pinstripe suit. Splayed diagonally across his bed, he groped for a phone as it chimed somewhere in the soft glow of LED charging lights. "Dammit, where the . . ." He finally saw his cell on the nightstand, its front panel glowing through a cocktail napkin with a cell number and lipstick smeared across it. He swatted away the napkin and grabbed the handset. "Yeah?"

A pause.

He sat up and flicked on the nightstand lamp. "Shit. I am. Yeah. Yes." He looked around. "Now?" He glanced at his watch, then reluctantly nodded. "All right. Fine. I'll meet you downstairs."

Two minutes later Clarke, wearing jeans and an untucked white button-down shirt, opened his red townhome door in bare feet to reveal an austere, well-dressed woman in her fifties coming up his stone steps. A black Lincoln Town Car idled at the curb outside—double-parked on his Georgetown street. The driver and another suited man watched her go inside. She waved them off, then muttered to Clarke, "Get inside before you catch cold, Henry."

She entered the foyer in a commanding fashion as Clarke closed the door and followed in her wake. "It's three in the morning, Marta. Couldn't this have waited a few hours?"

"You smell like gin." She sniffed. "And perfume. Are we alone?"

"Just the staff. With your nose I'm surprised you can't smell them too."

She dismissed his jibe with a wave and kept walking, examining the high plaster ceilings, the Federalist furniture, carved marble mantel, and original art. "I'd forgotten about this place. A bit traditional for a man your age."

He was tucking in his shirt. "It's been in my family a long time. Reminds me of my mother."

"I wouldn't have figured you for the sentimental type. Although I'm sure this place works wonders on K Street girls." She had already entered his study and grabbed the remote. She appeared to know the layout of the place.

"How bad is it?" He stood in the doorway.

She powered on his plasma TV, flipping through satellite channels. She came first to BBC One. Scenes of Middle East horror filled the screen. Streets running with blood as viewed from the air. The chyron at the bottom of the screen proclaimed, "*U.S. drone attack on Shia shrine kills thousands; thousands more injured."* The female anchor weighed in: *". . . official statement, but condemnations of the attack have come swiftly from China, Russia, and heads of state throughout the Muslim world."*

The live image switched to recorded amateur video showing a low-flying Reaper drone launching missiles against the dense crowds around the shrines. The U.S. stars-and-bars insignia was clearly visible on the fuselage.

"The incident took place in full view of tens of thousands of pilgrims moving on foot through the Iraqi city of Karbala. Although Pentagon officials deny U.S. involvement, pieces of the wreckage carried away by locals bear U. S. markings and serial numbers. Many view this attack as an act of American revenge for a deadly series of terror bombings in the continental United States—including one that claimed the life of Virginia senator Aaron Arkin and six staffers eight weeks ago. One Middle Eastern diplomat described today's events as 'a blind giant lashing out against unseen attackers.'"

"Holy . . . what the hell happened?"

"Have you read *Black Swan* yet?"

"I saw the movie."

She cast a dark look at him.

"What?" He shrugged. "It's not the first time the U.S. has bombed the wrong people, Marta. This is a big mistake, but it'll blow over."

"No. This time is different. . . ." She clicked the remote to surf news channels, from Al Jazeera to Russian English-language television, then to American cable news. Coverage of the attack was everywhere. Shots of injured being rushed to hospitals in Red Crescent vans. Screaming women and children. Most of America had not yet woken up to its latest public relations disaster. "U.S. Reaper Drone Massacres Shiite Pilgrims" and more crassly: "The Empire Strikes Back."

One looped video sequence showed drone wreckage raining down in fiery pieces over the city, the reporter in midsentence: *". . . above the city immediately afterward by an enraged Iraqi military."*

She nodded to herself. "Destroyed, of course. Pieces paraded by civilians on TV. The chance of getting that wreckage back: slim to none."

He sighed. "It's a terrible accident, but we'll get past it."

She muted the television. "It wasn't an accident. This was an attack on the United States."

Clarke frowned in confusion.

"It wasn't our drone, Henry."

He sank into a wing chair. "What do you mean it wasn't ours? Who else has Reaper drones? Britain?"

"I mean it wasn't a friendly Reaper drone." She narrowed her eyes at the screen. "I'd be curious to know how they got it past our radar. I suppose they could have launched it from a nearby desert road. Gorgon Stare would have been useful here. That's a funding angle we should pursue in committee. Make a note of that."

Clarke glanced around for a pad of paper but almost immediately gave up and frowned at her. "You're saying someone copied a Reaper drone?"

"It would hardly be necessary to 'copy' one. Nearly half of them have been lost in action—crashed or shot down. Not all of them recovered. Parts and pieces moving through the black markets of Central Asia."

"Seriously?"

"Technology spreads, Henry. That's what it does. That's why constant progress is necessary. Why we must always stay one step ahead. This is a teaching moment for those willing to learn."

He nodded toward the news, which now panned across screaming, injured children in a hospital ward. "This could be very bad for Brand America."

"Yes, and that's why it's critical we encourage these older drones to proliferate. Otherwise whenever there's a drone strike—like this—the world will blame the United States. That must change."

He watched the muted television for a moment—the looped replay of the mystery drone launching its missiles. "Do you think this attack is related to the terror bombings here in the States?"

She ignored the question and instead presented one of her own. "How does this disaster affect our clients?"

Clarke grimaced. "It's not good. It'll damage public perception of unmanned aircraft."

"Unless we successfully deflect responsibility."

"With powerful visuals like this circulating, that'll be a tough sell."

"You leave that to me. Just make sure your people are ready to work their mimetic magic."

They both stared at images of tiny, shroud-wrapped bodies being carried through an angry crowd.

CHAPTER 2

Warning Order

A black MH-47 Chinook helicopter raced in darkness along the slopes of a steep valley lined by snowcapped mountains. Pale moonlight reflected off the peaks and silhouetted the large chopper momentarily before it nosed steeply into blackness, descending rapidly in a combat landing. As it continued its erratic maneuvers, blinding green-white flares spat out of its tail every few seconds. Soon the pilot pulled the nose of the chopper up, bringing it down toward a blacked-out forward operating base studded with satellite dishes and radio antennas. The chopper rotated in a cloud of dust, then deftly touched down on a gravel landing zone.

As the turbine engines wound down, the rear ramp descended, and a dozen heavily armed U.S. Army Special Forces soldiers in black body armor and face masks emerged, pulling along a hooded prisoner wearing a mud-spattered *shalwar kameez* and *chapan*—his hands secured behind his back with PlastiCuffs.

One of the soldiers shouted, *"Paatsezhey!"* and shoved the prisoner along.

The group moved swiftly past concentric rings of HESCO bastions toward the heart of the camp, where a forest of antenna masts stood next to prefab structures. As they passed, indigenous workers in green smocks looked up from their duties building new fortifications, leaning on their shovels to steal a glance at the knot of soldiers.

The soldiers pushed their prisoner silently past armed sentries into an inner ring of defenses, toward an unmarked building secured with razor wire fencing. A sentry opened the doors to admit them into a vestibule, where still more sentries opened an interior door. No one spoke or saluted as the group moved swiftly through.

In a moment the door shut behind them, and they stood in a Spartan room lined with equipment shelving, rows of radios in charging stations, and weapons in wall racks. One of the soldiers drew a knife and cut the PlastiCuffs from their prisoner's wrists, while another soldier pulled the black hood from the man's head.

The prisoner calmly oriented himself as he rubbed his wrists. His long black beard and mustache with close-cropped hair lent him a distinctly Talibanesque air, which his lean frame and weathered skin only accentuated. He stared straight ahead with steel blue eyes.

The lead soldier nodded to him. "Welcome back, Odin."

The bearded man answered in perfect Midwestern English, "Good to be back, Staff Sergeant."

"Follow me. Can we get you anything?"

Odin shook his head as they walked down a hall lined by doorways. Several officers nodded with respect as he passed by. Before long they came to a wooden door. The staff sergeant knocked twice, and then entered a briefing room containing a single folding table. Plywood wall sections displayed sector maps and LCD panels displayed live satellite and surveillance images. Soft radio chatter kept up a steady background noise.

"I have Odin for you, Colonel."

"It's about goddamned time."

Looking up from the table was a man in his sixties wearing a blue Oxford cloth shirt and a dark blue blazer with khaki slacks, a laptop open next to him. His eyes were hard and his manner imposing. His powerful-looking hands hinted at the old commando he no doubt was.

The staff sergeant left without a word, closing the door behind him. Odin stood to attention and saluted. "You wanted to see me, Colonel."

"Have you forgotten whose side you're on, Master Sergeant?"

"No, sir."

"Well, it sure as hell looks that way. I'm in a class-five political shit storm because of you."

"In the proper context my methods—"

"Your methods have caused lasting damage to this mission. Here's a clue, son: You're supposed to disrupt enemy operations—not our operations."

"What I did made strategic sense."

"No, you thought it made sense—and it's not your job to think. It's your job to kill the enemy."

"I was taught that a special operator needs to think for himself—both strategically and tactically. To adapt to the situation on the ground or be overcome by events. Sir."

The colonel studied Odin. "How does warning an insurgent leader about an impending CIA missile strike make good strategic sense? My S-2 reports that the man's current whereabouts are unknown. This individual will now live to fight another day—thanks to you."

Odin was silent.

"How do you justify your actions, Master Sergeant?"

Odin considered the question. "Sooner or later we will leave this place. And we need to leave behind more than just radicalized young men who've known only war. The tribal elder I saved is widely respected in those capillary valleys, and he's a moderate compared to the people who would succeed him—although I don't imagine that was obvious in the aerial imagery."

"Task Force Steel says he's the hub of an insurgent network."

"Yes, in reaction to our military occupation of his land. But when we're not around he kills foreign fighters and narco-traffickers. If we get the hell out of this guy's way, he'll do our work for us."

"Nonetheless—"

"We don't need conventional forces here, Colonel. Men like me can work the ground unseen, play political factions against each other, use proxies. As it stands, our patrols and bases are just targets, and the more firepower we use, the more enemies we create."

"That's enough." The colonel's stare bored into Odin for several moments. "How did your team conceal its movements from our drones?"

"We created decoy targets in their flight path—remotely fired mortars. Insurgents do it all the time to frame rivals. We made the snatch while our drones were distracted."

The colonel continued silently observing Odin. "You've made your distaste for drones widely known at battalion."

"Drones are useful for recon, but they can't replace a human being on the ground. And if you ask me, these missile strikes do more harm than good. Take that disaster in Karbala—suicide bombings and IED attacks have already increased in every theater of operations. It's been a recruiting bonanza for our enemies."

"Pentagon says it wasn't our drone."

"We both know that hardly matters. So you tell me: Are drones helping us or hurting us, Colonel?"

The colonel seemed familiar with this sort of intense debate with his subordinates. He remained calm. "Like it or not, Sergeant, fifty other nations are developing their own drones as fast as they can." He paused. "Which is, in fact, why I've called you here."

Odin frowned in confusion.

"Are you familiar with the term *lethal autonomy*?"

Odin nodded. "Autonomous combat drones."

"Yes. Drones that fly themselves and make a kill decision without direct human involvement."

Odin considered this with some dismay. "That's a major RMA, sir."

"Tell me *why* it's a revolution in military affairs."

"Because it would combine all the worst aspects of cyber war—anonymity and scalability—with the physical violence of kinetic war. A successful design could be stolen and cheaply punched out by the tens of thousands in offshore factories, then sent anonymously against anyone without fear of retribution."

The colonel regarded Odin then nodded to himself, apparently having made a decision. "I have a mission for your team, Master Sergeant. A mission that requires someone who, as you so aptly put it, can think for himself, both strategically and tactically. I'm adding you to the BIGOT list for a highly compartmentalized SAP, code-named Project Ancile. You'll be one of only three people who know it exists, and you are to report to me and only me."

"What's my objective?"

The colonel closed his laptop and focused his gaze on Odin. "You are to discover the source of the drone attacks on the continental United States."

"You're referring to the terror bombings, sir?"

"That's a cover story. The truth is more worrisome. We think whoever was behind the Karbala attack is also behind the CONUS attacks."

Odin considered the implications.

"One more thing." The colonel paused for emphasis. "You are to pursue your mission no matter where it leads you—even if you are commanded to stop. You must continue, and you must succeed. Do you understand me, Master Sergeant?"

Odin nodded. "Yes, I believe I do, sir."

CHAPTER 3

Raconteur

"**G**ood afternoon, ladies and gentlemen. My name is Joshua Strickland, team lead for visual intelligence development here at the Stanford Vision Lab. I'd like to thank you all for coming today."

Strickland stood at the head of a darkened, windowless lecture hall in the basement of the Gates Computer Science Building. Beside him the camera-eye logo of the Vision Lab filled a large projection screen. In the PowerPoint afterglow he saw familiar and unfamiliar faces among a small audience seated primarily in the front two rows. He focused on the serious faces seated just before him.

"An especially warm welcome to our distinguished guests from the Transformational Convergence Technology Office. Thanks also to our faculty advisor, Doctor Lei Li, without whose support we would not be presenting to you today."

There was timid applause from somewhere in the darkness.

Strickland paused to collect his thoughts. So much was riding on this. He took a breath then began, "What you're about to see is a visual intelligence technology we call Raconteur." A click of his wireless remote, and the slide changed to an animation of dozens, then hundreds, and then thousands of individual video insets, swarming. It was a vast stream of graphic data. "Visual intelligence is often confused with 'computer vision'—but it's much more than that. Visual intelligence means giving machines the ability not merely to identify objects in images—which has been possible for years—but the cognitive ability to discern what's occurring in a scene. Concept detection, integrated cognition, interpolation—prediction. What could have happened, and what might happen next. It means giving machines not only the ability to see but to understand what they see."

He searched the faces of those front and center. "Why is this important?"

He clicked the remote, and the slide changed to surveillance images of London subway bombers moving through stations and standing in railcars. "In an increasingly dangerous world, video surveillance represents society's best hope to detect threats before they materialize. But this flood of visual imagery means an exponential increase in the volume of surveillance video that must be analyzed—and analyzed real-time if it is to be of use not just in reviewing criminal acts after the fact but in preventing criminal acts."

The image changed to that of a burned-out Starbucks on an urban street. Then another photo from a newspaper showing a burned-out SUV beneath the headline SENATOR ASSASSINATED IN TERROR BOMBING. "We need only consider the recent unsolved terror bombings here in the United States to recognize how critical visual intelligence is to our future."

Strickland scanned the faces of his audience. They were with him.

"How do we imbue machines with this ability? We do this by emulating the way humans process spatiotemporal events. Human visual cognition is closely attuned to change, and it's these changes that create what we call 'attention states.' We acquire 'attention states' from video imagery through an algorithmic mechanism that includes notions of focus of attention, markers placed on salient objects, and the critical relationships between those objects in terms of motion and contact. These are necessary to distinguish individual events from one another. A series of attentional states over time then becomes a visual attention trace—or VAT—which begins to form the elements of a story. One that can be programmatically narrated through machine-readable text—text that can then be algorithmically searched for relevance, in real time, by an 'audience' of other, simpler programs. This is why we call our system 'Raconteur'—because it tells the story of what's happening in a way that common systems can understand. And like any good storyteller, 'Raconteur' remembers how the current scene fits into the whole."

Strickland knew that his combination of youth and poise would be an advantage here. Disruptive technology was like that. Now, at twenty-two, he was leading a team that was about to revolutionize visual image processing. Although he wasn't the driving force behind the innovations, he did know how to spot and recruit talent to his work teams. If history was any guide, that was the primary skill necessary for success in Silicon Valley. Being able to spot a good idea and knowing who could make it work. Removing obstacles and inspiring others, that was the biggest part of innovation.

"We have worked with DARPA's technical staff to coordinate the following demonstration, in strict adherence to the Mind's-Eye Project guidelines. Please remember that our system has not been previously exposed to the images that you—and it—are about to see. We look forward to taking your questions after the test. Until then, ladies and gentlemen, I give you 'Raconteur,' the storyteller. . . ."

More light applause as the screen went black.

Strickland stepped aside as two smaller screens glowed to life up front—one bearing the title "TCTO Phase 1—Recognition Test." The other screen displayed a blinking cursor.

Strickland moved to the side to stand with his project team, bracing for whatever came next. He cast a tense look at his development lead, Vijay Prakash, but the handsome, dour Bengali ignored Strickland's arched eyebrows and looked to the screen. The rest of the grad student crew—Sourav Chatterjee, Gerhard Koepple, Wang Bao-Rong, and Nikolay Kasheyev—nodded in acknowledgment of the moment. Then they all turned to watch the screens too.

The words "TCTO Phase 1—Recognition Test" soon appeared also on the right-hand screen. The twin projections were set up so that whatever appeared in the left-hand screen, Raconteur would have to make sense of and describe in text on the right-hand screen.

Strickland felt relief wash over him as he stood in the darkness. Failing simple character recognition while reading the title card would have killed them, but then, OCR was handled by a licensed library, not their code. Still, he knew the DARPA judges wouldn't cut them any slack for choosing a bad library.

But the test was already moving on. No time to ponder disaster scenarios. The left-hand screen changed to black-and-white surveillance video. It depicted a woman walking down an office hallway carrying a cardboard records box.

Strickland tensed again. He'd seen the VI algorithms work a hundred thousand times and had a pretty good idea how they functioned, but they'd never been run live in front of such an important audience. What happened next would decide the next several years of his life—of their lives— and quite possibly the trajectory of Strickland's career. He focused on the blinking cursor on the right-hand screen—the Raconteur output panel.

As the video continued, text began to appear. . . .

Person carries object along corridor.

Murmurs of approval swept through the room, but Strickland remained tense. *C'mon. Do it. Do it, baby. . . .*

The cursor then began expanding on the details.

Woman carries box along corridor.

More murmurs and some clapping. Strickland cast a glance at the DARPA managers, who were nodding and talking softly among themselves. Taking notes. A wave of relief flowed through him. He'd had no idea how clenched he was, but now that initial impressions were good, the judges would be more receptive if there was a later glitch. He told himself that no matter what happened from here on, they had at least avoided a meltdown. They had gotten on the scoreboard.

The scene changed to an exterior; an American soldier standing on a littered street in some Middle Eastern slum, weapon slung and motioning to unseen people. A small—possibly Iraqi—child entered the frame behind him. Strickland felt the dread returning, as the text scrolled. . . .

Armed person . . . approached by child.

More applause and some actual shouts of excitement.

Strickland felt a smile crease his face before he clamped down on it. Too early to celebrate.

Uniformed soldier approached by child in street.

The hoots continued. So far so good, but Strickland knew the difficulty levels were only going to increase. As he watched, the system mistook another soldier entering the frame as a possible threat—*#ALERT—armed person.* Not too far off the truth, though.

The control frame faded to black and displayed the title: "TCTO Phase 1—Interpolation Test."

Here we go. The complexity of visual concepts ramped up fast. It was why their system focused on deriving context first while interpreting a scene, and why it never forgot what it had seen previously. That was key to avoiding a lot of useless processing. Humans walking down a city sidewalk, for example, do not suddenly expect to see a mountain vista or a rolling sea all around them. That would be impossible—thus, even if these things appeared, they were likely to be graphical representations like ads, not the actual thing. Daisy-chaining events made it possible to take the known and use it as a base camp from which to explore the unknown—pushing that frontier back just a little at a time, like ants exploring terrain.

As Strickland knew, even a person with Down syndrome was a generalized genius compared to special-purpose computer algorithms. Breaking things down to their simplest elements was the only way to accomplish anything useful. Prakash had worked out the architecture, and the design made Strickland's head hurt. But if the damned thing worked, he'd forgive all of the man's arrogance.

The scene on the left changed to a woman in a burka—a *burka*! What U.S. troops called a "BMO," short for "black moving object." DARPA bastards. No face, no clear view of her arms or torso. On-screen she resembled a walking bag. But if memory served, Vijay and Gerhard's gait detection code should help assign the attribute of "human" to walking objects—and along with "humanity" came implied geometry, potential actions, and patterns of movement. The burka woman was moving along a narrow village road carrying what appeared to be a plastic water jug on her head.

The room waited with bated breath. Then the text started scrolling. *Person carries object down street.*

Okay, so far so good.

The woman entered a dwelling through a doorway on the left, and the system correctly described her disappearance. Then all was quiet for a moment, until she reemerged without the jug on her head. This was the real test. Cognition.

#ALERT—DROPPED—ITEM: Person observed carrying object into building and leaving without it.

Strickland felt the importance of this moment as loud applause filled the room. They had just passed the bomber test. Years of work flashed before him. He felt the backslaps of his teammates, and he turned to their smiling faces in the semidarkness. He even grabbed hands and side-hugged Prakash. They'd never gotten along well—always struggling for the reins. But this moment was what they'd been working for. Even the eternally serious Prakash gave the barest hint of a smile. A smirk, really.

Strickland had to admit the guy knew what he was doing. "Great work, Vijay."

Prakash nodded. "It's a start."

Prick. Couldn't he enjoy anything?

There were calls for quiet as the test continued, but a warm tingling had settled across Strickland. They would get their research grant. He knew it now. The excited discussions among the judges told him they'd outperformed anything they'd ever seen. His professional career had begun, and he would forever remember this moment. He couldn't wait to tell Sandra.

But then he remembered that they weren't seeing each other anymore.

Strickland popped the cork on a bottle of cheap champagne and let foam spew in all directions as his research mates screamed in jubilation. Back in the KSL lab cluster on the second floor, there was much to celebrate. The lab was an open workspace with HD digital video cameras clamped to brackets and on tripods scattered here and there, rack servers in one corner, their LED lights flickering as though in time to the music. LCD monitors on desks and mounted to the ceiling scrolled Raconteur-generated text of the festivities . . . most of it not too far off—but then they would now have a federal grant to perfect it, wouldn't they?

What they'd believed to be groundbreaking work had been recognized. The venture capital arm of a U.S. intelligence agency had tentatively agreed to finance their research project, but along with that came top-level introductions to other private venture firms. His team now represented the very bleeding edge in the field of visual intelligence. All their personal rancor and disagreements had been for a purpose, and now the entire crew shouted another toast, enjoying the moment—Chatterjee, Koepple, Prakash, Wang, Kasheyev—a truly international team. And then there were the other lab teams in the cluster, along with their faculty advisors. There were spouses and significant others, as well—turning it into a full-scale party. Strickland wished he had someone to share it with too. But that would come in time, especially now that success had found him. In a few years he hoped to be a partner in some venture capital firm on Sand Hill Road. He was on his way.

Strickland stepped up onto an office chair as someone steadied it for him. He raised his glass and Lei Li, their mentor, called out for quiet—with everyone suddenly shouting, "Speech! Speech!"

In a few moments the music got turned down, and in the sudden silence Strickland raised a plastic cup sloshing with champagne. "Guys, I want you to know what an honor it's been to work with this team. I'm aware that the brilliance lies not with me, but with all of you"—he pointed—"Sourav, Gerhard, Bao, Nik, and of course, the inimitable Vijay." There was applause and cheers with each name.

Prakash stood near the wall, arms crossed, watching Strickland with something approaching disdain. Prakash wore his trademark khaki pants and blue Oxford button-down shirt. His hair, as always, closely cut and perfect. Bollywood good looks.

What was the deal with this guy? Why couldn't he just loosen up? Strickland tried to ignore him. "I think it's fitting that in a building where Google was born—bringing Web search to the world—visual intelligence would also be born, bringing the ability to search reality in real time. You guys will make history, and I'm just glad to be along for the ride."

"Hear, hear!" Another cheer went up and glasses were drained. The music came up again, and the crowd resumed shouted conversations, while lab members mugged before the video cameras.

Strickland noticed Prakash still staring daggers at him, so he waded through the crowd to him. "Vijay, what's wrong with you, man? You look like Kolkata just lost the cricket finals or something."

Prakash eyed him. "Speaking as one of the 'brilliant' team members, I don't appreciate you monopolizing the conversation with DARPA. We make decisions as a team, Josh. The only reason you have the title of 'team lead' is because you're good at dealing with suits, and it keeps you out of my way."

"I was just setting a date for the next meeting. We'll confirm it by e-mail later."

"We need to be involved in every decision that occurs—no matter how small."

"We're not a hive mind, Vijay. Occasionally tasks need to be delegated, and I don't see the point of bothering you with—"

Prakash got in his face, finger jabbing. "This is not the first time I've had to remind you. I do not work for you, Josh, and I expect you to represent the interests of the team, not just yourself."

"Whoa, whoa! Hold on a second. We all agreed from the get-go that since I'm the extrovert that it would be best if I did the talking, especially with the defense folks. That's what I've been doing." He gestured back to the chair he'd been standing on. "Did I not just lay literally all of the credit onto everyone else's shoulders?"

"And rightly so. The next time we communicate with the U.S. government, I expect to be copied, Josh."

He studied Prakash's face. Did he know? There had indeed been a few other communications, but it had only been an oversight. "Look, I don't know what you think I'm up to, but in case you haven't noticed, you're sort of critical to this project. I can't screw you without screwing myself. You're on the patent applications."

Strickland wondered if Prakash's highly competitive upbringing was behind this. He knew that the guy's father was a real type-A businessman— a real ballbuster who practically rode his sons with a riding crop. Old school. Very class conscious too.

Was that it? Strickland sometimes wondered if Prakash thought less of him simply because Strickland was straight middle class—the son of schoolteachers. He'd seen photos of the Prakash summerhouse in the south of France, and photos of Prakash literally in a polo outfit, holding the reins of a pony—like he was friends with the British royals or something. It was easy to forget that this guy might just look at him like he was one of the help.

The more he thought about it, the more it irritated him. He raised his cup again to Prakash and gave him an obnoxious wink, aiming a finger pistol at him in oily salesman fashion. "Who loves ya, guy? Eh? Who loves ya!"

Someone came up from behind and ruffled Prakash's hair, laughing. Strickland took the opportunity to step away, heading outside for some air. He worked the room on the way out, and by the time he made it to one of the hallway doors, he could see the light on in one of the tiny, window-less offices that surrounded the lab cluster. There sat the childlike form of Nikolay Kasheyev, their visual processing expert, sitting at his desk.

Kasheyev had some sort of pituitary condition that gave him the appearance of a twelve-year-old, even though he was in his mid-twenties. He was often told he was a child prodigy, and every time people made that mistake, Strickland winced on his behalf. But the Russian seemed used to it.

He could see Kasheyev examining multiplexed video streams, tiled into squares on his screen. Strickland rapped his knuckles on the office doorframe. "Hey, Nik, why aren't you joining the party, man?"

Kasheyev spoke without turning around. "The ravens are back."

"What ravens?"

Kasheyev finally bothered to turn around. "You never listen to me, do you?"

Strickland was too busy wondering how much Kasheyev's eyeglasses cost. It seemed that among the team members, only Strickland had come from humble circumstances. Everyone else seemed to have parents with money. No one else had had to work through their undergraduate years. At least not at menial jobs. It seemed like Kasheyev wasn't even aware that they'd probably laid the groundwork for becoming wealthy men today. It was as though it barely mattered to him.

"Josh."

"Ah. Of course I listen to you. I just don't retain what you say."

Kasheyev pointed to an array of six video images tiled on his screen—surveillance cameras that Strickland knew were being "watched" at all times by Raconteur algorithms. They'd had the system running more or less continually (in progressive versions) for almost two years, watching the public spaces all around the Gates building. Watching the comings and goings of students, automobiles, everything. That was part of the power of this system: *persistent surveillance*. Watching over time. Noticing patterns and changes to those patterns. Continuing to deduce meaning from what was seen, storing the symbolic representations, and sending alerts—in this case to Kasheyev's iPhone—whenever anomalies were detected. Specific alerts could be created, and apparently Kasheyev had started fixating on these birds. It was the least of his eccentricities.

Kasheyev tapped at one of the images, where what appeared to be a black raven gazed at their offices from a tree branch. Clearly the video was running, because Strickland could see the leaves of the tree swaying in a slight breeze.

Strickland leaned in to examine the screen, and then examined the Raconteur log, highlighted for the entry. *Raven perched in tree.*

"Okay, Raconteur recognized a species of bird. We're amazing."

"That's because it searched tagged Web images for comparisons—object identification is not really my point. It's that there have never been ravens in these trees. And, look, there's another raven here, up near the Packard Building to the south. . . ." He clicked around the screen and brought up a larger image of another raven perched on the parapet of the architecturally modern electrical engineering building across the street. He scrolled backward in time, and Strickland could see that as the sun rose and set, the twin, but lone, ravens returned day after day—but then one day, they weren't there. "It started a week ago. And they've come back every day since."

Strickland recognized that this was one of the problems inherent in working with brilliant people: They were half-mad. Fixations on details or finding links between disconnected phenomena was a mania with some of them. He patted Kasheyev on the shoulder. "There's this thing called 'migration,' Nik."

Kasheyev looked at Strickland like he was an idiot. "Ravens don't migrate. Adult birds like this have a range that spans miles. They don't stay in one spot unless they're a mated pair with a nest. And I don't see a nest."

"Fascinating. These birds are way more interesting than our new research funding. I say we drop everything and—"

"Look . . ." Kasheyev zoomed in on one of the ravens sitting in the tree, and then up to one of its legs. There was some sort of tag or transponder on it.

Strickland shrugged. "Okay, someone's doing research on ravens. This is a university."

"That's what I thought too. Ravens are very bright birds, Josh."

"Maybe they're here on a scholarship."

"No one is doing research on raven populations here. I checked."

"Jesus, I thought we were working on visual intelligence software, not stalking ravens."

"Take a closer look at the tag on its leg. . . ." He zoomed in the high-def digital image. Then he split the screen and showed a close-up of the other bird on the opposite side of the building.

The objects on their legs looked like identical black squares.

Strickland sighed, and was happy when he noticed Wang Bao-Rong, their twentysomething Taiwanese narrow-AI expert, motioning for them to follow as he walked past in the hallway.

"What's going on?"

Wang was tossing a brain-shaped squeaky toy in the air as he walked. "Conference call with the lawyers."

"Oh!" Strickland pulled Kasheyev from the seat. "C'mon, Nik! The birds can wait, man." He fell in with the rest of the crew, still sipping champagne.

Stanford University graduate science teams had already founded Hewlett-Packard, Cisco, Yahoo!, and, of course, Google. And the five patent applications Strickland's team had filed for Raconteur were potentially worth billions—especially now that the federal government was signing on to fund their work. This was the culmination of everything he'd worked for.

The team piled into a conference room, where Prakash was already standing, arms akimbo, in front of a speakerphone. Strickland was the last in and closed the door behind him.

Prakash barked at the phone. "Okay, John. The team's all here." Prakash looked up. "Guys, this is John Wolstein at Hartmann, Blithe, and Peale."

A voice came over the speaker. *"Hey, guys."*

Everyone chimed in greetings.

Strickland spoke up. "Tell us the good news, John."

There was a moment of silence. Then, *"Well, I wish I could do that, but I'm afraid there's a problem."*

A hot flash ran across Strickland's skin. Adrenaline surge. The intellectual property was everything. They'd already done a preliminary patent search. The path was clear. No one had ever taken Prakash's novel approach.

Prakash frowned at the phone. "What do you mean, 'problem'? What problem?"

Strickland realized that this was what Prakash was good at. He'd chew this lawyer a new asshole.

"You have prior art problems, Vijay. Big sections of your source code base are already public knowledge—available online."

The room went utterly silent. The static on the phone line was the only sound.

"You guys still there?"

"What the hell are you talking about? That's impossible! Where online?"

"Several forums. A code search turned up a half-dozen sites that carried

parts of your source code verbatim. Even some of the comments were there in the code. I don't know how it got there or—"

"Goddammit!" The words burst from Prakash as he glared around the room.

"Vijay, I'm just telling you what the facts are."

"I designed this code from scratch. There's no 'inspiration' from somewhere else. It is mine."

Strickland might have argued for more credit under different circumstances, but right now he felt like he'd been Tasered. He was just staring at the speakerphone, hearing the pounding of his heart in his ears. Hearing his future evaporate. He could see Prakash's tanned face turning red, veins appearing—as though the man were about to explode.

Gerhard Koepple, always even-tempered, looked ashen-faced. Wang, Kasheyev, and Chatterjee were sitting down, running their hands through their hair as if they'd just heard a close relative had died.

Strickland croaked out, "Where? Where online, John?"

"I'm sending you a link right now—"

Prakash broke in. "You'll send it to all of us. Not just Josh. Do you understand?"

"Yeah, okay, fine, Vijay. Listen, getting mad at me isn't going to help."

"Just send the damned message."

"Okay." A pause. *"It's headed your way."*

Strickland chimed in again. "John, where does this leave us? What happens now?"

There was silence for a moment. *"Nothing happens. I'm going to submit a report to Doctor Lei that the patents are not enforceable. And I expect the patent office will come to the same determination. I don't know what, if any, effect this will have on your Ph.D. theses, but that's the situation. My condolences. However this happened—and I'm not saying that you guys copied work from somewhere else—but however it happened, this code is now public domain. You won't be able to patent it unless this prior art issue is resolved."*

Prakash grabbed the phone and ripped it off its base on the table—tearing out the phone cord—and hurled it against the window. The glass vibrated with a thud as the phone blasted into pieces.

"Jesus, Vijay! Calm down! I wanted to ask him more questions!"

Prakash ignored Strickland and stormed out of the conference room to the office nearby that he shared with Wang.

Strickland was right on his heels, closely followed by the rest of the team. "Vijay." He felt his iPhone vibrate in his pocket, meaning he'd probably received an e-mail, but he wanted to deal with Vijay first.

Prakash was logging on to his computer and opening e-mail. He double-clicked on the top message as the others gathered around. There was verbiage from their lawyer, along with several links below the words "Prior Art." The first one was for a website somewhere in Russia, judging by the ".ru" domain.

Chatterjee leaned in and placed his hand between Prakash and the screen. "Not directly! Use a VM, dude."

Prakash looked like he was about to bite Chatterjee's head off for a moment before he took a breath, nodded, and copied the first URL to the clipboard. "This is a just a bloody Xenon connection, Sourav! And the machine's got nothing critical on it." But he nonetheless launched a virtual machine, opened a browser, and pasted the address into the URL line.

Everyone was waiting with bated breath as an offshore warez site named "Sourcebomber.ru" came on-screen. There, filling one section, was the source code to their attentiveness state class. Even Strickland, who'd not worked as much on the code as the rest of the crew, recognized it as Prakash's work—or at least they'd always thought of it as his. Strickland was beginning to wonder whether the rich kid from Bengal really was the talented software architect everyone considered him to be—but of course, that was ridiculous. Prakash had gotten into Stanford! He'd aced undergraduate CS classes. Serious geniuses had worked closely with Prakash and come away impressed.

Strickland was barely able to concentrate as Prakash's quivering hand scrolled down the page as function after function, class after class, of their precious source code was revealed on this public forum. It was like finding the love of their life in a gang-bang porno.

That's when Prakash really lost it. He picked up the flat-panel monitor and tore it off the desk. The team scattered as he began smashing it into the wall. Pieces of plastic and glass flew everywhere. He was screaming like an animal.

Their faculty advisor, the elfin Doctor Lei Li, came in shouting at Prakash. That's when Strickland realized that none of them had called her into the conference room. She had a stake in this too. But they'd thought it was just going to be a routine call.

She was screaming at him. "Vijay! Calm down! What's going on?"

"The bloody source code is out on the Internet! Raconteur is free-ware now! It's fucking unpatentable! Someone on this team is responsible!"

The rest of the team displayed the early stages of grief. Prakash had passed them all and gone straight to rage.

Kasheyev stared unseeing at Prakash's empty desk. "Or someone stole it from us."

Prakash focused on the boyish Russian. "Stole it? Do you think with idiots like Strickland and Wang around anyone would have to steal our code?"

Strickland had more riding on this than anyone else here. Prakash was talking crazy. "Whoa, wait a second—"

Prakash got into Kasheyev's face. "How could anyone steal it? Our servers aren't even on SUNet. There are no wireless devices on them. I've been checking the logs on the Merakis for months, looking for rogue connections and transfers."

Doctor Lei frowned. "How are you able to do that? You don't have rights—"

He ignored her. "And the only code of ours that gets near a network connection is already obfuscated and compiled. Except for the code my 'teammates' have in their possession." He pointed at where the monitor had been. "You saw that code. It was our uncompiled source—and recent source at that. Comments and all!"

Strickland felt a sinking feeling. He did indeed have a fairly recent copy of the source code—on the Leland network, on the cluster in the basement. But then, so, too, did the others. Didn't they? Did they actually not trust the hardwired network? And only their team had access to that share. Strickland suddenly realized that Prakash was studying his face.

And he had apparently come to a conclusion based on what he read there. "You son of a bitch!"

Strickland felt warm pressure on his face as the world spun out of control. It was several moments before he realized he was on the floor, feeling pain on his lips and the back of his head. He came to his senses with Koepple and Wang trying to get him to his feet. Prakash was nowhere to be seen, and neither were Chatterjee and Doctor Lei.

Kasheyev leaned into Strickland's line of view and placed an ice-filled paper towel that smelled of champagne onto his face. "You okay, Josh?"

His lips hurt like hell. One tooth felt loose. Strickland looked down to see blood had run down his white shirtfront. "What the hell, man . . ."

Wang was shaking his head. "Vijay has finally lost it."

Koepple was still looking pale—not his normal unflappable self. Perhaps he, too, was realizing just how completely fucked they were.

Strickland felt tears rising. What was he, a pussy? But he couldn't help it. This had been his ticket. These other guys had serious technical talent. Strickland was smart but not as technically brilliant as these other guys. He needed people like this to employ his own talents—people and management skills. If his doctoral thesis was rejected due to plagiarism, of all things . . . Jesus Christ.

Strickland looked up at the others. "Why did Vijay hit me?"

Koepple shrugged. "Why *did* he hit you, Josh? Is there a reason?"

"Oh, don't you start."

Kasheyev motioned for them to be quiet, and then turned to Strickland. "I don't think it was you, Josh. I think we need to look at the evidence here. This is a vision intelligence system. I have cameras in these rooms. No one can approach the project servers without our knowing about it. Vijay is right about that. And if no outsider physically got to those machines, then—"

"The damned project servers are in the middle of a party right now! There must be forty people in the lab cluster! Why the hell is everyone focusing on me? Because little Lord Fauntleroy popped a gasket and needs to find someone to blame? And why not the least talented coder in the bunch? Why not the guy who's had the least to do with the code? Do you realize how this fucks me? Do you realize how totally screwed my life is now?"

The whole team looked embarrassed.

Kasheyev patted Strickland's knee. "Sorry, Josh." With a last look he walked out, followed by Koepple.

Wang lingered a moment to point to Strickland's face. "You might want to think about pressing charges, Josh. We were witnesses."

Strickland shrugged. It was likely that Doctor Lei would already bring Prakash up on disciplinary charges. And besides, what was the point? Now his face looked the way he felt inside.

Wang walked out too, leaving him alone.

Strickland turned in the office chair to face what was actually a rather beautiful day out the window. From his position on the second floor, he could see a tree just outside, and a raven sitting on a branch there—staring at him. After a moment it flew away.

CHAPTER 4

Intrusion Detection

Joshua Strickland slumped in an office chair in the deserted lab cluster. Eyes closed, he listened intently to Rage Against the Machine. It was late. Very late. The place was littered with plastic cups, wine and beer bottles, and pizza boxes. It had cleared out pretty quickly after the intellectual property spill, but that had been hours ago. Hours and hours. Strickland glanced at his watch—then realized he wasn't wearing one. That he was, in fact, "philosophically opposed to wearing watches." What a poser he was. Lately he had begun to annoy even himself.

A nearly empty bottle of champagne hung in his hand. No, that wasn't quite right. He examined the foil label.

Sparkling wine.

The French were sticklers about their intellectual property too. He upended the bottle into his mouth, finishing off the last inch or so, then tossed it against the far wall, where it ricocheted into a trash can.

Not drunk enough by half. He groped among the bottles on the nearest desk until he came away with another half-empty. More of the cheap shit. But then, that's all he'd be drinking from now on. No first-round-funding-leading-to-an-eventual-IPO for him.

He thought about his student loans. About his other debts. It was nearly a hundred thousand by now. Did he even have a thesis to defend anymore? Did this incident violate the terms of his partial scholarship? Surely, someone could establish that his team really had written the Raconteur code before copies appeared online. Couldn't they?

He'd started wondering whether they'd actually written the software—and by "they" he meant Prakash. Prakash and Kasheyev. And maybe Koepple.

Strickland had always been the smartest kid in his high school, but when he'd come to Stanford, he was suddenly the slow guy. It was like swimming in white water here—a constant struggle to keep from drowning in knowledge, while for others it was easy. Or at least it seemed easy.

No, scratch that. He knew a lot of people were working hard to keep their place here.

Stop feeling sorry for yourself. You're no idiot.

The truth was that Strickland sought out supergeniuses—people who were obviously going places. That's what he'd seen in Prakash, wasn't it? And Kasheyev? The others just came with the package. Strickland supposed they thought the same of him.

But Strickland did have skills they lacked, didn't he? Unlike them he was outgoing and persuasive. A motivator of people. He could focus work groups.

He paused for a moment.

He was a parasite, wasn't he? *Fuck.* If he was honest with himself, he was the least valuable member of the Raconteur team. If they'd never met him, the software would probably have looked exactly like it did right now—Prakash's vision. Strickland had spent hours and hours studying the team's source code, intent on comprehending each class. Each function and subroutine. Damn, their code was elegant. Brief. Tight. Integrated. Epic poetry for machines. Strickland was still trying to understand all its subtle details and interconnections. He couldn't imagine having actually developed it.

In truth, Strickland's recklessness with the source code might have sunk all their hopes for youthful success. But was it really that reckless to store the code on their own department's servers?

What would it have taken to steal the project files from the Leland cluster? Someone with inside access, obviously. The server's log files might show who and when.

Unless they covered their tracks. But then he realized that these were probably virtual servers—part of a cloud. And even if that wasn't the case, the computer science department was crawling with arch hackers. People who could design microchips on the back of a cocktail napkin. He wasn't likely to find evidence they didn't want found.

And what the hell was he thinking—someone with inside access? What if it was someone who'd stolen the code from a misplaced USB drive? From a laptop or a wireless home network? Who was to say it was Strickland who had screwed up? What if it was Prakash? Judgmental prick.

Strickland slid his tongue across his front teeth. One still felt loose. The swelling on his lips had gone down, but if he weren't drunk, he guessed he'd probably be in serious pain right now.

Bottom line: There really wasn't much chance of finding out how the code got out. He was no computer forensics expert. Maybe Prakash and his rich family could hire one, but their hiring a lawyer to sue Strickland seemed more likely.

A thought suddenly occurred to him. What if whoever stole the source code was still stealing it?

Strickland sat upright—suddenly alert.

What if he could insert something in the source code that "phoned-home" if they stole it again? A smile spread across his lips—and he stopped himself as the pain spiked. He slid the wine bottle across the nearest desk and marched unsteadily over to the nearest workstation. Man, he actually was pretty drunk.

Strickland logged on to SUNet, then navigated to his own share on the Leland cluster, where he'd stored several versions of the Raconteur C++ source code. He perused the various "cpp" files. How to go about this? Prakash's code was so damned tightly integrated, and Strickland was pretty drunk. *KISS—keep-it-simple-shithead.* That was the best policy. But then, all Strickland had to do was add something that would run whenever the Raconteur service was executed. That meant during initialization, when constants and classes were instantiated.

What about stealth? *Screw that.* He was in no shape to develop a rootkit. His consciousness felt as though it were swimming hard just to stay above the alcohol line in his skull. He stared unsteadily at the screen. *Focus, you asshat.* Marshaling a few sober brain cells took all his concentration.

Software connecting to a remote host on start-up wasn't unusual. Checking for updates is all. Nothing to be alarmed about. He could write a tiny remote procedure call to pass back whatever info he wanted from the client via HTTP—from wherever his software was executing. The IP address of whoever stole the code, for starters. Maybe some details on the offending machine's operating system and language. Maybe a list of network shares and—

No. Keep-it-simple. Just a small XML-RPC client to send the data. He had a C++ library lying around that he could include in the Raconteur code base; that way he could fold his little messaging routine in without much trouble. Then he'd just set up a companion RPC server running on one of his own Web servers to pick up any XML messages sent from clients. The HTTP traffic would look just like standard Web surfing to the thief's firewall.

But wouldn't they notice Strickland's addition to the code? Perhaps not. If someone had stolen the Raconteur software, that meant they trusted the source, right? And the phone-home code only had to run successfully once. Just the one time to find out where it had been spirited away to.

Strickland launched Emacs and pondered what C++ project file to open first. Where should he make this change? He decided to slip the code into one of Raconteur's ancillary services—a visual trace library. There he added a new subroutine that formed the XML, gathering client IP address, local time, and local operating system, then issuing it to an RPC server he'd set up next. Lastly, he incremented the Raconteur project version—making a bullshit notation about fixing a possible memory leak. He used Prakash's initials to avoid arousing suspicion. After all, he'd rarely posted any changes that made it into the final source code. In fact, he'd have to admit he'd never made any meaningful contributions to the code itself. Until now.

Then Strickland took the better part of an hour coding the companion RPC server that would detect and process incoming pings from his phone-home code. It took that long mostly because he was so drunk he had trouble typing. He hosted it on a Web server he'd used as a summer intern at some Cupertino start-up. Error trapping? Bah. But it seemed to work, and it would gather any incoming data into a text file.

Now it was time to post his revised Raconteur source code to the network. Strickland manually copied this version, as he had all previous ones, into a new directory, following his previous folder-naming conventions. He did this outside of the official version control system just as he had in the past, so that this new directory wouldn't seem unusual to anyone monitoring the share. Strickland had been doing it to avoid Prakash and the others' knowing how much after-hours analysis of their code he'd needed just to keep up. So in that sense, Prakash had his own judgmental nature to blame for Strickland's placing the code in jeopardy in the first place—or was that just a rationalization?

That was it, then. The booby-trapped source code had been posted. Strickland stared at the screen, then closed the window with a single click. The die had been cast. Now he found himself staring at the desktop. He was all keyed up, and late or not, he decided he wasn't ready to head back to his studio apartment—to stare at ironic garage-sale clown paintings. They wouldn't seem so ironic a few years from now. Instead he decided to build a service to alert him to any data coming back from his surreptitious phone-home code. It felt good to be writing software again, and he decided to write the detection service in C#. Prakash always railed against .NET, saying real programmers didn't use managed code. *Fuck him.*

Strickland set up an app on one of his research domains that would place the IP addresses of incoming pings onto a world map. *Might as well make it slick.*

When he was done he nodded. He felt pretty good about himself.

Hanging out with all these supergeniuses it was easy to forget that a little deviousness could make up for a lot of IQ points. Maybe he wasn't the next Sergey Brin or Larry Page, but he'd do okay. He'd recover from this.

As he stared at the screen, at some point he nodded off to sleep.

Strickland jolted awake as the iPhone in his pocket sounded a klaxon warning—the sound effect he'd assigned for incoming messages from his phone-home code. He shook his head clear as the klaxon sound effect played again. He looked around the lab cluster to notice it was still deserted. What time was it?

The klaxon again. He pulled the phone out of his pocket, and, sure enough, there was an e-mail from his Web service. It had been less than thirty minutes since he'd posted the revised source code for Raconteur on the Leland SharePoint.

Thirty minutes.

Someone—or some software bot—was monitoring his SharePoint for changes. That meant he had been compromised. But by whom? Strickland switched over to his desktop, logged on, and then checked his mapping Web page. There, on a digital globe, he saw where the IP address of the machine that had just run his modified code resolved to: Shenyang, China.

He stared at the screen for several minutes without moving. The Chinese were stealing the Raconteur source code. They'd somehow slipped a back door into the Stanford network. While Strickland pondered what his next steps should be, the klaxon sounded again. He peered at his phone. Another message. He stabbed the refresh button on the Web page, and another IP address had been added to the map. This one in Washington, D.C.

What the hell?

Seconds later another klaxon alert sounded. And then another. Strickland clicked the map refresh again, and now there were dots on the map in St. Petersburg, Russia, and Colorado Springs, Colorado.

Another klaxon alert. Refresh. Now a dot over Hyderabad, India. As the minutes passed, Strickland watched as their visual intelligence software quickly spread across the world. By dawn there were twenty dots on the map, spread across China, the U.S., Europe, Russia, and Japan. It was the map to a covert cyber espionage pipeline. Who the hell were these people?

Strickland did a Whois lookup on the Washington, D.C., IP address and saw that the domain was registered to a company named Mirror Strategies. A quick check showed them to be a public relations firm. But then, it was much more likely they were being used as an unwitting proxy—most likely compromised themselves by the people doing the data theft. Perhaps their network was just a drop zone for stolen files from around the globe. The thieves could even recompile the source code remotely for added safety. Strickland would have no way of knowing just who was behind this—Chinese, Russians, Americans . . . who could tell? And who was to say it was even a government that was doing it? It could be just a cyber crime gang. Grad students like him, perhaps. Privateers for a foreign government, or just hackers doing it for shits and giggles.

Christ. Strickland's mind was racing. What did this mean? Well, for one thing, he could prove that their work had been—and was indeed still being—stolen. And that meant that they could avoid disciplinary action from the university. Hold it: They might even have a legal case against the university at this point. Would Stanford then be willing to underwrite an effort to find out who had done this to them? To find the people, companies, or governments responsible for this? In fact, DARPA would need to know. The Department of Defense would need to know. This had national security implications.

First Strickland had to call the team. His team. Whether Prakash was enraged at him or not, they needed to collectively decide on a course of action. Barely thirty minutes had elapsed after Strickland posted his revised code until it appeared half a world away. Someone had methodically targeted them. This was deliberate espionage. Strickland was just the weakest link, but it was likely that, had he not made the mistake, whoever it was would have kept searching until they found a way in.

On a brighter note that meant Strickland was not entirely responsible for this. It was no accident—it was someone's mission. Deliberate. Targeted. Espionage. Someone was watching their research with great interest. That meant there was still value here.

Strickland picked up his phone and checked the time—four-thirty in the morning. This couldn't wait, so he called the calmest person on the team: Gerhard Keopple. Maybe Koepple could convince the others to reconvene. . . .

Infuriatingly, it took over twenty-four hours for Strickland to get the entire team to agree to a meeting. Prakash had been the lone holdout, and it required the combined efforts of Koepple and Kasheyev and finally even Professor Lei to convince him to show up. Bao-Rong and Chatterjee weren't a problem. Like Strickland, they weren't really critical team members. They were ready to hear what anyone could do to salvage this situation— and their academic careers.

Strickland had told them only that he'd discovered how the code had been stolen—and by whom. In fact, the discovery had made him paranoid, and he refused to hold the meeting at their offices. Instead he'd insisted on a public place in the quad just north of Memorial Church. The wide paved courtyard there had a rosette pattern in its center, and that's where they found themselves standing in the predawn light as the occasional university worker walked past them on the way to the church or points beyond. Here they could see anyone approaching from a long way off.

Kasheyev betrayed no emotion. "How's your face, Josh?"

He hadn't thought about it all day. "Fine. I'm fine."

Professor Lei nudged Prakash. "I think you have something to say to Josh."

Prakash sighed impatiently and refused to look Strickland in the eye as he spoke. "I apologize for striking you, Josh. It was wrong, and I regret it."

Strickland nodded. "That sounds very . . . well rehearsed, but apology accepted."

Professor Lei raised her eyebrows. "So we're meeting out here why, Josh—because you think the offices are bugged?"

Strickland nodded. "The university network's been compromised—possibly by a foreign government. I've got the proof."

Prakash stared. "Oh, it's foreigners now."

Professor Lei interjected, "Vijay, let's hear—"

"Why should we trust a damn thing he says?"

Koepple cast an annoyed look at him. "C'mon, Vijay."

"Josh could be spinning tales of espionage to get himself off the hook. To make himself out like he's some sort of hero."

Strickland was starting to feel badly treated. "Someone is interested in our work, Vijay. Is that so hard to believe? We both know how much it could be worth. Somehow someone found out about it and focused on obtaining it."

"And they found you."

"Maybe that's true, but that doesn't mean that other members of this team weren't also compromised. Does anyone else here have copies of the Raconteur source code stashed somewhere?"

The team looked from one to the other. It had suddenly gotten quiet.

"I rest my case. Doctor Lei, we'll need the university to provide support—quietly, so that whoever's doing this won't know that we're aware of the compromise. But this is now a matter of national security."

She nodded. "What do you have in mind?"

"I say we uncover who these people are. Use all our collective skills to reveal their identities and see what the Defense Department wants to do about it. Forget lawyers. I don't think lawyers can help us."

The others exchanged looks.

Kasheyev shook his head. "It's too late, Josh. The code is already out there."

"Maybe, but that doesn't mean this is over. This isn't just any network breach. Our work has defense applications. And that means it's a matter of national security—which means other options are on the table."

There were murmurs among the others.

Professor Lei looked doubtful. "I don't think you know what you're getting into, Josh."

"We put too much into this just to walk away. If someone's trying to steal our future, I say we fight back." He looked to the rest of the team.

"Are you guys with me, or are you just going to take this? Because I, for one, am not going quietly."

They looked uncertainly to each other.

Prakash was the first to speak up, but not without first letting out an irritated sigh. "Count me in. You might be an idiot, but at least you're willing to do something."

Strickland cast a give-me-a-break look at him.

Prakash shrugged. "I'm ready to do whatever it takes to get back what's rightfully mine."

Strickland nodded. Prakash nodded grimly back.

"Well, if Vijay and I can agree on something for once, how about the rest of you?"

Strickland never got his answer.

Reality itself suddenly disintegrated around them all.

On the observation deck of Hoover Tower less than a quarter mile away, Odin lowered his Leupold binoculars to reveal blue eyes framed by a thick black beard and the brim of a Red Sox baseball cap. He surveyed the main quad beside the Memorial Church where flames, body parts, and a blackened section of cobblestones seemed to be all that remained of the men who'd stood there just moments before. The glass windows of the church had shattered in an explosion. A nearby palm tree was burning. There were shouts in the distance, car alarms wailing, but nothing stirred in the courtyard.

He looked up to scan the dawn sky still speckled with stars. In a few moments he saw a distant flash. Odin counted softly to himself as he stowed the binoculars. "One thousand eight, one thousand nine, one thousand ten . . ."

Still counting, he withdrew a cell phone from his jacket pocket and keyed a number from memory.

The boom of the distant aerial explosion echoed off the buildings like a hammer blow. He stopped counting, having reached "twelve," and noted the direction of the explosion. Odin let the noise fade before he spoke into the handset. "Our client just received an air mail package." He listened. "No one's left in the office. I need to catch the next flight out."

As he spoke, a large raven flapped down to perch on the tower railing next to him. It had a small transponder strapped to its leg and a nearly invisible wire filament headset hovering above its head. Odin extended his hand, and the black bird *caw*ed its harsh call as it climbed onto his arm. It fluffed the feathers at its throat and let out a *keek-keek* sound.

He lifted the raven and studied it as he spoke into the phone. "Schedule the next meeting as soon as possible. Our deadline was just accelerated."

He proceeded toward the tower steps, still holding the raven. Behind him a column of black smoke rose against the dawn light as horrified screams intermingled with the sound of approaching sirens.

CHAPTER 5

Omen

It was war, then. She had modeled this behavior and detected the cues—but even so, the swiftness of the assault caught her off-guard. Perhaps the stigmergic propagation rate needed to be tweaked.

Professor Linda McKinney stared intently at a procession of salmon-colored, dark-eyed weaver ants, coursing like blood cells along branching pathways. They scurried against a craquelure background of mango bark on highways only they could see, surging into combat against black ants many times their size—swarming over their enemy. The video image revealed the carnage in ultrahigh resolution. The dead were piling up.

Weaver ants—*Oecophylla longinoda*. Along with mankind they were one of the few extirpator species on earth—meaning they deliberately sought out and destroyed rival organisms (including their own species) to maintain absolute control of their territory.

McKinney zoomed the camera in on a growing knot of weavers, watching as dozens of workers swarmed a much larger, black ant—a *Dorylus* major, the warrior caste of the driver army ant (which the locals called *siafu*). The monstrous black ant had one of the weavers in its mandibles, but following a timeless script, the much smaller and faster weavers grabbed hold of their enemy, first immobilizing the massive intruder—and then tearing its legs off. They dropped it among the dead and moved on to their next victim.

Defeating a siafu army ant colony in battle was no mean feat. Here in Africa, even humans steered clear of siafu, which occasionally swarmed in wave fronts twenty million strong into huts and farms. Anything that could not escape their grasp would die. There were authenticated accounts of siafu killing humans who'd passed out drunk, unattended infants, and goats or cows that were tied in place. First suffocated by thousands of ants crawling into their mouth and lungs, the strangled victims would have their flesh removed in hours, leaving only bones behind. There was no stopping the swarm. You just had to get out of the way. And yet, as fearsome as they were, even siafu army ants fled from the weavers.

Weavers were so aggressive that McKinney would hear them in their multitudes, drumming their legs against tree leaves in alarm, sounding like raindrops as she walked through the mango orchards. Gathering their troops. Collectively, they dominated the treetops of Africa—while their close cousins *Oecophylla smaragdina* dominated the trees of Asia and Australia. What made them even more fascinating to McKinney was that their reign had already lasted more than a hundred million years. Human civilization was barely a blip on their radar screen.

Weaver society was so durable, so adaptable, that these ants had survived ice ages, extinction-level events—like the asteroid impact that doomed the dinosaurs at the end of the Cretaceous period, sixty-six million years ago. In fact, more than merely surviving, the weavers had thrived. In terms of biomass, they now rivaled that of humanity itself. In numbers they were counted in trillions. They were one of the most successful and enduring species on the face of the planet. That was one of the reasons she had spent her adult life studying them. There was an ancient knowledge of sustainability here on a scale humans could only aspire to. And they were fascinating in so many other ways.

McKinney had originally been drawn to myrmecology because of social insects' unique evolutionary strategy; where most organisms had a single body, Hymenoptera—the order of social insects that included wasps, bees, and ants—were in effect a single organism consisting of millions of separate bodies. The physician Lewis Thomas once described ants as "a brain with a million legs." It was like being able to send your hand to go get things while you were off doing something else. The great myrmecologist E. O. Wilson proposed that ants were a "superorganism"—an organism that transcended the limitations of a single body to enact a collective will. And that will had an intelligence superior to that of the individual ants themselves. Precisely how this occurred was still unknown, and it was a mystery that McKinney had dedicated her career to unraveling.

Studying the screen, she keyed observations into her laptop and spoke via speakerphone to a graduate student several miles away. "Mike, check the lens on camera nine. There's an occlusion that's confusing the tracking software."

"Got it. Rich, can you move the lift closer?"

Another voice came in over the line. "There in a sec."

"Thanks."

McKinney zoomed the image out, displaying dozens of thumbnail video insets on the panoramic HD monitor that, when tiled together, outlined an entire mango tree as a three-dimensional model. She rotated the model as though it were a video game—the difference being that the tree was real and the images real-time. The tree stood on the verdant hillsides near the Marikitanda Research Station, where McKinney ran her field lab. The mango tree's entire surface was being recorded in real time from dozens of separate digital video cameras placed on scaffolding around it. Software was stitching the imagery together into a single live 3-D image wrapped around the tree. Just one nest out of this colony's domain of a dozen trees, covering nearly eight hundred square meters of ground with nearly a half million ants in all. It had taken years of research and grant applications for her to get this system up and running—and to obtain such up-close and complete imagery of an entire weaver nest in real time. Of the superorganism in motion. And all to test whether her software model of weaver society was accurate. And, in turn, whether it could form the basis of a general model of Hymenoptera intelligence. That, in turn, might reveal secrets as to the very nature of intelligence itself.

McKinney turned on the tracking overlay and now saw glowing red dots hovering above individual weaver ants. She wanted to confirm that the computer vision software was accurately identifying individual weavers, and correctly distinguishing them from their much larger and darker siafu enemies. The enemy ants were denoted with blue dots by the tracking software. It seemed to be doing a fair job of telling the ants apart. McKinney would use the red dots from the data set to analyze weaver swarming attack. The idea was to capture the geometry of weaver movements, recording their collective action for analysis against her Myrmidon computer model. It would be interesting to see how her behavioral algorithms held up.

She smiled. Either way, this kicked ass. She was finally getting the raw data she needed to refine her model. To understand the processing power of insect societies. How intelligence could emerge from relatively unintelligent agents and amass into a collective mind.

With only a quarter million neurons in an individual weaver ant's brain, a single ant "knew" very little—especially compared to the one hundred billion neurons in an average human brain. And yet, multiplied by a half million ants, the number of neurons in a colony began to approximate the raw, collective processing power of the human brain.

An ant colony exhibited nothing like a human's sophistication, of course, but there definitely was a specialized intelligence. One that could plan and deliberately act. She'd seen that with other ant species like *Atta laevigata,* whose gigantic colonies excavated in Brazil extended twenty feet belowground with populations in the millions. These were cities able to regulate oxygen flow and temperature, able to farm fungi, dispose of waste.

But McKinney had especially seen evidence of collective intelligence in the nation-state-like domain of the weavers, where they maintained not one but dozens of hand-woven leaf nests in strategic locations throughout their territory and kept "livestock" in the form of mealy bugs (*Cataenococcus hispidus*). Outlying weaver nests were "barracks," garrisoned to fight any intruders on the borders of their territory. If an enemy appeared, workers would summon reinforcements from these castles, and within minutes even intruders a thousand times the size of a single weaver would be surrounded, immobilized, torn apart, then ingested. But more intriguing still was the way weavers waged all-out preemptive wars of extermination against members of their own species. This was a behavior that on earth was exhibited only by the most complex societies of humans and of ants.

Was the collective processing of individual ant brains a primordial, measurable manifestation of a singularity—a collective mind that comes into being whenever information processing achieves critical mass? These and other questions fascinated McKinney—and with the Myrmidon computer model she was on her way to finding some answers.

There was a knock on her lab door.

"Busy. What is it?"

The door opened, and she could hear the sounds of daily activity in the research station outside. A familiar man's voice spoke behind her. "Hey, I know this is none of my concern, but weren't you going to take Adwele climbing up E-39?"

McKinney froze at her keyboard. "Oh, God . . ." She checked her watch.

"Relax. You said one o'clock, and it's five till."

McKinney swiveled in her office chair to face a handsome young entomologist in a stained bowling shirt standing in the doorway. "Jesus, I completely lost track of time." She got up and started grabbing rope bags, packs, helmets, and other climbing gear from nearby metal shelving.

"Don't mention it."

She cast a glance his way. "Sorry, Haloren. Thanks for the heads-up."

"I didn't do it for you. I did it for the kid." He gestured to the computer monitors. "See, 'cause I know how engrossed you can get with your vicious little friends. I'm the same way with dung beetles."

She laughed. "No, you're not."

"If you're suggesting I wouldn't have chosen my line of study if I'd known I was going to be picking larvae out of monkey shit all day, you'd be wrong. It's fucking fascinating. Come over to my cabin some night and I'll show you."

"Yeah, I'll take a pass, thanks." McKinney knew that most of the women researchers found Haloren's sarcasm and self-deprecating humor charming. He was a few years younger than she, in his late twenties, and handsome in a rakish way, but also cocky and too self-amused. He mocked everything and, most infuriatingly, was usually right about things that didn't rise to her notice.

"Who's your friend?"

McKinney followed Haloren's pointed finger to the open window next to her workstation. Sitting there on the branch of a colorful bougain-villaea was a large black raven, staring calmly back at them. "I didn't even notice him."

"Check it out, he's tagged."

McKinney could see a leg band and tiny transponder glittering in the sun. "Someone with funding."

"The few. The lucky few." Haloren leaned against her desk. "You know, the Arabs say ravens are the harbinger of omens."

"Save it for your grad students." McKinney leaned in to the speaker-phone on her desk. "Guys, I'll be back in a few hours. I had an appoint-ment I forgot. Keep the video running and work out any glitches as best you can in the meantime."

There was a chuckle on the other end. *"No problem, Professor."*

Haloren gave her a look. "Those guys were listening the whole time?"

McKinney shrugged and hung up. She then leaned out to grab the window handle and took one last look at the oddly calm-looking raven, only a few feet away. She'd never thought of ravens as being this big. It was easily the size of a hawk, with a powerful, thick beak that looked like it could crush walnuts. Deep black, penetrating eyes, studying her. It had a tiny, wirelike feather hovering over its head, like a black filament rooted somewhere in the feathers of its neck.

It cocked its head at her with an eerie, deliberate focus.

She took a close look at the transponder on its leg and could see a grid of tiny metallic dots. McKinney looked back up at the raven, who was still watching her. "Hi, there. Where are you from?"

The bird cocked its head again, and then let out a perfect imitation of a chain saw.

McKinney laughed and looked to Haloren in surprise. "I didn't know ravens could do sound effects."

"Yeah, they're great at mimicry. My thesis advisor kept a raven. Pain in the ass. Regularly trashed his office, and it hated my guts." Haloren waved his hands. "Shoo! Shoo!"

"So maybe it's the sound of loggers he's imitating?"

"Probably."

She turned back to face the raven, but it had taken off, leaving a wagging branch behind. "Why'd you scare him away?" She shut and locked the window.

Haloren held the office door open for her, but pointedly didn't offer to help lug the forty pounds of climbing gear she was hauling. "After you . . ."

McKinney marched through the door. "Lock it."

"Got it. Got it."

In a few moments they were walking fast on the bustling dirt road running down the center of the research station. Local Maasai people in both Western clothes and traditional *kanga* nodded to them and smiled as they walked past. Haloren engaged them in Swahili, getting laughs out of several. Some of the Maasai were texting on cell phones, getting current cattle and mango market prices from town—an odd mix of the modern and the traditional.

Haloren kept pace easily alongside her, encumbered as she was. "You mind helping with this gear?"

"I would, but I'm a firm believer in the equality of my female colleagues. Hey, speaking of that: Doesn't Adwele already have a mother?"

"Yes, but he's missing a father."

"You applying for the position?"

"Back off, Bruce. He's a smart kid, and he'll need all the help he can get. Babu didn't leave much behind."

"I'm just curious whether you're doing it for Adwele or for yourself. You will be leaving at some point, you know."

McKinney studied Haloren for a moment, then nodded as she realized he really was just looking after Adwele's best interests. "I get what you're saying, but Babu was a good friend. He kept me safe on more than a few research trips. If I can help his family, I will. Even after I go home."

Haloren studied her too. Then he stopped suddenly. "All right, then. I'll leave you to it."

"Hey!"

Haloren turned.

"I promise not to tell anyone you're not really an asshole."

He saluted before heading off. "Much appreciated."

She smirked, shaking her head as she watched him fall in alongside another researcher heading in the other direction.

McKinney hung in an arborist saddle sixty feet above the jungle floor. A cacophony of tropical birds and vervet monkeys echoed in the trees around her. She shaded her eyes against sunlight glittering between the leaves overhead and examined the tree's crown, looking for weaver nests. Fortunately she didn't see any.

The lowest branches of this Outeniqua yellowwood tree—or *Afrocarpus falcatus*—were still twenty feet above her. Her rope hung down from a branch even farther up. She had launched a throw line over it with a crossbow and hauled her climbing rope up after it, securing both ends using climbing knots and a dual line technique she'd learned as a grad student to hook up her harness.

Readjusting her position, McKinney gazed out across the jungle from this hilltop tree at the densely forested peaks of the Usambara Mountains still shrouded in mist in the distance. There was an immense diversity of sights and smells. It was always breathtaking up here. She never failed to notice how beautiful these mountains were, wrapped in low cloud cover and jungle canopy—humid and profuse with life. Reveling in the natural world was as close to the spiritual as McKinney got. She knew it was on this continent—possibly in this very jungle—that the first hominids arose, beginning the journey that separated mankind from the other animals. Becoming self-aware. She felt humbled by the vast stretch of history this place had seen.

She looked down to track the progress of her companion, a sinewy African boy of about ten. He, too, wore a rock-climbing helmet and sat in a climbing saddle suspended from a separate rope. He was laboriously working his way up—his booted foot looped through a rope stirrup. The boy grunted as he pushed up with his leg, ascending another few inches, then readjusting his knots.

McKinney pointed. "Don't grab the Blake's Hitch, or you'll lose ground. Keep your hands below it. That's better, Adwele. Good." She smiled at him. "How you holding up? Need a rest?"

He shook his head. "No, miss. I'm good to go."

She nodded. Adwele was always good to go, ready to learn something new. Unafraid. "Don't push too hard. Take your time and concentrate on form."

He glanced down. Then looked up, flashing a white smile. "Look how high we are!"

"Check that out. . . ." She leaned back on her rope and pointed at the hills. "This is the way birds see the Amani."

Adwele looked out at a view he'd never seen, though he'd lived his entire life here. A grin spread across his face.

McKinney could see the wonder in his eyes, his growing fascination with the natural world. She saw so much of herself in him. It gave her pause.

A maternal pang was all it was, she knew. The lost decade of her post-doc work, the long hours and low pay of an associate professor. While other people were settling down, she'd been traveling in the remote regions of the world doing field research. It was an adventurous life, but not one suited to being a parent. Besides, there were already enough people in the world, and what she was leaving behind for future generations was her research. She took a deep breath.

"Let me see how your knots are holding up." She walked the tree trunk to come alongside him. McKinney checked Adwele's rig section by section. "Stopper knot's still solid. Nice bridge. Figure-eight looks good." She examined the Prusik knot wrapped around the main line and pushed the loops more tightly together. "Was this slipping when you ascended?"

"A little."

"Keep it snug like this, and it won't slip even if the rope gets wet." McKinney glanced below them. "About time to add another safety knot too. Every ten feet. Remember."

"Yes, miss." Adwele nodded and deftly tied a slipknot into the rope that trailed away beneath him. There were similar knots at intervals in the line below.

She rapped on his helmet with her gloved hand. "You're becoming a pro. Now, remember, it's important to follow all of the steps. What happens when we get careless?"

"Hospital or worse."

McKinney nodded. "Yes. Very good."

"Why does Professor Haloren use a metal tool to climb instead of all these knots?"

"You mean an ascender? Because Professor Haloren is lazy."

Adwele laughed. "He says you're cheap."

"Equipment can malfunction, and when it does, you'd better know how to do this yourself. Once you can tie these knots without thinking, you can use an ascender if you like."

Adwele was already gazing past her, up into the tree's crown. He pointed. "Look, a kipepeo."

McKinney followed his arm to see a pink, parchmentlike butterfly flexing its wings on the leaf of a nearby tree. "*Salamis parhassus*. Also called 'the Mother of Pearl Salamis.'"

Adwele took a small notebook and pen that hung by a short cord to a carabiner on his harness. He flipped through the pages and entered a tick mark. He counted. "Fourteen more than last year so far, and there's still a month to go. Is it the butterfly farmers at Marikitanda?"

"Could be. Although it could also be because you're surveying more."

Adwele nodded as he put his notebook away. "My sister says I cannot become a scientist. She says it is a white man's job, but I told her that you're a woman, and you are a scientist."

McKinney gave him a serious look, then planted her feet firmly on the tree trunk, far above the jungle floor. "Do you know why I love science, Adwele?"

He shook his head.

"Because science is the best tool we have for finding truth. For instance, to the naked eye you and I look very different, but it took science to help us see that there's almost no genetic difference between us. And that's a great truth. Remember that." She slapped him on the helmet playfully. "It's what you put in here that counts." And she poked him in the chest. "And what's in here. Don't let anyone ever tell you you can't try for something, Adwele. No one knows what you're capable of yet—not even you."

"Yes, miss."

"Time to head back."

He nodded.

"What's the first step when descending?"

Adwele thought for a moment, then looked down to the base of the tree. He cupped a gloved hand over his mouth and shouted, "Down check!"

McKinney looked down to see an Amani Reserve ranger named Akida wave back and give a thumbs-up.

"Clear!"

She looked back at Adwele. "Okay, good. Remember, we do this slow and steady so we don't overheat the rope. Two fingers on top of the hitch, with your control hand holding the line. Depress the Blake's Hitch lightly, and remove the safety knots as we reach them. . . ."

Walking the mile or so back to the research camp, McKinney shared the load with Akida, but Adwele insisted on carrying his own pack, struggling as he went. McKinney kept a short length of throw line over her back in a European coil and turned back to watch Adwele.

Navigating around a tree, Adwele started falling backward with the added weight. "Help me, miss!"

McKinney grabbed his rope bag and helped him reseat it on his shoulders. "You got it?"

"I'm good."

She exchanged grins with Akida, the Amani ranger who brought up the rear. They could both see traits of Babu in the son.

They continued walking the path home. Adwele walked behind her. "My mother says you are too pretty to keep your hair short. You should let it grow so that you can find a husband."

"Uh, thanks for the advice, but I'm in Africa to do research. And where I come from, women don't need to rely on a man for a living." She pointed down at driver ants swarming in a thick line along the edge of the path. "Look."

Adwele stopped to watch the swarm. "Siafu."

"Yes." McKinney pointed. "Do you know that almost every ant you see is female?"

"Even the siafu warriors?"

McKinney nodded. "That's right. All of the workers, the warriors, and the queen, they're all girls. The nursery workers determine the caste of the young by how they feed them, but the only time they make boy ants is when they want to create a new colony."

"Then they need boys sometimes, eh?"

McKinney laughed. Adwele never missed anything. "I guess that's true. C'mon, smart guy. . . ." She held out her hand to keep them moving. Her gaze happened on a large raven observing them from a tree branch overhead. She was surprised for a moment until she realized that the Amani no doubt held more than a few ravens. Perhaps she was only just starting to notice them.

CHAPTER 6

Wake-up Call

It was hot and humid in the darkness. Another scorching night at the research station. Early December, but Tanzania's hot dry season appeared to be coming on early. McKinney lay on her cot in a Cornell T-shirt and gym shorts beneath mosquito netting. Unable to sleep, she had rolled her shirt up and was fanning her exposed midriff with a Harvard report on social algorithms. Dripping with sweat, she listened to the sounds of the jungle all around her: animal calls and a relentless thrum of crickets.

Way out here there was no air-conditioning. Not that they couldn't have it, but it was frowned upon by hard-core field researchers (and grant committees). The technology that did make it out to the bush was always surprising. For instance, she got four bars on her cell phone in the Amani, but adequate medical clinics were rare.

God, it's hot.

Although her windows were open, they were placed high up the walls with a thick wire mesh for security reasons, inhibiting airflow. There was also a brass whistle on top of the Pelican case next to her cot that she was supposed to use to summon the station's several askaris in case of trouble. They'd had thieves in the night before, but since the American drone incident in Iraq, the university had doubled the security detail (presumably since a third of Tanzania's population was Muslim, and the American embassy had been bombed before).

She knew the cost of the added security would be coming out of all their research budgets, and she pondered whether it was another overreaction. They were far from Dar es Salaam, the old capital, and the researchers had had great relations for decades with the local Maasai tribesmen (most of whom weren't either Christian or Muslim, but worshiped their own monotheist god, Enkai.)

Speaking of god: God, it's hot.

She recalled how the big tourist hotels in Dar es Salaam deeply refrigerated the guest rooms with air-conditioning to keep out malarial *Anopheles gambiae* mosquitoes. She always had to bundle up like an Inuit when she stayed there, even if it was scorching outside. Right now that sounded pretty good. So did a cold beer.

Her mind wandered, as it often did on these hot, sleepless nights—and as always it eventually gravitated to family. To her mother. And then to her father. McKinney had been in a remote region of Borneo when her mother took ill, and she hadn't gotten back in time. The pain of that was always there on nights like this.

She rolled onto her side and looked at the framed photographs next to the glow of her recharging phone. A photo of her father, her mother, and two older brothers arm-in-arm. How much had she missed in all this time in the field? There was another photo of her, taken while skydiving. Her one hundredth jump, goggles on and thumbs-up in free fall somewhere over Virginia. Her jump partner, Brian Kirkland, had taken the photo. She was no longer with him. Long-distance relationships were always hard. He was a great guy. Married now with a kid.

Should she take a teaching position at the university? Give up field research? She thought of Adwele and his father, Babu, a ranger at the Amani Reserve. Killed by poachers. How would Adwele manage without a father? He was such a bright kid. But was Haloren right? Was McKinney taking an interest in Adwele for her own selfish reasons? Trying to fill a void? That was the worst thing about Haloren: As annoying as he could be, he was disturbingly perceptive.

An odd, unfamiliar humming sound intruded on her thoughts. McKinney looked up toward the window screen on the far side of her small room.

But the sound was already gone.

Jungle sounds. She lay back down and thought of large nocturnal flying insects. A *Goliathus albosignatus*? Goliath beetles had been known to reach four and half inches long. But she'd never seen one around the station. It would be great to catch one.

There was the sound again—this time coming from the window on her left.

McKinney rolled over and gazed up at the screen near the rafters. There was something just outside the window, a hum almost inaudible against the background jungle noise. And there—a shimmering in the night air. Now gone.

The odd humming sound moved, heading to the window above her bed.

Interesting. Maybe something rare? McKinney sat up and grabbed for an LED flashlight next to the brass whistle. Moving away from the window, she crawled to the foot of the bed and turned to stare up at the window screen.

Certainly not a bat. She cycled through her encyclopedic knowledge of local species, but couldn't map the sound. A consistent, soft hum.

Then, something reflected one of the station security lights—a gleaming carapace six inches across, rising slowly above the window frame. Methodically. Like a willful intelligence.

"What the hell . . . ?" She kicked on the LED flashlight. But the beam reflected back against the metal screen, blinding her worse than if she'd never turned the thing on at all. The object hummed quickly away.

"Dammit!" She clicked off the light, but now her night vision was ruined. "Just goddammit . . ." McKinney pulled on sneakers and got to her feet, pacing in the darkness, trying to figure out what to do next. She was wide awake now and just stood there, listening.

What she heard next shocked her: a boy's voice, soft and low just outside her cabin. "Help me, miss. Help me!"

A familiar voice.

McKinney felt adrenaline surge in her bloodstream. She called out, "Adwele?" She grabbed the brass whistle next to her bed and looped the chain around her neck.

His voice was unmistakable this time. "Help me, miss!"

Without thinking McKinney unbolted her door and ran out into the gravel lane bounded by blooming bougainvillaea, dark gray in the moonlight. She clicked on the flashlight and scanned the darkness. "Adwele! What's wrong? Where are you?"

The voice called back from behind the cabin. "Help me, miss!"

McKinney ran between her cabin and the next, calling out. "Adwele, where are you? What's going on?"

But the boy's voice was receding now, heading into the jungle. "Miss, help me. Help me!"

McKinney ran after his voice, struggling to put the brass whistle to her lips as she sprinted into the dense brush of the jungle, branches smacking her face. Before she could blow on it, she ran headlong into something laid across the path that caught her in the shins. She stumbled onto the jungle floor—but held on to the flashlight. She had it clenched tightly in her hand.

The voice was just next to her now. Above her. "Help me, miss. . . ."

"Adwele!" McKinney rolled over and aimed the flashlight up into the nearest tree. Sitting on a branch there was a large black raven, its eyes glowing white with reflected light. It cocked its head and opened its beak, delivering a perfect imitation of the boy she knew.

"Help me, miss! Help me."

A feeling of illogical terror gripped McKinney—a nonhuman intelligence had just tricked her. "Oh, my God . . ."

The raven flew off into the night.

And then the world exploded. Behind her a sound so loud and sharp that she felt it more than heard it as the shock wave passed through her body, blasting through the trees and kicking up a wave of dust in a blinding flash. Setting her ears ringing.

McKinney sucked for air and rolled onto her back to gaze fifty meters behind her at the research station.

Where her cabin had been there was now a raging inferno amid shattered wooden beams. Large pieces of fiery debris were still raining down, crashing into the trees. McKinney struggled to sit up—and to process what she was looking at.

An explosion.

Whistles were sounding in the research station now. Shadows of people running against the flames, shouting as the alarm went up. She was having difficulty comprehending what had just happened.

And then she felt a sharp sting in her right side. When she raised her hand to it, McKinney's fingers encountered a metal dart protruding from her T-shirt, and before she could react, she fell back onto the jungle floor. Warm syrup now seemed to be moving through her veins, and as her head lolled to the side, she saw a human form dressed in black, its face hooded, coming toward her at a crouch. Some sort of pistol in gloved hands. Black goggles over the eyes.

Curious. It was the only emotion she could seem to muster as a second hooded form in black approached from the other direction. A gloved hand grabbed her flashlight and turned it off. Someone forced one of her eyes open wide and put two fingers against her throat as if taking her pulse.

A calm voice nearby spoke softly. "Odin to Safari-One-Six. Touchdown secure. We are Oscar Mike to extraction point."

McKinney's eyes focused on a sturdy climbing boot kneeling inches from her face. A brand-new Hanwag. She'd always wanted Hanwags. That was a damned fine boot. Her vision began to fade.

In fact, it was the best boot money could buy. . . .

CHAPTER 7

The Activity

At some point McKinney became aware that she was strapped into an airplane seat, a stethoscope pressing against her shirt.

A man's voice close by: "Breathing normal. Pulse steady." The stethoscope went away. "Blood pressure one-seventeen over seventy-six." The sound of Velcro tearing and she felt pressure release from her left arm. "She's stable."

Another man's voice. Deeper. "Thanks, Mooch."

McKinney saw she was now wearing a gray flight suit, but she focused on her wrists. She was literally strapped into an airplane seat—her hands secured to the armrests by plastic zip-ties. The dull roar of turboprop engines throbbed around her. The window shade was down, so she couldn't tell if it was day or night. She gazed forward at the dimly lit cabin. A couple of empty rows ahead of her, then a bulkhead. She sat in the aisle seat on the right side. An asymmetrical layout—two seats right of the aisle, one seat on the left. Some sort of commuter plane. The height and dimensions of the cabin seemed familiar. Before she realized it, she heard her own voice say, "A Twin Otter."

That deep voice again, somewhere close by. "You know your bush planes."

She was still fuzzy, answering the unknown voice reflexively. "We used to jump from DHC-6s."

"Why'd you quit?"

"I promised my dad. After Mom died." McKinney's eyes wandered to the seat just across the aisle to see a trim, well-proportioned man sitting there. He had gray-blue eyes with a sun-worn face partly concealed by a Red Sox ball cap and a long black beard and mustache. The hat made him look like a rookie trade from the Taliban league. Otherwise, he was dressed in faded jeans with a weathered cameraman's vest overrun with pockets. The man looked vaguely Mediterranean . . . or perhaps Central Asian? Or maybe he was just really tanned. It was hard to tell. His accent was perfect Midwestern American.

Oddly, he was now whispering soothing words to a large raven that stood on an armrest next to him. The man carefully removed a small transponder from around the raven's leg as he spoke to it. The bird responded with soft *keek-keek* sounds and fluffed its throat and head feathers into punk-rocker spikes.

Woozy as she was, McKinney suspected the bird to be a hallucination, so she focused on the bearded man. "What happened? Has there been an accident?"

He glanced at her as he stroked the raven's head. "No, everyone's okay. You're safe now."

"I remember an explosion." She winced and grabbed her side. "Why am I in so much pain?" There was a stabbing sensation in her ribs. In fact, her whole body felt bruised.

"That's the Naloxone—it blocks opioid receptors."

"Nalox . . . why was I . . . what . . . ?" She was having trouble thinking.

"It was necessary to counteract the sufentanil. You'll be sensitive to pain until it wears off."

She shook her head in an attempt to wake up and finally succeeded in focusing her vision on the raven. The large black bird was apparently real, and it was studying her right back. The memory of the raven outside her window returned to her.

"I remember a bird. And an explosion."

"That was Huginn you saw. This is Muninn." On her confused frown he added, "Norse mythology. The god Odin had two ravens, Huginn and Muninn—'thought' and 'memory.' They flew across the land bringing him news of the world of men."

"And they do that?"

He opened his hand to reveal a tiny transponder bracelet. McKinney could see what appeared to be a grid of copper leads on the surface of the device.

"Plenoptic camera. Called a 'computational' camera in the trade—lets us change the focal length after an image is taken, remove occlusions through synthetic aperture tracking. Lets us clearly view surveillance subjects through light cover—window screens and foliage."

"How long have you been watching me?"

"Long enough to know you wouldn't hesitate to help Adwele."

"Your raven manipulated me."

"Huginn saved your life. Spotter drones can be difficult for us to detect, but he has a knack."

"Spotter drones? Who are you?" She tugged at her restraints. "And why the hell am I strapped into this chair?"

"You call me Odin." He spoke next to the raven. "Muninn, eat. Go on."

The bird *cawed*, and hopped away toward the back of the plane.

McKinney gave him a look like she'd entered a madhouse.

"Your restraints are a precaution. Some people react badly to the drugs. Get hysterical. Never a good thing on an airplane."

She tried to keep her voice calm, despite her mounting temper. "I'm not hysterical."

He studied her, then cast a look at someone behind them. "Mooch."

She heard movement, then the *swip* of steel being drawn as a handsome, neatly groomed man in his twenties with cocoa brown skin leaned over her. He looked of South Asian/Indian descent, and wore a crisp white *galabia* and white *taqiyah* skullcap. A stethoscope hung around his neck. He deftly slipped a razor-sharp killing knife through both her wrist straps. In a moment she was free, rubbing her wrists as "Mooch" disappeared again behind her.

McKinney looked around the whole cabin now that she could turn around. Half the interior was cargo space packed with metal cases and electronics equipment. Another bearded man, with pale skin and wild brown rock-star hair, sat one row back. He looked possibly Albanian or Russian with a soft, slightly rounded face and wide-set eyes. He wore faded jeans and a heavy metal band's T-shirt covered with Arab script. He also had tattoos of horses and fiery skulls running the length of both forearms. He was unaccountably tuning a kora—a traditional West African stringed instrument. Behind him sat a rather plain, olive-skinned woman in a maroon hijab and sari. She was holding a copy of *Small Arms Review* but had looked up to meet McKinney's gaze. The woman nodded and went back to reading.

Beyond her was a twentysomething Eurasian kid with hipster glasses and a soul patch. He wore khakis and a dark green pullover, along with a headset and mouthpiece. He was busy at an electronics console in the cargo area.

"Who are you people? Where is this plane headed?"

Odin extended his hand to the row behind him. "Foxy, pass me the Rover."

The Albanian man sighed and set aside the kora to dig through a satchel on the floor. "Take it easy on her, boss."

"The Rover, please. Thank you." In a moment Odin came back with a ruggedized computer tablet. He tapped the screen a few times, then held it up for McKinney to see. The device was already playing what appeared to be black-and-white aerial footage, a view from a thousand feet up, orbiting a jungle village.

McKinney recognized it. "The Marikitanda Research Station."

"FLIR imagery taken from an MC-12 about twenty minutes ago." He pointed with his scarred, calloused hand. "See this?"

"My cabin."

"Right. Watch."

McKinney saw a luminous human form run from her cabin. This was apparently infrared imagery, highlighting heat sources. She watched herself sprint into the jungle, where she was soon lost beneath the dense canopy. Moments later an object streaked into the frame and impacted on her cabin—whiting out the screen.

She looked up at Odin. "I don't understand what's happening."

"You were the target of a drone attack tonight, Professor McKinney."

"A drone attack—wait, you know my name."

"We know everything about you. Age thirty-two, born in Knoxville, Tennessee, undergraduate degree in evolutionary biology, UCLA, masters and postdoc work in entomology, Cornell University. Recently acquired a full professorship and a research grant for your work modeling Hymenoptera social systems. You're a Bills fan. You hate peas. Shall I go on?"

She stared blankly at him.

Foxy was again tuning the kora as he muttered, "Social media's a bitch. . . ."

McKinney was now fully awake. "You said a drone attack." She narrowed her eyes at Odin. "How were you . . . why were you here?"

"Like I said, we've been surveilling you for several days."

"But why?" McKinney then shouted, "And why the hell didn't you warn me? I could have been killed!"

"Calm down."

"I'll calm down when someone explains to me what the hell is going on. Why was I drugged and kidnapped?"

Odin spoke in soothing tones. "The research station has armed security, Professor. What would have happened if you called out for help? Innocent guards could have been hurt trying to defend you."

"Who are you people? Why would a drone attack me?"

He held up a calming hand. "We're here to help you."

"Then you should have warned me instead of—"

Odin shook his head. "This is a secret operation, Professor. I needed to be certain they were targeting you. We had to wait until the last possible moment."

"That who was targeting me?"

"That's what we're trying to find out." Odin turned the tablet screen back toward him and started tapping at it again. "Until tonight we haven't been able to predict the target of these drone attacks in advance. But you solved that for us."

"What the hell are you talking about?"

"Let's take it one step at a time."

"Why would someone send a drone after me? I study ants."

"Here . . ." He turned the Rover back toward her.

McKinney could now see a close-up infrared view of her own bungalow and its corrugated tin roof. There, hovering around her window, was a dimly visible object. A pizza-pan-sized four-rotor flying . . . thing. She could barely make it out as it moved from window to window with the thoroughness of a bee at a flowering bush.

She stared at the screen in disbelief. "None of this makes any sense."

"Looks like a modified Chinese F50 airframe, but that doesn't really tell us anything about its firmware or who sent it. I could buy a hundred of these off the back of some truck in Dubai or Moscow."

She was still watching the evil-looking insect float outside her living quarters, her own glowing heat signature visible in bed through the window.

"As near as we can tell, the parent drone sniffs out its victims by their IMEI."

McKinney still watched the screen. "I don't know what that is."

"International mobile equipment identity. Every mobile phone has a unique number burned in at the factory. That ID can be used to pinpoint the location of a specific phone anywhere in the world within fifty meters."

McKinney had a vivid image of her iPhone charging next to her bed.

"But that's not accurate enough to deliver ordnance. So the parent drone carries a spotter that it launches to confirm the presence of the target. The spotter descends, and we think it searches the vicinity, looking for the victim's face—probably uses a cheap pocket camera face-detection chip to make a list of human faces that it compares with target photos it already has in memory. We'll know more if we can catch it."

"Where would it get my photo?"

"Facebook, LinkedIn, university profile. That's a trivial problem."

She watched in horror as the spotter drone suddenly projected a grid of hundreds of infrared dots across the interior of her cabin—across her very body—in a light spectrum she hadn't seen as she lay in the darkness.

"Registration grid. Once the target is confirmed, it uses an IR laser to send a coded signal back to the parent, clearing it to attack. That's how we knew when to make our move."

McKinney saw her own form shining an LED flashlight beam out her screen that didn't show up in infrared, but the video focused on the quadracopter spotter drone, which floated away. A bright light blinked rapidly on its back in a complex sequence.

"The spotter then moves to a safe distance to film the strike, confirm detonation of ordnance, fatalities, so on. ELINT suggests that it then connects to the nearest Wi-Fi hotspot it can hijack to upload the video to a predetermined Web domain before the spotter also self-destructs." He looked to the back of the plane. "Did we stop that video upload, Hoov?"

The Eurasian guy at the electronics console answered. "We did. There was a connection to our open Wi-Fi access point just before the attack. It performed a test upload—which I let past—and afterwards a large encrypted file was transferred . . . which I trapped."

"Bingo. That means they don't have shit. No damage assessment." Odin handed the ruggedized tablet over to her, but his gaze stayed on Hoov. "What else do you have for me?"

Hoov was studying several screens of his own. "Judging from the impact radius, I'd say it's another fifteen-kilo laser-guided fuel-air bomb."

"Foxy, we'll need to insert a mop-up crew into the TPDF to get the bomb fragments."

Foxy answered. "Already in the works."

"And the parent drone—please tell me we got clear video for once."

Everyone turned to face Hoov expectantly.

Hoov milked the pregnant silence, then smiled. "Channel Two."

Odin clapped once and grabbed the Rover. He tapped the screen for a few moments as the others crowded around him, looking over his shoulder from the seat backs. It was obvious that they'd been trying to get a look at their quarry for some time. Their eyes went wide and they nodded in satisfaction.

Odin looked up. "Goddammit, good job, Hoov. There's our enemy, people. At long last we meet."

The woman in the hijab poked her ringed index finger. "South African Bateleur?"

Foxy shook his head. "Not with that wing configuration. Looks more like a Rustom-H to me. Or maybe an Indian Aura."

Odin was shaking his head. "No, it's another knock-off. Maybe built with stolen tech."

He turned the Rover to face McKinney. "Here's what would have killed you tonight, Professor. . . ."

She studied the black-and-white image. It was like seeing footage of Bigfoot; a vaguely familiar drone shape—straight wings, with canards, and a rear-facing propeller. It was filmed off to the side and from below, where a bomblike object was visible on a hard-point on its belly. The perspective of the image was changing slowly, as though taken from another aircraft that was moving in a different direction.

The rest of the group seemed pretty satisfied, but McKinney grimaced. "Why didn't you shoot it down before it attacked me?"

"Not the plan. It's important that they don't know we're tracking them. Not yet, at any rate. And by intercepting their spotter's video upload, they won't know whether you're alive or dead."

"Can't you trace it"—she rolled her hand in thought—"by radio signals or something? Find out who's controlling it?"

Odin looked grim. "That's the problem: No one is controlling it. These drones are autonomous—programmed to find and kill their victim, and then to self-destruct. So far it's been impossible to get a good look at one, much less capture it intact. But we're working on that last part, and thanks to you we made some progress tonight." He turned back to Hoov. "When did we lose it?"

"Disappeared from the radar screen nine clicks south of Target One at an altitude of twenty-two thousand feet."

Foxy murmured, "Figures."

Odin didn't seem surprised either. "Any luck catching the spotter?"

"Negative. It flew off after the bomb strike. Tin Man and Smokey are beating the bush trying to find it, but all hell's broken loose at the research station. Armed guards are running around with flashlights."

"Pull 'em out. See what our operatives can find tomorrow. In the meantime upload everything to the gateway, and tell Expert Four I want a written assessment by the time I return."

"Will do."

McKinney was still trying to process the insanity of her situation. "Let me get this straight: Someone tried to kill me with a self-piloting suicide drone?"

"I know this must all seem very strange."

She looked at him like he was certifiably insane.

"Okay. Maybe it is very strange. But now there's a tool to cheaply eliminate people without facing consequences. That means this is about to spread."

McKinney was still trying to grapple with it. "But . . . I've seen documentaries on plane crashes—can't you go through the wreckage and find out—"

"What? That the parts were made in China? Everything's made in China. Whoever's doing this is using off-the-shelf components—the same chips and circuit boards used in computers and game consoles. What we need to do is get ahold of the firmware that runs them—their brain. But immediately after they attack, these drones climb to about twenty or twenty-five thousand feet—then self-destruct. And when I say 'self-destruct,' I mean they shred themselves. Explosive residue on the few pieces we've found shows it's pentaerythritol tetranitrate—Primacord—basically explosive rope. Used for cutting steel."

Foxy twanged the kora. "What the Finnish army calls *anopin pyykki-naru*—'mother-in-law's clothesline.'" Another twang for emphasis.

Odin cast a look at him, then turned back to McKinney. "A chemical trace dead-ended to a batch of det-cord stolen from a demolition project in Cyprus two years ago—no suspects. The explosive cuts the drone into confetti, and at that altitude the wreckage spreads across twenty square miles. What we've found so far wouldn't fill a garbage bag."

Hoov called out from the back of the plane. "No suspicious radio traffic during the event."

"As expected."

McKinney held up her hand to silence them. "What. The. Hell. Is going on? Why is someone trying to kill me?"

The Albanian guy named Foxy raised his eyebrows. "You really don't know?"

"Because I'm an American? Because of the Karbala attack? If that's the case, you need to evacuate the entire research station."

Odin drummed his fingers on his armrest. "Unfortunately it's more personal than that. Someone is targeting you specifically, Professor Mc-Kinney."

She was utterly at a loss. "I study ants."

"That is the reason someone's trying to kill you. Because of your particular expertise."

"My expertise . . ." McKinney leaned back in her seat and just stared at him for a moment. "Who the hell are you people?"

"We're with the U.S. military."

"The U.S. military."

"Yes."

She eyed them. "You don't look like U.S. military."

"Well, that's kind of the whole point."

"I want to see credentials. Now."

"That's not how this works."

"Well, it's how I work. I'm sort of funny that way."

"We're the people who just saved you from certain death. That's all you need to know about us."

"As far as I know, you kidnapped me, blew up my cabin with a stick of dynamite, and put together some drone highlight reels."

Odin looked back at Foxy.

Foxy shrugged. "She's got a point." He lowered the kora and dug into his bag. In a moment he produced a folder, which he passed forward.

Odin took the folder. "I don't have any latitude to tell you who we are. That could put our mission in jeopardy." He withdrew a document, glanced at it, and then passed it along to her. "Are you familiar with any of these people, Professor McKinney?"

Still irritated, she hesitated before accepting the piece of paper. It was a printout of the front page of *The New York Times,* just a few days old. The headline read SIX DIE IN STANFORD BOMBING. The names of several of the victims had been helpfully highlighted in yellow by someone: Lei Li, Vijay Prakash, Gerhard Koepple . . .

"God, there's been a bombing at Stanford now too?"

"Were you familiar with these researchers or their work?"

"No. I've never heard of them."

"You're sure, Professor? Never bumped into them at a conference? Never read any of their academic papers?"

"No, I haven't. I'm sure."

Odin took the printout back. "You have one thing in common with these researchers, Professor. Both your work and theirs was found on a file server in Shenyang, China. Part of a cyber espionage pipeline that was spiriting advanced technology out of the West. At first we suspected North Korea's Unit 121, a cyber warfare group, but that's not where the trail led us."

She was speechless.

"The people who stole the Stanford researchers' work also made a point of taking yours."

"But my research isn't secret. I make it available to the entire scientific community."

"Well, they had your work and your tools before you published. Which means they broke into Cornell's network. Which means you were one of only two researchers in the world they were interested in. We have people searching for the network breach at Cornell, but what I'm concerned with is what knowledge you have that they wanted. And now that they've tried to cover their tracks by killing you, we know it's important to whatever they're planning."

"This is insane. I study insects."

"You develop behavioral computer models as part of your research."

"Yes. Simulations—modeling the social systems of certain insects."

"In fact, you're currently developing a computer model that simulates the swarming behavior of weaver ants."

She narrowed her eyes at him. "And that's what they're after?"

"Your work has direct application to a strategy being pursued by America's enemies. I came here to brief you, Professor McKinney."

"What do you mean 'brief me'? Brief me about what?"

"About the terror bombings in the United States."

"What about them?"

"They're not terror bombings."

She stopped short and looked around. No help.

"Over the past several months someone has been carrying out drone strikes in the continental United States. They're not intended to terrorize. They're targeted assassinations, meant to eliminate specific people. This is next generation warfare, Professor, and we're facing a very sophisticated adversary. Someone who's trying to remain hidden—and who thinks you know too much about their systems."

Again she was speechless.

He stared back at her, unreadable.

She finally nodded her head ruefully. "Did you really think we could just fire missiles into other countries, assassinating people from the air, without it coming back to haunt us? You flouted international law, and now you act amazed that—"

"Be that as it may—"

"I appreciate you rescuing me, but I don't appreciate you involving me in your . . . war, or whatever it is. I perform basic research on the natural world."

He turned more serious. "As one human being to another, I'm asking for your assistance."

"I turned down all military-funded research grants for a reason. I want no part of this 'permanent war' you people are selling. We should be investing in education and health care, not war."

He flipped through the folder in his hand. "You contribute to human rights groups and antiwar organizations."

"And I suppose you think that makes me some sort of traitor."

"No. It gives me hope that you'll help us."

"That makes no sense."

"Yes, it does." He leaned close to her. "We have reason to think these enemy drones might be using a software model based on the behavior of weaver ants. A model developed by you."

She felt the warm surge of adrenaline. "My God . . ."

He started dealing out full-color photographs into her lap. Photos of carbonized and torn bodies, maimed and injured people at bombing scenes—some of them children. "Scores of innocent people are dead. Politicians, scholars, human rights activists, business leaders, students. Someone has bypassed America's defenses to kill these specific people. And more die every week. What you need to do is tell me how to stop it."

She searched for anything to say as she gazed in horror at the images. "But I don't . . . I have no idea how my work could—"

"Tell me why someone would choose to imbue a machine with the mind of a weaver ant. What's so special about them? Why weavers?"

She felt nauseous, on the verge of tears, looking at the photo of a dead child. A twisted and burned stroller lay nearby. "Because the weaver ant is quite possibly the most warlike creature on the face of the earth."

CHAPTER 8

Lost in Action

Chet Warner had no desire to travel anywhere with the Pakistani army, let alone into the densely crowded slums of Lyari Town. It was like strapping on a deer costume to go out hiking on the opening day of hunting season.

One of the eighteen constituent towns in the city of Karachi, Lyari was a tangled warren of alleys, broken streets, and dilapidated buildings alongside the harbor on the west end of the city. Notwithstanding Pakistan's population of Taliban sympathizers and Islamic fundamentalists, and orderly military neighborhoods, Lyari was controlled by narcotics gangs armed with machine guns and rocket-propelled grenades; not even the police dared cross into it. Going in with the army seemed not much wiser, since the chief distinction between the police and the army was the color of their armored cars. Warner wouldn't even have considered going there if it weren't for Colonel Kayani's personal assurances that Langley would be pleased.

Warner glanced over to the ornately uniformed Pakistani army colonel sitting across from him inside the cramped BRDM-2 armored car. Kayani must be expecting a photo op, since he had never dressed like this before. It made Warner feel more at ease.

He tried to distract his chronically loose bowels by peering through the narrow bulletproof portal in the side of the BRDM. The convoy was rolling along the Lyari Expressway that followed the river of the same name. As he looked out, the river was just a dusty no-man's-land several hundred yards wide, bisected by a narrow channel of raw sewage and industrial effluent that reeked of ammonia. On the far side lay the Sindh Industrial and Trading Estate—or SITE town—a place every bit as fetching as its name implied.

Karachi had never been Warner's choice, but then, he hadn't distinguished himself in those early years, and accepting a clandestine service post seemed like a way to beef up his résumé—to get some respect. Then, just a few months after he arrived, the Russians started pulling out of Afghanistan. Colleagues sounded surprised he hadn't known Pakistan was going to be a career dead-end. He pondered a long list of missed opportunities and unproductive, low-profile assignments that followed. It had taken him one divorce and a decade of patience to work his way Stateside once more.

Then, on September 11—*bam*. Suddenly Pakistan was important again, and so were Warner's years of field experience and extensive army connections there. He soon found himself managing crews operating secretly out of remote places like Shamsi, Dalbandin, Jacobabad, and Pasni. Young teams. Technical teams. Experts doing split operations to launch and maintain unmanned surveillance drones that were being flown from inside trailers. Nobody knew then how important those little toys were going to become. If he was honest with himself, Warner knew that was probably why he'd been given the assignment; it was at first just a sideshow. Now, by chance, it was the main event.

Those days just after 9/11 were heady times, and he'd finally had a chance to shine. But as always, time marched on and new people with new skills followed the path he'd blazed. Drones were high profile now. Before long he found himself politically outmaneuvered by younger, more technologically adept Ivy Leaguers. The Garden Party set. His age-old nemesis.

When he looked back on his career, that had been the one consistent theme: being outmaneuvered. His ex-wife had called him timid, even though he'd spent half his life in war zones. Now here he was in Karachi again. Right where he'd started—and he'd been a lot more adventurous back in his twenties. Now he just kept worrying about oral-fecal disease transmission and kidnapping.

The colonel tapped Warner's knee and laughed, shouting over the diesel engine of their armored car. "You should not be anxious, you know. Everything has been arranged for maximum safety."

"Whenever you say things like that, Anil, you make me nervous. It sounds suspiciously like tempting fate."

The colonel laughed uproariously. "Fates be damned, my friend. You will be very happy. This will put the whole bin Laden issue behind us. You will see."

He'd known the colonel for twenty-five years—way back when he'd been a CIA paper-pusher, and Anil had been an ISI liaison. Back before Warner's expertise and long-standing connections made him a valuable consultant. Now both in their fifties, they saw the prospect of retirement just over the horizon. A low-end condo on the Texas Riviera was never far from Warner's thoughts. Now was the time to swing for the fences. One last pay grade boost before going to the consulting side.

The four-wheeled armored BRDM-2 slowed down, and Warner took a deep breath. They were cutting in on Tannery Road. From here things would only get dicier. This was PPP territory. Crawling through traffic would make them a sitting duck. One RPG at close range, and the passenger compartment would get punctured by a white-hot jet of molten metal that would ricochet around until everyone inside looked like undercooked meat loaf. He'd seen the tiny holes those armor-piercing warheads made in the hull of a tank. Why blast a huge hole when all you want to get at is the juicy center? But then, the convoy still seemed to be making good time. And they weren't dead yet.

He peered out the portal again, and judging from the numerous heavily armed police he saw on the streets outside, Warner realized that the roads must have been blocked to civilian traffic. So much for the element of surprise. . . .

In a few minutes their vehicle slowed again and swerved right, down a tight lane. Warner's view became a blur of passing masonry through the side portal. The sharp knock of a business sign being struck and bent back as they rolled past a shop front. All he could hear were sirens, car horns, and the rattle of the BRDM's diesel engine. They were effectively blind. If someone hit them now, they'd never see it coming.

But no harm came to them, and in a few moments the vehicle rolled to a halt.

Kayani clapped Warner on the back. "We are here, my friend. I have something very special to show you."

A soldier opened the heavy metal door, and what should have been fresh air flowing in was instead the familiar smell of the Third World—smoke, rotting garbage, and raw sewage. It was an odor Warner didn't wax nostalgic about. If only he'd been young when 9/11 happened. What sort of career would he have had then? All these young guys out here now with their high-tech equipment. The contractors with their expense accounts and liberal rules of engagement. It still paid to work relationships, though. He still had some advantages the tech wizards did not.

Kayani motioned for Warner to follow as they passed a gauntlet of worried-looking soldiers training G3s at the upper stories of tenements all around them. There nonetheless were hundreds of curious faces peering from ledges and window frames down on them. Faces whispering to each other.

Warner ducked down and hoped his tan from years of deep-sea fishing would conceal his nationality long enough for him to get to cover. But by now it had to be apparent he was some sort of VIP on a tour. A glance ahead showed that Kayani was leading him through the corrugated tin gate of a warehouse/garage. It was a ramshackle place, with garbage strewn in the alleyways and near the entrance. As he entered, Warner had to slide between rusted Bedford trucks, covered in dust. They still retained some of their outrageously ornate decorations, but parts had been cannibalized. Here the smell of oil and rotting wood overcame the reek of sewage.

Just beyond these trucks lay another doorway, a subdoor within another larger gate. This is where Kayani stood beaming next to half a dozen soldiers. Warner could see bright work lights inside.

"This way . . ." Kayani entered, and Warner stepped through behind him. Inside he saw a surprisingly large workshop—easily fifty feet long and nearly as wide, with a tall ceiling hung with chains and winches. What rooted him in place was that the entire workshop was littered with the wreckage and components of what appeared to be American drone aircraft. Disembodied wings with American markings leaned against the far wall. There were entire drone sections, fuselage components, and electrical and optical assemblies, stretching along heavy wooden tables covered in clear plastic tarps.

"Holy mother of . . ."

Warner walked along the tables past oscilloscopes, soldering irons, and assorted tools littered across half a dozen workstations. Wrecked fuselage sections were in various states of disassembly, their components arrayed like the results of an electrical autopsy. Legal pads with scrawled notes in Arabic—not Urdu or Pashto, but Arabic—along with hasty diagrams were visible on the workbenches. He flipped aside a plastic tarpaulin and saw the rear section of an MQ-1 Predator, the downward-angled fins and propeller twisted from crash impact. He ran his hands along the ground power panel in the side of the fuselage, wiping away dirt and dust. Given the political waves this discovery would make, Warner had to be certain this was the real thing—absolutely certain.

He examined the panel. There was the release consent switch, still set to armed. The battery-off button, manual engine start switch, ground power. He pulled the tarp farther back to reveal the front section of the same or perhaps another MQ-1, the fuselage smashed, with dirt and pieces of branches confusing things even more. He tried to get his bearings, tapping each subassembly as he found it: the synthetic aperture radar antenna, a damaged Ku-band satellite dish. The APX-100 IFF transponder was missing and so was the video recording unit, but he found the primary control module, partially disassembled. Glancing up at the rest of the shop he saw at least four more MQ-1s.

Colonel Kayani smiled broadly. "Did I not promise it would be worth the trip, my friend? Of course, the Pakistani government has no reason to hide this from you. We have no use for American drones because we have our own Mukhbar and Burraq drones—of more advanced design."

Warner stared at the walls in open wonder. And there, in front of him, hung what looked to be a large wiring schematic indicating the individual subsystems of an MQ-9 Reaper drone. The diagram was roughly quarter scale, and printed on professional blueprint paper. Warner could see the computer workstations and color plotters close at hand. They had the plans for an MQ-9. A Reaper.

This was a full-scale reverse engineering operation. He was nearly speechless.

"Well, what do you think?"

Warner, still wide-eyed, spoke without looking at Kayani. "I think I just got promoted."

CHAPTER 9

Influence Operations

Henry Clarke undid the buttons on his Balmain jacket as he cast an arm over the back of a leather sofa in Marta's K Street corner office. The tall windows had an expansive view over the broad intersections of Vermont and K Street, just off McPherson Square. It was a beautiful, sunny winter day, and he wondered where he should eat later—and with whom.

Marta, as usual, stood behind her desk, no chair in sight, pacing as she listened to someone on the phone, interjecting with the occasional "No. Yes. Yes." She glanced up at the far wall in measured intervals.

Clarke's gaze wandered to a dozen flat-panel television screens occupying the wall across from Marta's desk, in between bookshelves and framed vanity photos of her standing alongside senators, presidents, and celebrity CEOs. Every one of those television screens was tuned to a cable news channel with the sound turned down and closed captioning turned on. It was a collage with variations on the same story—the drone "discovery" in Karachi, and a rehash of the drone attack in Iraq.

Clarke wondered about that.

Marta edged closer to her phone's base station. "Get back to me when the hearing ends. Yes." Marta hung up the phone and stood staring at him.

Clarke spread his hands toward the footage from Pakistan. "Well, what a coincidence."

"There are no coincidences."

"I don't think the Arab street's going to buy it."

"It's not meant for the goddamned Arab street. It's intended for Main Street."

Clarke shrugged. "Personally, I would have leaked bootleg video onto the Web first—give it illicit appeal. Coming from mainstream media makes it look suspect to a younger demo."

"Suspect? You forget that the only voting your generation does is of the up-and-down variety. It might seem like an ancient Kabuki dance to you, but traditional media is where actual registered voters get their information. In response to the discovery, we've got talking heads pushing for greater homeland security and funds for autonomous UAVs. And meanwhile I see this. . . ." She curled a finger at him and walked over to the windows.

Clarke sighed and followed her. They stood side by side looking down onto the green expanse of McPherson Square below. There, a few hundred protestors had gathered with signs and banners, the largest of which Clarke could just make out: *America—The Biggest Terrorist.*

"Comic Sans. Never a good choice."

"It's not their choice of font that concerns me. It's that this attitude might spread."

"Frankly, I'm surprised anyone still bothers to protest in the street. It requires so many people."

Marta glared at him.

He held up a finger and walked over to his Dior Homme leather satchel and withdrew his iPad. With a few clicks he flipped it to show her a map of the D.C. metro area with clusters of thousands of red dots on it. "Look, cell phone geolocation data shows very few clustering anomalies for this hour and climate. And that's holding up pretty much across all major metro areas. It's gone down six percentage points since news of the Karachi workshop hit the Web, and it's trending downward. If people are protesting, they aren't doing it in the streets." He circled his finger over a few clusters of dots. "Some potential protest knots in Portland and Austin, but defiance-related tag cloud groupings in social media put us within the three-sigma rule—meaning roughly sixty-eight percent of the values lie within one standard deviation of the mean." Clarke gazed down at the protestors in McPherson Square. "Meaning everything's normal. I wouldn't worry about them—they're not the reality. Just a statistical outlier."

She stared down at the protestors, unconvinced. "You're the social media director. It's your job to contain this shit, and here I am looking at a counter-messaging campaign in my own backyard."

"If it makes you feel better, do it the old-fashioned way—have your guy hire a dozen drug addicts down at the train station to join the protest. A few dirty, scary people ranting and raving on television. It'll reverse the message to a boomer demographic. Or just ignore it. What happens on the streets doesn't matter anymore."

Marta stood glowering. "Don't these people have jobs?"

"Probably not. Some of your clients might have had something to do with that."

She looked up at him and grunted, then returned to her expansive desk. "Don't get too smug, Henry. You and your sock puppet army are just another tool. The basic principles of public relations never change."

He slipped his iPad back in its case. "Perhaps, but you never had metrics like this before me. I can tell you moment by moment how your message is playing with not just a national but an international audience."

"Part of the audience, Henry. Only part."

"The part that matters, Marta."

"I can't remember if I was as self-important as you when I was your age, but I do know I never learned anything by talking."

"Well, that's one of the benefits of social media. We can automate the talking." He zipped his satchel shut and tossed it back onto the sofa. "How are your votes lining up on the Hill?"

"The bill is moving fast through the Appropriation subcommittees, but it's been tied up in the House Permanent Select Committee on Intelligence. Some congresswoman from Ohio, or wherever the fuck, with qualms about automating war—as if the Chinese or the Iranians had any qualms about it."

"If she's come out publicly against it, our opposition team will already have a file on her. Do you need us to move on her?"

"Not yet. We'll work back channels for now. But if I can't sell it to the intel committees, I'll appeal directly to the public. So get your people ready. If I can convince the working class that taxing corporations is destroying the country, I can sell autonomous weapons. Even if we have to spread the manufacturing over something like thirty-five, forty states."

"A few thousand jobs won't help you sell it to the public. They need to know what's in it for them."

"That stopping the bombings here in the U.S. will be difficult without autonomous systems. The Defense Department is already drowning in surveillance video. And then there's the limitations on satellite bandwidth. That's what's preventing us from deploying ten thousand drones over Central Asia and the Middle East—JSOC alone is blowing through a hundred million dollars a month in commercial satellite bandwidth. They've maxed out available capacity, and it needs to escalate fast. That means drone autonomy is preordained. And then there's always saving American lives."

Clarke shrugged. "It all sounds complicated. And in some ways, Marta, the fact that people think these are regular, old-fashioned terror bombings works against you. There's a significant demo that believes our drone attacks overseas are causing these attacks, and the sooner we reveal these bombings as drone attacks, the sooner that demo can be flipped."

"Patience, Henry. This gives us leverage against politicians who think they'll get punished by the electorate for letting drones successfully attack us. For some reason, it's a popular notion that American voters won't react adversely to acts of medieval barbarism, but that somehow high-tech attacks will freak them out. Undermines feelings of American exceptionalism."

Clarke shrugged. "They might be right. What if the public panics?"

"Oh, please, why does everyone always worry about the public panicking? No politician is ever safer than when bombs are falling."

Suddenly a window-rattling BOOM echoed across the city. It silenced them both. The sound faded away.

Clarke looked up. "Another bombing." He grabbed his satchel again and liberated his iPad as he headed back toward the window.

Marta was close on his heels as several lines on Marta's phone lit up. She ignored the phone as she studied the horizon. The clear winter day helped her see a column of black smoke rising from several miles away. "Other side of the river. This could move things along."

"It was damned close. Don't you ever worry that one of these things is going to come flying through your window? It scares the hell out of me."

"There's no point worrying about dying, Henry. We're all going to die eventually."

"Well, at least you got a chance to live first." Clarke was tapping furiously at his iPad. "Twitter should have something in a second. I follow every media analyst in the Beltway, and they've always got their ears to the ground. Here. Crystal City, down by Reagan International." He read out loud. "Flames visible upper floor office tower. Broken windows. Bodies." He looked up. "Everyone races to have the first Tweet in a disaster."

Marta nodded to herself. "Defense contractors—across the highway from the Pentagon."

"An attack near the Pentagon—how the hell did they get past air defenses?"

"Could be stealth. Or it could be stand-off weapons. Or maybe they've been attacking all week without our knowing it, and this one got through."

Clarke was still busy jabbing at the tablet. "I'm telling you, until the public knows what's really going on, they will not see how a fleet of UCAVs will protect them from terrorists planting bombs with backpacks. They won't make the connection."

She gestured out the window. "The terrorists are striking at America's military industrial complex again—and after what was just discovered in Karachi. One senator already dead. It's building up pressure that begs for catharsis. You need to understand the power of revelation, Henry. The public assumes the truth is always being kept from them, and when the truth is finally 'uncovered,' they'll be more than willing to accept it. They'll embrace it." She turned and went back to her desk, watching the cable news channels silently tiled on the opposite wall. There was still nothing on them about the attack on Washington just a few minutes old.

Clarke noticed it and chuckled to himself. "Old media will get to it eventually, I'm sure."

Amid her ringing phones she called to him. "Get out of here and go create me a groundswell of popular support, please. I might need it, after all."

He smirked as he exited. "I thought you might."

CHAPTER 10

Deconfliction

Linda McKinney stared out the window of a clerk's office at a U.S. Army air base in Wiesbaden, Germany. At least that's what they told her this place was. It was night, the offices deserted. The runway quiet. Blinding vapor lights illuminated the snow-blown tarmac outside. Inside Christmas decorations hung from doorways. Photographs of children and unit logistics awards studded the desks.

The phones were dead. Tapping keys and pressing line buttons achieved nothing. They were inert. Likewise with the computers. All the hard drives appeared to have been pulled, and there were small locked safes beneath each desk. Every drawer was locked too. They had things battened down tightly.

McKinney parted the window blinds so she could see the tarmac more clearly. Uniformed servicemen rushed about in olive drab parkas as wind gusted around them. Young Americans of diverse ethnicity, pointing and talking as they pushed pallets of equipment on hydraulic jacks. Occasionally laughing as their breath stabbed plumes in the cold air. Their words were inaudible through the double-paned glass.

None of it seemed real. Everything had happened so fast. Right now in Tanzania it was the hot dry season—a time for getting research finished before the spring rains. Here it was snowing. She pondered the fate of her weaver project now that the government had abducted her. It had taken her years to get the funding.

She realized she was being selfish, but she couldn't resist a bout of self-pity. Yet, it could have been far worse. If Odin and his team hadn't rescued her, she'd be dead, and there would have been no project, period.

So her work was being misused by someone to attack the United States. Over a hundred people were dead. She recalled images of the carnage—photos of burned bodies—not the sanitized video from the news, but graphic images of the grievously wounded. What had been in the headlines as terror bombs all these months had ultimately been traced back to her own research. And now, after a short flight to the Tanzanian air base at Morogoro, they'd boarded a waiting, unmarked Gulfstream V jet and flown seven hours here to Germany. She'd sat almost the entire way in brooding silence. Mercifully they left her alone with her thoughts.

Not even twenty-four hours had elapsed since she'd been lying in blissful ignorance on a lumpy cot in Africa. Hard to believe that that humid, cramped little cabin, along with everything in it—along with her foreseeable future—had been incinerated in a flash. None of this seemed real. Not even the room she stood in.

McKinney thought back on all the times she'd experienced this feeling of sudden, surreal dislocation, of everything being torn up. Heading out into the unknown. That was her entire childhood. Her dad worked as a chemical engineer helping to design oil refineries—a job that had taken their family around the world. It had given her diverse life experience at an early age. As an outgoing, curious girl, she thrived on it, gathering insects, plants, and friends from every continent to add to her collection— a collection that grew into a lifelong fascination with the people and creatures of this world. To this day she maintained friendships from her years in South America, Eastern Europe, Africa, Australia, Asia.

Her childhood experiences taught her one thing above all: that the world was not filled with danger. Danger was there sometimes, but it wasn't the norm. The common thread she'd found in every culture was that the majority of people were decent and simply wanted to raise their children in peace. That basic desire was what linked us all.

Which was why America's recent, all-encompassing fear puzzled McKinney. She felt like someone who'd returned from a long, inspiring journey only to discover that an old friend had gone crazy-paranoid. She barely recognized what America had become.

And now that old friend was telling her that her work was somehow the latest threat.

And how was any of this her fault? She'd been doing primary research on the natural world. *Are we afraid of ants now?* Ant society went back a hundred million years—kind of hard to view it as a pressing emergency all of a sudden. And how on earth were we supposed to contain knowledge—especially in a world where others were rapidly eliminating America's technological edge? This wasn't something that could be stopped.

She heard a knock, and the office door opened behind her. She didn't bother to turn around. In a moment the bearded "Odin" came up alongside her. He also parted the blinds and looked out.

"Your plane will be ready soon."

"My plane?"

"You're headed back to the States."

She nodded, brooding. "I see." They hadn't exchanged a word since their chat on the Otter. She'd been too shocked, too amazed. But in the intervening hours McKinney had begun to process some of the implications.

"I need to call my father as soon as possible to let him know that I'm okay. These phone lines are all dead."

"You're not fully grasping the situation."

"Look, Odin—or whatever your name is—I need to call my father."

"Isolation protocol. Until further notice, in accordance with Title Ten of the U.S. legal code, you're prohibited from all contact with anyone on the outside."

She stared at him in disbelief but tried to maintain her composure in the face of mounting anger. "There's no reason to treat me like this. I will gladly tell you everything that I know about my research, but you need to realize that I've just disappeared in an explosion. My family needs to know that I'm okay."

He shook his head. "That won't be possible. The U.S. State Department reported Professor Linda McKinney missing after a bombing in East Africa. The attack was believed to be retaliation for Karbala."

"Oh, my God . . ." McKinney felt tears coming on, but she didn't want to seem weak in front of him. Her voice sounded clenched, barely in control. "The death of my mother nearly killed my father. You have no idea what this will do to him. Please, just let me—"

"I know that you actually dying would have been worse. And since Foxy and I risked our necks to save you . . . you're welcome."

McKinney paused to get her voice under control. The anger helped. "I'm grateful for you saving me, but there's no reason why I can't—"

"There are hundreds of reasons."

McKinney stared at him, and then shook her head. "No. I will not permit you to make me feel guilty about this. I wasn't researching biochemical weapons, I was studying the natural world. How people misuse basic research isn't—"

"Rationalization is a useful survival instinct, but it won't make any difference with me."

McKinney glared at him. She felt the walls closing in.

He let a moment of silence pass. "I'm guessing you have questions."

McKinney took another deep breath to calm herself. "Where am I going?"

"You've been attached to a special access program. Our mission is to identify the source of these drone attacks. We think you can help us predict the behavior of these things, which may help us get ahold of one intact—along with all its source code—which could lead us to its creators."

She searched for a reasonable reaction to unreasonable circumstances and came up empty. Nothing in her broad life experience had prepared her for this.

He studied her, and after a moment his hard expression softened a bit. He motioned for her to sit down on the edge of a nearby desk. "Can I get you some water or a cup of coffee? Tea?"

She shook her head as she leaned back onto the desk.

He sat across from her and folded his arms. "Let me explain how I found you. Maybe that will clarify why you don't want to reach out to anyone you care about right now. The people behind these drones are desperate to remain anonymous. It's that anonymity which prevents us from focusing our firepower on them. They will do literally anything to keep it that way—that includes hurting people you love to get to you."

She nodded slowly. "Okay, I understand. This is just all very strange."

"Do you know what a ROM chip is?"

"Yes, I think so."

"It's a read-only memory chip. Stores machine code, logic that controls electronic devices. A few months back an FBI forensics team at the scene of a Texas bombing dredged up a small piece of wreckage floating in a golf course pond. It was part of an enemy drone that had self-destructed at high altitude over Dallas."

McKinney recalled the news from some months back. "I remember—the oil company executives. That was a drone attack too?"

"All nineteen of them have been. And there were a dozen others that didn't succeed."

"My God."

"That piece of wreckage the FBI found included an off-the-shelf circuit board with a ROM chip attached. DOD eggheads put the chip into a logic analyzer and decompiled its machine code into human readable form. It was advanced stuff—visual intelligence algorithms. Cyber defense folks searched to see if anything similar was out on the public Web. They got a match to code on warez sites in both Russia and China—but the compiler fingerprint for the executables pointed back to the United States. Again, this isn't my specialty, but the cyber warfare folks can extract culture codes, MAC addresses, debug time-stamp formats and compiler paths embedded in executables. That led us back to a project at Stanford University's Vision Lab."

"You mean those researchers who were killed." McKinney was starting to focus on the problem at hand. It felt good to absorb information. It kept her mind off her own troubles.

"Right. That Stanford team included Russian, Chinese, and Indian foreign nationals—any one of whom could have leaked the code overseas."

She gave him a look. "Or an American could have sold it."

"Either way. I used proxies to let the Stanford team know their code had been stolen and posted on warez sites—to see if one of them would report back to a handler. That worked to some degree, and we were able to follow the trail to a server in Shenyang, China—where we also discovered your weaver ant software model. That's why I came for you."

"You seem to have glossed over the part where the Stanford team got blown up."

He paused. "It's possible no one on the Stanford team was a spy. Their project lead—an American—discovered that their network had been compromised—and he managed to trace the source of the theft. That turned out to be a gold mine of intelligence for us, but he was careless. Apparently whoever is behind this detected his trick, and the next time the team got together they were on the receiving end of a laser-guided bomb."

McKinney narrowed her eyes. "He was careless? Did he even know what he was dealing with? Did you warn him?"

"There wasn't time, Professor."

"Your tampering got them all killed."

"This is a war. There will be casualties."

"Don't beat yourself up."

"For all I knew, they might have been involved with these drone attacks. If so, tipping them off would have given them a chance to scatter and cover their trails."

"How can you be sure I'm not involved in these attacks? Oh, that's right—I'm a white chick, so I must be innocent. I did grow up all over the world, you know. I could have been turned to the 'dark side' in some madrassa."

"Are you finished?"

"I hope the rest of your mission has been more inspired than what you've told me so far."

He eyed her with some irritation. "I made a mistake with the Stanford researchers, and I had to get to you before the drone builders did. I am responsible for getting the Stanford team killed. I know that. We're doing the best we can, Professor, with incomplete information and very little time."

McKinney sighed and held up her hands. "I didn't mean to imply you don't care about those people." McKinney searched for some sense in what was going on. "But there are thousands of swarming algorithms around. Why would these people choose mine? I'm hardly the world expert on swarming intelligence."

"Maybe it has something to do with weavers in particular. Aggression. Maybe they chose yours by chance, or convenience, or some connection we can't see yet. But what matters is that they did take yours. If you know anything about the strategies of America's geopolitical rivals, then you'd know that swarming is a central theme. Whoever used this visual intelligence software to give a drone eyes is also planning on using your software to make them into a cohesive military force. An anonymous swarm that will prevent us from bringing our firepower to bear on our real attackers."

McKinney stopped short, then fixed her gaze on him. "Did you just say they were *planning* on using my swarming algorithm? I thought you said my weaver model had already been used?"

Odin showed no emotion. "I told you what was necessary to bring you under U.S. jurisdiction with as little drama as possible."

McKinney felt the rage building. "Jesus!" She paced angrily. "I get it now. You pile the guilt of killing a hundred people onto my shoulders so I'll meekly submit out of remorse for all the suffering I've caused. You manipulative asshole!"

"Professor, calm down. It doesn't change the reality of the situation."

"What else aren't you telling me?"

"A great deal."

"You admit it?"

"This is a life-and-death struggle. There's no time for social niceties."

"Like honesty. How convenient that must be for you. That's the problem with all these wars you people keep getting us into."

"As a biologist, you, of all people, know that conflict is a fact of life. Competition is the mechanism of evolution."

"There is a great deal more to evolutionary biology than survival of the fittest—although that's all anyone seems to remember. One of Darwin's contemporaries was Alfred Russel Wallace, who had even more profound lessons about evolution—that humans are social creatures. That we coevolve with other species as part of a fabric of interwoven and interdependent life-forms. The world isn't entirely about competition and dominance. And species that cooperate with others succeed better than those who do not. That's what civilization is, cooperation."

"And if there's not enough for everyone, who gets to live? Who gets to reproduce? How is that decided in the wild?"

"We need to aspire to being more than just animals—because unlike animals humans have the capacity to destroy the earth. In fact, we're already destroying it—and what you're doing isn't helping."

Odin glowered at her. "It's not necessary that you like me, Professor. But I can tell you from personal experience that every population has a criminal element—people who will do anything to gain and keep power. Whoever's behind this, they are such people, and they're building a robot army that will follow their every command. I'd like your help in stopping them."

She stared at him, then finally turned away. It had felt good to vent, but that didn't change the reality of her situation. "So what are you, then? CIA?"

"I told you, we can't discuss what I am."

"You're asking that I blindly follow orders. I'm not allowed to know from whom—and you've already lied to me. What you're asking is that I be an obedient machine. Isn't that what you're trying to stop?"

He gritted his teeth in frustration.

"This is a matter of trust. I don't trust you, Odin. You've given me no reason to trust you. How do I even know you're who you say you are?" She gestured to the office around her. "And as if the U.S. military has never done anything immoral or unethical. Convince me. Convince me, or throw me in prison—because I'm not going to help someone I don't trust."

He ran his hand through his long, unruly hair. "Christ, you're a piece of work. The file said you'd be difficult." He exhaled in irritation. "Fine. We're an elite intelligence unit of the U.S. Army."

"Special Forces."

"No. Special Forces is publicly acknowledged to exist. We don't officially exist."

"Delta Force . . ."

"Look, no. Not Delta Force. That's a counterterrorism unit. We go in before them. Alone and quietly. We uncover the reality on the ground. That's all I'm trying to do, Professor."

McKinney eyed him suspiciously. "What's your rank?"

"What does it matter?"

"I want to know who I'm dealing with."

"I'm a master sergeant."

"They sent a sergeant? I would have thought that tracking down the drones attacking America would have rated at least a lieutenant."

"What is this, a class thing?"

"No, but it occurs to me that officers go to officer training school, where they presumably learn how to manage groups of people and complex operations—where they learn ethics. I mean, I study bugs, and I went to school for half my life."

"For your information, I gave up all possibility of promotion to serve in this unit. Everyone in my unit is a sergeant—and we'll stay sergeants our entire career."

She was confused.

"Commissioned officers receive their commission from the Congress. That means the civilian government is answerable for their conduct. Noncommissioned officers answer only to the military high command. Our rank has to do with government exposure."

"Meaning you skip around the globe breaking laws, and they'll disown you if you're caught."

"Meaning I'm the guy who has to solve problems whether there's an international legal framework for them or not. And for drones, there is not."

McKinney felt convinced he was telling the truth, if only because the answer made her mad. "No uniforms, apparently."

"Blending in is what we do."

"Did it ever occur to you that the presence of American units like yours in foreign countries is precisely what's causing these drone attacks against us?"

"And you really think the world would be a peaceful place if we left it alone?"

"I wasn't arguing that the world is filled with unicorns and rainbows. I've spent a decade in the Third World. I'm no stranger to corruption and lawlessness in places like Africa. In fact, I'm godmother to a boy whose father was murdered by ivory poachers. So, I get that civil society needs to be defended by people with guns—but those people cannot be above the law. And you just described to me why you're a sergeant—in order to better skirt international laws."

"Okay. You don't trust your government. But if you think drones in American hands are frightening, imagine them controlled by North Korea, or Burma, or narco-traffickers, or Dominionists, or AT&T. If you want to lobby for some international legal framework for these machines, more power to you—but until you civilians sort this shit out, I and my team have to deal with it. It's not a fucking theory with me, okay? I'm concerned about whether humans will be combatants on future battlefields, or just targets. It matters a whole goddamned lot to me, maybe even more than it does to you, so I'd appreciate you setting aside your objections and pitching the fuck in."

McKinney was taken aback. She had apparently managed to get under his skin. Finally. She nodded. "All right. Okay. Just laying my cards on the table."

"Thank you."

Foxy, the wild-haired Albanian man with the heavy metal T-shirt, ducked his head into the office. "Knock, knock. Sorry to interrupt the high velocity data exchange, but you need to see this, Odin."

"What is it?"

"Cable news. They found something in Pakistan."

"What?"

"Drones."

"Goddammit."

Odin cast a look to McKinney, and then nodded. "No time like the present, Professor."

They headed toward the door.

Odin gestured to the Albanian soldier. "Professor, this is Foxy, my two-IC. If you need anything, and I'm not available, you talk to him."

Foxy extended a calloused hand. "Pleased to meet you, Professor. Wish it was under better circumstances."

"You and me both."

Odin led them down a tiled institutional hallway. They soon arrived at an austere recreation room at the end of the deserted office wing. There, on sturdy sofas, sat Mooch, Hoov, and the woman she'd seen earlier wearing a maroon hijab and a chocolate brown abaya. There was also a Caucasian man, short and stocky, with a thick reddish-brown beard—possibly Scotch-Irish. The group was staring at a television bolted at an angle to the drop ceiling. The woman was leaning back with her sandaled feet up on a coffee table. She nodded to McKinney.

McKinney nodded back.

When Odin entered everyone stood, but all eyes were still glued to the television, where an American cable news channel was showing video of a workshop filled with aircraft components—wings and fuselages. Odin studied the screen.

Foxy spoke over the anchor's voice. "Found a workshop in good ol' Karachi. Reverse-engineering operation for American drone wreckage. The story is that whoever ran it was behind the attack in Karbala."

"Who found it?" Odin was watching the screen impassively.

"Pakistani military. Maybe ISI. They tipped off CIA." Foxy pointed at the rough, leaked video footage. "There's a Predator tail. A few pieces of Reapers in the back."

Odin turned to him. "I call bullshit."

Foxy nodded. "No doubt."

McKinney looked at him with surprise. "Why do you think it's fake?"

"Too perfect. One of our drones commits an atrocity, and a week later we find a barnful of evidence that we've been framed by insurgents?" Odin shook his head, accentuating the length of his beard. "I'd say it's an influence operation. Even if it's true, most people abroad won't believe it. Foxy, work your connections at CIA. Try to find out who's hypnotizing the chickens. In the meantime, we proceed under the supposition it's an IO focused at a domestic audience."

Foxy frowned. "What if it's the real deal? Shouldn't we send someone to examine the site?"

"Too risky. They'll be closely watching whoever goes there. If the same extremely careful people carrying out the drone attacks Stateside are behind the Karbala attack, then they probably intended us to find this orgy of evidence—which means it's worse than useless; it's a deception. And if they weren't behind Karbala, then this has no bearing on our mission."

Above them a Ford pickup truck commercial had come on, depicting trucks towing improbable loads up improbable inclines in improbable ways.

Odin made a slashing gesture across his throat, and someone muted the television. He placed his hand on McKinney's shoulder. "Everyone. Cornell University professor Linda McKinney is now a member of this team. You are to defend her with your lives. From this point onward, you will refer to her as Expert Six or simply as 'Professor.' Is that understood?"

The team members nodded.

"Professor, this is my team. You've already met Foxy." He pointed to the woman in the maroon hijab. "Ripper. Human intel. Pay no attention to her outfit. She's about as Muslim as a Vegas casino." He pointed at the Eurasian kid who worked the electronics board on the plane. "This is Hoov. Signals intelligence—our knob turner."

Hoov displayed mild impatience. "He means commo—I trained with the 704th—"

"Hoov, this isn't your goddamned high school reunion."

Hoov nodded and closed his mouth.

Odin gestured next to the handsome Asian Indian man whom McKinney recognized as being the one with the stethoscope—and who had cut her loose on the plane. "Mooch, team surgeon."

McKinney and he exchanged polite nods.

Odin now pointed to the red-bearded man she hadn't seen on the plane. "And this is Tin Man. Human intel."

Odin turned to McKinney. "We'll hook up Stateside with the last two team members, Troll and Smokey. They handle signals and human intel." He grabbed the television remote and killed the TV. "All right, listen up. I want you all ready to ship out the moment the tail numbers on the C-37 have been repainted." He looked at his watch. "Make good use of the time en route to examine every bit of intel we got from last night's operation. I want detailed reports and recommendations when I get back."

McKinney glanced at the others, then at Odin. "You're not heading back to the U.S.?"

Odin shook his head. "Hoov and I will catch up with you all later. There's somewhere I need to go first."

CHAPTER 11

Eye in the Sky

Kinshasa and Brazzaville were the quintessential Third World cities of the twenty-first century. Large—with a combined population around thirteen million—and growing rapidly, they teemed with young men and guns. As the capitals of neighboring nations, they occupied opposite banks of the Congo River but nonetheless formed a single metropolitan area. They were essentially Africa's liver—circulating the population of the riverine interior through a pitiless Darwinian filter.

Without an urban plan sprawling shantytowns accreted around the colonial and corporate buildings in the heart of downtown. These shantytowns were some of the most crime-ridden and dangerous places in all of Africa.

The common refrain from the West was that only economic development and modernization could address such problems, but Odin knew that the modern world itself was what made this region of Africa so violent. That was because the Democratic Republic of the Congo contained nearly eighty percent of the world's supply of coltan—the mineral of the information age. Coltan was the industrial name for *columbite–tantalite*, a dull black metallic mineral from which the elements niobium and tantalum were extracted. The tantalum from coltan was used to manufacture electronic capacitors, which were needed to make cell phones, DVD players, video game systems, and computers. And at one hundred U.S. dollars per pound on the street, coltan had financed a civil war that since 1998 had killed an estimated five and a half million people. These were World War II–level casualties.

But the information age was selective about its information, and the same industrial world that fueled the conflict barely registered this war's existence. The U.S. and British only grew interested when the Congolese government attempted to nationalize the coltan mines—at which point the war became an intolerable human crisis. It now simmered in dozens of local embers, ready to flare up the moment the opportunity arose. Alternately stoking and dousing those embers was what would keep local governments disorganized and the cheap coltan flowing.

There were Westerners who looked with concern at the suffering of burgeoning Third World populations, but Odin knew that Mother Nature wasn't the nurturing type. In fact, she might view the stable populations of the West as a failure—a rebellion against primordial order. Nature wanted only one thing: for creatures to produce viable offspring. After that, you were genetically dead. Nature had no more use for you. Your extended lifespan, your biography, your Hummel figurine collection, were all just taking up space. By some cosmic joke, nearly the entire scope of human experience was at odds with the biological world.

So by Nature's measure both Kinshasa and Brazzaville were a resounding success. Happiness and contentment weren't in great supply, but there were lots of young people, eager to lay the groundwork for another generation. The rage here was of a type Odin had seen in all the shantytowns and slums of the world: Young men without prospects were not happy about their situation. In the vast game of Darwinian musical chairs, whenever the music stopped there were large numbers of people without a seat—and some smartass had sold them guns.

This was the root of most conflict in the world—people asserting their will to survive, to flourish, and to procreate. Evil had nothing to do with it. And although he'd worked these hidden conflicts for years, Odin knew that most fighting was just a symptom of another problem: too many people competing for limited resources. And yet fighting wouldn't resolve this either. Rwanda, for example, was still the most densely populated country in sub-Saharan Africa even after the genocide. No, the best way he knew of to defuse these conflicts was to provide opportunities and education to women. Independence. Once that took, population growth would ebb, and actual plans could be made for the future.

This was not a methodology favored by weapons manufacturers.

Odin stood at the visitors' railing and studied a glowing constellation of high-definition screens arrayed around the control room. Sprawling shantytowns simmered below the surveillance platforms. A populace unaware that they were the test subjects for a grand experiment.

"Have you ever seen EITS in action, Master Sergeant?"

"I have not, General."

A uniformed African-American JSOC brigadier general stood in the center of the control room as green-badge contractors in shirtsleeves manned most of the workstations in cubicles around him. The general took a sip from a white al-Qaeda–branded coffee mug. "Welcome to Stuttgart. What you're looking at is nothing less than the future of low-intensity conflict management."

"I appreciate you taking time for me, sir."

"Always happy to assist The Activity." He looked up at the screens lining the walls. "You might occupy a different command silo, but our systems could be a tremendous help in your group's line of work." The general reached out and straightened the visitor's badge on Odin's lanyard. It said merely Visitor.

"I'm eager to see what they can do, sir."

The general took another sip from his al-Qaeda mug.

Odin had seen these mugs many times before in command centers. They were much sought after by the REMF crowd. Al-Qaeda was, after all, mostly a media organization—one with a Web presence that would put Ashton Kutcher to shame. They rolled out their own branded characters and products to jihadists worldwide on a regular basis. They even had professional-looking magazines and journals, along with podcast reality shows, making jihadi documentaries with Western video-editing software.

Both sides could claim it as ironic with entirely different emphasis. If even terrorists ran franchise operations, maybe there was some common ground, after all.

Odin glanced up again at the array of high-definition screens and across the rows of control board operators. Dozens of people manning supporting systems. "I was told this is a test bed—a prototype—but it looks operational."

"In a limited geographical zone, it is. This is a joint public-private SAP. Major private sector partners helped build this operations center to showcase what a truly unified twenty-first-century command looks like. We think this technology has a tremendous future."

"We, sir?"

"It's difficult not to take a proprietary interest. My staff and I have contributed time and effort to make sure this system meets real-world operational requirements."

Odin actually knew quite a bit about the systems integrated into EITS, such as the Gorgon Stare, along with all the other systems that defense contractors were developing: automated 3-D mapping of Third World cities, building by building; as well as ARGUS-IR, the Autonomous Real-time Ground Ubiquitous Surveillance-Infrared system. They were networked, unmanned suborbital camera-and-narrow-aperture-radar platforms—airborne optics tiling together live, highly detailed imagery of a broad swath of terrain in real time. A persistent unblinking eye creating a digital, three-dimensional model of reality as it happened.

Odin nodded up at the main screen—a broad view of the smoke-shrouded shantytowns of Brazzaville. He'd run ops there numerous times in the past decade. "What are we looking at?"

"You don't recognize it?"

"After a while all these shit-holes look alike, sir."

The general raised an eyebrow. "The location isn't important. It's what the systems can do that's important. Compared with a platform like Gorgon Stare, the imagery from a Predator drone is like taking Polaroid pictures through a goddamned straw. We can zoom in on any portion of a vast battle space—each airborne asset has one hundred and sixty-five individually controlled high-resolution cameras. Multiple assets can be networked to programmatically tile together contiguous, high-resolution surveillance of broad swaths of terrain in real time. Synthetic aperture radar allows us to see through both clouds and darkness. This is an all-seeing eye, Master Sergeant, permanently recording all activity below from a height of sixty thousand feet—well above the weapon range of these populations."

Odin nodded. No doubt the names from Greek mythology encouraged the impression of an unassailable Mount Olympus. "The technology, was it developed in the States or—"

"International partnership, but in full accordance with DOD EAR, ITAR, and OFAC export control requirements. Our international partners are just as eager to see counterterrorism operations succeed under every regional command."

"And these are live images."

"Live. Everything you see on the main screen is live, real world. But live imagery is the least of it." The general moved over to a workstation manned by a uniformed JSOC first lieutenant wearing a headset—a strapping blond kid with clear skin and good posture. "Gartner, replay that truck sequence in sector H-Six we were looking at."

The lieutenant immediately paused the imagery on his screen and tapped in some coordinates.

The general watched intently but spoke to Odin. "The critical difference of EITS over previous surveillance systems is that this high-resolution video imagery is retained over time in a data cloud, allowing analysts to 'rewind' the entire battle space—to see what might have taken place in a given locale over time."

As Odin watched the nearby monitor, the image zoomed in to a tiny corner in the vast shantytown. People were walking past, but then they stopped in midstride. The video rapidly began to rewind, people and vehicles moving backward, until a faded red Toyota pickup moved into frame. The image then halted and began to play forward again, showing several armed men loading crates onto the truck bed.

Lieutenant Gartner was clearly used to doing demos with the general, because he was already doing what the general was about to ask.

"We can move in for a close-up of faces . . ."

The screen had already done so.

". . . and we can even rotate the view."

The image was already circling around to the other side of the men—not in a smooth pan, but in fifteen-degree leaps of POV.

Still, it was an impressive technical achievement. Odin remained emotionless. "How far back in time can you go?"

"As far back as we want to allocate storage space. We can even flag certain regions for long-term storage. Trouble spots."

The image was already zooming out to the large city view. Live again.

"We use algorithms to parse human activity—tracking the pulse and character of a place. Automating what we call 'pattern of life' analysis. Compiling a fingerprint, a signature of a city's normal routine. Airborne persistent video pattern-recognition systems will be *big* in this surveillance effort—Bayesian algorithmic models . . ."

The general was still talking as Odin watched a constellation of red glowing dots and squares superimposed on the vast city, like ants.

"This layer represents observable human activity. The dots are people, the squares vehicles. Over time the subsystem differentiates which part of the imagery is static city and which is dynamic human activity. But it goes further. Within that human activity layer, EITS begins to accumulate experience of the patterns of human living that represent a city's background noise—its norm. What travel patterns are followed each day from location to location—with each dot being tracked representing a trip marker that's added to the database. The totality of trips weaving a pattern of behavior. How consistent is this pattern? What portion of residents follow a routine, leaving and returning to the same places on a general schedule? Which portion of the population has no regular schedule? That lets us focus on areas of suspicious activity—a common point somewhere in the city where individuals who'd been present at earlier 'trouble spots' might later congregate, a place that might be the lair of an insurgent group—the sort of intel that your group would previously have had to obtain through HUMINT—can now be gleaned from observing the totality of human activity. Remembering it over time. Seeing everything. Forgetting nothing."

Odin watched the companion imagery as Lieutenant Gartner played impressive visual accompaniment to the general's pitch. Odin appeared deep in thought. "Our PIR usually involves locating a specific individual, and for that cell phone SIGINT suffices. Our knob turners can isolate known voice patterns, trace the—"

"You mean as long as you can run manned listening flights over the target area, and we already do that with unmanned airships that can stay aloft for weeks." The general nudged Lieutenant Gartner aside and clicked through a few menus to bring up another information layer.

The screen suddenly flipped to an entirely new field of hundreds of thousands of clustered dots, moving through the city.

"Every cell phone's IMEI and the base transceiver stations that serve them. This system simplifies eavesdropping. Just identify the phone you want"—he zoomed in and clicked on an ID number moving through central Brazzaville—"and you can record the subject's communications." The sound of foreign chatter came in over the speakers.

The general relinquished control to Gartner again and turned to face Odin. "Think about the combination of persistent telecom and video surveillance—being able to go back in time to see what happened on a street corner two months ago, before you even realized that someone was a person of interest." The general gestured to an image of the huge city, clustered with dots. "This system displays the social map of an entire city from the communications and geolocation data of its citizens. . . ."

Lieutenant Gartner heard his cue and started making link-analysis webs visible on screen—dense strands that depicted the social network of the city's populace.

The general was pacing, gesturing to the screen as he engaged in a rehearsed soliloquy. "A detailed social encyclopedia. Autodetection of suspicious activity . . ."

Gartner made certain the big screen did exactly that—showing a knot of young Congolese men pouring gasoline onto tires stuffed around another man's torso, then setting it alight to horrific effect.

"Now we know not only the cell phones of this group but also their faces"—the image zoomed in to a leader in sunglasses and a beret—"their leaders. Their vehicles, their confederates—in short, everything."

While the general talked, Odin wondered how much money they'd spent on this. In Vietnam it had taken an average of fifty thousand bullets to eliminate one Vietcong soldier. Had we upped the ante here? And what was the false positive rate? How many noninsurgents—people who simply matched a misguided pattern—were flagged by the system and handed over to security services or contractor hit squads for imagined or predicted crimes? Certainly, it was not in the interests of the folks running the system to admit it made mistakes.

Of course, Odin knew a system like EITS was not intended to resolve conflicts. It was intended merely to manage them. To keep violence disorganized, channeled, and isolated long enough to permit uninterrupted resource extraction. Once that was finished, the locals would be left to their own devices again. Rinse and repeat, and you pretty much understood the conflict map of the globe. This system let them know more about the locals than the locals knew about themselves. And it was just the beginning. There was no reason this couldn't be done everywhere—including America, as Odin well knew. The only question was whether it had already been implemented there, in full or in part.

Odin interrupted the general, midpitch. "I was told there's an autonomous strike capability to this system, General. Is that not the case?"

The general halted, took another sip of coffee, and nodded. "We both know lethal autonomy is inevitable, Sergeant. However, at the moment, we're not using armed systems over this AO. This is a surveillance platform only."

"Autonomous drones are part of the design specification, correct?"

"For surveillance, yes. Unmanned systems are how we coordinate complete coverage of the target area."

"But weapons could be integrated."

The general put his coffee mug down and studied Odin. "Kill-decision drones are a thorny issue, Master Sergeant. For the foreseeable future we're keeping a human in the loop."

"Is this the only implementation of the EITS system currently in use, General?"

"What are you looking for, Sergeant?"

Odin drummed his fingers on the railing while staring up at the screens. Then he focused his gaze on the general. "We both know the days of manned combat aircraft are numbered. Autonomous drones will be cheaper, more maneuverable, and expendable. And remotely piloted drones will be useless against a sophisticated adversary like China, Russia, Iran, or North Korea—they'll just jam our link signal. That means we need to integrate autonomous drones into our military units. For patrolling and reacting to incursions."

The general nodded and grabbed his coffee mug again. "We're in agreement, then. It's just a question of how long it will take Washington to realize it."

They studied each other for a few moments in silence as the clattering of computer keyboards and soft radio chatter sounded around the control room.

The general gestured to the screens. "Impressive, isn't it?"

Odin pondered the imagery. "I just have one concern, General."

"And what's that?"

"America pays for the difficult R and D to design these systems, and once they're designed, they might get away from us. And then there's the second- and third-order effects of technology like this. Surveillance drift nets create opposition—opposition from a public that doesn't want technological domination. They'll innovate ways to evade it, and it's quite possible we could wind up causing more conflict than if we'd never built it."

The general just stared at him.

"Just a thought. . . ."

CHAPTER 12

Underground Drive

Linda McKinney disembarked from a white, unmarked private jet, descending the steps into a cold winter night. Though idling, the plane's engines were still deafening, its navigation and strobe lights flashing.

A freezing wind gusted across the desolate tarmac of a municipal airport. A private terminal building stood off to the left, beyond which she could see a drab concrete elevated highway. Closer was a parking lot beyond a length of chain-link fence and a sealed white metal hangar. Other than that all she could see was a series of yellow-tinged parking lot lights extending into the distance.

McKinney zipped up a red Gore-Tex coat and matching knit cap emblazoned with a white company logo in bold letters: Ancile Services. She had no idea what it was or why everyone else was now wearing similar coats—though theirs were in black.

Other team members shuffled past her carrying duffels and backpacks. The woman, Ripper, nodded as she passed by. Her long black hair flowed freely now, with multiple ear piercings visible. Very much American. That had been a swift transformation.

Hoov and Mooch ducked by, opening the jet's cargo hatch. Tin Man and Ripper seemed to be heading toward the nearby hangar.

Foxy patted McKinney on the shoulder and shouted over the jet roar as he passed by. "Coming?"

"Where to?"

He motioned with two gloved fingers toward the hangar, and McKinney fell in line behind him. It was shocking how completely American he looked now in a company coat and hipster eyeglasses. He had the African kora slung over his back, but it looked more like a goofy souvenir in this context. As they got farther from the plane's engine noise, she asked, "Where are we?"

He cast a glance back at her. "Kansas City."

"My passport. All my identification was destroyed in—"

"That's not a problem, Professor."

"What is this, a military base?"

"Private jetport."

Ahead, Tin Man was turning a key in a lock near the main hangar door. The large doors opened a few feet, and the team moved quickly inside. Fluorescent lights were already flickering on, revealing two white panel vans in a cavernous empty space.

Foxy ushered McKinney inside the hangar and gave several quick hand signals to Hoov and Mooch. They were rolling equipment cases in from the jet, which was already taxiing away down the tarmac.

What followed was a frenzy of wordless activity as the team pulled the cases inside and started popping latches. Hoov put batteries in a disposable cell phone. After a moment he tapped in a number and spoke quickly as he peered through the narrow opening in the hangar doors. "We just got in. What's overhead?"

McKinney watched the others pulling electronic gear out of the cases. One of the devices looked like a standard metal detection wand— like something you'd search for land mines with. Other gear included what looked like an oscilloscope. They were installing batteries and powering up without saying a word to each other. Moments later Ripper had donned a headset and was waving the boom of the device along the sides of the nearest van.

McKinney met Foxy's gaze.

He nodded toward Ripper and Tin Man—who were doing a similar sweep on the second van. "Nonlinear junction detector. Finds uninvited guests."

"You really think they could have tracked us all this way?"

"Standard procedure, Professor. We always watch our backs." Foxy pointed straight up. "We need to sanitize the airspace before we move to base."

Hoov walked up, still clutching the phone. "There's a Predator orbiting forty-three clicks southeast of here. NORAD says it's U.S. Customs and Border Protection, but Troll's not sure. There's also a DEA flight out of Wichita fifty clicks to the east, but it could be scanning frequencies."

"Spy sats?"

"Nothing overhead for another nineteen minutes."

Ripper pulled off her headset and moved away from the vans. "Vans are clean."

Foxy nodded and tapped McKinney on the shoulder. "You're with me, Professor."

She followed Foxy toward the first van as Tin Man tossed him the keys. "Meet you back at the office. Take the long way home."

"Wilco. Keep your eyes peeled."

Foxy got in the van and McKinney uncertainly climbed in on the passenger side. The vehicle smelled brand-new. Foxy stowed the kora and his canvas satchel behind his seat and started the van. "Buckle up, Professor, this isn't Africa."

"Oh." She buckled her seat belt.

Nearby, Tin Man opened the rear hangar doors on the far side of the space. He ducked his head out the opening, then gave a thumbs-up sign.

Foxy drove through the doors out into the deserted parking lot and toward the front entrance to the small airport.

McKinney had been under the impression that American airports had more security than this, but apparently private jet terminals did things differently. There was only an unmanned parking gate between them and the tarmac. It made her wonder about the security she endured in major airports.

Foxy drove them past an obvious highway entrance ramp marked *Rt. 169/Downtown Kansas City*, and instead drove through a narrow tunnel beneath the highway, to emerge on the other side amid gritty, deserted industrial streets.

McKinney had never been to Kansas City before. She scanned the dark horizon, searching for the inevitable downtown of lofty bank towers, but all she could see were security lights on warehouses and factories along with the occasional billboard—the generic Americanness she remembered. The van's dashboard clock read 1:23 A.M. There was almost no traffic on the surface roads. The light industrial businesses, retail outlets, warehouses, and junkyards to either side were fenced and graffiti tagged, but it looked more orderly than any East African city.

Foxy repeatedly checked the rear- and side-view mirrors and glanced down every side road and alley they passed. His oddly calm paranoia was freaking her out. McKinney hadn't slept a wink on either the flight from Africa or the flight from Germany. She felt half-crazed from exhaustion and stress, and Foxy's behavior wasn't helping. All she could think about was how her father would deal with the news of her disappearance. Let's face it—her death. That's what any sane person would think if someone disappeared in an explosion. And what about Adwele? How would he cope with the death of yet another significant adult in his life? First his father, and now McKinney . . .

She suddenly noticed Foxy staring at her. "You okay, Professor?"

"Somebody blew up my world." She shrugged. "I'm doing great, Foxy. Just super."

He nodded. "You want my advice?"

"No offense, but I really don't."

"Well, I'll give it to you anyway. You just won the world's worst lottery, that's all. It's nothing you did—so don't focus on things beyond your control. Focus only on what you can control. That's served me well over the years."

McKinney considered his words. Actually it was pretty decent advice. She studied Foxy. "Thanks for saving my life. Back in Africa, I mean."

"Don't mention it."

"You actually know how to play that kora?"

Foxy gave her a disbelieving look and laughed. "Of course I play it. I can play most instruments I put my mind to. I will say, though, these twenty-one-string instruments are tricky. You ever hear of Foday Musa Suso?"

"Maybe. African?"

"Originally Gambian; moved to Chicago decades ago. I've been trying some of his songs. I haven't had much practice lately because my last kora got blown up. Along with some people I knew."

McKinney felt the normalcy drain out of the conversation. She could suddenly see in his face the hardened mien of an elite soldier. "I'm sorry to hear that."

In a few moments his seriousness passed, and he cast a grin her way. "This trip gave me the chance to grab a new one."

"I wouldn't have guessed a person in your line of work would be a musician."

"With music you can speak to anyone."

She leaned back in her seat. "Then music is a tool."

He frowned briefly at her. "That's not the right word. Look, what we do isn't what you think. Human intelligence, what we call HUMINT, mostly involves making connections with people—not hurting them. You never know what opportunities come from making friends. And music is a great way to make friends in strange places. Take the Arab heavy metal scene, for example. . . ."

"There's an Arab heavy metal scene?"

He nodded and smiled wistfully. "Oh, hell, yes. That's my music. The soul of disaffection. You won't find any more sincerity than in heavy metal music in a repressive society. When we get a chance, I'll play some for you." He patted the T-shirt he was wearing. "This is a Saudi Arabian band named Eltoba, but I'm a big fan of Arsames—Iranian death metal— and, uh, Mordab is good too. Oh, there's a kick-ass Bahraini Arabic death black metal band named Narjahanam. I saw them in an underground rave in Manama last year. Damned near got arrested. Their name means 'the fire of hell,' and, man, you can feel the youthful rage from these guys—not the sanitized, feigned shit coming from suburban kids trying to cash in. I mean fuck-it-all *rage* with a purpose."

McKinney found herself grinning uneasily. "You should be the Middle East correspondent for *Rolling Stone*."

"That would be problematic, but . . . oh, there's Acrassicauda, Iraq's sole heavy metal band—which is a start. But, hey, my personal favorite at the moment is an Afghan folk metal band—"

"Afghanistan has *folk metal*? You're pulling my leg now."

"Seriously, you can bridge any gap with music. It's an Afghan folk metal band named Al Qaynah; a mind-blowing combination of traditional central Asian instruments—like the rubab, the tanbūr—with a driving heavy metal foundation. Like all good art it challenges people. Takes them outside their comfort zone."

"Should I even ask what brought you to these places?"

He shrugged. "I'll tell you this much: I saw the Arab Spring coming. You could hear it in the younger generation's music. You could see it in their eyes; in how they used technology to express themselves artistically, creatively. State Department? The CIA? NSA? For all their satellites and garden party spies, they somehow missed a huge wave of popular outrage with the status quo. No, to understand a people, you need to wade into their culture. It's culture that tells their tale. And music is culture."

McKinney realized there was a lot more going on with Foxy than had first appeared.

"For instance, most people don't realize that British punk rock stemmed from a youthful backlash against survivors' guilt from the Holocaust."

"Oh, my God!" McKinney gave him an annoyed look. "Would you please just drive. Where are we going, anyway?"

"It isn't far."

"Why did we split up?"

Foxy nodded. "We always take separate vehicles and different routes back to base. The others will get in well after us."

"Who could possibly notice us among all the other people in this city?"

"You might be surprised what anomalies can be detected against background noise. That's why we have vans like this drive from the airport several times a day even if there's no one to collect." He took stock of her reaction. "I can tell nobody's tried to kill you before, Professor. It tends to change one's view on what constitutes reasonable precautions."

"Well, it looks like I don't have much choice in the matter."

"I hope you don't feel any more like a prisoner than the rest of us. We're all stuck on this operation until it's finished—that includes the other civilian experts. No holiday with the family for us either. I'd like to start thinking of you as another member of the team, if that's okay."

"Other civilian experts? So you've pressed other people into service?"

"None are in your unique situation, but you'll meet the other folks; subject matter experts, most of them with top-secret clearances."

"So they had a choice."

"Not after they were briefed."

He was driving down a cracked concrete boulevard now with a grass median peppered with patches of dirty snow. They passed a gravel quarry. The area was starting to get seedier. A truck stop stood at the far side, and a large riverfront casino was visible farther on, its brilliant signage threatening to induce seizures in any nocturnal creatures wandering about.

McKinney noticed a low, wooded hillside rising to the left. It surprised her, since she'd always thought of the Midwest as flat. There were obviously some hills here. She took note of the license plates on a passing car: Missouri. That's right. Kansas City wasn't in Kansas—it was in Missouri. Or at least part of it was. They didn't appear to be deceiving her about where they were. She spotted another truck: Kansas plates.

The *click-click* of the van's blinker sounded, and the van slowed. They crossed left over some railroad tracks and seemingly straight toward a grassy hillside. Oddly, even a spur from the railroad line curved along with them as the road led toward a white stone cliff face that cut into the hill.

McKinney looked up at an illuminated sign that read SubTropolis. It was bolted above the concrete-framed entrance of a tunnel. Flags of the world were on display on angled poles above the entrance. The opening was at least twenty feet high and fifty feet across. A roadway large enough to accommodate two semitrucks side by side led into the hillside. In fact, McKinney could also see farther down along the well-lit cliff face where the railroad tracks led into the underground as well. Whole trains could apparently enter the hill.

Foxy opened his passenger window and swiped a magnetic card at a reader, and the roll-up metal security gate started to rise.

"What is this place?"

"The office. Got a roof of solid limestone a hundred feet thick. Three times stronger than concrete. No drone missile can hit us down here. Odin doesn't like to take chances."

Foxy pulled through the gate and immediately the massive tunnel opened up into a brightly lit grid of solid rock pillars and interior buildings. There were signs bolted to the rock walls pointing the direction and bay numbers for various manufacturing businesses, warehouses, and shipping companies. The roadway curved downward slightly, and then straightened into a main thoroughfare, punctuated by yellowish metal-halide lights. The place was a vast subterranean business park.

McKinney had never heard of such a thing. Every hundred feet or so there was a massive, chiseled column of solid stone, twenty feet square, but otherwise the place just seemed to stretch on endlessly in three directions beneath the hillside—bright lights trailing to a vanishing point. "My God, this place is huge."

Foxy nodded. "Six miles of road. Fifty-five million square feet of space. Only ten of that's been improved for use, and only half of that's occupied."

McKinney craned her neck to check out the endless rows of pillars. "How on earth . . . ?"

"They've been mining limestone here since the forties. Somebody had the bright idea that, since this rock formation has been here for about two hundred and eighty million years, it would be a stable environment for archival storage, data centers, things like that. No worries about tornadoes either. Hell, there are all sorts of businesses down here. Packaging companies, light fixture companies. They can roll semitrucks and railcars right inside too. It's got major advantages for this operation. For one, it's impossible to observe what we're doing from the air or satellites, and there are several entrances—lots of comings and goings at all hours. And we're centrally located—a short flight to most of the country."

Foxy cut the van left down a side tunnel, and they were soon cruising down another cavern road that led to a vanishing point. "We operate under unofficial cover—oil and gas exploration firms, microwave communications companies. Things like that. Gives us what's called 'status for cover'—meaning a reason to be someplace. Allows us to move around in the countryside with heavy equipment without drawing attention. Here we are. . . ."

Foxy slowed the van, and then turned right down another side passage. Here the floor opened out into an endless grid of stone columns— but the lights ended. They now headed off into utter blackness. Their headlights seemed to be swallowed by the vast dark.

McKinney found herself leaning forward in her seat. "I'll bet there are some interesting fossils in here."

"Yeah, well, I wouldn't know anything about that. All I know is that it's a good place for an isolation facility. We've got a quarter million square feet far away from all the other tenants. That way we don't get visitors, and no one notices us. We're way the hell out in the darkness, and nobody's going to wander on over to borrow a cup of sugar. Look . . ." He pointed at the stone floor stretching out beneath the headlights.

McKinney could see a single security lamp in the distance.

"Porch light's on, so the coast is clear."

They drew closer to the light and finally pulled up to a rolltop door in a long white corrugated steel wall that rose from rock floor to rock ceiling. It stretched out into the darkness in both directions. Several cameras focused on the entrance. Foxy waved, and the rolltop door began to rise, clattering with an echoing racket amid all the exposed rock.

She could see a company logo for Ancile Services, text with a simple shield shape; the same logo emblazoned on her coat. There was a suite number next to the garage door, along with a mail drop and an intercom. It all looked quite innocuous. Underground buildings apparently had to be fashioned down here to make the spaces functional and comfortable. The perimeter wall looked similar to what other businesses had built, although there appeared to be domed security camera enclosures at intervals along the perimeter.

McKinney was surprised when what lay behind the rolltop gate was just more darkness.

Foxy nodded forward. "Buffer area—a hundred-foot-wide exterior perimeter to prevent anyone listening in on what we're up to." He pulled the van through the doorway, and the gate descended behind them.

As they drove ahead into the dark, something came swimming out the blackness. Literally swimming through the air was a small shark, replete with teeth and fins, its tail working furiously as it swam to investigate the incoming van.

McKinney peered closely at it. "What the hell . . . ?"

Moments later several more sharks "swam" out the darkness, converging on the van like a school of fish.

She laughed in confusion. "Okay . . . what are those things?"

"Air swimmers—cheap children's toy that Expert Five converted for security purposes. It's a neutral-buoyancy balloon with a power tail fin. I don't know how many he's got flying out here, but they patrol the buffer space for intruders."

Sure enough, now dozens more of the things were sweeping in out of the dark all around them to investigate the lights and movement of the van, bumping up against the windows as though the van were a submarine.

McKinney couldn't help but admire them. "They're swarming." She noticed also a little payload beneath the shark-shaped dirigibles, a rectangular piece of black plastic—and the reflection of a camera lens.

Foxy nodded. "Yeah, Five's an AI expert. You'll like him. From what I understand, his fish here explore a space, memorize the layout, and then they use some sort of routing algorithm to patrol."

"A foraging pattern. Do you know what species they're modeling?"

"I sure don't. All I know is they explore the space and remember the layout. When they encounter something that wasn't there before, they send up an alarm. Flying around independently makes it difficult to blind them with lasers or other countermeasures. They swim to a charging station too." He chuckled. "Freaky how much it looks like fish feeding."

"So an antidrone unit is being guarded by drones."

"Fire with fire."

"Oh, there's a clown fish." McKinney pointed.

"Yeah, it's getting crowded. C'mon, move it." Foxy tapped the horn as he nudged through the gathering wall of fish. "Everyone else is probably asleep, but I'll get you squared away in your quarters."

"We stay down here full-time?"

He shrugged. "It's not so bad. Nothing's more comfy than knowing you're not gonna get blown up in your sleep."

McKinney pondered that for a moment as she watched another flying shark "swim" past the right side of the van.

In a few moments they pulled up to another corrugated steel wall and a rolltop gate, this one unmarked. The gate rose automatically to reveal a brightly lit garage bay over a hundred feet long and half as wide, containing several large trucks, heavy equipment, and other gear. The floor was painted gray and marked with yellow parking and lane lines. Metalworking equipment, welding rigs, and workbenches were scattered about the place. Interior walls sectioned off the garage, and several doors led off into other areas of the complex.

Standing in the middle of the garage and pointing with two gloved hands to an open space was an athletic Latino in his twenties. He had tattoos of two different women on either bicep and small, pretzel-like ears that lay flush against his crew-cut head. He wore a blue Ancile Services polo shirt with jeans, and tan combat boots—as well as a small black submachine gun slung against his chest.

"Home sweet home." Foxy pulled the van into a space and killed the engine.

The rolltop gate was still rumbling closed as the Latino came up to the van. McKinney nodded to him, and he nodded back. The air was about sixty-five degrees and smelled powerfully of cut stone.

Foxy exchanged a complex, full-body handshake with the man. "Smokey, how the hell are you, man?"

"All right. All right."

Foxy gestured to McKinney. "Smokey, this is—"

"I know who it is, dipshit." He removed a shooting glove and extended his hand. "Professor. Pleasure. They call me Smokey. You didn't see me in Africa, but I was on the ground. Glad to see you made it out okay."

Foxy was busy grabbing gear. "You ever find that F50?"

"Naw, it was crazy back there, son. People with guns runnin' around."

McKinney felt her eyes drooping in exhaustion.

Foxy slapped Smokey on the shoulder. "Hey, looks like the professor needs some rack time. So do I."

"All right, we'll catch up later."

They left Smokey behind and headed toward double doors. As McKinney padded across the floor, it occurred to her it wasn't concrete. It was solid rock, probably hundreds of feet thick, ground flat by mining equipment and polished. Their shoes made almost no sound as they walked across it.

Looking around at the other vehicles in the large garage, McKinney noticed some were marked with the same Ancile Services shield logo she wore, while others were painted teal green and marked with U.S. Forest Service insignia. There were also a couple of four-wheel-drive Dodge Power Wagon crew-cab pickups in the process of being painted with Bureau of Land Management livery—the word *Ranger* partially stenciled and taped out along the side. All of the vehicles were rugged-looking; obviously made for off-road work, with the largest trucks being ten-ton, four-wheel-drive monstrosities. She'd seen similar Unimog trucks in Africa used by pricey European or South African tour groups. Apparently no expense had been spared on this place; there were three gleaming multi-ton Amerigo four-wheel-drive survey trucks with sensors and antennas sticking up from a windowed control room in their cargo area. They looked like oil company seismic trucks, but they were partially disassembled in places with welding equipment stored close by and modifications half-finished.

McKinney gestured to the vehicles and looked at Foxy quizzically.

"Need-to-know, Professor."

"You realize that conducting covert military operations inside the United States is illegal."

"Someone's attacking us, Professor. When that happens we get to shoot back. No sense panicking everyone in the meantime."

They pushed through the doors and entered a plain white hallway that smelled strongly of spackling, fresh paint, and adhesives. The whole place was brand-new. It had the look of a medical office building. Foxy brought her ahead and to the right, down a side corridor.

"Your hooch is this way. . . ."

McKinney's head kept darting about. "This whole place was built just for this project?"

Foxy sighed. "Yeah, and let me tell you, top-secret general contractors don't come cheap."

They turned a corner to see a man with tightly curled gray hair standing with his back to them in the middle of the hallway; he was dressed in a sweater and slacks, holding a tablet computer in his hands while he watched a lawn mower–sized unmanned electric vehicle with large, off-road wheels weaving through doorways, following some sort of search pattern.

Foxy called out, "You're up late."

The man kept his eyes on the vehicle. "Tinkering is sleep for me." He turned as they reached him.

He was balding, with an aquiline nose. A wiry, intense-looking sixty-year-old. He regarded McKinney with something like disdain.

Foxy gestured to McKinney. "Expert One, meet Expert Six."

The man stared intently as he extended his hand. "Brian Singleton, Professor Emeritus, Computer Engineering and Robotics, Carnegie Mellon University."

Foxy rolled his eyes. "Goddammit, Singleton, how many times do I have to tell you, no names?"

"I'll be damned if I'm going to cower behind some puerile alias."

"It could compromise your personal safety, not to mention—"

"Let these terrorists do their damnedest." Singleton focused his gaze back on McKinney, but he addressed his talk to Foxy. "The report said she's a myrmecologist. Don't tell me this young woman was brought here because of Odin's fixation on swarming again."

"One, what Odin does or doesn't do isn't my—"

"Because it's a waste of time." Singleton's eyes stayed on McKinney as she watched his vehicle whizzing around the hallways unattended behind him. "The drones we're facing are premeditated hunters, not swarming hordes." He gestured behind him at his nimble vehicle. "Hunting alone. We can't waste time on conjecture."

McKinney stared right back at him. "I'm not here by choice, and I have no intention of trying to push an agenda on you."

"Good. Because I won't allow us to be sidetracked."

"Fine."

"People are dying."

"I got it. Okay? Let it go."

Foxy interceded. "Stop busting balls." He gestured to the hallway. "You wanna call off your premeditated hunter?"

Singleton kept his gaze on McKinney for a second more, and then nodded. He clapped his hands sharply, and the unmanned vehicle stopped in its tracks.

Foxy pushed past with McKinney. "Thank you. See you in the morning."

"Good night."

After they rounded the corner McKinney shook her head ruefully. "I knew there was a reason I liked fieldwork."

Foxy chuckled. "Oh, he's all right once you get to know him. Just been here a while, that's all." Foxy led her to a row of blond-wood doors. They stopped at one with the number six engraved on a plastic plaque. "Here we are."

McKinney narrowed her eyes to see that someone had even printed the number in raised Braille letters underneath. She ran her finger along the dots.

Foxy opened the door. "Yes, we are ADA compliant." He turned on the lights. They buzzed on to illuminate a Spartan dormitory-style room with sturdy, brand-new furniture. A bed, dresser, and a desk with a laptop already sitting on it—hardwired with a CAT-5 cable to a jack in the wall. A flat-panel television hung opposite the bed. It was a room she'd never in a million years conceived she'd be in. She was still trying to grasp the surreality of all this and half expected to hear the night sounds of the jungle. Here there was only the sterile buzzing of lights.

Foxy walked to the desk and opened the laptop. "Yours for the duration. It has most of the software that was on your old laptop."

"Do I even want to ask how you know what was on my old laptop?"

"You can ask Hoov tomorrow. He might have some firewall advice." He gestured to the laptop again. "There's a team wiki on our intranet that'll tell you everything you need to know about the mission. Welcome to government service."

"A covert military operation with a wiki."

Foxy headed to the door. "It's only going to get stranger from here on, Professor. So I suggest you get some sleep. Your bathroom's over there. Toiletries too. Clothes and shoes in the bureau and closet. The alarm clock will sound at oh six hundred hours. Everyone gathers in the team room at seven. You can grab breakfast before then—I'll send someone around. If you need sleeping aids or anything else, ring this button by the door." He regarded her tired eyes. "Any questions?"

She shook her head wearily.

"Super . . ." He gave her a two-finger salute. "See you in about five hours, then." And closed the door behind him.

She stared at the dead bolt, and then walked over to turn it with a satisfying *clack*. Just the sight of the slug of steel entering the frame, sealing her off, brought her stress level down by half.

McKinney then sat on the edge of the bed and put her hands to her face. This was insanity.

She noticed the remote control for the television on the nightstand. She grabbed it and clicked the power button. The television blinked to life on the Weather Channel. A meteorologist was waving her hands above the northeast, showing a high-pressure system moving in from the Great Lakes. It was a window of normalcy viewed from inside a loony bin.

She clicked the channel button and cable news came up. Video of a burning office building, windows blackened and blasted out. The chyron scrolling on the bottom read, ". . . *attack in D.C. Six dead. Twelve injured . . .*"

McKinney felt it almost personally.

The anchorwoman spoke over the video: "*. . . time in the heart of America's defense sector close by the Pentagon. The bomb claimed the lives of Alerion Aerospace CEO Brad Oliphant Jr. along with several board members and executives. As a parts supplier for several Pentagon drone aircraft programs, security analysts speculate that Alerion was targeted by extremists intent on exacting revenge for the recent Karbala shrine attack, despite new evidence supporting an American denial of responsibility.*

Although al-Qaeda and other terror organizations have voiced support for today's attack, authorities confirm that no credible group has yet to claim responsibility for—"

Click.

Another cable news station. An inset photo of the same burning office building next to the anchorman, who was in midstory. "*. . . explosion could be heard throughout the capital city and, for some, brought back awful memories of 9/11. It is a city under siege this hour, as residents cope with the realization that they now live in a combat zone.*"

Click.

Another news channel. Images of the injured being rolled on gurneys to waiting ambulances. Fire trucks. The anchorman's voice authoritative: "*Parts of D.C. are in lockdown as investigators comb through the scene, reviewing surveillance videos for some clue as to how the bombers were able to bypass security.*"

McKinney nodded to herself. A smart bomb doesn't go through security. She wondered if this was a planted story or whether most government officials really didn't know the truth either.

Click.

More news. Same story.

Click.

News again. Was that the only thing on this damned system? Weather and news?

Click.

News commentary. Several pundits sitting across from each other at a desk that would look at home on the Starship *Enterprise*, weighing in on recent events. A bald man with a crooked tie was talking fast. "*. . . ourselves is why, after over a decade in the War on Terror, literally trillions of dollars and thousands of American dead and tens of thousands of injured— after all that blood and treasure—and literally hundreds of thousands of civilian dead overseas, why are we now as helpless against these terrorists as we were on 9/11?*"

Another pundit: "*That's not the big issue here, Howard. I mean, given all the privacy and civil liberties that we've given up, we now effectively live in a surveillance state—cameras on every street corner, in every place of business and office building, mass wiretapping—and yet the government is no closer to finding these terrorists. You look at the Spanish train bombings, the London Underground bombings—they had surveillance video in a matter of hours that led to the perpetrators. Yet here it's been months and nearly two dozen attacks—"*

The host interjected, *"Well, there have been arrests."*

"But the bombings continue, and we've had no convictions. We've had several suspects released, in fact."

The host changed direction. *"Instead, word on Capitol Hill is that House and Senate intelligence committees are examining an emergency defense appropriation reported to be in the tens of billions of dollars to create a drone air defense system, which makes me wonder how much more we could possibly spend on security that isn't—"*

Click.

The Weather Channel again. McKinney tossed the remote onto the nightstand and collapsed onto the bed, listening to the soothing voice of the weatherwoman. . . .

". . . scattered showers across much of southeast Asia and the Indonesian archipelago. While a high-pressure system eases down over the Kamchatka Peninsula . . ."

CHAPTER 13

Close Hold

Linda McKinney exited her room to the sound of arguing. As she rounded the corner, she came upon Foxy and Singleton squared off again, while two large ravens squabbled over the wreckage of Singleton's hunter vehicle on the floor in the middle of the hallway. The birds were using their thick black beaks to tear wires out of the autonomous vehicle's central circuit board. Pieces of plastic littered the floor.

"When is Odin going to get these flying rats under control?"

"You know they like to wreck things. I can't keep windshield wipers on the trucks when they get bored. Besides, I thought your 'hunter-killer' could look after itself."

"It's idiocy having these birds flying around down here. They steal chips and components."

Foxy and Singleton both turned to see McKinney. Foxy nodded. "Morning."

"Morning." McKinney looked down to see the ravens flapping their wings, *cawing* loudly as Singleton tried to move in to salvage his machine.

Foxy thumbed down the hall. "Team room's that way. You'll find breakfast there."

"Thanks." McKinney nodded and stepped past, trying to stifle a shared grin with Foxy as the birds snapped at Singleton's fingers. He tried to shoo them away.

Like the rest of the underground offices the brightly lit team room was new enough that it still smelled of fresh paint. However, it didn't have a drop ceiling; instead exposed limestone stood three times McKinney's height above. The scoured and striated rock was painted white and criss-crossed by fire sprinkler pipes and bright fluorescent work lights. The work area was huge. A dozen people in jeans and variously colored Ancile Services polo shirts sat around a series of large tables that had been pushed together to create a broad and long work surface littered with thousands of documents, photographs, and blueprints, as well as machine-milled foam models of what appeared to be unmanned aircraft and machine parts. There were also diagrams of corporate and residential buildings detailing explosive damage, dotted with callouts and captions unreadable at this distance. A dozen identical laptops were open and running with people clicking away at keyboards. Half a dozen more people sat or stood at tables running along the room's perimeter. The walls were hung with large plotter-printed diagrams, maps, and blueprints depicting the United States, maps of commercial flight paths, radar and military installations, and printouts of surveillance imagery. There were also silhouettes of hun-dreds of drone aircraft pinned to the walls—way more, in fact, than McKinney had known existed. The silhouettes were categorized by country: Argentina, Bulgaria, China, the Czech Republic, France, Germany, Greece, India, Iran, Israel, Italy, Japan, Latvia, Pakistan, Poland, Russia, Serbia, Singapore, South Africa, South Korea, Spain, Taiwan, Turkey, the UK, the U.S.—and on, and on. There were hundreds of drones on the walls.

Clearly thousands of man-hours had already been expended on this project, and everyone seemed to be busy working their portion of it.

Odin stood at the head of the table with his arms crossed. He nodded silently to her as she examined the team room.

Among the other team members it was impossible to tell who was military and who was civilian. Long hair and beards certainly didn't indi-cate a civilian background, since Odin and Foxy had both.

There was a plump forty-something Asian man—Korean, she

guessed—conversing with a lanky blond guy who, although boyish, was probably in his thirties. She exchanged nods with him as she laid her assigned laptop on the table and took an open seat. There was lots of room.

Glancing along the table she saw a pear-shaped African-American man in his thirties gesturing to a laptop screen, while another Asian man listened in, slighter in build and more fair-complexioned—most likely Japanese. The Japanese man gave McKinney a knowing, sympathetic nod. Two other individuals at the edge of the room—a Caucasian man and a Latina in their early twenties—were arguing about something involving radio signals. A collection of computers and signal processing equipment lined their workstation.

The last team member at the table, a sophisticated-looking African-American woman in her late twenties or early thirties, with short hair, smiled in greeting. Her eyeglasses went way beyond functional into stylish-expensive territory. "Have you had breakfast yet? There's food just beyond the pillar."

McKinney shook her head. "No, I'm fine, thanks. Not much of an appetite."

A series of clocks on one wall showed the time in a dozen cities of the world. It was nearly seven A.M. local time.

"So, what is this, mission control?"

The woman nodded. "Joint operations center—the JOC. People from different disciplines and commands under Odin's op-con." On McKinney's squint she added, "Sorry. Military speak. It means 'operational control.' He's in charge here."

"He made that pretty clear."

She smiled sympathetically. "They pick assertive types to head these missions." She reached across to extend her hand. "I'm Snowcap, team psychologist."

McKinney shook the woman's hand. "Surprised to see a psychologist here."

Snowcap nodded. "These operations usually include a psyops component—managing public response to frightening news. I've been briefed on your situation. These things can be stressful even for trained military personnel. Let me know if you need help. Foxy mentioned you're having trouble sleeping. I can prescribe something, if you like."

"No. I'm good, thanks." As McKinney settled in, she noticed a sign in large red letters painted on the wall across from her: *No Mundungus This Area*.

Before she could ask Snowcap about it, Odin stood and dropped a pad of paper onto the table. His voice boomed out. "All right, let's get started."

Everyone stopped what they were doing and focused on him. The two radio folks at the edge grabbed a seat at the main table. Behind Odin, Singleton emerged from behind a large whiteboard hung on a massive pillar of stone. He was stirring cream into his coffee as he calmly took his seat next to Odin, near the head of the table.

Odin gestured to McKinney. "As you can see, we have a new team member. Expert Six is the myrmecologist who developed the swarming algorithms we found on the Shenyang server—algorithms based on the African weaver ant, her particular field of study. Which means her work is of specific interest to the enemy. Which is no doubt why they tried to kill her thirty-six hours ago."

Most of the team nodded at her with respect.

Singleton cleared his throat. "You realize they might simply be using her algorithms because they were readily obtainable."

The others groaned, tossing pieces of paper in his direction.

Singleton held up his hands calmly. "I'm just saying that if they'd been able to get their hands on a more sophisticated model, they would have."

The Korean scientist scowled. "I suppose you think they should have used your code instead."

"I've looked at Six's swarming model, and I don't see how it would be useful in a hardware context without major modifications."

McKinney looked across the table at him. "I didn't write it with hardware in mind. I had no idea that it would be used in any context other than pure research."

"Clearly. Not to mention the fact that we haven't seen swarming behavior in these attacks. So far what we've seen is precision bombing of carefully selected targets. That doesn't approximate the indiscriminate foraging of Hymenoptera."

Odin stared at him. "Everyone on this team has expertise relevant to the mission." He looked to McKinney but pointed at Singleton. "One is an expert on robotics and visual intelligence. More complex autonomous systems." Then he pointed past McKinney to the Japanese man. "Expert Five, artificial intelligence."

McKinney brightened. "I saw your flying fish swarm when I came in last night. Pretty cool."

The man smiled. "Thanks. More of an experiment, really."

Odin pointed to the African-American man. "Expert Four, drone design." He crossed the table to the thin blond man. "Expert Two, aerospace and electrical engineering." Next to him, the Korean man. "Expert Three, computer engineering." He pointed to the woman across from McKinney. "Snowcap, our MI and psyops liaison." Then to the two signals people. "Gumball and Leggo, signals intelligence. And of course, you know Foxy."

Singleton immediately waded into the silence that followed, gazing across the table at McKinney. "It's not my intention to offend you, Six, but your software isn't exactly munitions-grade AI. I don't want us wasting time on theoretical swarming applications."

McKinney made a point of meeting his gaze. "I'm not offended by rational discussion. I gather we're all here to solve this problem."

Odin spoke to the room. "Swarming strategies have historically won sixty-one percent of all battles—and an even greater percentage in urban terrain. Think Grozny, Stalingrad, etc."

Singleton was undeterred. "But we're facing more sophisticated, singular weapon systems."

"Which to me aren't as worrisome as what might be coming."

Singleton scoffed. "You're not seriously suggesting we let these assassinations continue unopposed?"

"Don't try my patience. The enemy is interested in autonomous swarming—which has the potential to transform the conduct of warfare. We will listen to what Six knows."

Odin gestured to McKinney. "As a matter of fact, Professor, would you please come up and give the team a primer on your software model and maybe weaver ants in general?"

McKinney sighed, realizing how tired she was. But then, she'd taught many a class exhausted when she was a TA and then an associate professor. She nodded and stood, heading to the nearby whiteboard bolted to the wall-like stone pillar. It was covered with green dry-erase ink, diagrams of circuits, and logic work-flows.

She turned to the team. "Mind if I erase this?"

Singleton pursed his lips. "Hmm. I'm still working through some things there."

McKinney put the eraser back on the tray. "Fine. I guess I can—"

Foxy was already wheeling a portable whiteboard in from the edge of the room. He slid it in front of the first one.

"Thanks." She grabbed a marker and faced out to the assembled experts sitting around the room. One of the stranger speaking engagements she'd had. She looked to the Japanese scientist, the AI specialist. "Five, quite a bit of this will be elementary for you. I apologize in advance."

"Not at all. I'm interested to hear it."

"Well . . ." She took a moment to gather her thoughts. "Ant colony optimization—or ACO—models have been around since the early nineties. Mathematical representations of ant behavior are widely used in private enterprise to optimize complex logistics problems, like delivery truck routing, computer network routing, and market analysis. Antlike swarming intelligence is best illustrated by a classic combinatorial optimization challenge known as the Traveling Salesman Problem. . . ."

McKinney drew a series of dots on the board. "Given a list of cities"— she started connecting the dots with a single traveling line—"how do you find the shortest possible route that visits each city only once?" Her onboard solution quickly failed to do so, and she looked up. "Sounds simple, but it's not; it's what's known as a nondeterministic polynomial-time hard problem—meaning it's very difficult for humans to achieve. Ants solve this problem routinely. They will always find the shortest possible route to a food source, and as experiments using the Towers of Hanoi Problem set show, if that path is obstructed, they can adapt and find the next shortest route. And so on. They do all this without centralized control and without conscious intent.

"In many ways, individual ants are similar to individual neurons in the human brain. The fact that individual ants—let's call them *agents*—follow fairly predictable behaviors, means that *metaheuristics* can simulate their actions with considerable accuracy."

Snowcap held up her hand. "A metaheuristic is . . . ?"

"It's an iterative computation method designed to improve a candidate solution. It's a form of genetic or evolutionary programming. For example, here's a basic ant algorithm for detecting the edges of pheromone trails. It was developed way back in 1992 by Marco Dorigo. . . ." She started scrawling on the board.

$$p_{xy}^k = \frac{\left(\tau_{xy}^\alpha\right)\left(\eta_{xy}^\beta\right)}{\sum\left(\tau_{xy}^\alpha\right)\left(\eta_{xy}^\beta\right)}$$

McKinney pointed at the formula. "An ant is a simple computational agent that iteratively constructs a solution for the problem at hand. At each iteration, each individual ant moves from a state x to state y, which represents a more complete intermediate solution. Thus, for each ant"—she pointed at the formula—"k, the probability p_{xy}^k of moving from state x to state y depends on the combination of two values—namely the attractiveness η_{xy} of the move, as computed by some heuristic indicating a priori desirability of that move, and the trail level τ_{xy} of the move, indicating how beneficial it has been in the past to make that particular move."

Odin grimaced. "I think we might be getting too deep in the weeds here, Professor. How does your model function?"

McKinney nodded and erased the algorithm. "Right. Sorry. Just wanted to lay a foundation."

"You can put the gory details up on the wiki."

"Now, my work in particular . . ." McKinney thought for a moment, and then wrote two Latin names on the board. "*Oecophylla longinoda* and *Oecophylla smaragdina*—two closely related arboreal ant species that dominate the tropical forests of Africa, Asia, and Australia—otherwise known as the weaver ant due to their practice of weaving leaf nests with larval silk. They're of the order"—she wrote on the board again with her clear, Arialesque print—"Hymenoptera, which includes bees and wasps. Weaver ants are what's known as a eusocial insect, meaning they exhibit the highest level of social organization in nature.

"I developed Myrmidon, my weaver computer model, based on years of direct field observations." McKinney paced before the board. "Unlike most ant species, weaver ants are fiercely territorial. They attack any intruders into their domain—no matter what the odds. Climb into a weaver tree, and you will be attacked. They swarm enemies with suicidal disregard. That strategy is not evolutionarily problematic because, as with many colony insects, weaver workers don't reproduce—only the queens pass on their genetic material. Thus, workers always fight to the death— the colony is their legacy.

"A single weaver colony might span dozens of trees and include hundreds of nests built throughout their territory in an integrated network. From here they launch attacks, raise young, and care for livestock, other insects that they raise for nectar."

The team members looked surprised at this last part.

McKinney drew another series of points similar to the Traveling Salesman Problem and started connecting them. "Weavers maintain a flexible network of routes between their population centers. And unlike most ants, they have excellent vision. They also have better memories than regimented species such as army ants. Individual weaver ants can accrue 'experience' which informs later actions."

Expert Five piped in. "So they're like a neural network."

McKinney nodded. "Precisely. Weavers process experience via *mushroom bodies. . . .*" She drew the outline of an ant's head, inside of which she drew several large blobs. The largest, occupying the bottom center, she shaded in. "These are brain structures found in almost all insects, and they manage context-dependent learning and memory processes. Their size correlates with the degree of a species' level of social organization. The larger the mushroom body in the brain, the more socially organized an insect society is. As we'd expect, weaver ants have an unusually large mushroom body, which endows weaver workers with above average memory.

"That memory sharpens the iterative component of weaver swarming intelligence. Because swarming intelligence is all about data exchange. What we call"—she wrote a word on the board—"*stigmergy*. Stigmergy is where individual parts of a system communicate indirectly by modifying the local environment. In the case of weaver ants, they exchange data mostly through pheromones." She started drawing lines that represented ant paths. "If they encounter a source of food or an enemy, they return to the nearest nest, all the while laying down a specific mix of chemical pheromones in a trail that communicates both what they've encountered—food or threat—and the degree to which they encountered it—lots of food or a big threat. Half a million individual agents moving about simultaneously doing this creates a network of these trails, known as the colony's *pheromone matrix*, holding dozens of different encoded messages. This matrix fades over time, which means it represents in effect the colony's current knowledge. As weavers encounter these trails, they're recruited to address whatever message the trail communicates—for example, to harvest food or fight intruders. As they move along the trail, they reinforce the chemical message—sort of like upvoting something on Reddit or 'Liking' someone's Facebook status. As that pheromone message gets stronger, it recruits still more workers to the cause, and soon, clusters of ants begin to form at the site of the threat or opportunity."

Expert Two, the blond man, nodded. "Meaning it goes viral."

McKinney nodded. "Basically, yes. In this way, weavers manage everything from nest building, food collection, colony defense, and so on. At each iteration of their activity, each ant builds a solution by applying a constructive procedure that uses the common memory of the colony—that is, the *pheromone matrix*. So, although individual weaver ants have very little processing power, collectively they perform complex management feats."

McKinney dropped the marker in the tray at the base of the whiteboard. "In fact, if I were going to create an autonomous drone—and I had no ethical constraints—swarming intelligence would be a logical choice. Lots of simple computational agents reacting to each other via stigmergic processes. That's why weaver ants don't need a large brain to solve complex puzzles. They can solve problems because they can afford to try every solution at random until they discover one that works. A creature with a single body can't do that. A mistake could mean biological death. But the death of hundreds of workers to a colony numbering in the hundreds of thousands is irrelevant. In fact, the colony is the real organism, not the individual."

Expert Five interjected, "Then we would expect swarming drones to be cheap and disposable."

McKinney nodded. "And individually, not very smart. The demise of one or dozens or hundreds might not mean the demise of the group—and the survivors would be informed by the experience of swarm mates around them."

Singleton scribbled on his notepad. "You sound intrigued by the possibilities."

"I find weaver ants fascinating. But I wouldn't want to meet them scaled up in size and given weapons. It would be an insanely foolish thing to build."

Odin stood up again. "Thank you, Professor."

Singleton cleared his throat. "All of this would be incredibly useful information if we were facing hundreds of thousands of swarming robots—which we are not. Can we get down to business now?"

Odin just stared at Singleton for a moment. "Now that we know what risks we might face from swarming intelligence, let's review recent operations." Odin turned to the African-American scientist at the far end of the table. "Four, tell me what you learned from the Tanzanian video."

The man put on glasses and started examining his laptop screen. "Pretty amazing to finally see one of these things flying, Odin. Your hunch about the target was dead on." He glanced up at McKinney. "No offense intended, Six."

"None taken."

He tapped a combination of keys, and what was on his screen moved to a larger flat-screen monitor hanging on the wall where everyone could see it. It was the black-and-white FLIR footage of the drone that had attacked McKinney in Africa.

"From what we can tell, Odin, this isn't an extant design." He pointed at various features with a laser pointer. "Forward canards. Midsection dome. Slightly swept wing. What we're looking at here is a Frankenstein machine— something put together from all sorts of different drone designs."

"What's the prognosis for recovering wreckage?"

"In the Amani jungle reserve? Approaching zero. Whole armies have disappeared in there."

"What about its radar track? Where did it come from?"

"Came on radar off the east coast of Africa, near Zanzibar."

"HUMINT?"

"CIA's got some local stringers asking around, but that's gonna take time. Could be weeks till we hear anything."

"What about ships in the area?"

"There were dozens of ships and small craft. It's near a major African port, but there were no satellite assets overhead at the time."

The Korean scientist nodded. "The enemy's probably monitoring orbit schedules."

"Okay, so even though we were in the right time and place, we still have no idea where these things are originating."

The African-American scientist nodded sadly. "It'll be worse here in the States. The drones mix in with domestic air traffic—small private planes. There are thousands of unregistered private airstrips—runways on ranches and commercial and private lands that aren't attended by flight controllers or anyone else. Radar echoes alone aren't going to identify these things, and since they are remotely controlled we can't listen for unique radio signatures."

The Korean scientist nodded. "None of them have been picked up by DEA drones or coastal radar, so they might be being built and launched domestically. But with just two dozen attacks over three months, we don't have much data to work with. There's too much terrain to cover."

The blond scientist added with a slight Germanic accent, "Without an intact specimen—"

The Korean scientist next to him shook his head vigorously. "The moment we try to grab it, it'll explode in our faces—making it next to impossible to determine who built it, how it operates, and how to defend against it."

Odin glanced down at the notes on his pad of paper and crossed an item off a list. "That's being handled, Two. Next comes target prediction. Where are we?"

The Japanese researcher shook his head. "Nowhere, Odin. We've run the previous bombing victims through tens of thousands of link analysis filters, searching for any recognizable pattern or connection, but there's nothing. A human rights activist, a financier, oil company executives . . ." He threw up his hands. "None of them knew each other or had interactions of any type. They didn't work for the same companies or even in the same industry. They had no common financial interests, enemies, religious or political affiliations, social interests. Exchanged no communications. Not all of them were American, and on paper some of them would have been political adversaries—for example, the human rights activist in Chicago and the private prison lobbyist in Houston. Or the financial journalists killed in the New York café bombing or the retired East German Communist party boss living in Queens."

Odin pondered it. "What were the journalists working on when they died?"

"Corruption at major investment houses. The activist was doing a documentary on sweatshops in Syria." He shrugged. "If you're going by a list of people they criticized—well, it's a long list. It's in the hundreds. We certainly can't use it to predict an attack. We sliced and diced the data just about any way we can think of, and the only clear pattern is that these drones don't attack in high winds, rain, or snow."

A murmur swept though the group as several wrote that down.

"None of you guys noticed that?"

Odin looked up from his notepad. "Praying for rain isn't a solution. What else have you got?"

"Other than that . . . I guess we're still dead in the water."

"Not entirely." Odin tapped the intercom on a phone sitting on the table nearby.

A voice came over the speaker. *"You ready?"*

"Yeah, get in here."

"There in a sec."

McKinney couldn't help but notice that Odin was looking at her. She raised her eyebrows.

The others looked to her as well.

Odin paused a moment before speaking to her. "Your value, Professor, lies not only in what you know, but also in what you represent."

She looked at him askew. "I'm not following you."

The team room door opened, and Hoov, the Eurasian communications specialist from the plane in Africa, entered carrying a laptop case. He pulled up a chair and deposited the case on the table between Odin and McKinney.

Odin gestured to him. "You remember Hoov. He's been examining an image we took of your laptop several days ago—before the attack."

"You broke into my quarters."

Hoov shook his head dismissively. "Not necessary, Professor. I was able to remotely access your system."

"Oh, well . . . that's okay, then."

"Tell her what you found, Hoov."

Hoov nodded and addressed McKinney. "Three different classes of malware—one a fairly common ZeuS/Zbot Trojan variant, but two of them were a bit more exotic. Not known in the wild, and sophisticated. They both utilized a previously unknown OS vulnerability—what's known as a zero-day—which means we're dealing with serious people."

"Get to the point, Hoov."

"Okay. Professor, your computer is infected with the same rare, stealthy malware that compromised the Stanford servers."

McKinney wasn't surprised. "Okay, so they stole my work the same way they stole the Stanford researchers' work."

"Correct."

"How long do you think they've been inside my machine?"

"Hard to say. But . . ." Hoov looked to Odin.

Odin leaned in. "I've got a cyber team ready to trace the espionage pipeline this malware serves whenever I give the word. But I don't want to do that just yet."

"Why not?"

"It would risk detection, and I don't want them to abandon this pipeline like they did the Stanford one. Right now they're still searching for you. That's valuable to us."

McKinney narrowed her eyes at him.

"They're not positive you're dead. They'll be looking to see if you pop up again. We can use that."

"I don't like where this is going."

"If they suddenly discovered you're not dead, for example, and are here in the United States working with the U.S. military . . ."

"Jesus!" McKinney pushed back from the table and stood up. "You didn't bring me here for my expertise. You brought me here as bait!"

The other researchers turned to look at Odin with varying degrees of concern.

He held up his hands. "Wait a second. If we can get them to send a drone after you, that means we can predict where a drone attack will occur in advance. Which is what we've already spent months preparing for. It means we have a shot at catching one of these things."

"No matter how many times you assure me you're telling me the truth—"

"Whether you like it or not, until we find out who's sending these drones, you're not safe—and neither is anyone you care about. That means there's no going home for you until you help us trace these things back to their maker."

"I can only imagine what happens to me now if I refuse. Do you strap me to a telephone pole somewhere and chum the Internet with my data until drones come to kill me?"

Odin stared impassively. "I was sort of hoping we wouldn't have to use straps. . . ."

CHAPTER 14

Insomnia

It was well past midnight, and Linda McKinney hadn't slept in three days. Instead she was sitting at the desk in her room in front of the government-issued laptop. Oddly, it had no brand markings on it. She flipped up the lid and was surprised to see it was already powered on. The main page of a wiki was on-screen.

In the dim screen light McKinney could see her logon and password info on a printed security card next to the laptop, along with a "security best-practices" guide. She minimized the wiki page and noticed an Ubuntu desktop arranged much like the one on her own laptop. Okay, at least they were using open-source software, and they'd spied on her enough to install Code::Blocks on this loaner machine. No doubt her weaver ant simulation project files would be on here as well. She was actually impressed that the government folks were this competent.

She double-clicked on the Firefox browser icon. Not surprisingly, it didn't bring her to the Internet. No getting to the outside world. Instead it went to the same intranet project wiki page that was already open. The title "Task Force Ancile" headed the page with the company's shield logo. Along the left side were links to various categories: intelligence, video, interdiction, and many more.

A top-secret operation with a logo. She thought that was funny.

McKinney clicked on the word *Ancile,* and a definition popped up describing the Ancile as the legendary shield of the Roman god of war, Mars. The text said Rome would be master of the world as long as the shield was preserved.

Master of the world, eh?

Ruling the world wasn't on her personal list of priorities. She back-clicked and surveyed the categories of information available on the main project page. There were various headings: *Robotics, AI algorithms, Forensic analysis,* and many more.

She clicked on a link entitled *Attack Scenes.* It brought her to a page with dozens of thumbnail images. Brief introductory text described them as videos uploaded to various offshore aggregation websites. They appeared to be video clips of actual attacks as they happened, presumably filmed by spotter drones—like the one that had hovered outside her cabin back in Tanzania.

McKinney clicked on the first video thumbnail. It expanded to a full-screen high-def digital video of several men playing golf on a lush green course somewhere. There was no sound. Even now the angle was changing subtly, as though being filmed from a moving object. The men stood around the manicured green watching one of their number getting ready to putt.

Suddenly an instantaneous blast ripped the scene apart. McKinney recoiled in horror as body parts rained down in every direction. Strangely, there was no crater in the grass, which was now smoking, yet slick with blood. It appeared that the bomb detonated above the ground, to devastating effect. She closed the window and just stared at the main page. There were at least a dozen more.

"Dear God."

She didn't want to see any more of that. How had the videos been discovered? And by whom? The comments section still seemed to be hashing out the answer. Logons with call-sign names she didn't recognize, but also the occasional one she did—Expert Three, Hoov, Gumball.

She backtracked to the main wiki page and followed the link to a diagram of all the drone attacks. It showed a map of the United States overlaid by a couple of dozen red dots scattered mostly on the coasts— although some were deep in the Midwest. As she moved her mouse over the dots, basic details of each attack popped up: date, GPS coordinates, number of dead and injured, and a hyperlink for more information. She clicked on a link for a bombing in Urbana, Illinois. She remembered its having been reported as a terrorist bombing in a park months ago. Six dead. A dozen injured. A dedicated page popped up with the names and photos of victims, grisly high-res photos of the scene. She scrolled down to see vast amounts of information, and another bustling comments section.

Looking at all the death and suffering that had occurred, McKinney couldn't help but feel she was being petty in having suspicions. But then, they'd made a special effort to get her to view this, hadn't they? Her contribution to the effort was apparently going to be as cannon fodder.

She pushed away from the desk.

McKinney stared at the ceiling in the alarm clock's blue LED light. The cold glow cast fantastical shadows on the acoustic tile above her. She heard the whoosh of air flowing through the HVAC system and the occasional mysterious sounds of far-off activity—heavy trucks, echoed shouting, and clanging metal. She tried to imagine what was going on elsewhere in this secret place. A place that didn't officially exist and where no one she knew could find her. Isolation protocol.

It was 1:47 in the morning according to the blue digits on the nightstand. The sheets and blankets were crisp and smelled new. The mattress firm. She felt truly clean for the first time in months. No dust or humidity down here, and the bathroom was new. The hot water came down in torrents. Properly focused, it could probably quell a riot. Everything in the room had the cool precision of Scandinavia.

She sat up in bed. This whole place just felt wrong. She couldn't quite put her finger on what was eating at her. Why she couldn't sleep. Why she hadn't slept since the attack. She grabbed the TV remote and switched on the television. The Weather Channel blinked into existence on the far wall. Soothing music played over a list of international cities and temperatures. After a few moments she changed channels to the first of several cable news networks in rotation.

More beating of war drums. People being warned to report suspicious activity. More details of yesterday's bombing in D.C. Updated fatalities from the Karbala bombing—4,300 dead. She changed channels several more times. Nation-under-siege hysteria was everywhere. Even the commercials were for pepper spray and burglar alarm systems. She stopped on one channel where a congresswoman from Ohio was speaking on the floor. *". . . in a rush to make sweeping changes we'll regret. We've been down this road before, and we're no safer for it. Sixty-five billion dollars over the next four years for a fleet of autonomous drones to defend the homeland. Again, money that could be put toward education, health care, or infrastructure. Drones are not going to stop these bombings. In fact, our drones might be the root cause of these bombings. . . ."*

McKinney cast off the covers and sat on the edge of the bed. The news had moved on to another story, but she hadn't. She turned it off.

Our drones might be the root cause of these bombings.

And sixty-five billion dollars for drones being pushed as an emergency defense. The ultimate automated cash machine—drones could be both the hero and the enemy, and who would ever know? *Sixty-five billion dollars.* And that was probably just the start.

McKinney got up and walked aimlessly around the room, feeling the cool stone on her feet. What reason did she have to believe what they'd told her?

She was a scientist, and science required evidence to sustain a hypothesis. The operative hypothesis being that this was a government-sanctioned top-secret military operation to defend against deadly drone attacks. But where was the proof to sustain that hypothesis? Over the past decade, half a dozen illegal black ops run by rogue elements in the military had been revealed—assassinations, torture. . . . Maybe these people weren't even with the military—maybe they were private operators, looking to influence government policy. Maybe they were agents of a foreign government. What did she really know?

She thought back over the past forty-eight hours. They had flown here in private aircraft, to a private air terminal at Kansas City—bypassing customs and Homeland Security entirely. Smugglers could have done the same. Did she really know she'd been at an army base back in Wiesbaden—or that it was even Germany? It was dark. She saw a couple of men outside in uniform. She saw offices and army insignias, but truthfully, how did she know that wasn't just some airport office somewhere? She hadn't seen any military cargo planes or fighter jets.

The attacks were real enough—they'd been in the news for months—but if these were the people behind them, they could easily have provided all this footage to her. But why would they need to deceive her? Could they be trying to trick her into helping them? The iterations of conjecture were stacking up fast.

What did she really know?

She felt confident she was in Kansas—the highway signs, the cars and businesses on the way in. She was in the United States. There was supposed to be rule of law here.

She padded over to the bathroom and ran some cold water in the sink. She leaned over and splashed her face. Was this just lack of sleep making her paranoid?

Why not be paranoid? She'd been kidnapped—and by people with a serious amount of resources who seemed focused on robotic war using her social insect algorithms. And getting ready to use her as bait for a drone attack—one they might be running as well, for all she knew.

McKinney walked around the room, looking for cameras. Nothing apparent. But then she knew cameras could fit on the head of a pin now. She caught sight of herself in the mirror above the bureau dresser—looking like a prisoner with her short brown hair, in her Cornell T-shirt and sweats, or like some New York branch of the Baader-Meinhof gang. Lean and crazed. The blue light and shadows made her look twice as dramatic. She burst out laughing—almost hysterically—for several moments. If her father and her brothers could see her now, what would they say? Caught up in international espionage. Absolutely laughable.

She grew serious again. McKinney had to know what was going on in this place. Asking questions wasn't enough. It was time to acquire some hard evidence.

She approached the hallway door and pressed her ear against the wood, listening for any movement outside. Everything was quiet. Satisfied, she carefully turned the dead bolt and then the lever handle. She pulled the door open wide enough to look out both ways down the corridor. She heard only the light buzz of overhead lights. No cameras visible, although there were sensors up on the walls, smoke detectors, sprinkler heads, and the like.

The coast seemed clear, so she stepped out into the hall and started moving left, in the direction she'd entered the day before with Foxy. As she passed the other numbered doors, she heard the sound of snoring from somewhere. It faded as she continued, and soon she came to a T-intersection marked by fire doors held open by magnetic retainers. She peered around the corner.

The adjoining corridor was wider, and the sound of metal clanging and occasional shouts was louder to the left, toward the garage. She turned the other direction, where the hallway continued to another T-intersection with no doors in sight. She decided to walk purposefully in the center of the hallway, head held high. Nonchalant.

Once at the corner she headed decisively left and bumped straight into a closed door. It had some sort of electronic sensor lock with a glowing red LED light over its handle. McKinney turned back the other way without skipping a beat and headed down the white hallway lined with blond wood doors. The other end of the corridor also terminated in a closed door, but she didn't see any red LEDs over its door handle. She marched toward it.

On the way she passed another door, behind which she could hear muffled talking. She slowed to listen and heard radio static, then indecipherable radio voices. Then several people talking in a foreign language. McKinney cautiously approached the door and pressed her ear to it.

A man's voice was talking in a guttural language she didn't recognize. Maybe Russian?

The sudden piercing *caw* of a raven close by made her literally jump and turn. There, perched on a fire extinguisher sign jutting out from the wall, was a large black raven, examining her curiously.

"You scared the crap out of me." She approached the bird, while it continued to regard her calmly. McKinney could see the raven wore some sort of fiber-optic headset that was barely visible until she got within a few feet. The bird stepped out onto the edge of the sign and flapped its wings, *caw*ing again.

"No one likes a snitch, Huginn."

The bird *caw*ed back.

A familiar voice spoke nearby. "That's Muninn."

Startled again, McKinney turned to see Odin standing in the corridor, not far behind her.

"Can't sleep?"

She marched up to him. "I heard someone talking in a foreign language behind that door."

"You still don't trust me?"

She pointed. "The more I think about it, the more suspicious I am. Why aren't we on a military base? Why can't anyone show me government credentials or any proof who you are? Why am I locked up here?"

Odin nodded slowly. He appeared to be carefully considering his answer.

Muninn *caw*ed again behind her.

McKinney pointed at the bird. "And what the hell are you doing using animals? How is this ethical?"

"You need sleep, Professor."

"What I need is proof that I'm not helping bad people do bad things."

He pointed to the raven. "Huginn and Muninn fly outside every day and always return of their own free will. If they regarded you as a friend, they wouldn't have sounded the alarm."

"You're using them."

Odin extended his arm and Muninn flew over to perch upon it, then climbed onto his shoulder. "That's a cynical view of symbiosis."

"Training ravens to help fight your wars is hardly symbiosis."

"I sometimes wonder who's training who. You know what they say about field research: 'Never study an animal smarter than yourself.'" He approached the door McKinney had been listening at and pounded heavily on the wood.

The radio chatter beyond stopped, and they heard heavy footsteps approach the door. It pulled open a crack, and a wrinkled, gray-haired man with a ponytail and liver spots answered. A cigarette was tucked in the corner of his mouth, smoke curling around him. He spoke in a slight Russian accent. "What the hell are you pounding on door for? You scared the hell out of me." The man's eyes darted from Odin to McKinney, and his expression turned to a slight grin. He pulled the cigarette out of his mouth and opened the door further. "Well, good evening, dear lady. . . ." He extended his hand, but Odin interrupted him.

"Knock it off, Rocky. Tell the good professor here why you speak Russian."

The man scowled and opened the door all the way. "Because I'm Russian, you asshole. Why?" Behind him McKinney could see an electronics lab littered with circuit boards and drone aircraft components.

"Where are you from?"

"What's this all about?"

"It's a simple question."

The man huffed. "Is FBI doing this nonsense again?"

"Answer the question."

"My brother and I defected 1989. My clearances are in order, and anyone who says otherwise can kiss my Ukrainian ass." He started poking Odin in the chest. "And that includes you. You think you intimidate me? I'll take that bird of yours and shove it straight up your JSOC ass. I was held by KGB for a year in Smolensk. There's not a man in the world who can—"

Odin held up his hands. "Rocky! Okay, man. I just wanted to put something to rest. It's cool. We'll get out of your hair." Odin gestured to McKinney and started heading back down the hall.

. Rocky leaned out into the hall. "You haven't introduced me to your lovely young friend, Odin."

"Need-to-know, Rocky."

"Ah . . . fuck you and your secrets. I have better secrets." He went back into his lab and slammed the door.

McKinney sighed as she walked alongside Odin.

"If it will put your mind at ease, Professor, wander around the facility. I can't open every door for you, but you can talk to whomever you find. Pump them for information if it helps you sleep."

She nodded to herself. "I'll do that."

Odin turned down a side corridor. "Don't stay up all night. We're going to need to brief you on the baiting operation tomorrow. At no point will you be in actual danger."

"Why am I not convinced of that?"

"Tomorrow." Then he was gone.

For several minutes afterward McKinney walked the halls, but since most of the doors were locked she found herself heading toward the garage and the sound of metalwork under way. At first she just peered through the small wire-mesh windows in the doors, but then she walked through the double doors and out into the garage. Half a dozen workers were busy modifying vehicles to either side, with flashes of welding equipment and pounding of mallets as they made adjustments. Foxy stood talking to Smokey over a clipboard, both of them with submachine guns slung across their chests.

Foxy was flipping through pages on the clipboard. "Tell 'em they have four days to get their mission loads palletized and over to SOAR so they can calculate centers of gravity. Weapons go 'air only'—no ordnance overland."

Smokey nudged his head toward McKinney, and Foxy turned with some surprise to see her.

"Looking for something, Professor?"

"Can't sleep. Odin said I could look around. You can check with him."

"All right." Foxy smiled, and then held a hand to his right ear, speaking softly to the air while Smokey watched her. She could see a small wire corkscrewing down from Foxy's ear into his collar. After a moment he looked up and shrugged. "Suit yourself, Professor. Let me know if I can help with anything."

She nodded absently, but she was already looking around the motor pool. A couple of the trucks that had been here when she arrived were gone. She couldn't remember which ones. Before she reached halfway in the line of vehicles, she stopped to watch another military tech in his twenties digging through a bundle of wire he'd pulled from the side panel of a large four-wheel-drive truck. He was a clean-cut kid referring to a wiring diagram and using a voltmeter to test connections.

He noticed her watching him.

"Quite a project you've got there."

"It's the job, ma'am." The kid had a southern accent that she couldn't quite place. Texas? Georgia?

McKinney approached the ten-ton truck, running her hand along its gleaming fender. His eyes darted toward her furtively.

It was actually an impressive truck. Brand-new and with a broad chrome grille and a crew cab that could probably accommodate four or more people. It was branded with the shield logo of Ancile Services and looked ruggedized for overland seismic work, with the door handle at about eye height. However, most of the cargo area was taken up with what looked like a multiton electrical generator with twin oversized exhaust pipes. The side panels of the generator were open, exposing circuit boards, switch boxes, and bundles of wires that the tech was examining.

She nodded toward the bundles of wires. "How'd you learn to do all this?"

He glanced up. "The training, ma'am." He grunted as he reached deep into the equipment panel.

"What are you guys doing out here, anyway?"

He paused. "Can't discuss that, ma'am."

She nodded slowly. "All right. . . ." She ran her finger along the truck again and started wandering back along the garage, examining the vehicles on the far side.

McKinney wandered past a large four-wheel-drive U.S. Forest Service fire control truck. It had an extended four-person passenger cab and equipment panels along the length of its enclosed cargo bay—all teal green. Whatever modifications were being done to it were either finished or not yet started. Her eye strayed past it to the workbench just beyond—where a key fob hung on a peg from a metal carabiner.

She glanced back toward Foxy and Smokey, who were still engrossed over lists on the clipboard, then over at the kid working on the nearby truck. He was focused on wiring. McKinney purposefully walked over to the workbench and slipped the key chain from its peg. It bore a plastic tag marked International 7400 DT530 in bold black letters. She turned to see the International logo on the nearby truck's large chrome grille.

She took a deep breath. Was she really considering this? Was it lack of sleep?

But then again, if these people were who they said they were, this would only be an inconvenience. If they weren't, then she might be saving lives—her own among them.

McKinney climbed the steel step near the cab and opened the driver's door. With one last furtive look around she got in and flexed her fingers over the steering wheel. After gathering her courage, she reached out and pulled the cab door closed. Another swift motion, and she stabbed the power door-lock button.

She put the key fob into the ignition and cranked the engine until it came to life with a rattling diesel roar. A glance in the tall rearview mirrors showed the young tech dropping his wiring diagram and running toward her truck.

McKinney released the parking brake, then depressed the clutch and smoothly threw the shifter into first. She revved the engine and popped the clutch, launching the massive truck forward. The young tech was almost up to the cab, but stepped back and appeared to be shouting for help now.

It all seemed surreal in the haze of her exhaustion, but she really seemed to be doing this. She was mounting an escape.

McKinney was already slamming the truck into second gear. Even under the circumstances, she had to admire the quality of the equipment. It was nothing like the ancient five-ton Mercedes trucks she'd driven on rough mountain roads in remote stretches of Africa or the jungles of the Amazon. This thing was brand-new.

She glanced out the passenger rearview mirror and could see Foxy and Smokey running forward, submachine guns ready in their hands. The words tumbled out of her mouth unbidden. "Please don't shoot." She had to be too valuable to them for that. She had to be.

McKinney brought the truck surging toward the workbench and the corrugated steel perimeter wall that enclosed this building-in-a-cave. She remembered that the empty buffer zone was patrolled by Expert Five's automated fish. Then it was a straight shot to the second perimeter wall— and to freedom.

She plowed the truck through the sheet metal wall with a thunderous crash that echoed in the cavernous space, with pieces of metal hardware clanging away. In the confines of the mine the noise was deafening.

But the massive Fire Service truck plowed through the wall like paper. The green paint of the hood was scarred and scratched, but otherwise she was already hurtling off into the darkness of the buffer zone.

The engine roared as she put the truck into third gear and kicked on the headlights—then the overhead lights and sirens. They wailed away like a banshee in the confines of the mine, the lights exposing the exterior perimeter wall ahead as she weaved past a huge stone pillar.

Dozens of flying sharks swam slowly toward her, but she plowed right through them before they could get out of the way. Some went under the tires and others got stuck in her grille and rearview mirror brackets. The truck was still accelerating. Thirty-five miles an hour now.

A glance at her side-view mirror festooned with shark balloons and she could see that she'd sheared away a long section of the prefab wall behind her. Men were rushing around the garage area. She turned forward again. "C'mon! Move!"

She smashed the truck through the second perimeter wall at forty-five miles an hour, wincing as the second thunderous clatter of steel panels and brackets blasted aside. McKinney then spun the wheel to the right, to bring the truck back in the direction she remembered as the entrance. The high center of gravity of the off-road truck made it lean into the turn, the tires screeching on the slick stone floor. She eased off and slalomed a bit to regain control.

McKinney slammed the shifter into fourth and started picking up speed. The twenty-foot-wide pillars of stone raced past on either side. The truck roared through the darkness, while McKinney searched for signs of civilization.

But headlights soon appeared in her rearview mirror.

"Shit." That hadn't taken long. Something smaller. Faster.

Looking forward again, she saw lights ahead—the inhabited areas of SubTropolis. And that meant marked roads. She pressed the pedal down and kept accelerating.

The headlights behind her had almost caught up by the time she merged onto a marked road with a friendly Exit sign. She eased up on the gas, realizing only now that the air brakes hadn't had time to charge completely. The truck fishtailed and shuddered as she tried to slow it down heading into a curving turn, scraping against one of the massive pillars in a shower of sparks.

"Get it together, Linda. . . ." But now she had the truck racing down an established roadway; someone up ahead was pulling over to let her fire truck past. She leaned on the horn as well, roaring past.

McKinney glanced at her speedometer and realized she was going sixty in a twenty-five-mile-an-hour zone. But a glance at her rearview mirror again made her stomp the accelerator down. It looked like one of the Bureau of Land Management Forest Ranger pickups was a hundred feet off her tail. It also had its sirens and rack lights on, the headlights alternating on and off.

McKinney roared toward a subterranean intersection with a stop sign. She started to ride the brakes and downshift. A glance in the rearview again. She shook her head. It wasn't right to kill someone to save herself. She downshifted further and continued to slow, hoping her sirens would warn people as she approached.

McKinney slow-stopped her way through the intersection, and was already accelerating on the far side when she saw the BLM Ranger pickup pull alongside her. Smokey leaned out the window, shouting at her. She could see an automatic pistol in his inside hand, still concealed within the vehicle. McKinney cranked the wheel to the left, veering into them.

The forest ranger vehicle slammed on its brakes and just narrowly avoided being smashed against the stone tunnel wall.

McKinney turned forward as she emerged from the tunnel mouth into a cold Kansas night. She let out a howl of joy and tried to orient herself.

She recognized some of the area from when they came in. There was a truck stop across the wide road on the far side of railroad tracks. A strip of brown grass patched with dirty snow divided the poorly maintained concrete highway.

There were trucks and cars out here now, but she still drove aggressively, fire truck sirens blaring. She crossed the highway, dodging in front of an approaching semitruck and roaring across the railroad crossing.

A glance in her rearview mirror showed the Ranger following close behind. To any normal person this would look like two emergency vehicles racing to a call. She had no idea where to go—only that she had to find a large crowd of people. Lots of witnesses—or police.

McKinney followed a surface road and was surprised to see, of all things, a gambling casino close at hand. She dimly recalled passing it on the way in from the airstrip.

It loomed there along the banks of the Missouri River—the Ameristar, an island of stucco and concrete in a sea of parking lots. She knew one thing about casinos: They had loads of armed security. Beyond it McKinney could see the sparse skyline of what must be downtown Kansas City. *Hallelujah.* Civilization.

She accelerated toward the casino entrance and hung a right at an absurd, cartoonishly large replica of a locomotive, glittering with lights and a marquee. *Nickel Slots! $3.99 Prime Rib.*

After years abroad in the Third World, she just had to laugh at the absurdity of this situation. Lack of sleep had her half out of her mind.

The forest ranger vehicle came up on her again, but she kept yawing from side to side on the main casino road to prevent them from pulling alongside. Fortunately, they weren't trying to shoot her tires out. Perhaps they were more concerned about getting the truck back in drivable condition. Other cars leaving and entering the casino pulled over to let the erratic emergency vehicles pass.

They were now approaching the stucco portico of the casino's main entrance, flanked by glittering neon towers. McKinney roared under its roof and toward the valet station, where cars and a few taxis were parked or idling.

A glance in her rearview showed the forest ranger vehicle slowing and hanging a U-turn. She felt relief flood over her. She'd done it. She'd escaped. Turning forward she realized just how fast she was still going and pounded on the brake. The fire service truck shuddered, screeching as it collided with a concrete crash pylon just short of the nearest waiting taxi. She lurched forward in her seat, but no air bags deployed.

Dozens of people ran toward the truck. All faces turned to her. Security guards and parking valets. She slumped back in her seat, suddenly overwhelmed by intense weariness. She suspected it was the beginning of her body's parasympathetic backlash to the adrenaline surge.

Not yet. This isn't finished. Not yet.

She killed the engine, the sirens, and all the lights, then undid her seat belt and climbed down from the cab. Half a dozen men had reached her—a guy in a suit, a couple of old men, a security guard, uniformed parking valets.

"You all right, honey?" A balding middle-aged security guard with a big belly was holding her arm.

She wriggled free. "I'm fine. Call the FBI! Kidnappers are pursuing me. They're in that federal ranger's truck behind me!"

The guard frowned at her as scores more people gathered around them. One of the other people in the crowd pointed back toward the entrance. "It's driving away."

"Where?" The guard grabbed her arm again and moved to look down the casino drive. "You were running away from federal rangers?"

McKinney got in his face. "If they were real rangers, why are they fleeing a crash scene? Why are they trying to get away?"

He studied her face, and the gathering crowd seemed to be mulling it over. McKinney looked up to realize that she'd really wrecked the truck. The front wheels were six inches off the ground, the bumper and front grille staved in by the pylon, which had torn out of the ground at a forty-five degree angle. Even the sidewalk was buckled.

More armed security guards had arrived, and they were starting to push the crowd of onlookers away. The oldest and apparently most senior of the security guards came up. He was completely bald and looked like an ex-soldier himself, now in his sixties. "What the hell. Ya lose control of her, honey?"

Before the first security guard could speak, McKinney answered, "Call the FBI! I was escaping from kidnappers."

He frowned and pointed at the U.S. Forest Service truck. "Where the hell did you get a Forest Service truck?"

She was surrounded by a dozen armed security guards in brown shirts, slacks, badges, belts, and nightsticks now. What might normally feel alarming felt greatly reassuring. Her heart rate was returning to normal, but she suddenly felt exhausted.

The senior security guard was staring at her, still surprised.

She spelled it out for him. "Call. The. F. B. I.!"

He patted her on the arm. "Let's start out with the police, honey."

CHAPTER 15

Closed Loop

Twenty-four hours and a bit of sleep later McKinney sat in a holding room at the FBI Kansas City field office. Half the far wall was a mirror. The other walls were white-painted cinder blocks with initials and profanity here and there etched into the surface. She tried to imagine who could conceive of—let alone succeed—in sneaking razor blades into an FBI interrogation room. This was not a world she was familiar with.

The single table was bolted to the floor, along with several sturdy resin chairs, also bolted in place. Smooth edges. Nothing to hang oneself or cut oneself with. They'd taken her cheap watch when they processed her. She never wore jewelry in the field, but the FBI agents who booked her had looked at her with suspicion when they found she had no jewelry on. *What kind of woman has no jewelry?* Drug addicts, presumably.

After what seemed like an eternity, the single door to the interview room finally opened and a pair of clean-cut men in suits entered. They weren't smiling. One held a folder, and they both stood across the table from her, while the door slammed decisively behind them on its own, drowning out the brief interlude of footsteps and hallway chatter.

"Ms."—he looked at the folder—"McKinney, I'm Special Agent Tierney, this is Special Agent Harrison."

She nodded to them. "Gentlemen."

"How is it you're here?"

"In my written statement I—"

"The State Department lists you as 'missing, presumed dead,' somewhere in Africa. And yet you show up here, claiming to have information about the terror bombings in the U.S."

"I do have information related to the bombings."

"Related to the bombings? How's that different?"

"The bombings aren't what they appear."

"You do know that providing false statements to federal officers is a felony?"

"Why on earth would I lie about this?"

"Well, it's just that among other things, you have a criminal record."

McKinney was surprised. "I'd hardly call my record criminal."

"Marijuana possession, disorderly conduct."

"I can't believe we're discussing this. I was arrested with a thousand other people at a demonstration. And marijuana? Hello, I went to college."

"So you don't think drug laws apply to you?"

"That's not—look, can we get to the very critical thing I'm trying to tell you?"

He was reading through the file. "You disappeared under suspicious circumstances with a substantial life insurance policy." He looked up. "And you have considerable student loan debt."

"I can't believe this."

"You stole and wrecked a U.S. Forest Service truck—"

"It's not a Forest Service truck, and I had to use it to escape."

"Because you claim you were kidnapped"—reading again—"'possibly by a top-secret military operation . . . or a terrorist cell. One or the other.'" He looked up. "Is that right?"

The other agent just snorted.

"Look, I'm a published entomology professor with Cornell University. You can go to the university's website, search for me, and you will find a photo of me and everything. I'm not some kook. I'm a world-class expert on ants—myrmecology. I've given you my social security number, my—"

"Yeah. We confirmed your identity through fingerprints. That's not the problem. I'm just confused . . . how did you get back into the United States?" He flipped through the papers in the folder. "You departed Newark for Johannesburg, en route to Tanzania, two and a half months ago, and customs records show you haven't returned. American Airlines shows you booked for a return flight later this month."

"I explain that in my statement."

"Indulge me. I'd like to make sure your story is consistent. How'd this go down again?"

She sighed in frustration. "I was kidnapped and brought back to the U.S. against my will."

They both leaned against the wall. "You were kidnapped—in Africa—and brought to Kansas City? Was this before or after the bombing?"

"I know it sounds crazy, but—"

"Why would the government 'kidnap' you? And if they did, why didn't they update your passport status? And how did you get hold of a Forest Service truck?"

"It's not a Forest Service truck. I was kidnapped by some sort of well-funded, secret military operation. They had a motor pool filled with vehicles from false front companies and different government agencies." She pointed at the Ancile Services polo shirt she still wore. "This shirt, for example. Ancile Services is supposed to be an oil exploration company, but it's a front for this secret operation."

Agent Tierney nodded slowly. "I see."

Harrison let a slight smile escape. "Presumably, they had a pressing ant problem."

She stared at them. "They claimed my weaver ant software model was being used to power autonomous combat drones."

"Ah. That's right. You do mention that the terror bombings are unmanned drone attacks."

"I have no idea whether that's true or not, but that's what they told me. For all I know these people are the ones behind the attacks."

"You mean the terror bombings? I thought you said these were government people who kidnapped you?"

"Possibly. I don't know. I never saw any proof that they were government people, and even if they were military, it might still be an illegal military operation. It wouldn't be the first time the U.S. military was involved in something illegal."

Tierney glared at her, then started flipping through the folder. "Let's talk about your antiwar activity. . . ."

"Oh, for godsakes! This has nothing to do with—"

"Let's just go through it. Who do you think was to blame for 9/11, Professor McKinney? Do you think the U.S. government was behind 9/11?"

"I can't believe you're asking me that."

"Because they obviously were?"

"No!"

Tierney spread his hands. "Can you give us any details about this supposed top-secret government operation, then? Where are they located?"

"I said I'm not certain it's a government operation."

"Okay, fine—this nefarious plot, then. Can you tell us where their secret lair is?"

"Yes, I know where they are."

"Then why didn't you put that in your statement? We could already have checked it out."

McKinney grimaced. "Because it might actually be a government operation. They said they were trying to prevent these drone attacks." She cast an uncertain look at them. "Do you gentlemen have . . . I guess . . . top-secret clearances?"

They groaned and shook their heads. Tierney leaned onto the table in front of her. "Professor. We get the-government's-out-to-get-me and I'll-tell-secrets-if-you-let-me-go crap on a daily basis. Look at it from our point of view. In fact, you're a scientist; look at it from a scientific point of view. Which do you think is more likely: a) that you were kidnapped in Africa by the CIA—"

"I never said it was the CIA."

"Or whoever, then, and brought here to work on a secret drone project—or b) you got in legal trouble in Africa, possibly narcotics-related, faked your death, and snuck back into the U.S., say, through Mexico, high on drugs, and stole a truck?"

She took a deep breath and tried to control her temper. In truth, she had to admit that Occam's razor would favor his hypothesis.

"Do you still take drugs, Professor?"

"No! I was a sophomore in college. Give me a drug test if you don't believe me."

"Oh, we will. You do realize you're in serious legal trouble?"

"I'm starting to realize that, yes. I'd like to call a lawyer."

"Well, you waived your right to have an attorney present during questioning."

"No, I didn't—when did I do that?"

"When you were brought in, you kept insisting that you immediately speak with an agent, and you didn't listen to what was being said to you while you were being processed." He pointed to her signature on one of the documents in the folder.

McKinney realized what a serious turn things had just taken.

Tierney continued, reading from the folder now, "You crashed a stolen federal vehicle, made false statements to federal officers—"

"I'm telling you the truth. I can prove it."

"So prove it, then."

There was a knock on the door, and then it opened slightly. Agent Harrison hurried over to it, putting his nose in the open space, conversing with someone. He turned, and the door opened, revealing a couple of men in nicer suits, putting their credentials away.

Harrison motioned for Agent Tierney to follow him. "Matt. C'mon. The SAIC says Homeland Security's got this."

Tierney looked back and suddenly straightened up. "Sir. How can we help you?"

"By leaving this room." The senior FBI agent held the door open for them while the Homeland Security agent stepped inside. He had a kinder face—a fatherly look, with a full head of gray, neatly groomed hair.

"Oh. Of course." Tierney glanced back at McKinney and headed for the door.

The Homeland Security agent grabbed the folder from him. "Speak no more of this with anyone. Your SAIC will debrief you."

"Yes, sir."

The agents headed out along with the local agent in charge, and the door closed behind them, leaving McKinney alone with the recent arrival.

He nodded and sat down across from her. "How you holding up, Linda?"

She studied him warily. "Not well. Who are you?"

"Agent Blake, Homeland Security." He produced his credentials again, handing them to her so she could inspect them closely. The gold shield and ID were enclosed in a quality black leather sleeve. "I flew here from Chicago once your report was flagged in the system."

After examining his credentials she handed them back. "From Chicago? Because of me?"

He nodded.

She dropped her head onto her hands. "Oh, thank God." She lifted her head up again. "Please tell me you believe me."

"Something in your written statement intrigues me—your theory about the terrorist bombings. You mention that they're actually drone strikes. Who told you this?"

"That's what the man commanding the operation told me. He goes by a—a call sign. 'Odin.'"

"Odin." It was unclear whether it was a declaration or a question.

"I don't know whether it's true or not." She studied his expression. "Is it?"

He took out a black leather-bound pad, from which he drew an expensive-looking silver pen. "I have no idea, but if there's a special military unit here in Kansas City, I should know about it. And I don't."

"If they're a legitimate defense operation, that's one thing, but . . . I'm a scientist. I needed corroboration before I—"

He patted her hand. "You did the right thing. We need to get this sorted out. You're lucky you got away—if what you're saying is true, they're very dangerous people. Can you tell me where their operation is headquartered?"

She sighed in relief and nodded vigorously. "Yes. They're in a place called SubTropolis—on the north bank of the Missouri River."

He nodded. "I know it. Homeland Security and the FBI use it for archival data storage."

"Then they might be legitimate?"

He jotted notes. "Let's stick with what we know."

"They said they chose it so that drone missiles couldn't hit them."

"Clever."

"You're with the government—can you call someone and find out if this is legitimate?"

"The federal government is a complex organism, Professor. Sometimes pieces of it become . . . cancerous. Dangerous. As a scientist, I'm sure you understand."

McKinney didn't know what to feel.

He squeezed her hand again. "I'm sure this has all been very stressful, but what's important is that you're safe now."

McKinney nodded. "What happens next?"

"I need to make arrangements. In the meantime, let's get you to a safe house. Someplace where no one with access to government systems can find out where you are."

She gave him a sideways look.

He smiled reassuringly. "I was thinking a downtown hotel under an assumed name. Room service, cable TV. I'll assign agents to guard you."

"You believe my story."

"Let's just—"

"Then what they told me about the drone attacks must be true. It's why you came down here so fast, isn't it?"

He stared at her, unreadable.

"I'd like to phone my father."

"I don't mean to alarm you, but if this is a rogue government agency we're dealing with, your life is in danger. And we'll need to get your family under protection as well. We need to get you into hiding, and I need to get you out of here as quietly as possible."

McKinney fidgeted in the back of an unmarked government sedan, Agent Blake at the wheel. The car moved through late-night traffic near downtown

Kansas City, Christmas decorations on the light poles. Blake had asked her to assume the posture of a suspect being transferred to Homeland Security custody, and accordingly they out-processed her and put her in a vehicle with a metal grille partition that separated her from the driver. Even worse, they'd handcuffed her like they would any other prisoner. She even had her hands chained to her waist, wearing a tan prisoner jumpsuit and booties. With each passing day her life just kept getting stranger.

"Now that we're away from the FBI office, can you please take these chains off me, Agent Blake?"

He shook his head. "We need to get well clear and make sure we're not being tailed first."

McKinney slumped and tried as best she could to get comfortable on the hard plastic seat. As they drove through downtown, she leaned her head against the window, watching the shop and office façades passing by. Normal life. There wasn't much foot traffic. It looked like the type of downtown that cleared out after dark—after the office workers left.

McKinney wondered if the Feds would raid the secret base. Was it still there? Perhaps Odin's whole team had picked up or destroyed the evidence and fled. A sudden fear gripped her that she'd been wrong or that the Feds would get involved in a shoot-out with the military team because of her—a miscommunication or misunderstanding that might wind up subverting America's defenses. Guilt nagged at her as she recalled the dead, burned bodies in those bombing photos. The face of one dead little girl in particular bothered her.

But what other choice had there been? She was a scientist. You don't just take people's word for things—you find out. She needed to corroborate their story, and they were unreasonable to expect that she'd do what they asked without official sanction that the operation was legitimate and legal. If the Feds raided the place and it turned out to be an illegal operation—or worse yet, that they were behind the drone attacks—or bombings, or whatever they were—then she would actually have helped stop a serious crime. Wouldn't she?

McKinney didn't feel any better. She realized that this was probably what intelligence work was like: no idea what the big picture was, and no clear best course.

She'd been lost in her own thoughts for a while when she suddenly noticed they were moving through a large, empty parking lot. Cones of bright light from towering lamp poles stabbed down at regular intervals. She could see passenger jets taking off in the distance. A car rental lot was visible several hundred yards away, as were illuminated billboards that only occur in the nether regions around airports—shuttle bus and mileage program ads, breakfast buffets. The usual corporate chain hotel logos glowed on towers not far off. Apparently Blake was bringing her to a hotel near the airport. Not a bad idea to remain anonymous.

The sedan slowed in the middle of the parking lot. Blake circled, looking warily in all directions.

McKinney leaned forward. "What are we doing?"

Blake ignored her.

"Agent Blake, what's going on?"

Without answering Blake stopped the car in the center of the lot, ignoring the parking lines. He got out.

"Hey!" McKinney leaned over to watch him walk out to the edge of the cone of light in his full-length greatcoat, scanning the horizon. "Hey, what's going on?" Her shouts were magnified in the plastic confines of the sedan's backseat. She tugged against the chain binding her handcuffed wrists to her waist. "Agent Blake!"

He continued to act as if she didn't exist.

McKinney glanced around. There were no other cars within two hundred yards of them. It was a vast, empty place beneath floodlights. The winter cold was already creeping into the car—her breath stabbing out vapor. She could hear the engine parts clicking as they cooled.

Agent Blake was now acting as if she were a nonperson, and a terrible realization began to sink in: that she had fallen in with dangerous people. That much was increasingly clear.

She lay back against the seat and tried to remember what normal life was like. Instead all she could remember was how instantaneous the blast wave had been on those attack videos—bodies disintegrated by industrial weaponry, as though they were made of paper.

Would anyone ever discover what happened to her, or would she just become another one of the disappeared in the world? The researcher who disappeared somewhere in Africa. That's Africa for you, people would say. She thought again of her father.

Just then something dark alighted on the trunk of the car.

McKinney recoiled in alarm but then turned to see a large raven marching around the trunk lid just beyond the rear window glass. It wore a small headset and what she now knew was a tiny video camera. Huginn or Muninn—she could never tell them apart. She didn't know whether she was happy to see him or frightened.

Blake was still scanning the horizon and hadn't noticed the bird. It flew off again unseen.

A moment later a vehicle's headlights approached and entered on the far side of the vast lot. It was an unmarked blue utility van.

Blake opened his coat, holding his hands up where they could be seen. Before long the van coasted to a stop behind Blake's car. She recognized a grim-faced Odin behind the wheel with his long black beard. He ignored her, instead scanning the area, keeping a wary eye on Blake.

Satisfied, he got out—the dome light not turning on—and he cautiously approached Blake's car. Odin wore some sort of insulated orange jumpsuit with a reflective vest and ID badge. It looked like an airport technician's outfit.

Blake moved to intercept him.

McKinney watched the men approach one another, keeping their hands visible. They converged next to the car, close enough for her to hear them through the glass.

Blake spoke first. "David Shaw. I'd ask what rock you crawled out from under, but the professor was kind enough to tell us."

Odin glanced at McKinney.

She couldn't help but feel ashamed.

Odin turned forward again. "I'm surprised she's still alive."

"Would you have shown yourself if she wasn't?"

"No."

Blake spread his hands. There you go.

"Homeland Security—is that your idea of a joke?"

"One must maintain a sense of humor in these trying times."

"Why'd they send you, Ritter?"

"To talk some sense into you."

"Or because they hoped I'd kill you."

Blake seemed uncertain for a moment.

"But I'm long finished doing their dirty work."

Blake relaxed a bit and smiled genially. "NorthCom isn't your territory. You're supposed to be over there keeping the savages busy."

"Maybe the savages back here need watching too."

"The old man's bitten off more than he can chew this time, David. This isn't Pakistan. Maybe you've been overseas so long you forget that it's a team sport here. And you're not on the team."

"I didn't come to talk. I came for the girl." He headed toward McKinney's sedan.

"Does she know you're using her?"

Odin turned. "Yeah. You might have noticed she tried to escape."

"You can't stop this, David. It's going to happen no matter what. They want it. Stop looking."

"You of all people know that isn't going to happen."

"Ah, never quit the hunt. Do you want to end up like Mouse? I hear they're still finding pieces of him over there."

Odin paused, but then regained his calm and reached the car door.

"What if they let you come home, David? Would you be willing to walk away?"

Odin stopped. He met McKinney's gaze for several moments. "Walk away." He nodded silently to himself. "And the professor here?"

"She's already dead, and you know it."

"Good-bye, Ritter."

"Everyone wants this, David. Everyone. You can't fight it."

Odin turned to appraise Ritter for a few moments. "See, that's the difference between you and me. I don't just fight the battles I know I can win." Odin opened the car's rear door.

McKinney glared at Blake—or Ritter, or whatever his name was. He seemed to have transformed into a completely different person. "How did he—"

"Not now." Odin pulled her up out of the rear seat by her waist chain and started moving her over to the blue van.

Blake called to them. "You can't prevent something whose time has come."

Odin opened the side door of the van. McKinney could see that it was an empty metal shell—no padding.

"I'm sorry. I had to know."

"Now you know."

He picked her up with powerful arms and tossed her into the cargo hold.

"Odin, I—"

He slammed the door, leaving her in the semidarkness, craning her neck to see the safety cage between her and the driver's compartment. Odin got in and started the van.

McKinney realized how relieved she was to see him.

He adjusted the rearview mirror to meet her gaze. "Happy now, Professor? The monsters of the deep know you by name."

She knelt and looked up at him. "I didn't have a choice. You gave me no good reason to trust you."

"Smart people are always difficult. Always looking for answers. And the answers always lead to more questions." He accelerated the van toward the parking lot exit, and she slid into the rear doors.

She crawled forward again. "Who was that man?"

"I rest my case."

"He said he was with Homeland Security."

"There are people who work for the people who run the world. He's one of them. I wouldn't be surprised if they send the Black Chinook for me now."

"You kidnapped me. You can't seriously have expected me to trust you."

"Why the hell did you trust them?"

"The FBI? Homeland Security?"

"You don't seem the brand-conscious type, Professor."

"Don't be glib. I needed independent verification that this was real."

"Oh, it's real, all right. Think of it as an iceberg; you only see what's on the surface. There are people beneath; people who built the systems that run everything."

"In the government?"

"What difference does it make whether they're in the government? They're larger than government. They're power. The world is a big system now. I don't think anyone knows who's in charge. But you can run afoul of various interests. That's for damn sure. And you just did."

She pondered that—then looked up at him again. "Shaw."

He met her eyes in the mirror.

"That's your real name: David Shaw."

He clenched his jaw for a few moments. "That was his idea of a warning—letting me know that they know who I am. They think it gives them power over me."

"But your family? Your—"

"It won't lead them to anything. That's why the colonel chose me."

They locked eyes in the mirror.

"'Shaw' was the name of the road they found me on. It's a common practice with foundlings at orphanages." He looked back to the road. "All names were made up at some point. I just know when and where mine was."

McKinney slumped against the sliding door as the van sped along a service road.

"Well, you poured some blood in the water tonight. Let's see what shows up."

That's when McKinney noticed they were actually moving along the airport tarmac, approaching a large propeller-driven aircraft. McKinney recognized it as a C-130 cargo plane. She'd seen them used on various research projects in remote locales, although she'd never been aboard one. There were vehicles and work lights around it. Silhouettes of people rushing around.

In a few moments the van rolled to a stop. Odin got out, but Smokey was already opening the sliding door. He stood in the doorway a moment. "Look who decided to join us."

She sighed resignedly as he pulled her up out of the van and onto her feet. They were parked next to the C-130's lowered rear cargo ramp. The plane itself was unmarked and painted drab brown. Tail numbers were the only markings. Other team members were busy loading gear, while Hoov scanned the skies with some sort of boxy optical device on a tripod.

But they all stopped for a moment at the sight of McKinney and broke into mock applause.

She looked guiltily to Odin. Hoov, Ripper, Mooch, and several more people she hadn't seen before were all dressed in civilian clothes with no guns in sight. At a hand signal from Odin, they immediately resumed loading cases and checking equipment.

Odin produced a key and started unlocking her chains and handcuffs. "You want to escape, Professor?" He tossed the handcuffs and chains into the van and closed the sliding door. He then gestured to the vast expanse of tarmac around them. "There! You're free to go. Best of luck to you." He stomped up the cargo ramp.

Foxy stood alongside McKinney as she watched Odin go. He whistled. "Impressive. You got under his skin."

She looked to Foxy. "I hope you don't take what I did personally."

Foxy held up a clipboard. "Well, let's see. Our electronic warfare truck's been impounded by the Feds, we had to destroy servers and prototypes we couldn't move, we lost our JOC, and we've had to dangerously accelerate the entire timeline. Basically you fucked everything up." Foxy looked up from the clipboard. "But on a personal note: That was seriously metal."

CHAPTER 16

Damage Control

"We have a problem, Henry."

Henry Clarke looked up from his Chateaubriand in surprise. He spoke while chewing. "Good to see you too, Marta." Clarke gestured with his fork to his date. "Emily, meet Marta. Marta, Emily."

The young woman smiled amiably, extending a dainty hand. "Nice to meet you."

Marta just stared at her—cherubic cheeks and straight blond Dutch hair hanging in bangs that ended just above the eyes. "I need to borrow Henry for a moment, my dear."

"Oh . . . Okay, I—"

Clarke nodded, stuffing one more piece of steak into his mouth. "Back in a sec."

Marta led Clarke toward a private room in the back of the busy restaurant. Her eyes swept the place. "I'm shocked to find you in a place like this. An overpriced strip mall."

"What can I say? She chose it."

"Ah, I see. Was it near her school?"

"Ha, ha. You know, it's very uncool to just keep showing up with little or no warning."

Marta brought them into the private room as two suited gentlemen in her security detail closed the doors behind them. The room was empty. "The schedule has changed. There's word of some rogue element loose out there that could corrupt the message. Before that happens, we need to be ready."

"When, ready?"

"Like whenever I say. Tomorrow. The day after. Whenever means whenever. Can your people deliver?"

Clarke sighed deeply. "Christ, I thought you told me 'have patience.' What happened to patience?"

"We don't have time for patience. The situation has changed, Henry. Serious people are on the move. So say good-night to your little friend and get your ass to the office. Be prepared to man a crisis center for the next few days."

Clarke nodded. "Okay. All right, I'll gather the troops." He paused as something occurred to him. "This 'rogue element'—they don't think we're actually behind the . . . 'troubles,' I hope?"

"Even if they did think so, it will shortly be moot. Let the serious people deal with that. Ours is a struggle for messaging supremacy, and we need to win."

"About them thinking we're behind this . . . was that a yes or a no?"

CHAPTER 17

Safari-One-Six

Linda McKinney had never ridden in the cargo bay of a C-130, and now that she had, it wasn't something she looked forward to repeating. The cavernous space reeked of jet fuel and the hydraulic fluid and oil from past vehicular cargo. Then there was the roar of aircraft engines. But at least on that last point, the team used wireless Etymotic headphones to reduce the noise and permit conversation. The headphones were also tapped into the pilot's address system, not that much info had been forthcoming from the flight deck. *"Prepare for takeoff"* had been about it.

After a while McKinney switched the headphones off, enjoying the unearthly silence. Looking around in the red-light semidarkness she could see the team sitting in jump seats to either side of the cargo bay, or moving about, checking on equipment. Foxy and Tin Man were cleaning assault weapons. She could see Foxy's African kora sitting atop a pile of gear—at least he'd managed to salvage that from the abandoned SubTropolis facility.

Farther forward Hoov was clicking away at a laptop. The aircraft's loadmaster was double-checking static lines and conferring with the flight engineer—who was busy moving about on other inscrutable duties. There was also some sort of signals workstation set up against the forward bulkhead, with twin flat screens showing radar and other sensor data. Two airmen in headsets sat there, monitoring and talking on radios.

McKinney sat by herself on one of the uncomfortable DayGlo nylon webbing jump seats. Like everyone else she wore an insulated gray aircrew jumpsuit to help keep back the cold, and cold it was. McKinney occasionally exhaled just to see how much vapor she could create. The cargo hold was pressurized, and she knew they had heaters, so she was unclear why they were keeping the temperature so low.

She'd spent the past hour trying to figure out their cargo. It looked like a gray fumigation tent folded and strapped onto a double-wide pallet that stood near the middle of the hold. Steel cables snaked from it into neatly rolled and bound coils on the floor, and then stretched to another, half-height pallet of solid concrete. This was apparently some sort of deadweight. McKinney guessed it was a parachute linked to a concrete weight, although the precise purpose of it escaped her. There were high-tension cables locking the concrete slab into place, along with some sort of quick-release lever. There were also a couple of pallets of equipment and supplies cocooned in plastic wrap farther forward that obviously weren't meant to be deployed in midair, since they didn't have static lines attached.

They'd been airborne for nearly an hour when McKinney noticed Odin emerge from the narrow door at the front left of the cargo hold with two paper cups of coffee. He approached and extended one to her.

She accepted it, powering on her headphones. "Thanks." Her own voice came back to her in radio timbre. She popped the cup lid to see that he'd added a touch of creamer.

His voice came through on the headphones. "I checked your FBI file to see how you like it."

She cocked an eye at him. "Very funny." She took a sip. It was hot and technically coffee. It would do. "Why the hell is it so cold in here?" She motioned to the exposed ducting and vents that traced along the interior.

"I want everyone ready for an intercept the moment it comes."

"How does freezing our asses off help that?"

He nodded toward the closed cargo door. "If we have to open that door, anyone not in an insulated flight suit is going into hypothermia in seconds. This makes sure everyone's ready."

"Where are we headed, anyway?"

"Need-to-know, Professor."

"Well . . . as the drone bait on your hook, I think I need to know."

"You want to know. That's not the same thing."

"What difference does it make?" She looked around the cargo hold. "Who can I tell?"

"The plane could crash. You could crawl from the wreckage and post on YouTube."

She gave him an exasperated look.

He took a sip of coffee, then grimaced. "Northern Utah. We've set up an interception team at a decommissioned missile base out in the desert. Anything that approaches us out there will be highly suspect. It's fifty miles from nowhere."

She recalled the videos of previous attacks—most of them above urban areas filled with air traffic. It would have been nearly impossible to tell friend from foe in time to intercept anything in a city. "You're really just going to put me out there, like meat on a stick?"

"I never said you had to actually be present."

"That's what being bait is."

"Your data and your likeness, Professor. That's all we need. That's why we scanned your head when you were unconscious on the Otter. We sent the digital model to special effects artists, and they created a simulacrum of you out of ballistics gel. Painted it, prepared the hair, clothes, everything."

"You're joking."

He shook his head. "You'll see it soon enough."

"But the spotter drone in Africa was sniffing for my phone—which got blown up."

"It was sniffing for your IMEI. We cloned that—and your headset Bluetooth ID. Hoov mirrored your laptop, and they'll set it up in a hangar there. We built a whole fake military research camp with generators, computers, the whole shebang, just in case they're watching with satellites."

"When did you do all this?"

"We've had the camp set up for weeks. We just needed the bait."

"Me."

"Or at least a representation of you."

She contemplated this as she sipped coffee. "Then you don't really need me anymore, do you?"

"Don't get carried away. We still have to fight these things, and you may be of some help there. Plus . . ." His voice trailed off.

She raised her eyebrows.

"You're a loose end to some people, Professor. I don't want to let you out of my sight." He gestured to the team in the semidarkness of the cargo hold. "These are the people I trust. I've seen how they behave under the worst possible circumstances. That's something that few people ever get to see in a person."

McKinney looked around the cargo hold at Hoov and Foxy laughing as they ribbed each other about something. She could see Tin Man and Mooch intensely focused on checking equipment.

"You can trust your life to these people. I do every day."

McKinney nodded appreciatively. "In case I haven't said it before: I really do appreciate everything you've done to keep me safe."

He nodded. "Just try to get some rest."

In the cold dawn they disembarked from the rear cargo ramp of the C-130 in the middle of a vast reddish desert with sweeping mesas, stone outcroppings, and barren mountains to the north. The sky was mottled with fiery cirrus clouds. It was beautiful. It had been a long time since she'd been in Utah—a hiking trip in Zion. This place had a similar desolate beauty.

Close by stood another C-130 cargo aircraft, this one painted in commercial livery—red stripes with a big A on the tail. It was parked near a fuel tanker truck on a rough dirt airstrip with the crew milling about doing routine maintenance. A Hughes Model 500 chopper was tied down in the distance. She'd ridden in one of those before on a heliskiing trip in Alaska. This one was painted bright red with an Ancile Services logo.

About a half mile to the east she could see a collection of buildings and sagebrush ringed by tattered-looking chain-link fencing and rusted Restricted signs. There were new antenna towers and satellite dishes there amid old corrugated tin buildings, a massive concrete bunker, and rusting pipelines and conduits. The whole area was peppered with dozens of heavy vehicles.

A new Jeep Rubicon approached them trailing a cloud of dust. Odin nodded at the Jeep's driver, a buff-looking Asian—possibly Thai or Indonesian—as it rolled to a stop in front of them.

"Troll, how we looking down here?"

"We're one hundred percent operational."

"Good." Odin caught a red object tossed at him by Hoov. Odin turned and offered it to McKinney. "Ski mask. Please put this on while you're on the ground, Professor."

She unfolded it. A cheap drugstore ski mask, red with white trim. "What for?"

"I don't want any drones sneaking in here and recognizing you before we're ready."

Troll opened the Jeep's doors. "We're not transmitting yet, Odin."

"Doesn't matter. Better safe than sorry. This has taken a lot of preparation."

McKinney realized he was right and pulled the mask on. The fabric was scratchy. She was ready to rob a liquor store now.

The team piled into the Jeep, with some of them standing on the sideboards as they headed into the nearby camp.

The place was a mixture of decay and modernity. Among the rust-stained, inscrutable concrete blocks sprouting twisted pipes and the buckshot-spattered outbuildings there were also parked heavy vehicles leveled and raised on hydraulic jacks, most with civilian markings. They were spread out in a way that would make it difficult to destroy them with a single bomb.

Scary that she was starting to notice these things—to think this way.

Odin nodded at the passing buildings. "White Sands missile facility. In the fifties they'd launch test missiles from here on a trajectory to Nevada. That's what the old track railings were for. And the heavy bunker."

They were passing teams of people now, most in civilian clothes, but some of them in gray camouflage uniforms and tan boots. They drove past a hangarlike building, inside of which was parked a Humvee with a bank of four missiles in a hydraulic rack launcher, pointing up at a forty-five-degree angle.

"AIM-120s—just in case."

"I thought you were trying to catch this thing."

"Like I said: just in case."

They drove toward the center of the makeshift camp and passed more heavy equipment. There was a large satellite truck with several dishes aimed to the south, a mysterious trailer with a steel mast that rose at least a hundred feet above it, the top clustered with cameras, receivers, microphones, and other objects. A large white radar dish also spun circles on the back of a flatbed truck with a command van close by. There were several military-like cargo trucks with huge off-road tires, piled with equipment and crates, as well as a Unicat passenger van parked to the side. She'd ridden in one like it on a long, grueling trip across West Africa. There were also several official vehicles—or at least they were marked that way. She recognized the two Bureau of Land Management Ranger Police SUVs and a couple of smaller U.S. Forest Service trucks. There was also a large semitruck with a full-sized shipping container on a flatbed trailer—dozens of thick cables leading out of it over to another equally huge generator truck, engines rumbling.

They finally pulled up to an off-road craft services van where cooks were busy serving an institutional breakfast buffet, of all things. There were dozens of people milling around here—both men and women. McKinney counted over forty people, and she knew she missed some.

"My God, this is quite an operation."

Foxy nodded. "Everyone thinks this shit just happens. War *is* logistics. And paperwork."

The Jeep rolled to a stop near the chow wagon. Everyone piled off, headed toward a serving tray. Odin called after them. "Guys!"

They all turned.

"Eat. Shit. And get back to the plane. We're on standby until further notice."

Aye, ayes rippled through the group.

McKinney got out as well, straightening the eye holes on her ski mask.

"Professor."

She turned to see Odin motion for her to follow as he headed into a corrugated metal hangar across the sandy roadway.

She caught up to him. "Hey, I could use something to eat."

"In a second. I want you to see something." He led her out the far side, through a large rolling door to a series of olive drab military tents. Odin led her through the open flaps, where several rather fashionably dressed people were placing computer monitors and chairs, and hanging maps. Natural gas heaters were keeping the tent warm.

An attractive woman with blond hair did a double take at the ski-masked McKinney, but Odin barked, "Ignore her. Keep working."

The woman immediately resumed what could only be described as set dressing.

Odin stopped and McKinney came up alongside him.

Two young men were adding finishing touches to what was a frighteningly real reproduction of herself—complete with hair and eye color. It was a simulacrum of her sitting at a desk, hands on her own laptop keyboard. Her twin wore a green polo shirt and jeans. One of the special effects artists was using an airbrush to touch up her neck, while the other one concealed wires beneath a mat on the ground.

"This is creepy as hell."

The men looked up at her. One of them smiled. "Thanks."

"What are the wires for?"

Odin answered. "Body heat. We know the spotter drones use IR, so your decoy needs to match the thermal signature of a human being. Between that"—he pointed at the iPhone sitting on the desk—"your cloned phone, your malware-infected laptop, and your physical likeness, we should be able to lure this thing in."

One of the artists pointed. "Odin, check this out." He plugged a wire in, and McKinney's twin's fingers clattered on her keyboard.

"Ha!" Odin chuckled. "Nice touch, Ian."

McKinney's mouth was dry just looking at her sacrificial twin. "When does this all start?"

"A few hours from now, I'll have your laptop 'accidentally' log on to a mobile broadband tower overlooking Interstate Seventy, at the top of that hill." Odin looked out at a distant antenna tower surrounded by fencing atop a nearby ridgeline. "That should let them know you're in the United States. And where."

"And what do you do if something comes?"

Odin studied the sky. "Let's get some breakfast. . . ."

CHAPTER 18

Firestorm

Falling asleep in the cargo bay of a C-130 was like trying to catch some shut-eye on the undercarriage of a passenger train. Even after three hours she hadn't managed a wink. McKinney stared out of one of the few round porthole windows, crystals frosting its edges. She could see a wide, barren canyonland below of eroded basins and distant brown mountains in the moonlight. The plane looked to be about twenty thousand feet up. It was a crisp, clear winter night.

Odin glanced over at her and spoke into his headset microphone. "We'll give it another twelve hours, and then change crews at Hill Air Force Base." His expression suddenly changed. He stopped and touched a hand to his headphones, listening to something she couldn't hear in her radio.

She searched his expression. "What is it?"

"Something is here." Odin turned to the others and circled his hand. "All units. All units. Bogey approaching White Sands Base at three o'clock."

The radio crackled. It was Foxy's voice—coming from farther forward in the C-130's payload bay. *"No unidentified radar contacts, Odin. The sky and ground are clear."*

Odin looked to Foxy across the pallets and the length of the cargo hold, talking on radios even though they could see each other. "Negative. I just got a transmission from Huginn. He's got a positive contact."

McKinney looked around and noticed she hadn't seen Odin's ravens on board. She gave him an incredulous face. "Huginn and Muninn are talking to you."

"Yes." Odin grabbed his rucksack from an overhead stowage rack and rummaged through it to produce a ruggedized tablet computer. "They've been on the ground at White Sands Base for over a day. I'm in contact via satellite radio."

"You're talking to your ravens over a radio?"

He nodded as he booted his equipment. "Training. They communicate direction, distance, and type of contact. Whatever this is, it's airborne, and coming in from the east. Navy SEAL teams command attack dogs via headset commands—the only difference here is that ravens are more intelligent." He logged on. "And can see and hear for miles and cover vast areas over any type of ground without being detected."

Foxy's voice came over the radio channel again. He was examining a tablet computer of his own over by the flight deck doorway. *"The only radar contacts the techs have in the east are dozens of miles out. American Airlines Flight 733 from Denver to Salt Lake City forty miles out at thirty-eight thousand feet, and two private aircraft, one eighteen miles out, heading north at four thousand, and another at twenty-two miles out heading southwest at five thousand feet. You sure it wasn't our MQ-1 they saw?"*

Odin looked across the cargo back. "Negative. How many times has Huginn been wrong, Foxy?"

Foxy said nothing.

McKinney stood and braced herself on an equipment rack as the plane bumped in turbulence. She looked over Odin's shoulder. "You're sounding the alarm on the report of a bird?"

"Huginn and Muninn don't act this way unless something is seriously wrong." He looked at the signals officers studying their radar console. "Those sensors don't reveal everything." Odin's tablet was now booted, and he turned the screen so she could see black-and-white thermal imagery from one of the raven's cameras. The birds were following something at low altitude. The rocks and scrub soared past in the imagery.

McKinney studied the screen. "A raven's-eye view."

Huginn was trailing the black silhouette of a bird of prey gliding over the desert terrain at an altitude of perhaps a hundred and fifty feet. The second raven, Muninn, sometimes entered the frame, meaning they were flying together.

McKinney studied the image. "Looks like a hawk."

Odin spoke into his radio. "You getting this, Foxy, Hoov?"

"Yeah, Odin, Prof's right. Looks like the twins sent up the alarm over another bird."

Odin studied the screen. "That hawk has one problem: It's got no heat signature." He pointed his gloved hand at the thermal image, and McKinney could clearly see the difference between the heat intensity of the second raven and the interloper.

Odin keyed another radio. "All units red alert. Bogey one thousand meters out and closing on White Sands Base from the east. Designate bogey Target One. Looks like a microdrone in the shape of a bird. Have the Predator swing around to track this thing. I want stable, detailed imagery on it, and port the video to the team at the JOC."

Another voice came through, possibly Hoov's. *"On it, Odin."*

Odin strapped on a MICH helmet with a monocle over his left eye, then handed the tablet to McKinney. He appeared to be watching from the helmet eyepiece. "Pretty goddamned clever. Even if it showed up on radar, its speed and profile would match that of a bird."

"A spotter drone."

"That would be my guess. It's too small to deliver any ordnance."

Foxy's voice again. *"Agreed, boss."*

Odin was adjusting channels on a satellite radio on his harness. "Okay, we're getting the Predator feed. Give them Huginn's coordinates, and they should be able to pick up the bogey from there."

"Got it."

He adjusted the radio. "The attack drone is probably still over the horizon and won't reveal itself unless this one finds who it's looking for."

"Me."

"Yes. Let's hope it takes our bait." He worked unseen commands on his monocle screen with a handheld controller, and suddenly her table computer showed a surveillance camera image of . . . herself, sitting in a well-lit converted hangar somewhere, motionless, except for her fingers clattering away at a keyboard in front of a large window.

McKinney sat down again, the tablet computer in her lap. She kept her eye on the image there. It felt eerie.

Odin appeared to be clicking through screens of his own. "We've got a Predator doing a mile-radius orbit of White Sands Base at ten thousand feet. I wanted to get clear video from a separate platform. We're much farther out and twice as high, but we've got lightning pods for our own thermal imaging."

"Lightning pods."

"High-resolution thermal optics in a pod on the wing. Here . . ."

Odin had brought up another thermal image on the tablet. This one was far more clear and stable than that from the ravens. The image showed what was now clearly an artificial bird with a small propeller mounted on the tail. Odin's ravens ducked in and out of the frame, dogging the interloper, shadowing it.

"Probably electric. Silent." Odin spoke into his headset. "Huginn, Muninn. Return. Return. Confirm."

One by one a seeming confirmation *caw* came in over the radio, and the ravens broke off from trailing the artificial bird on the tablet screen.

McKinney looked at him. "You're shitting me."

"I told you they were smart. I don't want them in the middle of this when the fireworks start."

The radio crackled. "*Odin, signals team says this thing just went into an orbit over White Sands Base. Looks like it detected either the professor's cell phone or the Bluetooth ID of her laptop.*"

Hoov's voice chimed in, "*It's probably getting a PID on her physical likeness now.*"

Odin added, "Stay alert, everyone. When it summons the attack drone, we won't have much time to intercept it."

Hoov's voice. *"Best bet's to head east. That's where the most likely radar tracks are."*

McKinney and Odin exchanged looks in the semidarkness as they waited and watched.

"Heads up."

Odin spoke into his mic. "What?"

"It's signaling."

The FLIR imagery showed a pulsating laser on the top of the birdlike minidrone. It was flashing rapidly in a variable pattern.

"All right, that's the attack signal."

Foxy's voice. *"Yeah, we see it."*

"Could it be signaling a satellite? What sats are overhead at the moment?"

"Got my hands full at the moment. I'll check later."

Odin spoke into his mic. "Tailhook, Tailhook. This is Odin. Do you copy?"

"This is Tailhook. Go ahead, Odin."

"Where are we in our orbit?"

"We're . . . about fifteen clicks southeast of White Sands Base."

"Copy that. You see those two echoes east of us? Head to a point midway between them. It's likely that the main attack drone will be coming in from the east."

"Copy that, Odin."

Foxy waved from over on the far side of the plane, where they manned the electronics console. His voice came over the radio. *"Odin. Whoo boy, we've got something interesting here. That northbound radar contact to the east just turned west on a vector that will run it right over White Sands."*

"Private plane?"

"Affirmative. VFR. No flight plan registered. It's fifteen miles out and coming in at just under two hundred knots. Altitude one-zero hundred."

Odin gave a look to McKinney but spoke into the radio. "Here we go. Battle stations, battle stations. Tailhook, you know what to do: Intercept that bogey from above and behind once you confirm it's a drone."

"Wilco, Odin. On our way."

McKinney grabbed the seat as the C-130 went into a steep, banked left turn and an equally steep descent. The g-forces were strong enough that the cargo would probably have stayed in place without straps. Odin remained planted as well, standing without even grabbing a handhold. He was apparently well used to airborne operations.

"Foxy, focus the plane's lightning pod on that bogey and get me a visual as soon as possible. Put it on channel four."

"Copy that."

"Hoov, have the techs review the radar tapes to track that bogey back to its source, and get a Ranger team airborne. We might be able to catch whoever launched this thing before they get far."

"Already on it. We just got the info from the FAA on that contact. Looks like it hooked north from a western course fifteen minutes ago. It first came on the radar screens over the Denver metro area. That's two hundred thirty-six miles from here."

"Damn. Whoever launched this thing would be long gone by now. Get the info to the local FBI office. Have them work with the FAA to pinpoint the exact GPS coordinates where it first came up to radar altitude. Hopefully we can get some surveillance video that shows where it was launched from."

"A city. It figures. Must have hid in all the private air traffic."

After a few moments the C-130 leveled out. The engines throttled up, and McKinney noticed several of the other team members scurrying around, prepping the pallets. Odin, too, was rummaging through Pelican cases and racks on the edge of the cargo bay.

She looked at him. "What happens next?"

"We hope this is our drone. If it is, we bag it before it can self-destruct." He pulled a black flight suit and parachute from a case and tossed them to her.

She caught them with both hands. The suit was as heavy as a dry scuba outfit but was made of thicker synthetic material. "What's this?"

"Cold-weather flight suit. If this is our target, we'll be opening the cargo door, and it'll be sixty below in here soon. Be sure to close every flap."

She put the tablet down and started pulling herself into the suit. It felt expensive, and she had no doubt it was military-grade special operations gear. She looked up to see Odin doing the same thing. "So how you planning on bagging this drone?"

"We're going to deploy an oversized air sock of sorts. NASA tech, specially made Kevlar, Nomex, and ceramic fabric—stuff designed for inflatable space-station sections to withstand micrometeorite impacts. Vented to release pressure. Should be relatively explosion-proof. We're going to trail that air sock two hundred meters behind this aircraft, then come in from above and behind the drone and scoop it up. If it explodes— as we think it will—almost all the wreckage should remain in the bag."

She nodded. "And that gets you a complete drone."

"The wreckage, anyway." He gestured to the huge block of concrete attached to the first pallet by steel cables. "After we net it, we push this deadweight out the back of the plane, which drags the whole thing down to earth."

The peculiar cargo now made sense, but then she narrowed her eyes at him. "We're going to intercept a flying bomb. Did I really need to be here for this?"

He pulled on his black hood, then pulled on a jump helmet with integral headphones of its own. "After your last stunt, you're not leaving my sight. Besides, with a drone incoming, the ground is not the safest place to be right now."

She nodded reluctantly and pulled off her own headphones. It suddenly got very loud—the engines howling. She pulled her own integral hood on and was soon quite warm despite the cold. McKinney examined the fabric and shouted, "What's this material?"

He shouted back, "Classified. Here . . ." He approached her with a sophisticated-looking facemask, flight helmet, and goggles. "Oxygen. In case we need to climb rapidly to chase this thing." He handed her the goggles first.

She nodded and put them on.

He placed the helmet on her head, took it off, made a few adjustments, and then put it on again. It was heavily padded and had integral earphones. In a moment she heard his radio voice again. "Have you ever used a PHAOS rig?"

She shook her head.

He clipped the aerodynamic oxygen mask onto her helmet. Then he rigged the oxygen bottle into the flight suit. He then held out her parachute pack.

"So you have paratrooper training."

He eyed her. "I've done a few jumps. . . ." Then he also held out the leg loops of a yellow nylon harness. The moment she stepped into it, he quickly buckled it around her. McKinney traced her hand from the harness to a strap that led to the ceiling.

Odin spoke as he worked. "Monkey cord. It'll keep you from falling out of the aircraft."

She nodded. "I've used them before."

He smacked her shoulder and gave a thumbs-up. "You're good to go. Just stay out of the way when all this stuff goes out the hatch." He gestured to the payload.

McKinney could see that the others had donned their high-altitude and parachute gear as well, along with helmets and monkey cords.

The pilot's voice came over the radio. *"Odin, this is Tailhook. We've got eyes on that cyclops. Repeat, eyes on the cyclops. Sending the image on channel four. Over."*

"Copy that, Tailhook." Odin clipped on his own monkey cord harness, then grabbed the tablet computer. He flipped to channel four.

McKinney leaned in to see a highly detailed black-and-white thermal image.

Odin nodded to himself, then keyed the radio. "Been looking for that son of a bitch for a while. Tango Yankee, Tailhook."

"Don't mention it."

There, on-screen, was the image of a delta-shaped unmanned aircraft, tracking above the badlands in the night, shades of gray on gray. It was visibly different from the drone that had tried to kill her in Africa: a flying wing with a propeller on its trailing edge. The wing surface itself appeared to be of patchwork material—at least on the thermal image. As though it was a hobby project.

Odin keyed the mic. "Foxy, get us as much video imagery as you can on our approach. If it self-destructs, this is all we're going to get. So I want video from every angle while we're bagging it. Top, sides, bottom. Got that?"

"*Odin, this is Tailhook. We're a mile behind this thing and coming up fast, but we're still going to be tight on time if we want to bag it before it drops its payload.*"

Odin exchanged hand signals with Foxy. "Copy that, Tailhook. Get us in there, man."

The plane lurched in sudden turbulence. McKinney grabbed Odin's arm to steady herself. She focused on the camera image. They were nearly on top of the drone, and she could see the texture on the composite surface.

Another voice came on the intercom. "*Stand clear of the cargo doors. Opening in three, two, one . . .*"

A loud sucking sound was followed by a rushing roar as the upper rear floor of the cargo bay raised up beneath the tail. A moment later the lower ramp leveled, with hydraulic pistons holding it in place to either side. McKinney could see Foxy and Tin Man moving toward the payload, while the loadmaster and flight engineer looked out the open cargo door with thermal binoculars at the yawning gulf behind them. The view of the vast Utah wilderness below them was beautiful in the crisp winter moonlight.

Odin walked toward the ramp. McKinney stood up but remained where she was as the plane passed close above the mystery drone. It was a hundred or more feet below them and a bit farther back, but the entire team was riveted by it—apparently never having seen their enemy with the naked eye.

Odin's voice came in over McKinney's headphones. "Let's hope One was right about these things not having eyes on the back of their heads."

In a moment Singleton's voice came over the radio in response. She hadn't seen him down at the camp, but he was evidently there. "*They're a Spartan, single-use platform. Their targets are all below them. Eyes above would mean they'd need software to interpret what they're seeing in a different context. It wouldn't be justified.*"

Odin nodded. "Thanks, One."

Behind him the loadmaster readied the first pallet with the folded tentlike object on it.

Foxy's voiced crackled. *"Tailhook, this is Foxy. We are deploying the interdiction bag. Get ready for some drag."*

"Copy that."

Odin motioned for McKinney to stand back, and he moved against the wall next to her. A moment later the small drag chute deployed, pulling the folded bag pallet toward the emptiness beyond the cargo door. In a moment it tipped off the edge and started unreeling steel cable that quickly pulled taut on the concrete pallet. The securing straps there snapped tight.

McKinney saw the loadmaster checking the cable assembly. He gave a thumbs-up. On Odin's handheld screen, a night-vision image showed the interdiction bag open like a parachute canopy at the end of a curving, one-hundred-meter length of steel cable behind the C-130.

The loadmaster radioed the pilot. *"Interdiction bag deployed. Tailhook, you are GO for interdiction."*

The pilot's voice came over moments later. *"TOC, interdiction bag deployed successfully. We're moving in to capture."*

"Copy that."

From this distance it looked like the bag was pathetically small. McKinney decided to edge closer to the ramp alongside Odin. He gave her a brief glance, but she was busy taking in the fantastic view. She could also see the drone more clearly from this vantage point. It was only a hundred or so meters back. It looked even less impressive up close, with perhaps a twenty-foot wingspan. She could hardly believe all this ruckus had been caused by this jury-rigged hobby aircraft.

The drone seemed to be inching back relative to the billowing containment bag, the pilot maneuvering it into position. The bag was aerodynamically stable, apparently due to small fins on its side. Hoov was watching the scene intently as he manipulated a handheld joystick. It occurred to McKinney that he must be controlling it.

The whole team watched in tense anticipation.

The pilot's voice crackled. *"Fifty meters."* A pause. *"Thirty meters."*

In the green night-vision camera image the unsuspecting drone eased back toward the bag.

The pilot's voice came over the radio. *"Odin, we're just three miles to Target One. Altitude ten thousand feet."*

"Just keep it steady."

On-screen the drone pulled up slightly, and a voice came over the radio. *"Bomb in! Bomb in! Target Two has deployed ordnance."*

Odin spoke. "JOC, you've got ordnance inbound. All personnel take cover."

Singleton's voice came back with a siren wailing in the background. *"Copy that, Odin."*

The drone began to climb steeply.

The pilot's voice. *"Pulling up. Keep it in the box. This fucker's climbing fast."*

Odin motioned for McKinney to get back and followed behind her toward their seats. She heard his voice in her headphones. "We need to bag it, Tailhook. You're running short on time."

"We'll get it."

The men in the cargo bay grabbed for handholds as the plane lurched upward, chasing the drone up into the sky. Suddenly the entire view through the open cargo bay was of the dark badlands below. Tin Man started sliding back, and Foxy reeled him in by his monkey cord.

Meanwhile, behind them the plane was managing to gain on the drone and center it back into the maw of the bag. The team in the cargo bay watched intently—and in a few moments the drone disappeared, enveloped by the bag.

"Bingo, TOC! Bogey's in the bag! Repeat bogey's in the bag!"

McKinney and Odin looked to each other.

The bag was edging sideways, and then the drone suddenly started taking evasive maneuvers. McKinney realized there was nothing to stop the wild drone from hurtling forward a couple of hundred meters into the cargo bay and exploding—taking them all out.

The pilot's voice came over the radio. *"This thing's going nuts."*

Odin waved to the crew. "Deploy the deadweight!"

"Stand clear!"

She saw the loadmaster kick the quick-release on the pallet of con-crete that formed the deadweight. It whipped along the rails from the drag of the interdiction bag. The huge block tumbled off into the night, and the bag fell down and behind with it.

"Interdiction successful. Bag in free fall."

A moment later a white flash pierced the night above the Utah desert, and a fiery light and smoke filled the bag. The boom followed soon after.

Foxy was training some sort of night-vision binoculars on the distant object. *"Drone just self-destructed, but the bag looks intact."*

She could hear cheers on the radio, and Odin and McKinney ex-changed relieved smiles. He pointed, and they watched the glowing inter-diction bag still falling from thousands of feet in the air. "Let's hope it has the answers we're looking for in it."

The pilot's voice crackled again. *"TOC, missile lock-on! Are any of you guys burning me?"*

Hoov's voice. *"Negative, Tailhook."*

Then, from somewhere low on the eastern horizon, a missile streaked across the night sky, burning like a flare as it arced upward toward them. McKinney felt the adrenal wave of fear spreading like heat down her legs. Even for a civilian, the sight of a missile ascending toward them was obvi-ously bad.

"Missile six o'clock low! Deploying angel fire."

McKinney watched amazed as suddenly the sky erupted in a fountain of blinding light, dozens of flares spreading out from the base of the C-130 and trailing behind them. Salvo after salvo of flares formed an angel wing pattern of smoke and green-white light behind them. The plane lurched to the right, throwing her against the wall. Then left. Mc-Kinney grabbed on to the equipment rack and looked behind them through the open cargo door.

Odin's voice came over the radio. "Godammit, Hoov, what the hell's out there?"

The missile raced past them wide on the left and detonated, creating a flash and a powerful *thump* that caused the plane to lurch.

The pilot's voice. *"Shit, we're hit."*

Odin raced forward, pulling on his monkey cord to steady himself.

McKinney watched in horror as a burning glow filled the left-side porthole windows, and a noticeable vibration set in on the floor. The C-130 yawed from side to side—still spitting flares every few seconds. The men in the cargo bay still looked incredibly calm to her, checking their monitors and grabbing fire extinguishers. It made McKinney straighten up, wondering what she should be doing.

The pilot's voice crackled as though announcing the in-flight movie. *"Shutting down engine one. I'm going to try for the base camp airstrip."*

Foxy's voice. *"Where'd the missile come from?"*

Hoov's voice answered. *"Nothing on radar."*

Odin was pulling gear from a Pelican case. "Did it come from the ground?"

"We've got an inconclusive echo moving across our six. Ah . . . now it's gone again."

"Opened its weapon bay. Expect another launch. How far out?"

"Three miles."

"All right. Team Ancile. Execute, execute, execute!" Odin turned to McKinney and unfastened her monkey cord harness. "Check your chute, but don't jump until I say."

"*Until* you say? What happened to the pilot trying to land?"

"Change of plans. Get busy, Professor!"

She pulled on the shoulder straps of her parachute and began securing it. It was apparently a military-grade HALO chute. She grabbed for handholds against the lurching of the plane as she familiarized herself with the location of the ripcord and the cutaway. A glance up told her that everyone else was checking their parachutes as well.

The pilot shouted again. *"Missile lock-on!"*

McKinney looked out the open cargo doors to see another missile streaking out of the darkness, rising fast from a low angle. Odin was staring out with what looked like thermal binoculars. "I've got eyes on two bogeys, six o'clock, low, four thousand meters. I think we got our answer, Foxy."

"Looks like it."

Odin started tapping in numbers on a wrist computer.

Flares spouted from the C-130 again, and it took evasive maneuvers that sent McKinney sprawling. She grabbed on to the equipment rack and pulled herself to her feet again.

What the hell am I doing here? The question kept repeating in her mind. She looked at that fiery glow in the left-side portholes and was relieved to see that it had almost gone away. She was tempted to run out and jump from the cargo ramp, but she resisted. She had to stay with the team. The image of Ritter's ghoulish eyes came back to her.

She's as good as dead, and you know it.

Odin's voice came over the radio channel. "Tailhook: Clear your people."

"Copy that, Odin."

Odin rummaged through equipment cases again. The other team members were hurriedly grabbing weapons and strapping on gear. "Move it, people!"

McKinney kept her eyes on the incoming missile as it streaked into the flares and past them without exploding. "Jesus Christ . . ."

The pilot's voice came over the radio. *"Setting autopilot to twenty-three thousand. All crew, bail out! Bail out!"*

The plane tilted into an upward climb, while Foxy stomped toward Odin along with a half-dozen crew and team members. Foxy held his kora by the neck, and as he approached he looked sadly at it. "Well, another one bites the dust." He tossed it out the cargo bay doors and into the abyss.

Odin gestured to Foxy with a slashing motion across his throat as he pulled the mic boom from his helmet. Then he shouted something directly into Foxy's ear for several moments. She couldn't hear it over the roar of the plane and her own insulating headphones, but after a moment Foxy nodded and motioned for the others to follow him.

He saluted McKinney. "See you in hell, Professor!"

The whole group went single file, launching one by one off the back ramp and into the moonlight over the Utah desert. McKinney watched them go and could see their silhouettes recede into the void. She felt like launching with them.

Odin grabbed her by the shoulders. "Not yet, Professor."

"Are you crazy? Someone's shooting missiles at us!"

"Remember that discussion we had about you being bait?" He was fiddling with a small nylon pack, clicking red buttons. "I left some parts out."

"Why in the hell do you keep lying to me?"

"Because whatever you knew, they now know."

The remaining flight crew came down from the deck and through the bulkhead door into the cargo bay. The navigator and copilot saluted Odin and jumped from the ramp one after the other. The pilot stopped and put a hand on his shoulder. *"Ship's clear. Happy hunting, Sergeant."*

Odin just thumbed toward the exit. The pilot nodded and ran off into the void.

Odin glanced down at his Rover tablet and showed it to McKinney.

It was an image from the surveillance camera watching her decoy. Where "she" had been, there was now only burning debris and fake body parts. Her stunt double was charred.

"My God."

Odin tossed a satchel with a blinking red light on it well forward through the bulkhead door. "Whatever these things are, they just shot down our Predator drone too."

McKinney held on to the equipment rack and glared at him. "Then what the hell are we still on this plane for?"

He pulled off his helmet and goggles and, from one of the Pelican cases, produced a full-faced aerodynamically designed black helmet with integrated tinted goggles and oxygen mask. It looked like something from a Star Wars convention. He pulled out a second one, flicked a switch, and shoved it into McKinney's arms, motioning toward his throat.

She sighed and tore off her helmet, goggles, and oxygen mask. The cold hit her face like fire. She quickly put the new helmet on and realized it had integrated thermal or night vision in the goggles. She felt his hand fumbling with switches at her neck and suddenly heard the hiss of oxygen flowing and his voice in her ears.

"—secure comms. Can you hear me?"

"Yeah, I hear you. What the hell's going on?"

He pointed out the back. She could see much more clearly in the night now, and that made it all the more alarming to see yet another missile streaking up toward them. But farther back she could also see twin pinpoints of heat glowing—distant aircraft following them.

She was about to jump toward the exit when she felt his rock-hard fingers gripping her shoulder.

"Think about it."

"Think about what? Let go of me!"

"Who knew we were here?" He was now hanging what appeared to be a belt-fed machine gun across his chest and cinching it tightly. It had a large boxlike magazine. He looked up at her as he adjusted a twin pistol harness as well.

She couldn't keep her eyes off the incoming missile. "We need to jump! Now!"

"It'll hit an engine."

"And what if the fuel tanks explode? What if a wing comes off?"

He was concentrating on prepping his gear. "I've seen a Talon take worse. . . ."

"Odin!" She started pulling him toward the edge of the cargo ramp and the vast space beneath them.

He held her back. "Not quite yet, Professor."

The plane was still vibrating from the earlier hit, and the two remaining plastic-wrapped equipment pallets were hopping around. McKinney hit the deck as the missile streaked in and detonated somewhere off the right side.

The plane lurched and yawed to the right, then developed a truly disconcerting undulating pattern. Piercing alarms started wailing. McKinney crawled to her feet again and could see thirty-foot flames and dark smoke trailing from the port wing—all portrayed in the black-and-white phosphorescence of her helmet's night vision.

"Steady . . ." He grabbed her arm and started walking slowly toward the lip of the cargo ramp. The Utah desert scrolled by fifteen thousand feet or more below them in the black-and-white world of her helmet. A glance up front.

Flames were licking through the bulkhead.

McKinney struggled against his grip, then tried a self-defense move she'd learned in a class that prepared female researchers for remote field-work overseas—a kick toward his groin.

Odin deflected it easily and got her in an armlock. "Cut it out, Professor. We're not quite at altitude yet." He looked out the back ramp at the incoming objects, then started tapping numbers into a small computer integrated into the wrist of his HALO suit.

She noticed that the plane was indeed still angled in a climb.

"I figure two minutes of free fall is the most we'll get. At a distance of three miles and a speed of three hundred knots, that should put us close enough."

"Close enough for what!"

She could see the reflected glow of the flames trailing behind the plane in his insectlike helmet eyes. He was like the devil incarnate, standing amid the fire and chaos, his voice calm, his legs absorbing the now violent shuddering of the aircraft. He rammed the bolt back on the machine gun.

"You're insane! You're going to get us both killed!"

"Look, I don't come to your job and tell you how to research ants."

He nodded back behind her, and she turned to see yet another air-to-air missile arcing up toward them, but now she could more clearly see where it was coming from. Two sleek flying wings were below them and closer now—a few miles away.

"The people behind this need to think we're dead, Professor, or we're going to be too busy looking over our shoulder to find anything." He raised his gloved hand to reveal a palm-sized trigger device. The flames glowed higher in his plastic eyes. "You ready?"

"Oh, my God . . ."

"We stay in close formation. Do not deploy your chute until I give you the signal."

"Screw formation! It's pitch black out there! If we collide—"

"Hey!" He grabbed her helmet and put his right in her face. "You've got a hundred and two USPA jumps under your belt and the best night-vision money can buy. No excuses for dying. We need to be well below radar before we deploy. If you deploy your chute early, they'll know we bailed before the crash. Which means they keep hunting you. Are we clear?"

She stood unsteadily.

There was a flash and another BOOM. The plane started yawing to the side again, rumbling.

"Goddamn you . . ."

"Go!" He let go of her arm.

McKinney spun to face air-forward as she leapt from the cargo ramp, spreading her arms and legs to stabilize into free fall. Odin was right behind her. The racing wind hit her as a wall of pressure, but the high-tech jumpsuit and helmet kept her insulated. She'd never worn anything so effective at cutting wind. She concentrated on her form, and it started to calm her mind. The view was breathtaking even in night vision.

The flaming C-130 cargo plane receded ahead and above them.

Odin glided slowly toward her as he raised the detonator in his gloved hand. He squeezed, and the big, stricken plane detonated in a blinding flash, followed by a blast wave. The plane came apart in a ball of flame. Odin tossed the detonator and motioned calmly for her to drift one-eighty as he coasted alongside.

She heard his voice in her earphones. *"Remember: Don't open your chute until I give the word."* He strained to bring the tightly strapped machine gun barrel down against the onrushing wind and scanned the eastern sky as they fell.

He extended one hand skillfully as a fin to swerve him ten yards away from her as they continued in free fall, the cold wind rushing past them at one hundred and twenty miles an hour. Seven or eight thousand feet below them, she could see they were dropping down toward two fast-moving objects headed in their direction. She matched Odin's movements as he extended and retracted his arms to guide himself faster, slower, left or right, adjusting an intercept course.

"This is insane. They'll kill us!"

His voice came through on her headphones. *"These are autonomous drones, Professor. I'm betting they're using visual intelligence software to understand what they're looking at."*

"So?"

"*Humans can't fly. Which means we can't be here. I'm betting they won't be able to figure out what we are. . . .*"

As they fell through twelve thousand feet, the drones passed below them and to the right by a couple of hundred meters. McKinney saw, more than heard, Odin's machine gun open up. Fiery tracer rounds raced out like brilliant white sparks in her night-vision goggles. The bullets stitched the sky around the approaching aircraft, and although the rounds went wide, she saw that the drones immediately reacted to the incoming projectiles, veering off to the right and left around them as Odin's fire chased them. One thundered past, headed for the falling, fiery wreckage of the C-130, but the other drone curved around, coming back to have another look at the attack coming from midair.

For a fleeting moment she clearly saw it as it whipped past them, followed by a thunder so loud she could hear it even within her helmet and all the rushing wind. These weren't propeller aircraft but jet fighters that looked like flying black manta rays, tails blazing with heat. And it was clearly an unmanned drone. There was no cockpit—and it definitely didn't look like a hobby kit.

She heard his voice in her headset. "*See that? Home-built drone, my ass. We caught the one they wanted us to catch.*"

"Then why did they send these too?"

"*There's something else going on. Something I'm not seeing yet.*"

She was distracted by all his shooting, the tracers spraying wildly out into the night. "Do you really expect to hit those things at these speeds and distances?"

He kept firing intermittently at the drone. "*If I can get them in close enough.*"

"Altitude!" She could see the ground closing in. They were already passing through nine thousand feet. She looked back up and realized they were well below the jet-powered drones. The one that had turned back toward them, though, was also arcing down to follow them in their vertical dive.

It was coming after them.

"*Come on down, fucker. . . .*"

"You're insane!" She clutched her ripcord but, at the last moment, held back, resisting the urge to deploy. Looking up she realized the drone might plow straight through her canopy.

Odin opened fire on the drone diving down from above them. His tracers spat upward like a fountain of sparks as the craft roared closer, now only a few hundred meters above and gaining fast, its array of buglike eyes staring down on them.

Several miles away Foxy, Ripper, Hoov, and the others folded up their parachutes on the desert floor and gazed up at the fireworks in the sky—tracers spreading into the stars as jet engines roared and fiery debris rained down farther on.

Foxy just shook his head. "Subtle, boss."

Hoov tapped him on the shoulder and showed him an image in the Rover tablet's screen. "They're raiding the camp."

Foxy could see dozens and dozens of FBI and Homeland Security vehicles rolling toward the JOC camp, rack lights flashing. He nodded to Hoov. "Time to regroup."

Ripper signaled to an approaching chopper.

Still falling through the night sky, Odin stabbed two gloved fingers toward his eyes. "*Stay with me, Professor. . . .*" Then he turned and kept firing at the drone looming in from above. The shell casings were starting to collect around them as they fell, and McKinney batted them away.

She saw a glow as something launched from the front of the drone. She barely had time to react by the time what must have been a missile raced just a few yards past them but detonated much farther below. She felt the blast wave as a white-hot light flare appeared in her night vision goggles—but the next-gen goggle phosphors recovered quickly, unlike the ones she'd used before on research trips. Soon they fell through an acrid smoke cloud and down into the night. The drone on their tail obliterated the smoke cloud as it howled through half a second later.

It was only a hundred meters behind them, and Odin's tracer rounds stitched across its front. Flames quickly burst from it, and it yawed off course, spinning wildly, trailing smoke.

McKinney glanced down to suddenly see the dark, cold terrain racing up to meet them. "David! Ground!"

He unstrapped the machine gun and hurled it away so it wouldn't tangle in his chute. It spun off into the darkness. "*Not yet, Professor.*"

The burning drone corkscrewed past them, plunging down toward the dark landscape. They fell through its trail of black smoke for a moment or two. It was so dense, she could smell burned plastic and aviation fuel even through her oxygen mask.

She was almost looking straight across at the horizon line now. "We're practically on deck!"

"*Easy . . . easy . . .*"

There was a fiery explosion on the desert below them, illuminating the terrain and showing just how low they were—not far above fifteen hundred feet.

"You're going to get us killed!"

His enclosed helmet made his face unreadable, but his voice sounded calm. "*Wait. . . .*"

Again she put her gloved hand around the ripcord. They were at BASE jumping height. Moments to impact. There would be no chance to deploy a secondary. A glance at Odin showed him measured, hand extended. *Wait . . . wait. . . .*

He made a cupping motion with one hand and shouted, "*Now!*"

She pulled the ripcord and closed her eyes as the chute drew her up sharply. When she looked up to see the canopy deployed fully overhead, she felt another rush of adrenaline combined with relief. It was the heady mix that had lured her to skydiving in the first place. She glanced down just in time to see the desert floor racing up to meet her.

McKinney pulled in on the canopy controls and got herself moving laterally just in time to come to a stumbling stop and roll over the sagebrush and sandy soil. She rolled to her feet, cursing, and unclipped the harness.

"What the hell's the matter with you?" she shouted into the radio.

She looked around for him and saw Odin sixty or seventy feet away, efficiently balling up his canopy. *"Bundle your kit."*

McKinney stared at his distant form for a moment, then started rolling and collapsing the parachute. "Do you realize how close you came to killing us?"

"Two hundred and thirty-three."

"Two hundred and thirty-three what?"

"HALO night jumps." His helmeted head turned toward her. *"Finish up, we gotta get moving. And kill your oxygen. There's fire here."*

McKinney cursed under her breath again, then searched for the valve on her small green oxygen bottle, cinching it closed. Then she pulled the free-fall helmet off, breathing the clean desert air. She was panting and tried to get her breathing under control. It was actually beautiful out. She looked up at a brilliant field of stars in the winter sky. She felt incredibly alive.

You're okay. Everything's okay.

She balled up the parachute silk and joined up with him. It was only then that she noticed a field of scattered fire burning in the desert not far off.

"C'mon." Odin led the way through sparse creosote bushes and desert scrub.

Before long they came to the first pieces of wreckage, still on fire. Odin tossed his parachute directly into the flames, motioning for her to do likewise. She tossed it in after his.

"Shouldn't we be escaping or something?"

He kicked a small piece of wreckage away from the flames, some sort of internal mechanical component, badly charred and twisted.

"Odin."

He kicked sandy soil onto it, smothering the flames. "I need to confirm something." He picked up the still-smoking device with his gloved hands, searching.

He pulled his helmet off and drew a small tactical flashlight from his flight suit pocket. The flashlight had a wad of duct tape on the handle end, on which he bit down as he placed it in his mouth. He clicked it on, aiming it with his head as he examined a small metal plate printed with numbers and a logo. McKinney looked over his shoulder.

He pulled the flashlight out of his mouth. "VisStar Inertial Gyroscope . . ." Odin looked up at her as he tossed the piece of wreckage away. "Black project aerospace. Military-grade. Doesn't mean they sent the thing, but it does mean we're dealing with insiders."

"But why would they leave so much evidence behind on the parts?"

"Because they don't care if they're found out. There's something major going on here that I'm not seeing. And that probably means politics." He started fishing through his flight suit zipper pockets.

"Ritter warned you that 'they all wanted this.' Who's they?"

"Ritter wouldn't know. He's just a messenger. They've got ten thousand like him. We'll need to connect the dots beyond Ritter."

She examined the sky above them, still brilliant with stars even with the fires burning nearby. "What about the other drone?"

The sound of jet engines was now gone. In fact, there were no aircraft sounds at all, just the lapping of flames with the occasional *pop*.

"Those were short-range air-to-air missiles—probably AIM-92s." On her frown he added, "They were gunning for aircraft, not ground targets."

"What about the first drone? The one we caught in the bag?"

He produced a GPS unit from his flight suit and started booting it up. "I don't know yet. It might have been sent by someone else. Did you happen to notice those drones swarming?"

"Are you joking?"

"Did you recognize any behavior from your weaver model?"

McKinney recalled the machines flying in formation "They were flying together. I wouldn't call two drones a swarm. They certainly didn't manifest any weaverlike recruitment pattern, if that's what you mean. And it's too small a group, too short a time frame." She gestured to the wreckage. "You think this has a black box flight recorder in it?"

"Probably, but they'll be coming for it. So we can't stick around." He examined the GPS screen. "We need to get to the rally point."

"Where's that?" McKinney looked around at the frozen, mountainous desert around them.

"Not close." He pointed at the mesas lining the horizon. "A lot of this is exposed rock. We won't leave tracks. We'll move across the heights and keep close to cover. There might be UAVs coming." He put a pair of thermal binoculars to his eyes and scanned the horizon. In a moment he put them away. "We're good for now. And about ten miles northwest of Green River as the raven flies. It's rough ground, and we need to make up time."

McKinney was still studying the burning wreckage.

"Congratulations on your first night jump, by the way."

She couldn't help but laugh and shake her head. "Wasn't fun."

"Still." He pointed toward the horizon. "South. Southeast around that ridge. Green River's probably eighteen miles on foot; it's gonna be a serious hump."

"You ever do a mile through Peruvian jungle?"

"As a matter of fact, I have." He started walking. "This area will be crawling with regular military and law enforcement soon. We need to be long gone by then."

He climbed the edge of a smooth, sloping outcropping of stone and motioned for her to follow. The rock formation continued as far as she could see by moon and starlight. He headed farther up the spine of rock, toward distant lights glittering against a jagged silhouette of mountains.

McKinney took a breath and hurried up the rock face after him.

CHAPTER 19

Hot Wash

Odin and McKinney moved at a steady pace across a vast expanse of undulating rock; above them was a brilliant field of stars. She could even see the Milky Way this far out from civilization. It had been a long time since she'd experienced a cold, clear night like this. Being able to be outside at night without getting eaten alive by malarial mosquitoes was a pleasure. It almost made her forget the circumstances of their journey. The temperature was down in the thirties, but she was more than warm enough in the HALO jumpsuit.

"Can I keep this thing as a souvenir?"

He just cast a look back at her.

"You can tell them it blew up in the crash."

"Keep moving." He turned back again. "Here . . ." He tossed her a plastic tube that she just barely caught. "Energy gel."

She examined the tube. "This classified too?"

"No, I got it at a sporting goods store."

She cracked it open and squeezed some of the saccharin-sweet substance into her mouth. "Yuck. It tastes like a scented candle."

"It'll give you energy and keep you hydrated. Take it all. We've got a long way to go."

She kept sucking on the tube.

The nearest stationary lights were miles away still. To the north they could also make out Interstate 70 and the truck lights moving over the vast desert landscape.

Odin occasionally stopped to scan the sky with thermal binoculars. Whether he was orienting himself or looking for danger, it was hard to tell.

Before long she heard a loud *caw* on the wind. McKinney and Odin turned to see both the ravens flutter down to land on rock outcroppings nearby.

A smile crossed his face. "Huginn. Muninn. Good."

The birds fluttered and *caw*ed again as if in response.

McKinney stood next to him, appraising the birds. "They found us. Even way out here."

"They can cover a lot of ground—with excellent night vision. And hearing. Their eyes are sharp enough to tell a golden hawk from a goshawk at a distance of two miles."

"Then they can hear approaching drones."

"Long before we can." He extended his hand to one of the ravens—it was always impossible for McKinney to tell them apart, although Odin seemed to be able to. The raven climbed onto his glove. He knelt and looked directly into its eyes. "Huginn. Scout. Muninn. Scout." He released the bird, letting it walk over to its mate.

The ravens made a few *keek-keek* sounds and flew off into the night sky in opposite directions.

She watched them go. "That's amazing." It did feel good to have friends in the sky, scouting for trouble. "When did the military start working with ravens?"

Odin looked up at her. "The military doesn't work with ravens. I do. I've known them both for twenty years, and if I'm lucky, I'll be with them another twenty."

"Twenty years? How long do they live?"

"They can live to be sixty."

McKinney did the math. "But that means you've known them since you were a kid."

He got to his feet. "We need to keep moving." Odin started upslope, and McKinney ran to catch up.

"How did that happen?"

He cast a look back at her. "I spent a lot of time in the woods."

McKinney recalled her own childhood explorations in distant woodlands and jungles—treks that inspired her career. She paused. "How's a kid in an orphanage spend a lot of time in the woods?"

"I ran away from foster homes a lot."

"Really?"

He nodded. "I was about twelve. Had a camp hidden in the woods, and this raven kept visiting me. I'd try to shoot him for food, but he'd fly away every time I grabbed my gun."

"You were twelve, and you had a gun."

"This was rural Pennsylvania. A .22 Ruger I stole from my foster father. Not the point. Every time I grabbed it, the raven would fly away. Or he'd put a tree trunk between him and me. He was smarter than I was."

They ran for a few moments in silence. It was the most McKinney had ever gotten from him, and she didn't want to interrupt.

Odin eventually continued. "I began to enjoy his company. He'd let out a warning whenever anyone else came near my camp. He started to lead me to carcasses in the woods. Deer that had been hit by cars. I realized he couldn't penetrate their hides. That's why he'd bring me—to cut them open for him. And that was our arrangement. I always shared with him after that. And he helped me survive."

"A symbiotic relationship."

"Not unusual for ravens. Back in school I learned all I could about them. Whenever I'd go back to those woods—even as a man—Huginn would recognize me. And later his mate, Muninn. They can remember individual humans for years. We're special to them."

"How so?"

They kept up a fast pace over the rocks. McKinney realized it was a good thing she was in excellent shape, because Odin was apparently used to covering ground fast.

"You familiar with the term *encephalization*, Professor?"

She nodded. "Sure. I'm a biologist. It's the amount of brain mass exceeding what would be expected, given body mass. It directly correlates to intelligence. Humans and dolphins are the most encephalized species, for example."

"And ravens."

She frowned. "I didn't know that about ravens."

He glanced back. "Like I said, I wanted to learn everything I could about them. For instance, why do they need to be smart—why smarter than, say, an eagle?" He slid down a rock face and kept talking as they moved.

McKinney contemplated the question. "It's true—brain tissue is metabolically expensive. So unless it's needed, excess brains don't appear in a species."

"Right. So why does a raven need a large brain?"

It was intriguing. McKinney realized she had no ready answer. "Okay, why?"

"To manage relationships with dangerous creatures."

McKinney considered this.

"Ravens thrive around human communities. That's been going on for tens of thousands of years. In fact, there's evidence they had a similar relationship with Neanderthal before we arrived on the scene."

"So what are you saying—they actively seek us out?"

"They seek out top-of-the-food-chain predators—and put us to work for them."

McKinney laughed. "I'd be interested in seeing the research."

"Assuming we survive, I'll be happy to show you." He scrambled up an escarpment.

"How do ravens get us to work for them exactly?"

"They lead predators to prey. Wolf packs will follow a raven and let it eat from their kill. Ravens helped ancient people find game too, and still do for modern Inuit people. So what I experienced as a boy has been going on since ancient times. They've gone to war alongside man as well—to feast on the dead. The Vikings revered them and put them on their banners. In every human culture throughout history ravens held a special place. They're mystical, mischievous, good or evil, but never just a bird. Ravens have observed us for so long they understand us. But one misjudgment interpreting our behavior, and they'll likely not live to make another. Working with predators is a dangerous game."

She nodded. "That's why they need to be smart. And the cooperation helps both species survive."

"Exactly."

McKinney looked up to see silhouettes sailing against the moonlight, watching over them. "And do you think they're really aware of this relationship?"

"I'm convinced of it. They can solve complex puzzles to reach food without direct experimentation. They use their large brain for conceptualizing reality; imagining scenarios and calculating likely outcomes. No other creature except man can do that."

"I must say you surprise me, Sergeant." McKinney caught his gaze reflected in moonlight. "So how does a man like you wind up as an elite commando?"

He considered the question. "I know your opinion of the military, Professor, but barring some unforeseen advance in human affairs, the implied threat of violence is the only thing holding civilization together."

"That's a pessimistic view."

"Where do you think political power originates?"

"Legitimate political power is derived from the consent of the governed."

"Ah, you're splitting hairs. Power is power." He glanced back to her. "If we're honest, power is derived from only one thing: physical force."

"I couldn't disagree more."

He came briefly to a stop, studying the terrain and sky with the thermal binoculars. "How's it go again? 'Governments are instituted among men, deriving their just powers from the consent of the governed.'"

"Yes. Exactly. As a soldier I'm glad you know that."

"And what if a government doesn't listen to the will of its people? Or a citizen doesn't follow the laws of their government? What then?"

"It doesn't necessarily result in violence."

He nodded. "Which is why human society mostly works; people avoid trouble. But behind every law is the implicit threat of force, and behind every vote is the implicit threat of rebellion. That's the bargain that holds a free society together. And no society with a wide power imbalance remains free for very long."

He motioned for them to keep moving, and in a moment they were bounding down a rocky slope.

McKinney was still troubled by his premise. "I'm not convinced that violence is the glue that binds us, Sergeant."

"I didn't say violence—I said the implicit threat of force. Think about it: Democracy only arose when the ability to employ force was decentralized. If you go back to the Middle Ages, the state-of-the-art weapon system was the armored knight. He cost a fortune to train, feed, and equip. But a mounted armored knight could overpower almost any number of peasants on a battlefield. And the distribution of political power in medieval society reflected that; authority was vested in a tiny minority, and the people had no choice but to obey.

"Then, with the advent of gunpowder, that all changed. Suddenly you didn't need a highly trained specialist warrior to win on the battlefield. All you needed was a warm body who could fire a gun. Anything they could aim at, they could kill. And at that point the edge in warfare went not to highly trained warriors, but to the side that could field the most people. At which point we saw the rise of nation-states—and nationalism as a concept—as the logistical requirement for fielding an ever-larger conscripted army. But this changed the political dynamic. The nobles could no longer ignore the demands of their subjects. Those subjects now had the power to kill them or refuse to fight in their wars, and so kings began to cede more political authority to representative bodies of the people—parliaments, and so on."

McKinney shook her head. "It's so like a soldier to come to the conclusion that the gun created democracy. You do remember how many African nations are awash with guns without even a hint at democracy, right?"

"My point is that with autonomous drones, you don't need the consent of citizens to use force—you just need money. And there might be no knowing who's behind that money either. Drones tell no tales."

McKinney examined the sky. "Ritter said, 'Everyone wants this.' Who's everyone?"

Odin grimaced. "There are dozens of nations joining in the drone arms race—and companies too. There are just too many advantages over manned systems. Armed conflict is about to change."

"We have to stop it."

"I don't think we can stop it, Professor."

McKinney was surprised by his admission. "Then you agree with Ritter."

He shook his head. "I didn't say that. We might not be able to stop it, but we can sure as hell alter its trajectory." He motioned for them to keep moving.

Odin stared downslope through binoculars in the predawn light, watching a bustling truck stop that served the nearby Interstate. He and McKinney were concealed in a drainage ditch. They had peeled off their free-fall and flight suits and stashed them under rocks near an old barbed wire fence post. The Ancile Services shirts and jeans they wore underneath were wet with sweat from their nightlong trek, making the cold wind that much colder. McKinney was now shivering, exhausted, hungry, and terribly thirsty. It had indeed been a tough hump.

Odin lowered the binoculars. "Interesting. Over by the gas pumps." He passed them to McKinney. She raised them to her eyes and noticed they had a built-in laser range finder. It showed their distance to the truck stop gas pumps as five hundred eighty-three meters. But what she saw at the pumps was unusual—several media satellite trucks idling or refueling, with camera crews and reporters sipping coffee and chatting. One was speaking into a camera under lights.

"Probably covering the plane crash."

One of the satellite trucks rolled out of the parking lot, headed back toward the Interstate.

"Hungry?"

"And thirsty."

"C'mon. . . ." He collected the binoculars from her and stowed them as they headed to the truck stop at the edge of a small Utah town.

McKinney scanned the horizon. "What about Huginn and Muninn?"

"They'll keep an eye out for trouble."

"Don't you need to feed them anything?"

"Not in the field. They're masters of survival. C'mon."

Odin knelt and produced an inch-thick wad of cash from a slot in the upper portion of his boot. He peeled off a few twenties and stowed the rest. "There are usually shower facilities in these truck stops—but also criminals. Don't talk to anyone you don't have to."

"I've dodged rebel checkpoints in Uganda. I think I can manage a Utah truck stop."

"We're coworkers traveling together, but you barely know me."

"If we get separated, where's this rally point you mentioned?"

"Don't get separated."

She gave him an irritated look. "How far?"

"A few hours, but I've cached equipment here. We always plan for the worst, and we're seldom disappointed." They walked past the long rows of diesel fuel pumps and trucks idling with their running lights lit here and there in the gravel parking lot. Women were standing on the steps of a semi cab talking to a trucker. The reporters and crews at the satellite trucks seemed to be winding down and getting ready to go.

McKinney and Odin entered the main truck stop concourse, ringed by a minimart, a Jack in the Box, Internet kiosks, a coffee shop, and shower/restrooms. It was early yet—about five-thirty in the morning—but the morning papers had arrived and were on display at the front of the minimart. The screaming headlines were unavoidable:

AMERICA UNDER DRONE ATTACK.

Odin and McKinney exchanged looks. He grabbed a couple of different papers and headed toward the cashier.

"Water too." McKinney raided the nearby glass case for several plastic bottles and followed.

He gestured to packaged sandwiches. "Grab some food."

She gathered a few processed-looking sandwiches that she wouldn't normally have touched. In her current state, though, they looked delicious.

They brought everything to the front. The cashier was an overweight fiftyish Caucasian woman with too much eye shadow. She shook her head sadly at the headlines as she rang them up. "Can you believe it? Drones've been attackin' us all this whole time? I'll tell you what, you just wait till they find out who's sendin' 'em. Somebody's gonna pay, is all I know."

Another customer, a sixtysomething trucker who sported a frazzled long beard, much like Odin's, and a feed company baseball cap, nodded. "Probably China. Hey, you got any a those American flags with the suction cups that go on the car?"

"No, we ain't got no flags, but I should have Sam buy some 'cause we'd sell out, right?"

"Damn straight."

She turned back to Odin. "That'll be twenty-three seventy-five, hon."

He paid and joined McKinney over by the shower entrance, as she opened the water and started taking measured sips. She handed one to him, but he was too busy reading the paper.

She looked around at the truck stop. "We've been gone a day . . . look at this place. . . ." She gestured at the people reading papers and glued to the flat-panel televisions above the coffee shop counter. Odin folded his paper back and pointed to a diagram captioned "Air Force Sets Trap for Enemy Drone." McKinney leaned in with widening eyes to examine it alongside him.

The diagram depicted the series of events above Utah with childlike simplicity. It showed a cartoonish cargo plane being shot down by the mystery drone over Utah's desert, with the enemy drone subsequently intercepted by twin jet-powered American drones. It was a cover story, one that introduced to the public a previously top-secret autonomous drone, known as the "Manta Ray," which was apparently the hero of the moment. It was everywhere in the news. A media blitz.

McKinney pointed at the stock photo of the jet-powered drone. "Look familiar?"

Odin nodded to himself. "Someone had this all ready to go."

"Probably the Pentagon."

"Don't be too hasty. War isn't a purely military endeavor—especially nowadays."

He walked toward the coffee shop and the televisions up near the ceiling above the counter. McKinney went with him, and they stood near several truckers, male and female alike, watching cable news. There was a live spot of a reporter standing in the Utah desert.

One of the truckers pointed. "That's down by Hanksville Junction, off the Twenty-four, twenty miles from here."

A murmur went through the crowd.

On-screen there was an inset of green, night-vision video showing tracer bullets flying in the night sky, missiles streaking overhead, and the C-130 exploding in midair, spiraling downward. It looped endlessly as the reporter spoke live in the other half of the screen.

"*. . . awoke to a dramatic scene in the night sky. Pentagon officials have refused to provide details of the operation, but the shoot-down of an enemy drone marks the first successful interception of what—instead of terror bombings—now appears to have been a wave of drone attacks on America's heartland. Attacks that have so far claimed one hundred and four lives and cost tens of millions of dollars in property damage. Attacks that likewise shed new light on the drone missile attack in Karbala, Iraq.*"

The lip-glossed news model back in the studio took her cue. "*What's surprising, Matt, is how easily these mystery drones penetrated American airspace. How long has the Pentagon known that these were drone strikes, as opposed to planted bombs?*"

"*That's not clear, Jenna, but word came this morning of a classified multibillion-dollar emergency defense appropriation that would clear the way for mass-production of the type of Manta Ray autonomous drone that proved so successful over Utah last night. That legislation will no doubt be fast-tracked in light of recent events.*"

McKinney nodded. "That's what this is about."

He watched, saying nothing.

The anchor then did her best impression of disarming feminine ignorance. *"What do you mean when you say these Manta Ray drones are autonomous, Matt?"*

"That means they aren't remotely piloted. They're programmed to hunt on their own."

"Why wouldn't the Pentagon use the remotely controlled Predator or Reaper drones that have been so effective over Pakistan and Afghanistan?"

The pretty female being lectured to by the man. McKinney felt like punching the screen in. "God, she's nauseating. . . ."

"Jenna, the Pentagon points to the scalability of these drones. They can be deployed in large numbers without the need of a human operator and ground control station."

"Automating combat aircraft sounds like a troubling shift."

"Actually, Pentagon officials stress that there's always a human in the loop to make what they call the 'kill decision'—whether to shoot or not. But the benefit of these autonomous drones is that, unlike human operators, they're ever-vigilant—and this is key: They aren't susceptible to radio jamming like the current Predator or Reaper drones."

"Radio jamming—what is that, Matt?"

McKinney balled her fists. "Is she supposed to be retarded?"

The man-in-the-field provided the answer. *"It's a key weakness of remotely piloted drones. Any technologically advanced opponent can simply jam the radio signals that permit you to communicate with your drone, rendering it useless. With this new generation of Manta Ray drones, they're fully autonomous, and so can continue a mission even if their radio communications are jammed."*

"So this provides us with greater security, while still keeping a human in the loop?"

"That's right, Jenna."

Odin walked away, shaking his head.

McKinney came up alongside him, pondering the situation. "They're screening 'Autonomous Drones for Dummies' on every channel."

"Molding public perceptions is what they're doing. Creating a new reality. This is the real campaign. The actual bombings were just prep."

McKinney looked across the faces watching the news—Caucasian,

Latino, Black, and Asian faces. All of them were watching attentively, followed by mutterings of "We'll get those sons-a-bitches" and "Don't fuck with the U-S-A."

"Apparently it's working."

"They're good at what they do. War is just one of their products." He headed for the rear exit doors. "C'mon, we've got to get to the rally point."

"Can we rest a bit and eat before we start walking again?"

"We're not walking, and time is a factor." He pushed through the truck stop concourse's rear doors and headed out through the parking spaces behind the building. He was searching for something, and moments later he focused on a late-model Ford Expedition with U.S. Forest Service markings and rack lights on top. He glanced around, then reached under the chassis to produce a magnetic key case. He removed a key fob and used it to pop the SUV's rear cargo door.

McKinney studied the vehicle. "You plan ahead."

"Multiple exfil routes and cover for action is standard operating procedure."

Just then both the ravens fluttered down and landed atop the SUV, pacing around.

McKinney was happy to see them. "Hi, guys. Is the coast clear?"

They *caw*ed at her in response.

Odin came up with two small suitcases. One he handed to her.

She took the bag. "What's this?"

"Forest service uniform and identification. It might not fit well, but it will fit. Head into the showers, get cleaned up, and change. We meet back here." He nodded to the ravens. "Back soon."

He locked the SUV with a flash of lights, and McKinney fell alongside as they walked back toward the truck stop.

CHAPTER 20

Oscar Mike

They drove for a couple of hours on Interstate 70, heading east toward Colorado. McKinney and Odin now wore U.S. Forest Service ranger uniforms replete with badges. The ravens paced about in a large wire cage that Odin had stored folded up in the cargo area. He had also stored food and water for them.

What little traffic there was on the highway consisted of isolated tractor-trailers. The landscape was as barren as anything McKinney had seen anywhere in her travels, a frozen and forlorn rock-scape with ice-capped mountains to the north.

Odin kept the police radio on, listening to the occasional Utah state trooper reporting status during traffic stops. They were seventy or more miles from the drone crash site now and had apparently escaped unnoticed.

Neither of them spoke. McKinney was too weary, and Odin seemed to be cogitating something. At some point she succumbed to exhaustion and fell into a deep, dreamless sleep.

When she awoke they were still on the highway, which now wound along a river in brown hills patched with snow. She looked around in the afternoon light.

"Where are we?"

"Outside Grand Junction, Colorado. Eat something. No telling when you'll get the next chance."

She inspected one of the shrink-wrapped sandwiches and started tearing it open with her teeth. "Anything on the scanner?"

He shook his head. "Not about us."

Before long they came down from the hills into the city of Grand Junction—a prosperous-looking oil town of mirrored glass buildings with a companion older downtown. But Odin blew through on the Interstate and headed out the far side. After a few minutes he took an exit onto a county road and headed into hills covered in snowy pines. The blue-white shadows of the Rockies were visible in the distance.

They passed only two other vehicles while traveling fifteen miles or so into steep forested hills. Odin slowed the SUV at the entrance to a rutted dirt road. There was a metal swing gate blocking it. He turned in and parked in front of it.

"We're here?" McKinney looked around.

"Hop behind the wheel. I'll open the gate." Odin got out and put his Forest Service hat on with military precision.

McKinney did likewise with somewhat less precision. It felt odd playing the role of park ranger. She had never worn a uniform in her life, and she now realized how they caused you to adopt a persona. You could almost "feel" the role you were supposed to play. She imagined that was something authority had always known.

Instead of unlocking the gate, Odin was counting off paces to the right of it. About twenty feet down the road he stopped and flipped over a flat rock in the woods with his boot. With a cautious glance to make sure no cars were coming, he knelt and rooted in a hidden cache to come up with what looked to be a walkie-talkie and an automatic pistol in a sealed Ziploc bag. He returned to the SUV and emptied the bag's contents onto the hood. He quickly slid the pistol into his Forest Service jacket.

McKinney noticed a packet of twenty-dollar bills, a U.S. passport, and several other items in the pile.

"You have stuff scattered all over the place."

"When things go wrong, you'll be shit out of luck if you haven't prepared." Odin then started keying numbers into the front of the radio. "Crypto codes—hang on." Finished, he keyed the mic and looked up the road. "Safari-One-Six, Safari-One-Six. This is Odin. Do you copy?"

They stared at each other across the hood of the idling SUV, listening to radio static.

Then a squawking voice. *"Odin, this is Safari-One-Six. I read you five-by-five. Sky is clear. Welcome home."*

Odin looked visibly relieved. "We're coming in. Odin out." He pocketed the radio. "Let's get off the road." He pulled a key out of the Ziploc bag as he approached the gate.

McKinney walked around and got behind the wheel of the SUV. Odin unlocked a thick padlock and pushed the gate in, motioning for her to drive through. He then relocked the gate behind them and got in on the passenger side, pushing the seat farther back with a thump. "We've a couple miles yet."

McKinney brought them down a road winding along the bottom of a ravine, which then opened into a canyon that followed a frozen creek. There was patchy snow in the pine forest around them, but only occasional ice on the dirt road. They bumped along at twenty miles an hour for a while until McKinney came around a curve and suddenly saw a man materialize out of thin air alongside the road. It took her a moment to realize that it was a soldier in a camouflage suit, lowering what appeared to be a mirrored shield. The combination of the two had given him something approaching invisibility. The soldier carried a large white sniper rifle in the crook of his arm, and signaled her to halt with the other as they approached.

McKinney brought the SUV to a stop and looked to Odin.

"It's us." He got out, and she did likewise.

A Polaris ATV was already coming down the road ahead with another sniper on it, rifle strapped over his back. The first man had pulled back the mask on his ghillie suit to reveal Foxy, grinning as he pulled his long hair out of his face. He slapped Odin on the back. "Startin' to worry about you guys."

"Everyone accounted for?"

He nodded. "Now that you two have arrived. But there's news too: Hoov says the mission's over. Task Force Ancile is supposed to stand down and return to FB."

"Stand down? On whose orders?"

The driver of the Polaris had stopped, engine idling, and pulled back his own ghillie suit hood to reveal Smokey. He nodded in greeting to McKinney.

Foxy shouldered his rifle. "Colonel sent word over JWICS. Says you're to report when you get in."

Odin exhaled as he contemplated this, sending a plume of vapor out over his beard.

Foxy looked dour. "They're shooting us down in more ways than one."

"We're still on mission. . . ." Odin headed back to the SUV.

"What? What do you mean?"

Odin marched toward the truck. "Let's get to the house."

Smokey and Foxy led the way on the Polaris, a mile or so down the dirt road where the ravine opened out to a small valley surrounded by wooded hills. The road forked, with the right branch descending toward the valley floor, but they followed the Polaris to the left, uphill to a big chalet built into the hillside and surrounded by sparse pine forest. The first-floor walls were of fieldstone, but stout logs formed the next two floors, with a pine-needle-covered slate roof and dormers rising above that. There was another Forest Service SUV parked near a closed garage door.

McKinney looked up through the windshield as she pulled to a stop.

Odin gestured as he got out. "Old FBI safe house. They used to debrief Russian and Cuban defectors here in the sixties and seventies." Odin opened the cargo bay and grabbed the raven cage.

Smokey and Foxy had already pushed through the tall oak doors into the foyer of the old chalet. "Hoov!"

McKinney and Odin followed them into a musty three-story entry hall lined with mounted elk and deer heads, balcony railings, and a large staircase. There was a huge fireplace on the far wall, and although it was cold in the house, there was no fire lit. Stacked along the wall were a dozen or so green Pelican equipment cases.

McKinney then stared up at a large antler chandelier hanging on chains overhead. "This place is a vegan's nightmare."

"Who's vegan?" Hoov entered the room from an interior door and nodded greetings.

Odin dispensed with pleasantries. "Get me an uplink to the colonel ASAP."

"On it." Hoov departed just as Ripper entered from a different doorway with Mooch. "Hey, Sarge." She was now wearing a flannel shirt, jeans, and hiking boots. "Is it true we're standing down?"

"No. How's our security?"

"We've got boom cameras topside and an RF-transmitter sensor perimeter established at the ridgeline, but there hasn't been any movement. No overflying aircraft."

"Have you swept the place?"

She nodded. "Nothing."

"Good." Odin deftly tossed his Forest Service campaign hat over a deer head's antlers. He then put the birdcage down and opened its door. "Huginn, Muninn. Explore." They hopped out of the cage.

McKinney couldn't help but notice that everyone was armed with pistols in nylon thigh holsters and scoped assault rifles hanging barrel-down on straps over their shoulders and combat harnesses with spare clips. "We expecting trouble?"

Odin spoke without looking up. "We're always expecting trouble."

McKinney heard a loud *caw* and looked up to see the ravens perched on the antler chandelier. "At least someone likes the decor."

Hoov entered again. "Colonel's up, Odin."

"Thanks." He headed after Hoov. "I want this recorded."

"Already rolling."

McKinney followed them both into what looked to be a rec or family room. This had another large fieldstone fireplace, and the walls were sprinkled with authentic-looking mountain bric-a-brac—snowshoes, muskets, kerosene lanterns, and framed portraits and photos of men posing with large dead animals. There was also a sizable bar along with a couple of sofas and a writing desk—on which Hoov had set up his electronics workstation. As with the rest of the place, the heavy drapes were drawn and the overhead lights and lamps on. Hoov's workstation consisted of several flat-panel monitors, a couple of ruggedized laptops, radio gear, and wires running out beneath the drapes—through a sliding glass door, perhaps. There was also a small video camera clipped to the top of one of the monitors, on which a red LED light glowed.

Staring out at them from the central monitor was a stern-looking, thick-necked man in his sixties, in a sport coat and button-down shirt, viewed from the waist up. The lines on his face were as intricate as the Utah desert seen from space.

Odin saluted. "Colonel."

The man nodded. "Glad to see your troop is all accounted for, Master Sergeant. Did Professor McKinney survive?"

"She did, sir. She's with us."

"Good. Task Force Ancile is to stand down immediately. You're all to return to Fort Bragg with whatever intel you have."

"Why'd they shoot down my plane, sir?"

"Let's call it a misunderstanding, Master Sergeant."

"I'd like to know what—"

"Return to base. It doesn't matter what happened before; now that the drones are public, there's been a reset. Joint Chiefs are letting Air Force take the lead. We're to stand down. It came from the very top."

Odin just stared for a moment. "Colonel, I think you need to—"

"It's not your job to think, Master Sergeant. It's your job to follow orders. Now, get to it."

The screen blinked out.

Odin kept staring at the dark screen.

Foxy sat down in his flowing ghillie suit on the arm of the sofa. "So that's it, then? Air Force shoots at us, and then we're under their op-con?"

Odin shook his head slowly. "Hoov."

Hoov looked up from his laptop screen and pulled his radio headphones off. "Yeah?"

Odin pointed at the screen. "Run it through Visuallistics."

Hoov frowned and tossed his headphones onto the desk. "You serious?"

Foxy could see the shock on Hoov's face. "Odin, what's up? Why would you suspect the colonel? I mean, this is the colonel. Mouse and he—"

"I don't suspect the colonel."

"Then I'm not following you."

"Just do it."

Foxy still looked confused.

Hoov was turning to another laptop. "That was a JWICS transmission—off our own damn satellite."

"Do I have to do it?"

McKinney looked from person to person. "What's going on?"

Foxy shrugged. "Odin thinks someone's running an IO on us."

"Which means . . ."

Hoov was opening the image of the colonel on another computer screen. "Influence operation. He thinks the video was doctored—which is fucking unlikely."

"But how would you know?"

"Digital forensics—software we use to check the validity of photos and video that informants send us. People sometimes add the faces of high-value targets to footage, looking for a reward." Hoov was clicking away as he spoke. "This works like weapon ballistics: Every brand of commercial camera has an electronic signature—subtle variations of resolution and compression pattern. This software tells me almost instantly the make and model of video camera that was used to make an image."

"How does knowing the camera help?"

"Once I know that, I can tell if any part of the image has been altered. I don't know how anyone could do that in real time, though. . . ." Hoov clicked away, and then stopped. He straightened. "Huh."

Odin, Foxy, and McKinney watched him closely.

Odin spoke first. "What is it?"

Hoov turned. "It hasn't been altered."

Odin looked relieved. "Good."

"I wasn't finished." He gestured to the screen. "It wasn't altered because it wasn't created by a camera. It was created by Image Metrics. He's a vocaloid."

"A what?"

Odin answered. "A computer-generated character."

The group gathered around the monitor. The colonel's image looked photographically real.

Foxy was shaking his head. "Fuck me. . . ."

Hoov ran his fingers through his close-cropped blond hair. "They must be using motion-capture. An actor on a green-screen or something. Sampled the colonel's voice patterns. They use this type of tech to do virtual pop stars in Japan, but I've never seen it this real. It's . . ." His voice trailed off.

"This is some seriously sophisticated shit, boss. And they're inside our satellite network?"

Odin stared at the screen. "We need to assume whoever's behind this is deeper in the system than we are. It also means they know where we are. The satellite uplink would have confirmed that."

Hoov was checking radar images on one of his screens. "The feed from NORAD doesn't show anything around us for fifty miles."

Foxy shook his head. "But why would you trust it?"

Hoov swiveled in his chair. "For the moment they think we believed the colonel's message, Odin. They'll be expecting us to return to Bragg."

"We'd never reach the base."

Foxy sat back down on the sofa arm. "Now I've seen everything."

Ripper and Tin Man entered the room and Foxy nodded to them. "Keep an eye on those perimeter alarms."

Ripper scowled in irritation. "What'd the colonel say?"

"The colonel's a goddamned cartoon. Keep an eye on the sensors."

As they exited with confused expressions, one of the ravens flew atop a tall bookshelf and plucked up a large, squirming beetle from a dark corner. The bird then flew down and perched on the lampshade next to McKinney. It held the beetle in its beak, legs still wriggling.

Foxy regarded the bird. "Good one, Huginn."

McKinney did a double-take on the insect.

Huginn cocked its head at her but did not start eating the huge black beetle in its mouth.

"What have you got there?"

Foxy looked up from the laptop screen again. "Dinner, look's like."

McKinney tried to approach the bird, but it walked to the other edge of the lampshade. She caught her breath. "Hang on a second."

Odin turned to face her. "What is it?"

"It's a South American flower beetle—its territory ends four thousand miles south of here." She plucked it from the raven's beak. Huginn didn't put up too much fuss. She examined the beetle as its wings beat furiously to escape. But McKinney was an old hand at handling live insects. The others gathered around her, and she pointed at what appeared to be a large third eye in the center of its head. "How did it get here?"

Odin leaned close to it.

"Someone get me a knife. . . ."

McKinney moved over to the bar, as Foxy started rooting around through drawers.

"Get me some tweezers and a couple pins if you can find them."

"Right." He handed her a loose razor blade he found in a utility drawer and kept searching. McKinney held up the huge beetle to the light as Odin sat on the barstool next to her.

It was immediately apparent that the bug had been "altered." McKinney pointed with the razor blade tip at two plastic objects underneath each wing. "I've seen this before."

"What do you mean you've seen it before? Where?"

"At an entomology conference a couple years ago. These are tiny generators, capturing the wing movement to power microelectronics."

Odin looked incredulous.

"It wasn't classified—it was brain research. They were looking for a research grant."

Foxy handed her several sewing needles in a mug and a pair of tweezers.

"Thanks." She put the razor blade down and grabbed a needle—sticking it straight through the beetle's brain, killing it, as she anchored the beetle to the bar top. Though dead, the insect's legs were still scrabbling at the wood.

"Hard core, Professor."

"We'll see. . . ." She then took the razor blade and started dissecting the beetle, peeling back the carapace to get at the brain. Almost immediately, she noticed fine fiber-optic threads leading from a tiny camera lens into an electronic device the size of a grain of rice. She used the tweezers to tease it away from the brain and up into the light.

It looked like a tiny CCTV camera and antenna assembly, with Asian characters printed on it.

Odin studied it. "We're through the looking glass, people."

"Chinese."

Odin pushed away from the bar. "That's just the camera's manufacturer, Foxy."

McKinney nodded. "The conference presentation was on 'brainjacking.' They insert the transmitter directly into the insect's brain— adding it at the larval stage so the insect grows around it. They leverage an existing nervous system to make a remote-controlled minidrone out of a living thing. All you do is activate the neurons that handle flying, turning, crawling, whatever, and the bug's own nervous system handles the rest. We all thought the guy was sick. Apparently he found a receptive audience in the military."

Odin took the camera from her and held it up to the light, then he ripped the antenna out. He looked around. "There's no telling how many more of those things there are in here."

Odin tossed the thing on the floor and crushed it under his boot. "This site is blown. We need to evac immediately. What's down at the airstrip?"

Foxy answered. "MD500 chopper and a Cessna Grand Caravan."

"In cover?"

"The Cessna's in the hangar."

"Fueled up?"

He nodded. "Wing tanks too."

"All right. Hoov . . ."

Hoov swiveled on his chair. "Yeah?"

"Destroy the uplink equipment and prepare to move out."

"You got—"

There was a series of deep *thwacks* as holes appeared in the heavy drapes and fist-sized divots blasted out of Hoov's chest. Then half of his head blasted apart, spraying McKinney and the sofa with gore. Hoov's body pitched forward, upending the coffee table.

"Sniper!"

CHAPTER 21

War Mask

McKinney was dimly aware of shouting and people hitting the floor around her as the world seemed to constrict to a tiny focal point on her shoes—which were covered in blood. Hoov's quivering body lay at her feet. She stared at the interior of his skull, even now coursing with blood that pooled across the floor. Blood was also oozing from several other holes in Hoov's chest, turning his entire blue Ancile polo shirt maroon.

That's when someone grabbed her bodily by the shoulders and hauled her over the back of the sofa. She didn't even feel the hard impact on the floor, but it must have brought her back to her senses. She looked up to see bullet holes systematically drilling into the foreheads of every human portrait and photograph on the wall that faced the covered window. Glass and splintered wood ricocheted around the room as bullet holes appeared with the speed and precision of a sewing machine. Two flat-panel monitors with the colonel's face displayed on them also got hit dead center, blasting apart.

"Stay down!" Whoever had grabbed McKinney was dragging her. She felt Odin's beard scratching her face as he pulled her behind the bar. His arm was as hard as a baseball bat, and he had a .45 tactical pistol in his other hand.

Someone shouted, "Sniper, Black, Alpha, Two!"

Odin responded in a booming voice. "Automated sniper station. Probably synth-app radar—stay away from perimeter walls!"

Foxy's voice. "Hoov's gone, Odin."

"I know."

A voice called out from the foyer. "Odin! Boomerang says the shots came from two locations near the center ridgeline. Plunging fire from six hundred and eighty-three meters and six hundred and twenty meters out."

"What are we facing?"

"Hard to identify the station model at this angle—both acoustic signatures look like .338s. They're in heavy cover and burning us with radar."

Foxy pounded the floor with his fist from behind the sofa. "They must have been here all along—waiting for confirmation that the team was all present."

Odin nodded. "Mark their location! And turn on a goddamned GPS jammer, Mooch! I don't want a JDAM down on our heads."

"On it!"

McKinney saw Ripper with her back to the bar next to them. The woman looked cool and focused as she pulled a metal canister from her harness.

Odin shouted, "Popping Mike Mike particle smoke!"

Ripper pulled the pin and tossed the now fiery canister over the bar into the room.

Odin talked over the hissing, expanding smoke cloud. "All right, listen up! We've drilled against this weapon system a hundred times. You all know what to do. Everyone to the foyer, in full AD gear, two minutes! On my mark!"

Looking down, McKinney realized she was completely spattered with gore. Chunks of what must have been brains came back on her fingers as she wiped her hands. The involuntary reaction was instant. She vomited onto the parquet floor behind the bar, sucking for air between retches. "Oh, my God . . ."

People talked to her rapidly from somewhere, but her body wouldn't let her hear. She had the dry heaves, crawling on her elbows.

Someone pulled her up sharply. Odin. He smacked her painfully on the scalp with his open hand. "Get your shit, together, Professor. I need you on deck."

The pain brought McKinney back to her senses but pissed her off. "Fuck you! I'm working it out." She rose to a crouch.

The smoke had almost filled the room, and it was getting hard to breathe.

Odin shouted, "Go! Go! Go!"

The team leapt into action, calling out with repeated "Go! Go! Go!" as a form of echolocation as they moved quickly out of the room.

Ripper tossed a bar towel to McKinney. "Move, Professor!" She motioned with her rifle, and McKinney rushed past as she wiped blood and brains off her neck and face—and ran into a choking cloud of smoke. As she emerged into the relatively clear air of the large foyer, Mooch grabbed her. "You injured?"

"No. It's not mine."

Foxy and Tin Man were already breaking open the large Pelican cases piled against the wall, while Ripper kept guard with her assault rifle, scanning every opening. Mooch was powering on electronics packages contained in ruggedized backpacks.

"COMJAM up."

Odin entered, dragging Hoov's body—a small rug covering its head. "We mourn later. Right now this operation has been compromised at a command level. This house is probably surrounded by class-one sniper stations—no doubt with more serious ordnance inbound. I need an immediate exfil plan."

Mooch answered first. "I say we make for the airstrip and fly out in the Caravan."

Foxy and the others were pulling strange weapons, armor, and gear out of the cases. "What about those jet-powered stealth drones? They could just shoot us down if we fly out."

Odin shook his head. "I think they brought those out for their big show. They don't have them in quantity yet. That's what their appropriations bill is for."

Ripper added, "And Odin took one out."

Foxy pulled what looked like a Roman shield with a mirrored surface out of one of the equipment cases. It had some sort of flexible fiber-optic viewing lens on a cable attached to its inner side. "Look, let's just dodge these sniper stations and light out into the back country on foot."

"Overland on foot it's two days to civilization, and the longer we stay in this area, the more shit they'll be able to throw at us. With TRACER radar they could pick us off even in dense cover. We need to get clear out of this region as fast as possible. That means exfil by air."

Smokey nodded. "He's right, Foxy. With the wing tanks on the Cessna we could do fifteen hundred miles easy."

"But to where?"

"We'll work that out once we're airborne. For now we just need to get out of this killbox."

"You wanna fly below radar in these hills?"

Ripper nodded. "I'll fly the bitch." To McKinney the woman's appearance seemed incongruent with her attitude—she didn't look tough. She looked like a pleasant neighbor. Someone who baked a mean casserole. But here she was, strapping on special-purpose body armor.

Foxy eyed her. "Have you flown one, Ripper? It's not a one-seventy-two."

"Fuck, yeah, I've flown one. Remember Caqueza?"

Mooch grimaced. "We were picking branches out of the landing gear."

"Well, is that low enough for you?"

"Then it's agreed." Odin pointed at Foxy. "If Ripper gets hit, you're pilot, Foxy. Then me."

McKinney noticed that while the conversation was going on, the team was suiting up in black body armor with odd, irregular edges and color patterns—green and brown splotches, textures. In particular they were strapping on outlandish helmets that looked almost like Pablo Picasso carnival masks—fearsome and highly asymmetrical.

Odin grabbed a thick plastic combat shotgun and jammed a plastic round drum clip into it. He chambered a shell. "They've got face detection running. Looks like they're set to shoot at any human likeness, regardless of thermal intensity—so I want complete facial cover. Mooch, help the professor into Hoov's cool suit."

"Oh . . ." McKinney looked down at Hoov's partially covered body. "I—"

"Not negotiable, Professor. Mooch!"

"On it."

Mooch pulled a black jumpsuit out of a nearby case and tore open the Velcro fasteners before handing it to McKinney. The thing looked almost like a deep-sea diving suit, except that it had raised ribs running all along its surface. The others had already put theirs on beneath their odd armor. They resembled an oil-rig dive team gearing up for performance art.

Mooch talked while he worked. "Cool suit—it helps conceal your thermal signature. Refrigerant flows through the bladders. You'll start getting cold if you're not moving, so let me know if your fingers start to feel numb." He was already strapping odd body plates onto her arms and legs.

She studied the plates. Their intent appeared to be disrupting the human outline—with special emphasis on the face. Mooch pulled a dense balaclava over her head.

"Radio earphones too. I want her jacked into team comms." Odin turned. "Foxy, Tin Man, get up to White, Bravo, Two and draw some fire. I want a map of every sniper station between us and the airstrip."

"What if they're mobile? It'd be a waste of time."

Mooch shook his head. "Look at the GBOSS images. They're dug in like ticks out there. They're not going anywhere."

"Right." Foxy pulled an uninflated pool toy from one case, and then he inserted an air canister into its base. The pool toy quickly inflated into a human bust—a Caucasian male in a suit. He affixed it to a plastic pole, then he and Tin Man ran upstairs with it.

"Watch your ears . . . firing!"

Odin aimed the shotgun at the skylight on the ceiling at the far side of the entry hall. BOOM! BOOM! BOOM! Glass rained down onto the floor planks ten feet away. The sky was now open above them. Odin leaned down to the ravens, who seemed unfazed by the gunfire. He held up an index finger. "Huginn. Recce. Recce. Muninn. Recce. Recce. Go!"

They *cawed* back at him loudly, then flew up through the skylight into the blue sky.

McKinney watched them go. "They could get shot, Odin."

He finished getting his asymmetrical armor on. "We know the OS of just about every autonomous sniper station on the market, Professor. They're made to kill people, not birds." He was watching his Rover tablet, an image from one of the birds' cameras. "The twins will do a mile orbit, and we'll see what's between us and the airstrip."

Several shots rang out in the distance—a crackling that echoed in the hills. It gave Odin pause. However, his video image kept running uninterrupted, and in a moment Smokey and Tin Man ran down with a deflated human decoy.

"Trigger-happy little bastards. We barely got near the wall with the decoy when they opened up on us—straight through the planks."

Mooch nodded to a bank of monitors on a nearby table. "There's your vector map, Odin."

Odin stooped to examine the video monitor. It showed a series of dots and glowing lines projected on the hillside, illustrating the path of incoming bullets. "Okay, two high on the ridge, eight hundred and nine hundred meters, one closer on this rise—about seven-eighty. Foxy, what do you think—Lapua Magnums?"

"That's what I'd use."

"All right." Odin clicked around the computer screen. "That gives the bullets a flight time of about a second, give or take." He stood up. "Even if they bracket us, that's too far for them to hit an evasive target. Foxy!"

"Yeah?"

"Take the mirror blind and mark targets with near-red. Smokey, Tin Man, assemble the M224 in defilade—behind the SUVs might be good. On Foxy's direction drop some seven-twenties on those two sniper stations. Clear us a path to the airstrip." He looked around. "Objections?"

Everyone nodded and murmured assent.

"All right, then. Do it."

They immediately launched into action, grabbing yet another equipment case and dragging it toward the front door.

McKinney gave Odin a quizzical look. "Then you've faced these things before?"

He nodded. "Our team has unique expertise, Professor. We illuminate them with a near-red laser for targeting—heatless light. It's based on insect bioluminescence, actually. Helps conceal our presence. These machines can see infrared light like we can see visible light, so we don't use it."

Foxy and the others, now in their cool suits, swiftly opened the front door, Foxy holding the mirrored, curving shield in front of him. Smokey and Tin Man followed him through the door, and although everyone tensed visibly as they ran out into the open, their cool suits and other equipment apparently made them invisible to the autosnipers in the hills.

McKinney moved over to the security monitors and watched over Mooch's shoulder. The screen showed Foxy moving to kneel behind the mirror shield in the driveway. Behind the SUV Smokey and Tin Man quickly opened the Pelican case and set up what looked to be a light mortar. In less than a minute Tin Man radioed in.

"All right, Foxy, burn Target One."

"Burning."

Smokey was monitoring some sort of electronic device that he then held against a mortar round Tin Man offered to him.

"Round programmed. Firing."

Tin Man dropped the mortar round into the tube, and they both ducked down with their mouths open.

The mortar blasted with a CHOOM sound that was audible inside the house.

Mooch tapped another monitor focused on the distant sniper station. It looked like an evergreen bush with a black pipe sticking out of it. But in a few seconds the bush exploded, revealing a shattered optical lens and a tripod mount as it tipped onto its side.

Mooch radioed. "Target One down."

"Copy that, Mooch."

They quickly acquired the second target and repeated the process, requiring two rounds this time until they were satisfied it was knocked out. The entire team in the foyer breathed in relief as Foxy radioed in.

"Targets eliminated."

Odin nodded. "All right, everyone. Let's move everything to the SUVs."

But suddenly a deep humming sound started to emanate from somewhere outside—somewhere away in the hills. They all looked at each other.

McKinney spoke first. "What is that?"

It sounded like a thousand weed whackers heard from a mile away.

Mooch examined the bank of camera monitors. "I don't see anything. And we're jamming common drone radio frequencies. And GPS signals."

Foxy's voice came in on the radio. *"Odin, we're hearing a strange sound out here. You got anything on the sensors?"*

The sound was getting louder. Odin studied the rover screen. "Foxy, get your team back inside. Now!"

On the video monitor they grabbed their gear and dragged it back toward the front door of the house.

To McKinney the humming started to take on the sound of bees. Very large bees.

Ripper was aiming her rifle from doorway to doorway on the balconies above them. "What the hell is that?"

Odin was studying the Rover screen. "We're gonna need a new plan." He turned the screen to face them. It was a raven's-eye view, flying over the forested hills—following what looked like a massive flock of black birds, thousands strong. Except that they didn't move like birds; they swarmed low through and around the trees, hugging the land. Following something. The raven perspective showed that the cloud was moving, in surges and leaps, straight toward the house.

Foxy frowned. "What the hell . . . ?"

McKinney studied the image. "Oh, my God . . ."

Foxy, Tin Man, and Smokey came back in through the double doors. Foxy lowered the mirror shield. "What is it?"

Odin stowed the Rover. "Batten down the hatches, people. We're about to get hit, and if it's what I think it is, it means we shoot everything that moves."

The team started grabbing extra ammunition from the Pelican cases.

Ripper pulled her smaller, lighter ammo clip out and slapped a heavy, translucent, twin-drum magazine into her weapon. "Smokey, you got any spare drums for a HK416?"

"No, I wasn't packing for an assault."

"Mooch! Bag Hoov's body. We're taking him with us."

"Right." Mooch got busy, removing a body bag from his rucksack.

"Foxy!"

"Yeah?"

"What's the most defensible room in this house from a swarm?"

"Probably the garage. Stone walls, covered by hillside on two sides. There's a jeep there—no top, though. And I don't have the keys."

The humming sound was wrapping around the house now—forcing them to shout. The sound of shattering glass came from upstairs—front, back, sides. Everyone aimed weapons upward.

Smokey eyed the balconies warily. "Fuck me. . . ."

"We move to the garage. Now!" Odin grabbed McKinney and started moving across the foyer. "Any expert advice, Professor?"

McKinney stared upward with dread like the others. "Yes. Don't let them find us."

Smokey brought up the rear. "Thanks for the tip."

Just then a series of gunshots boomed outside the tall front doors, the wood splintering in around the door hardware and hinges. Bullets whined past in the foyer, shattering a vase and breaking the glass of a cabinet.

"Move! Move! Move!"

The doors started to disintegrate as dozens more bullets ripped through the wood.

As they reached the entrance to a hallway, Ripper pointed, aiming her weapon up. "There!"

They looked up to see dozens of black buzzing objects pouring over the upstairs balconies from several directions. They looked like toys, two-foot-diameter quadracopters with wiry frames and a central hub—not unlike a winged insect.

They seemed to respond to Ripper's movement or her shout, because they immediately surged downward in a gathering cloud.

Ripper opened up with her HK, a blade of fire stabbing out as she panned the ceiling, shell cases clattering across the floor around her. McKinney was surprised that her earphones seemed to cancel the loudness of the weapon, while still allowing her to hear her teammates on the intrateam radio.

Odin was shouting, "Ripper, move!"

Pieces of shattered plastic and entire quadracopters were raining down now, smashing into the floor around her as she ran toward them—firing upward the entire way in an uninterrupted burst. Smokey and Tin Man were also ripping the ceiling with short bursts from their HKs.

Foxy rushed past them, dragging Hoov's body bag by a strap, headed down the hall.

As Ripper reached the doorway, one of the wiry drones fell nearby and a shot rang out close in. Ripper grabbed her leg and fell into the doorway, bleeding. "Dammit!"

Mooch grabbed her by the collar, dragging her down the corridor, as Tin Man and Smokey raked the floorboards, shattering the wounded drones moving around there.

"These fucking things . . ."

The team was losing ground. Already hundreds more drones were swarming in from above. The hum was deafening and didn't seem to get canceled by their headsets.

And then the front doors pushed open and scores more poured in from outside.

Odin's voice. "Fall back! Fall back! Tin Man, Smokey, cover the rear. I'll pop smoke."

McKinney ran down a hallway lined with closed doors just ahead of Odin. She sniffed the air and caught a pervasive peppery scent enveloping them, but she ran on.

Behind him Mooch was dragging the wounded Ripper—who was cursing and flailing.

"Goddammit, Mooch, I can fucking walk! Let me go!"

Foxy stood in a left-side doorway at the end of the hall, motioning for her to enter, his weapon raised. "Go! Go! Go!"

Behind them Smokey and Tin Man were falling back in bounding overwatch, firing madly as they retreated, riddling the walls and doors with bullets, cycling through their big drum clips.

The drones poured through the doorway after them, but the narrow opening made their position more defensible. The devices blasted apart in midair and tumbled across the floor as they came in, their pieces piling up. But their frames seemed to be made of thick metal wire or tubing, because they largely kept their shape even after their core was shot out. They lay like dead insects on their backs, spiky legs pointing upward.

Smokey glanced back, "What the hell's that smell? You smell that?"

Tin Man nodded. "Like weak pepper spray. It's burning my eyes."

Odin tossed a smoke canister into the foyer, and it issued billowing clouds. He called back, "Foxy! How's our ride?"

A muted voice shouted, "Working on it!"

Smokey dropped his large drum clip and shouted, "Reloading!"

That's when Odin noticed that the swarm was already surging through the smoke.

Tin Man fell back to another doorway. "Goddammit!"

Odin nodded. "That's millimeter-wave particle smoke—and it doesn't even slow them down." He raised his auto-shotgun and began raking the doorway with buckshot that seemed particularly effective. He shouted at the others, "We won't have enough ammo to knock down half this swarm."

Tin Man got in a kneeling position. "Heads up! Forty Mike Mike. Fire in the hole!" He fired the grenade launcher bolted to the underside of his HK out the end of the hall into the smoke-filled foyer. There was a muffled flash and pieces of drones ricocheted everywhere—but the cloud soon swarmed in again through the smoke.

Tin Man pulled the receiver open and slid another forty-millimeter grenade into it while Odin sprayed the doorway with buckshot. FOOM! Another grenade went into the foyer with similar results.

"How many of these fucking things are there?"

"Behind you!"

Odin and Smokey turned to see Foxy pointing at a bedroom door near them. Bullet holes were blasting through near the doorknob, punching out panels in the door. Then the wall.

"Fall back! Smokey, Tin Man, back!"

They ran past the doorway, firing into it, and the swarm surged into the corridor behind them. Flames were visible rising along the foyer walls.

McKinney ducked back into a stone-walled two-car garage where Foxy was busy under the dashboard of a late-model crocus yellow Jeep. It had no roof, just padded roll bars. "You're kidding me. . . ."

"It's all we got, Professor. Unless you think we stand a chance reaching the SUVs in the driveway."

"No, I don't." McKinney noticed Hoov's body bag lying in the small cargo area. She turned to see Ripper sitting in the jeep's doorway as Mooch examined her calf. He was wrapping it in bandages.

"Small-caliber bullet. It'll keep."

"I fucking told you." She was reloading her weapon.

"Did you see what it was?"

"Looks like a goddamned zip gun. They have rows of them. They try to get you in close. They've got these beady insect eyes. . . ."

McKinney sniffed the air again. "Does anyone else smell that?"

Ripper nodded. "Like cayenne pepper?"

Mooch cut the bandage. McKinney ducked her head out to look down the hallway.

Odin glanced back at her. Although his expression was impossible to see behind his asymmetrical mask, his posture indicated they couldn't hold out long. Behind him all hell was breaking loose, with Tin Man and Smokey spraying machine gun fire and lobbing grenades.

Odin turned forward again, firing at a drone that came in from the side door. One blast from his shotgun caused it to detonate, blasting all three men off their feet and peppering the walls with shrapnel.

McKinney raced forward to grab Odin.

He shoved the auto-shotgun in her hands. "Shoot!" And crawled to assist Smokey, who was tugging at the screaming Tin Man. Blood covered Tin Man's legs, and a metal spike protruded from his thigh. Smokey was also bleeding in several places.

McKinney raised the heavy combat shotgun as a wave of drones surged forward in a way that was all too familiar from her research. She never thought she'd be facing weavers on their own level, but now that she was, she was really beginning to hate them. She opened up, and the recoil on the auto-shotgun wasn't as bad as she expected. She kept the trigger down and panned the hallway over the heads of Odin and Smokey, who were dragging the screaming Tin Man back.

Dozens of drones blasted apart as she fell back firing. She was surprised how satisfying it felt.

In a moment Smokey was up again, firing with his HK. "Got it, Professor."

McKinney lowered the smoking shotgun and reached down to help Odin drag Tin Man into the garage. There, Mooch took over.

Tin Man was cursing. "Motherfucker! I fell on one and a spike went through my leg. Their legs are aluminum spikes or some shit."

It appeared that the spike had already been pulled from his leg, and Mooch was applying pressure.

McKinney looked up to see that Odin had gone back into the hallway, but now he and Smokey were falling back into the garage again— Smokey spraying with his HK, Odin using a pistol. In a moment they pulled the door closed behind them. Odin pounded it. It sounded solid. "Fire-rated door. Should give us a few minutes."

They were both bleeding in several places.

Almost immediately the door began to deform in points with a popping sound—bullets being fired into it from the other side.

"Maybe not that long." Odin looked ahead to the thick wooden gates of the garage door. The sound of bots surging against them rattled the doors.

McKinney held out his shotgun, and Odin grabbed it. "Thanks, Professor. Looks like we're even."

"Do you smell that?"

"The pepper?"

"Yeah. I think they're laying down a pheromone matrix—like weavers. They probably release it as an attack signal."

Odin nodded. "Interesting."

Mooch looked up from ministering to Tin Man. "How bad are you, Odin?"

"Bullet fragments. Nothing serious. Foxy!"

"What?"

"If you don't get that jeep started, we are fucked."

"I appreciate your encouragement, but the battery was dead. I'm rigging an alternate with the comm set."

Odin pulled the Rover tablet out of a pouch and looked at a raven's-eye image of the house—from hundreds of feet above.

McKinney watched over his shoulder. The house was almost lost beneath the black swarm. They hadn't even made a dent in it.

"What about Huginn and Muninn?"

"Ravens can outfly eagles. I'm betting they can outfly these things." Odin tapped the screen. "Well, your computer model seems to work, Professor."

"I'd like to get one. Examine it."

The team groaned.

Ripper muttered. "You can study it while it's chewing your fucking eyeballs out."

The jeep's ignition suddenly cycled, and the engine roared to life.

The group let up a shout. The hallway door was suddenly penetrated with a bullet hole. The projectile whined off the garage wall.

Odin motioned. "Load up! Professor, you're a maniac at the wheel. You drive."

"I don't know where I'm going—"

"Downhill. We'll handle defense. Do it! Go!"

McKinney crawled over the side into the driver's seat, strapping herself in.

Odin grabbed an aluminum baseball bat leaning against the wall. "Everyone grab a club. We can't use guns if they get in close quarters."

Smokey grabbed several hammers off a pegboard above a worktable and tossed them to teammates. "Here." Mooch grabbed a tire iron.

Everyone piled into the jeep, and with seven people it was tight. Foxy sat up front in the passenger seat, with Ripper, Mooch, and Tin Man pressed into the small backseat. Behind them, hanging on to the roll bars, were Odin and Smokey, trying to avoid kneeling on Hoov's bagged body.

The group with proper seats was fastening and cinching seat belts. Tightening gun slings.

"Don't take your helmets off. We've still got sniper stations out there." Odin nodded to Smokey and Mooch as he looped his combat harness around the roll bar. "And if you don't have a seat belt, strap yourself to something—we're going overland, and it's going to get rough."

Bullets blasted the doorknob out of the garage's interior door.

"You ready, Professor?"

She was examining the controls. Thankfully the jeep had an automatic transmission. One less thing to focus on. "Where am I going?"

"Just head downhill however you can. You can't miss the landing strip. Then make for the hangar at the south end."

"Who's opening these garage doors?"

"Blow through them. And whatever you do: Drive fast, and keep driving fast. Even if we're on fire and dead, keep driving fast. Do you understand?"

"Those instructions are pretty clear."

The interior door popped and shuddered.

He slapped her shoulder. "Now! Execute, execute, execute!"

McKinney put the jeep into drive and revved the engine. Apparently this was a six-cylinder, because the acceleration was good as they hurtled toward the green wooden garage doors.

The steel push bar of the jeep blasted back the twin doors, momentarily sweeping aside part of a seething black cloud— even smashing a few drones against the stone walls of the house. It was actually dark out because of the hundreds of drones, buzzing so loudly that the sound entered McKinney's middle ear—unnerving and terrifying.

She could barely make out the landscape ahead. The two Forest Service SUVs were parked off to the right, blocking the driveway behind a whirl of drones. So McKinney accelerated the jeep straight ahead into the cloud, aiming between two large pine trees at the edge of the gravel driveway.

Foxy next to her, along with several team members behind her, opened up with machine guns and shotguns, blasting apart the drones in front—which were quickly replaced by new ones pressing in.

They collided with the cloud of two-foot-wide machines, which ricocheted and bumped off the fenders and windshield. The impact was instantly followed by the crackling of gunfire and acrid, sulfurous smoke. Shouts of pain. Spattering of blood. The windshield pocked with a spider's web of cracks, and she heard bullets whining past nearby. Several loud *thwacks* came to her ears as pieces of plastic and tufts of upholstery foam popped into the air around her. The steering wheel suddenly felt sluggish, as if a tire—or several—were flat.

But she kept her foot hard on the accelerator, and the jeep roared on. And then suddenly they were hurtling into space, falling.

The jeep lurched up as it impacted lower on the hillside. Having jumped off the level parking area, they were now racing downslope through sparse pine forest at forty or fifty miles an hour. She cranked the wheel to the left to avoid a large rock, only to discover that steering on pine needles was like swimming through melted marshmallows. The front tires trembled as though flat, and it required every ounce of strength to keep the jeep under control.

But McKinney kept the pedal down as she slalomed between the trees. She glanced in the rearview mirror to see a black cloud hurtling through the forest after them—behind that the upper stories of the house were engulfed in flames. But as she looked left and right she saw clear air—no drones. The team was shouting, whether in relief, encouragement, or warning, she didn't know.

Odin's voice in her ear. "Keep heading downhill."

A burst of machine gun fire behind her.

"If you hit a dirt road, turn left. That'll lead you right to it."

"The front tires are flat."

"Just keep going!"

McKinney drove on, dodging trees, while the cloud maintained a distance of a couple of hundred feet behind them. She wondered about that. Was it the delay it took them to transmit the pursuit message to the others? Whatever the reason, it had given them time enough to break through.

In any event, there wasn't much margin for error. Get stuck in a rut or strike a tree, and they were all as good as dead. She focused as she slid and weaved the jeep between trees, running now over nearly level ground. And then a dirt road did appear through the trees ahead, almost perpendicular to her. McKinney started to angle the jeep, veering left. She could see a ditch next to the road and figured it would be safer to cross if she was running nearly parallel to it.

Heavy brush forced her hand, and she had no choice but to drive straight for the road, taking the ditch head-on. A jolting lurch, and they landed on the roadway, veering toward the far side. She corrected, and they were now racing on the road, headed downhill—and toward a tall, corrugated metal building with no windows.

Foxy smacked her arm. "Straight ahead, Professor."

Odin shouted, "Drive to the far side of the hangar. There's a door there. Foxy, you able to move okay?"

McKinney glanced over and for the first time noticed that Foxy appeared to have been shot in the side. His glove was spattered with blood.

"There's sure as hell no way I'm staying out here."

"Okay, even before the jeep stops, I want you to hop out and get that door open. We'll be right on your tail with the rest of the wounded."

McKinney was already racing around the side of the hangar building. It was easily seventy feet on a side. A level grass landing strip stretched out before them. She glanced in her rearview mirror and saw that the swarm of drones wasn't far behind. Perhaps a few hundred meters now.

"Keep our speed up!"

McKinney brought the jeep thumping on flat tires around the far side of the hangar, next to a steel door. She slid to a stop, unbuckling her seat belt. The hum of the swarm was already growing louder.

"Move! Move! Move!" Odin looked up and whistled at the ravens— which were already diving down to meet them.

Smokey hefted the body bag containing Hoov out of the cargo bay, while McKinney helped Odin pull Tin Man over the side of the jeep. Tin Man sucked it up and moved under his own steam while they helped him toward the door that Foxy was already unlocking. The others were close behind. Everyone was bleeding from major or minor wounds.

As they pushed through the doorway into a sizable hangar with a concrete floor, McKinney felt a wave of relief pass over her—even though the sound of drones smacking into the building like hail was already sweeping around from the far side.

"Close that door!"

Odin waited until Huginn and Muninn flew past, and then he pulled the metal door shut with a *boom*. The humming sound went down a few decibels.

The team was already rushing forward to a large single-engine plane that McKinney recognized—a Cessna Grand Caravan. She'd seen them used as bush cargo planes. This one was painted white with green and yellow stripes and looked fairly new.

"Smokey, secure the twins. There's a cage in the cargo hold."

"On it."

Ripper already had the cargo doors open, and she was limping around to the pilot door. Blood soaked her lower leg.

"You okay to fly, Ripper?"

She gave Odin a look. "Just get in the damn plane."

Smokey lifted Hoov's body bag into the hold and climbed up after it.

McKinney climbed in through the wide cargo door as the ravens flew in past her. Spatters of blood were already staining the floor and upholstery. She grabbed one of several seats in front of the cargo area, while Smokey urged the ravens into the safety of a black mesh cage. There were a few boxes and equipment cases, but the cargo bay was nearly empty.

Smokey looked up. "Should we toss the cargo?"

Ripper was flicking switches with headphones on. She shook her head. "No time."

Foxy climbed into the copilot seat and put on headphones too. "How we getting these hangar doors open?"

Ripper pointed.

Odin was standing next to the hangar doors, his hand over a switch. He held up an arm, giving several signs Ripper seemed to understand.

"Let's hope this damn hangar holds together long enough to pull this off."

The turboprop engine began to whine to life.

McKinney leaned forward. "You're starting the engine—in a closed hangar?"

"Like I said, Professor. Keep your fingers crossed."

The engine thundered to life, and Odin hit the hangar door switch. McKinney watched in horror as he raced the eighty or so feet toward them, the doors opening ever wider.

Foxy shouted, "Run, goddamn you!"

A cloud of drones started issuing through the widening opening between the twin hangar doors. Before the swarm could orient itself, Odin reached the open cargo door and leapt inside.

"Get the hatch!"

Smokey reached out to get the hatch as the swarm raced toward the plane. Several lead ones disintegrated amid sparks in the whirling propeller blade, but two slipped past in the high wind and tumbled into the passenger area before Smokey got the hatch closed.

Odin grabbed an equipment case as a weapon. "Look out! Get them!"

The buzzing, insectlike quadrocopters quickly righted themselves and launched around the passenger cabin, one rushing straight for Smokey's face. He bashed it aside with the butt of his HK416.

The other one streaked right toward McKinney, who was strapped into her seat. She knocked it away with her hand as it fired a bullet with a deafening bang that grazed her wrist. One moment later, and the bullet would have gone right between her eyes. She ducked and unbuckled her seat belt—unsure where the drone had gone. "Where is it?"

Ripper shouted, "Everybody hold on!" She rammed the throttle forward, and the plane surged ahead. Smokey, Odin, Mooch, and the two drones they were contending with slid back toward the rear of the Cessna as dozens of drone bodies clattered along the outside the fuselage or disappeared in a cloud of sparks into the plane's propeller.

Smokey pressed his boot down on one of the rotor mounts of the drone, pinning it to the floor. He then repeatedly smashed his rifle butt into its circuit board core—crushing its optic array. "Die, fucker!"

As he pounded the small machine, it fired its several small-caliber bullets from tubes on its metal frame—at least one bullet catching Smokey in the ankle before it died.

"Goddammit!" He toppled back.

They were roaring along the airstrip now, nearing eighty miles an hour. The tree line raced past, and the drone swarm fell behind.

Huginn and Muninn *caw*ed angrily inside their cage as Odin hurled a heavy equipment case at the remaining drone hovering toward the front. "Tin Man, get it!"

By now the cabin was spattered in blood as the wounded team clambered around trying to destroy the last drone.

But the device headed straight for McKinney. She deflected it with the trauma plates strapped to her arm, but it kept driving up against her, its electric blades humming.

She was both horrified and riveted by its appearance this close. It was a simple four-rotor helicopter with blade enclosures, but the frame seemed to be made of thick wire, ending in spiky legs. In the center pod, held in the metal frame, was a series of tightly packed circuit boards and a row of four lenses—its "eyes." Next to that, in racks, were what looked to be silver compressed-air canisters—the type of thing whipped cream was dispensed with. But these seemed to be spraying the air with some type of chemical that had a faint peppery smell—a pseudopheromone, marking her. And then stacked to either side of the core body were what turned out to be gun barrels.

This is what was *crack*ing at her as she struggled to kick it away. Bullets pinged off her trauma plates, but then she felt a piercing pain in her upper leg, just as Odin smashed the drone into the floor, and Mooch bashed its core in with his rifle butt.

"Dammit!" She'd never experienced such pain. McKinney writhed on the cabin floor now in a rapidly expanding pool of blood. She raised her gloved hand to see arterial blood spurting out of a hole on her inner thigh.

"Oh, my God . . ."

Mooch came up alongside her. "Professor's hit!"

Odin knelt down next to her as well.

Scenery raced by outside, and then McKinney felt gravity press her into the floor, and the trees at the edge of her vision disappeared. "Did we make it?"

Odin got close to her face. "You're going to be all right."

The pain was incredible. "Oh, God. Let me see it!"

"No, lay back."

She could feel someone cutting through her pant leg.

Odin turned. "Mooch, how's it look?"

"Femoral artery—close to the pelvis. Tourniquet's out. Keep the pressure on. Here."

She felt another pain as something was jabbed into her leg. And then a soothing feeling came over her. A warm sensation. Calm.

Odin's face was right next to hers. He seemed calm too. Normal. She was fading. Her consciousness was ebbing.

"Pass me that Hespan." The tearing of plastic.

Foxy's voice. "How is she?"

A serious look crossed Odin's face.

McKinney felt her vision narrow. Darkness ebbing in like rising water over her face. Hands on her side. Then on her back.

"I need to contain this bleeding. Or she isn't going to make it."

McKinney's focus faded. She tried to speak, but she was so tired now. She sank below the waves. Into the blackness. Into silence.

CHAPTER 22

Sanctuary

Linda McKinney awoke to a warm breeze wafting over her face. As her eyes came into focus, she could see gauzy white curtains trailing away from a row of tall windows, undulating with the flowing air. The sun shone in, blinding white. She lay beneath a crisp linen sheet in a proper bed with a sturdy headboard made of rough-hewn pine. Clean down pillows cradled her head. Thick wooden beams traversed the ceiling above her. The walls were of mortared stone. This was an old place. A cross hung from the wall above the bed, and along the wall nearby were framed icons of saints and sepia-toned photos of brown-skinned, black-haired ancestors in starched collars and black dresses.

McKinney felt a sting in her hand and noticed an IV drip running from a needle taped in place in the top of her right hand. It led to an IV bag on a stand nearby. Her right leg felt tight near her pelvis, as though wrapped in bandages—and a biting pain came to her from somewhere deep in her upper thigh. She felt the tautness of stitches.

There was a gentle *keek-keek* sound.

McKinney looked to the footboard. A large raven regarded her and extended its wings. It then ruffled its throat and head feathers. *Caw.*

McKinney's voice came out hoarsely. "Muninn." She wasn't sure why she knew the bird was female. Perhaps it was something in the bird's manner. She just felt like she knew.

The raven *caw*ed loudly several times, then flew off between the gauzy curtains and out the window.

There were footsteps, and the heavy bedroom door opened to reveal an elderly woman with a deeply tanned, timeworn face. Her long gray hair was wrapped tightly, and she wore a dress of rough brown cloth with a richly embroidered white apron and collar.

McKinney nodded to her.

The old woman spoke soothingly. *"Kehaca ti ictok."* She held up one hand.

McKinney tried to remember what Spanish she'd mastered on previous expeditions to South America. But then, she'd spent more time in the Amazon basin. Portuguese wasn't going to help. Even so, this didn't sound like Spanish. She cleared her throat and spoke in slow English. "Where is this place?"

The old woman smiled kindly, holding her arm and patting it gently. *"Ni we-wen ci."* She turned to the heavy oak door bound by black iron hinges. "Lalenia! Lalenia!" The old woman's powerful voice startled McKinney. Dogs barked from somewhere outside. McKinney tried to sit up a bit in bed.

More footsteps, and in a moment the heavy door opened again, revealing a much younger Latina in jeans and a white shirt. Her long black hair was tied back to reveal a beautiful almond-shaped face with mocha brown skin. She approached the bed and smiled, motioning to the old woman as she spoke in that same language. *"Wala seh yanok Ratón."*

Then the younger woman turned to McKinney and spoke in Spanish-accented English. "How do you feel, Professor McKinney?"

McKinney looked around the room. "Weak. Where am I?"

"You're in Tamaulipas near Kalitlen." At McKinney's blank stare she added, "Rural Mexico."

"How long have I been unconscious?"

The young woman leaned over to say something quietly to the elderly woman, who nodded and left. The young woman then approached the side of the bed, producing a penlight from her shirt pocket. "You've been unconscious for several days. You lost a great deal of blood, and we've been rebuilding your platelet count."

McKinney kept her eyes open as the woman checked her pupil dilation with the light. "I got shot."

"Yes, I know. The bullet nicked your femoral artery." The doctor lowered the penlight. "You were very lucky the damage wasn't worse."

McKinney remembered wrestling with a hellish toy—one whose brain she'd helped design. "Yes." She felt suddenly very tired.

"Mooch is a talented surgeon. He was able to stop the bleeding, but it was close. And having O-positive blood probably saved your life."

"Who are you?"

The woman placed a hand on her own chest. "I am Doctor Garza. You can call me Lalenia. We are in a very remote part of Mexico here. We don't engage in formalities."

"Your English is excellent."

"I went to medical school in the States."

"What was that other language?"

"That was Huastec, a Mayan dialect. My family has owned land here for generations. Rosario taught it to me when I was very young."

"Medical school. Your parents must be proud."

The young doctor became subdued. "My parents are no longer with me." She took McKinney's pulse, listening for several moments.

The door opened again, and this time a well-toned and muscular African-American man with a smooth bald head entered. He wore a Nike tank top shirt and cargo shorts. He was a striking male specimen in perfect physical shape. But what surprised McKinney was that he was missing both his legs beneath the knees. In their place were metal alloy prosthetic legs that he employed with such grace, she would never have known it if he weren't wearing shorts. The prosthetic limbs ended in brightly colored running shoes that he apparently tied on just like anyone else.

Lalenia brightened considerably when he entered. "Ratón, look who's up."

The muscular man smiled a tight, distorted smile as he walked to the end of McKinney's bed. She could see now that the right side of his face was disfigured from a grievous wound whose scar tissue pulled at the side of his mouth. A horrendous scar ran along the side of his head to a stunted ear. He also appeared to be missing his right eye and had in place a false eye as black as onyx. He placed his hands on the footboard and she could see he was missing several fingers from his left hand as well. He had once been a handsome man, but he seemed not to notice.

He met her gaze and nodded. Then he spoke in a deep, mellow voice. "So, you're the one who broke out of Odin's isolation facility." He started laughing midsentence. "That shows dash, Professor."

McKinney stared at him. "Ratón . . . Mouse. You're Mouse."

"You've heard of me."

"A man named Ritter mentioned you. He made it sound as though you were—"

"Dead?" He nodded. "On paper, I guess I am."

Lalenia walked over and kissed him on the cheek. "Not even close, baby."

McKinney could see how much they cared for each other. Whatever scars he bore, Lalenia clearly did not see them.

Mouse focused on McKinney. "You ran into some difficulties back in the States."

"Are we safe here?"

"Safe is relative. From them, perhaps, but only because you're in the middle of a war zone. The cartels killed thirteen thousand people here last year. There's more killing going on here than in Afghanistan."

McKinney was at a loss for words. "Are you serious?"

"Most Americans have no idea how bad the fighting is down here. This will be JSOC's next battlefield, Professor. Mark my words. Mexico's constitution might prohibit U.S. boots on the ground, but there are workarounds."

Odin walked in suddenly from the open doorway. He was wearing a faded gray T-shirt and jeans. He nodded to McKinney and let a slight grin escape. "I was worried about you for a while there."

McKinney suddenly felt the reality of the situation. "I'm still worried about me. I can't go home. And how long until they send machines here to kill us?"

He met her gaze and nodded grimly back. "Get some rest, Professor."

Exhaustion came quickly to McKinney for quite some time, and she slept often. A week later she was sitting in the courtyard of a substantial-looking stone hacienda with a terra-cotta tile roof, enjoying the sunshine. The Christmas holiday and New Year's had already come and gone, and she was morose with worry for her father. And for her brothers as well.

McKinney watched local children playing soccer in a dusty road nearby. She could see them through a wrought iron gate in a stone wall that enclosed one side of the courtyard. Their shouts brought back memories of Adwele playing with schoolmates in Tanzania. She wondered how he was coping with her sudden disappearance. Reaching out to him now would only put him in danger. She was helpless to do anything.

Instead, she stared into the distance. Beyond the houses were steep forested mountains, with clouds towering overhead. It was beautiful, but all she could think about was how to get back to her old life—and how impossible that now seemed.

Odin's voice broke her reverie. "They said you were up and about."

She looked up to see him standing in a nearby doorway.

"How are you feeling?"

McKinney shrugged. "Physically better. Psychologically, not so much."

Odin came up clutching something wrapped in a burlap sack. He laid it on the table between them and sat in one of the rattan chairs next to her. Then he poured a cup of coffee from a steel pot nearby.

"How do you know about this place?"

"Years ago. We came down on an operation for the GWOT." Seeing her confused expression he added, "The Global War on Terror. After 9/11 there were concerns about terrorists crossing the border, arms smuggling, that sort of thing. Turns out, the weapons were being smuggled the other way—from the U.S. to Mexico. We got caught up in a drug war."

McKinney studied him. "You perplex me."

"Why?"

"I just . . . why do you seek out war?"

He shrugged. "It's what I'm good at. And there's a bond you develop in war that's hard to find in civilian life. People you can trust your life to."

"But why get involved in Mexico's drug war?"

"'Cause we were here. There's a small number of vicious people destroying Mexican society to smuggle drugs into the U.S. Killing judges, reporters, men, women, children. We helped the locals who were trying to stop it. Those weren't our orders, but we weren't about to stand around and do nothing."

"And Mouse?"

Odin nodded. "He met Lalenia. She refused to leave after the cartels killed her parents and her brothers and uncles. After they met, Mouse was always looking for an excuse to return here."

"Is that how he . . . ?" She gestured to her legs.

"IED. Central Asia. A few years back. Lalenia came up to Virginia to help him through physical therapy." He pondered the memory. "Mouse was my commander, Professor. Team leader before me. He taught me everything I know. I needed his advice, and a safe place to regroup."

"Apparently they think he's dead."

Odin nodded. "He's a legend down here. *El Ratón*—the Mouse. The cartels respect him. They found out the hard way that he's an expert at insurgent warfare. He trained the locals to defend their land. To push the cartels out. Before that they were finding a dozen bodies in the street every morning. That's over now."

McKinney sat listening to the kids playing soccer for a while. The children laughing—untroubled by the momentous events of the world.

She gestured to the covered object in the center of the table. "What's in the sack?"

"Something you should see. I didn't want to alarm you until you were better."

"I've been alarmed ever since I met you."

"Okay, then . . ." He unfolded the burlap to reveal one of the black weaver-drone quadracopters that had attacked them in Colorado.

A slightly irrational fear gripped her. It was clearly dead—damaged and missing half its rotors. As a scientist, she was angered by irrational fears, so she tamped it down and leaned forward to look at the drone.

The core of it looked mostly intact, although none of the rotors at its four corners was still whole. The spikelike metal feet protruded menacingly, clearly sharpened like metal thorns.

"We managed to reconstruct this one by cannibalizing parts from the two that got into the plane cabin." He picked up the lightweight device. "It wasn't difficult. I get the feeling these were meant to be assembled by semiskilled workers. They're modular, cheap. Mostly dual-use off-the-shelf parts. Circuit boards. Memory chips. Batteries. Optical sensors."

She extended her hand, and he passed the dead drone to her. McKinney's curiosity had already bested her anxiety, and she peered into its recesses, rotating it around. The broken propellers flopped around at the ends of wires. Her nose caught the peppery scent she remembered from the Colorado swarm. "There's that smell again. Like cayenne pepper. I'd like to know the chemical composition."

Odin nodded. "Mouse knows a few local chemists. Ex-cartel people. I'll see if he can get it analyzed."

She kept sniffing and traced it to nozzles next to a row of silvery capsules in the frame. They looked like the nitrous oxide cartridges used for whipped cream or the CO_2 propellant in paintball guns. "Four capsules. Like the chemical glands of a weaver. Mixing them in varying proportions to communicate different messages. That would match ant behavior. It's how they lay down a pheromone matrix."

"So they were leaving a trail."

"It's probably how they incite each other to attack. Each new arrival at a scene reinforces the attack message by spraying more pheromone. But that also means they'd need some way to read each other's chemical pheromones."

"Like an electronic nose."

"Right." McKinney ran her finger along one of four forward-facing wire antennas that were studded with tiny microchips.

Odin peered closely right next to her.

"Weaver ants—ants in general, actually—have dozens of sensilla on their antennas. They detect all sorts of things, chemical traces, heat, humidity. If these devices are running my weaver model, then they'd respond to numeric pheromonal input values. It's virtual in my simulations, but here it could be a concentration measurement received from a hardware sensor. Weavers also transmit information to each other by touch, vibration." She ran her fingers along each antenna, noting half a dozen small nodules.

"They transmit data to each other physically as well?"

McKinney nodded. "It allows them to move information through the swarm separate of the pheromones."

"And we wouldn't be able to jam that communication with radio countermeasures either."

"I suppose that's true of both the chemical and touch communication. But also, I was wondering how they found us—how they detected we were in the house, and where."

"I was wondering about that too. These stupid little bots outperformed any system I've ever seen. We were wearing cool suits to hide our thermal signature and AD armor to conceal our human shape and faces. That fooled the sniper stations in the hills, but not these bastards. I was thinking maybe they reacted to noise or movement."

McKinney shook her head. "If they're using the weaver model I created, they'd focus on organic compound sensors. Ants have receptors in their antennas that help them identify food. Maybe—"

"You're saying they smelled us?"

"Or tasted us." She sighed. "I know it sounds silly, but that's part of what weavers do when they swarm. They detect food sources by trace chemicals— in much the same way as they read each other's pheromone messages."

Odin seemed to be contemplating something. "It doesn't sound silly at all, in fact."

"What?"

"There's a technology—well known in counterterrorism work, used by customs and Homeland Security. It's called 'C-Scout MAS.' We used it while hunting for high-value insurgent targets."

She examined one of the dead drone's antennas. "I don't know it."

"It's an electronic nose that sniffs the air to detect human presence. Apparently there are fifteen chemicals that indicate human presence by the breath we exhale—things like acetone, pentane, hexane, isoprene, benzene, heptane, alpha-Pinene. You get the idea. They appear in a specific ratio wherever people are breathing—the more concentrated it is, the closer people are or the more people there are."

"You're saying this technology is currently in use?"

"The detectors were on a microchip."

She manipulated the articulated antennas on the dead drone. "Then maybe these drones find people in their vicinity by the gases we exhale—just like weavers would detect food. That would actually work well with my model. They could be coded to identify whatever they're hunting by chemical signature—moving toward greater concentrations of the target scent and away from decreasing concentrations. That relatively simple algorithm is how my model works, and it manifests itself as complex hunting behavior when scaled up to a swarm of stigmergic agents."

"We were breathing fast. Keyed up. We must have seemed like glowing neon signs to these things."

McKinney was already looking more closely at the drone's innards.

The drone had an aluminum tube frame, in the center of which was a wire box acting as ribs protecting the core. There was a stack of computer boards there, vision sensors all around, thin antennas—both leading and trailing—and wiring. Then along both sides were what looked to be steel cylinders—four in all.

Odin tapped them. "Zip guns. These were thirty-eights. They slide in on tracks, so it looks like they can have various weapon loads. The other one had .410 shotgun shells."

"They're flying hand guns."

"Dirt-cheap, highly inaccurate guns—but effective enough in close quarters."

She examined what looked to be ports in the back. Charging sockets? There were also LED lights, all dead, but curious nonetheless. "If these run on my model, an appropriate number of workers would be 'feeding' the others. With weavers they pass along nectar—liquid food. Here, they probably pass along electricity, battery power. There seem to be electro-mechanical analogs for all the inputs and outputs of weaver swarm intelligence manifested in these things."

She tossed it back onto the table in disgust. "But it looks like a toy. An evil toy designed by some sick, twisted—"

"Those 'toys' nearly killed all of us, and if we hadn't fled, they would have. Lalenia pulled ten bullets out of our team, and that's with body armor on." He rewrapped the drone in its burlap shroud. "These things could be churned out of just about any contract factory in the industrialized world. Shipped anywhere by the thousands—just like toys."

She looked up at him. "Oh, it's worse than that. Those inputs and outputs—the stimuli and the response—they can take just about any morphology. These zip guns could just as easily be missiles. Those tiny rotors just as easily jet turbines."

He narrowed his eyes at her.

"Ants are what's called a 'polymorphic' species—they have various caste groups that can differ widely in size. For example, *Pheidologeton diversus*—the marauder ant—has supermajor warriors that are five hundred times the mass of one of their minor workers. And yet they are the same species and operate with the same brain—and belong to the same colony."

"You're saying these things could be easily scaled up using the same software brain."

She gestured to the dead drone on the table. "I'm saying this might just have been a low-cost test version. A prototype. They could easily be made bigger."

He contemplated this news. "Which means they will be. And I'll need to take action before that happens."

"Take action?" she asked. "I don't know if you've noticed, but we're all in hiding. The entire military-industrial complex wants us dead."

"Not the entire military-industrial complex." He looked calm and sipped his coffee. "Just part of it."

She threw up her hands. "Oh. Well, then it's the part that can monitor the FBI, fake your satellite communications, launch killer drones, and manipulate the media."

He nodded. "Most of the military's logistics have been privatized. Its computer systems. Its networks. Satellites. But there are still people behind it all, and most people who work in defense are just plain folks trying to protect their country. That's our advantage. We just need to uncover who's behind this. And I'm guessing it's not a large group. That's the appeal of these machines. They seem like something that would save American lives, but once built, they can be quietly controlled by a small number of unaccountable people. No coffins coming home from their secret wars." He nodded to himself again. "But finding a small number of unaccountable people is doable."

She stared at the table. "I don't share your optimism. Weaver ants have survived almost unchanged for a hundred million years because they dominate every environment. If someone's supersized them, and that design is out there—then what's to stop this from spreading? You remember what Ritter said: Everyone wants this."

"We were able to come to an international agreement about nuclear and biological weapons. So we should be able to come to some agreement about robotic weapons too."

"Odin!"

They both turned to see a group of young boys at the gate. The lead one rolled a soccer ball on the tips of his fingers. He wore a bright yellow soccer shirt with the number twelve on it, but the other boys were in a mishmash of clothing.

The lead boy called out, *"Mira, todavía tengo la pelota que me diste, quieres patear?"*

The other boys urged Odin on.

He turned to McKinney. "If you'll excuse me, I'm being challenged to a contest of skill." He stood and walked toward the gate. *"Bueno, Pelé, vamos a ver como las mueves. . . ."* He hopped the wall, and the knot of boys took off after him down the street, laughing as mangy dogs barked and ran alongside them.

McKinney grinned slightly, watching through the gate, as Odin kicked the ball around with a growing knot of boys. He leaned down and said something that made them all laugh uproariously. It was a side of Odin she'd never seen. He seemed a natural ringleader, and it was apparent these boys knew Odin. They were at ease around him. She found it hard to square this side of him with the elite warrior.

She nearly jumped out of her skin when another voice spoke right next to her. "Mind if I join you?"

McKinney turned to see Mouse standing in the doorway of the hacienda. "My God, you scared me; I didn't hear you come up."

Mouse sat where Odin had just been. "That's how I got my nickname." He looked at Odin directing the boys into teams in the quiet, dusty road. "Ah, soccer. My game has suffered a bit."

"I wouldn't have guessed he was good with kids."

Mouse nodded in the group's direction. "They look up to him. He understands what they're going through."

"What's that?"

"They're orphans."

McKinney now looked with concern at the young boys.

"Lalenia runs an orphanage for the children of the disappeared. It's a lot of kids."

McKinney looked into the street. "I knew David was an orphan, but I had no idea about these children."

Mouse observed her closely for several moments. "He told you his real name?" He turned to watch Odin playing referee of an impromptu soccer match. "That's interesting."

"He didn't exactly tell me. Another man said it in front of me. Some guy named Ritter—the same man who mentioned you. But David said his own name wasn't important—that 'Shaw' was just the street they found him on."

"He told you that much? And he brought you here. Are you two . . . ?"

She held up her hands. "Oh . . . no! No, we're just . . . colleagues."

"Didn't mean to embarrass you. It's just that he doesn't usually share information about himself. David doesn't trust people easily." Mouse studied her with his remaining good eye.

Nonetheless it felt like he was looking right through her. She squirmed.

"I worry that he's missing a big part of life."

"I imagine in his line of work trust doesn't come easily."

"You forget: I'm in the same line of work. And he came to us like this. As a kid, pretty much everyone who should have taken care of him, didn't. He had difficulties. Learning disabilities. Turns out instead of being stupid, he was just very, very smart. No one checked. He grew up in juvie halls."

McKinney watched Odin holding the ball up, the kids screaming with laughter. "Why are you telling me this?"

"Because that man is a brother to me. I love him like my own flesh and blood. David projects an image of invulnerability—like nothing can hurt him—but we both know that's not true."

McKinney nodded slowly and turned to see Odin bringing the soccer ball to one of the smaller boys.

Mouse took a deep breath and tapped the table. "The militia's having a celebration tonight. To welcome back the old team. I hope you'll come."

"I'm not really up for a celebration."

"There's no better time to celebrate friendship than when things are at their worst." With one last tap on the table he stood and silently departed.

In the cool evening air the courtyard of the hacienda was filled with locals dressed in a wide array of inexpensive, but new, clothing—men in modern slacks with bright print shirts, cowboy hats, and boots; the women in cotton dresses and shawls. The courtyard was strung with white lights, and a stage had been set up against a wall near the garden, on which a large band of guitarists, violinists, vocalists—and even a harpist—were playing. The audience had cleared away tables and was dancing joyously.

McKinney limped along with a cane and stood next to a large tree, observing the festivities. It was a type of Mexican music she'd never heard before. No horns—almost like country or bluegrass. With a lively beat.

The aroma of a whole pig roasting over a fire pit came to her, along with that of vegetables and fruit being grilled. Tequila and beer flowed, along with wine. There were smiling faces and laughter all around her. She remembered this from war-torn areas of the world. No one treasured happy moments more than those going through dark times. Mouse was right about that. Community was what sustained people.

At the far end of the courtyard, among armed militiamen, Odin's team was gathered in a circle, their arms around each other. Some of them looked seriously inebriated. McKinney could see the grief in their expressions. Smokey in particular wept as Odin rubbed his crew-cut head, comforting him. Foxy raised a beer bottle, and they all poured it onto the ground before them. It appeared to be a memorial rite for their fallen comrade.

Doctor Garza put her arm around McKinney. "How are you feeling, Professor?"

McKinney looked up. "Stiff, but I decided to take Mouse's advice."

"Good. You need to exercise the leg. No dancing, though."

McKinney laughed. "Don't worry." She gestured to the band. "I've never heard a mariachi band like this."

"That's because it's not mariachi. It's a *conjunto huasteco* ensemble— probably a little different to your ears. Oh, look. . . ." She pointed to Foxy, who had suddenly appeared onstage. He grabbed a small guitar as the band urged him to join them. "Foxy has a rare gift for the *son huasteco*. He must have some Mayan blood in him somewhere." She grinned mischievously.

McKinney noticed that the group of mourning commandos had already broken up, and Foxy was taking the stage as the audience cheered and shouted encouragement.

"Foxy, toca una canción!"

There was laughter and people clapping. McKinney couldn't help but smile. On the edge of the gathering there were children as well, dancing and playing. Their laughter was infectious, as they shouted for Foxy to play.

Foxy started boldly strumming his borrowed Spanish guitar, and the crowd roared their approval as he fell in with the rest of the band. But soon he began to play around their music, weaving rhythms in and out as people cheered. He began to sing with a rich baritone voice. It was stirring, passionate music, whose lyrics McKinney couldn't understand. But that wasn't quite true. She could feel the bittersweet story in the emotion of music. It was just as Foxy had said back in Kansas City. Music transcended language.

McKinney had to admit the man had talent, all the more surprising given his headbanger proclivities. But she could see the truth in his belief that music connected people. All around them was joy, even amid sadness.

Mouse suddenly appeared out of the crowd and took Doctor Garza's hand. "Señorita . . ."

Garza laughed and turned to McKinney as he led her to the dance floor. "Excuse me, Professor."

McKinney smiled. "By all means."

But just then she also felt a tap on her shoulder. She turned to see Odin. He stood silently for a moment as others moved around them.

McKinney motioned to her cane. "Doctor says I shouldn't—"

"Follow me." Instead of heading to the dance floor, he motioned for her to follow him as he headed toward the edge of the crowd. "I need you to see something."

"Now?"

"Yes. Our guests are only here for tonight." He was already moving ahead, and she limped after him with the cane. In a few moments it was apparent that he was leading her toward a barn not far from the main house. On the way, just beyond the lights and noise of the celebration, she was surprised to see armed militiamen standing guard in the darkness. They all nodded to Odin as he passed. It reminded her about another truth of war—there were no time-outs.

When they reached the barn, Odin brought her through a gap in the open doors into what appeared to be a workshop. Two men were gathered around a well-lit workbench there, one a younger Asian man, the other a distinguished-looking Mexican man in his fifties. Both were clearly dressed for the party but were now busy examining the damaged drone Odin's team had reassembled from their encounter in Colorado.

The men both looked up as Odin and McKinney approached.

Odin nodded to them, gesturing to McKinney. "Gustavo, Tegu, this is the professor."

They both nodded back and extended their hands. "Professor."

Odin turned to McKinney. "Tegu used to manage communications for smugglers, and Gustavo was a senior chemist for the drug cartel that controlled this region."

"You're a chemist?"

Gustavo shrugged. "It was not my goal to work for the cartels, Professor. I was a chemical engineer, but then, sometimes we're not given a choice. I have a wife and children."

"I'm sorry. I didn't mean to imply . . ."

Odin gestured to the workbench. "I sent chemical samples and asked Tegu to bring some equipment and have a look at our little friend—see if your theory about pheromones panned out."

McKinney moved up to the workbench and could see Tegu using some sort of voltmeter to test connections on the black drone. "And what have you found?"

Gustavo answered instead, picking up one of the aluminum cylinders, but gesturing to the dead drone. "Fascinating design. This appears to be a chemical-dispensing, chemical-reading electromechanical machine. The pepper scent you smell is a diluted mixture of oleoresin capsicum, the active ingredient in pepper spray. This cylinder here contains o-chlorobenzalmalononitrile. It's a lacrimator found in teargas. Both very common chemicals you might find present at any riot or civil disturbance." Then Gustavo held up the remaining capsules. "But these two cylinders are the interesting ones. They contain what are known as chemical taggants, used by law enforcement agencies like your DEA and ATF to invisibly mark narcotics, or cash—or anything, really. We have run into these before." He held up one metal cylinder for them all to see. "Perfluorocarbons—chemical structures that do not appear in nature. Odorless, colorless, and which dissipate at a predictable, measurable rate. You can reliably determine how much time has elapsed since they were applied."

McKinney looked to Odin. "That's just like the pheromone matrix of ants. The message dissipates over time. And is unique."

Gustavo palmed the cylinders. "These are cyclic perfluorocarbon tracers that can be detected in concentrations as little as one in ten-to-the-fifteenth parts. This one is perfluoromethylhexane, and the other is perfluoro-1, 3-dimethylcyclohexane. These two chemicals, combined, could create a unique chemical signature—like a code."

McKinney nodded to herself. "A colony-specific identifier. They could use it to identify their colony mates, and to organize colony activity."

Tegu looked up from soldering several microchips to wire leads. Though Asian, he spoke English with no accent whatsoever. "Well, quite a few of the microchips on these antennas generate an electrical signal in the presence of a specific chemical signature." He held up the evil-looking drone. "I managed to power it back up." On McKinney's alarmed look he smiled. "Don't worry, I removed the gun barrels first. But it is a vicious little fucker. . . ."

He held the drone up to McKinney's face, and they immediately heard the firing pins on the gun rails clicking maniacally as it tried to kill her.

"Face-detection chip. Goes for a head shot if it can. I don't know where you found this thing, but whoever designed it should seriously consider anger management counseling."

Odin leaned in. "What about the chemical detector?"

"Oh, yes." Tegu held up what looked like a modified voltmeter—the one he'd just been soldering. "Gustavo and I ran some tests and discovered which chips on these antennas are responsible for detecting the perfluorocarbons." He ran his hand along the antenna that he'd grafted onto the voltmeter. "I removed the antenna and attached it onto this old voltmeter." He pointed at the green LED numeric display. "The antenna detects the presence of these chemical taggants, and I've wired it so this display shows their concentration level."

McKinney accepted the jury-rigged detector and held it up to the perfluorocarbon canisters. The LED readout immediately raced up into the hundreds. As she pulled it away from them, the readout started to count downward. "Meaning we can now follow their trail."

Odin collected the cylinders from Gustavo. "Meaning we can hunt them. Hopefully back to their source."

CHAPTER 23

Collateral Damage

Henry Clarke sat in a damask armchair next to his bed in an Egyptian cotton robe. A bottle of Dalmore fifty-year-old single malt was open on the table in front of him. A crystal glass of Scotch chilled by cold granite stones stood half-full in his hand.

He could hear the gentle breathing of a young woman in his bed nearby—sound asleep beneath the silk and down. He glanced back at her lush red hair. Her perfect alabaster skin. Clarke considered what a positive reflection she was on him, and he thought of places where he should be seen with her. He took another sip of the Dalmore.

The light of the sixty-inch plasma-screen television played over the girl's form in shadows. The TV was on a clever mechanism that concealed itself in the wall when not in use. Clarke had gotten tired of waiting the several seconds it took for it to rise from its hiding place, and now he left it uncovered all the time. There was a moral in there somewhere, but he couldn't fathom what it might be through the fog of Scotch. Perhaps: "Just because you *can*, doesn't mean . . ." No, that wasn't it.

The pattern of the shadows suddenly calmed—meaning the commercials were over. He turned to face the screen again. He liked watching the news in the middle of the night with the sound turned off. A vaguely mannish British anchorwoman spoke silently for several moments, and then the screen was taken over by U.S. senators and pundits. Now there was file footage of twin Manta Ray drones flying in formation—above the Statue of Liberty, no less! A twofer: a veiled 9/11 reference (guarding sacred ground), and a positive association with liberty. Marketing psychologists deep in the bowels of M & R had no doubt thought that one up.

But the news had moved on now to shots of American FBI and Alcohol, Tobacco and Firearms agents confiscating what looked to be remote control toy airplanes and vehicles—the larger ones that require a license to operate. We were declaring toys illegal now?

Clarke unmuted the TV with the remote. The anchor spoke with the video as a backdrop: "*. . . emergency legislation amending FCC Part Fifteen to restrict remotely piloted and autonomous vehicles in the United States—including those licensed to operate at fifty megahertz on the six-meter band. In anticipation of the change, federal agents seized stocks of remote control aircraft and rocketry equipment from special interest clubs and retailers, and also detained suspect individuals for questioning.*"

The video showed agents putting a handcuffed, balding Middle Eastern man in a Windbreaker into the back of a sedan on some grassy field. People in a nearby crowd—apparently fellow enthusiasts—were shouting angrily.

So they were restricting automation now? That was an odd development. He thought it risky to instill fear of the very thing they were pushing as the security solution. The footage depicted these hobbyists as suspicious. A fringe element that needed to be monitored. He could smell Marta's scent on this.

His cell phone vibrated, causing the young lady in his bed to stir. He reached over to the nightstand to grab it and spoke softly. "Yeah."

"*You're not in the office.*"

"I had plans. Everything's under control—you forget I can monitor operations from anywhere."

"*There's still value to being in the office.*"

"I see you're rolling out new product tonight. Not sure I see the rationale."

"What's not to understand? Certain knowledge needs to be branded subversive. These machines are no longer toys. It was the same with the Internet—at some point hacking became a national security matter. Drone use needs to be restricted to the professionals now."

Clarke frowned at something on-screen. "Well, it makes my job harder. I mean, they're questioning a high school kid for sending a camera to the edge of the atmosphere with a weather balloon."

"It could just as easily have been anthrax spores, Henry."

"Where the hell would a high school kid get anthrax spores? More importantly, why?"

"If hackers are the militia of cyber war, then hobbyists are their drone war cousins. It's safer for everyone if we scare them now. Put them on notice. Isolate them. Like we did with the WikiLeaks people."

"For the record, I think it's a mistake. It'll create a grassroots backlash that will take thousands of puppeteers weeks to dilute."

"Well, then I suggest you stop sipping Scotch and get your ass back to the office. . . ."

CHAPTER 24

Myrmidons

Linda McKinney spent her days wandering Lalenia's ranch in the warm, dry weather, using a hiking stick for support and as protection against stray dogs. Her strength had returned, and she could walk a considerable distance now. It was surprising how such a small hole had nearly drained all the life out of her.

But what life was left to her? Where could she go? She'd been recovering in Mexico for two months, and now it was almost March. She couldn't help thinking that there was no clear path home. Had they declared her dead? she wondered.

She thought about the antidrone team—or what was left of it. Foxy had flown off to Mexico City—gone to connect with informants, or buy weapons, or sell the plane—nobody would tell her which. Tin Man had gone away to get specialist treatment for his leg injury. Meanwhile Odin and Mouse spent most of their time together, running around the area on shadowy business. She didn't see Odin much.

Was this her life now? An expat American hiding in rural Mexico? She wondered when the hunt would resume. Or if it would resume.

In the meantime she walked. As she did, McKinney studied the ground. It was a habit she'd formed after a decade of field research. She had lately been monitoring Argentine ants—*Linepithema humile*. She noticed a trail of them and followed the tiny species back to its nest. Much smaller than weavers, they were nonetheless the most likely to give weavers trouble in the future. The reason was simple: They'd evolved into a single supercolony that spanned continents—trillions of members and possibly millions of queens. They were the Wal-Mart of ants—existing like a single, vast multinational corporation. Their numbers outstripped all others. Even far more ferocious ants simply could not kill all the Argentine ants, and eventually, their food sources were eaten out from under their mandibles.

The Argentine ants were reducing biodiversity. Other insects could not survive their onslaught, and the birds who ate those insects were also starting to suffer—and on up the food chain. Humans weren't the only ones capable of wrecking their ecosystem by succeeding too well, apparently.

And yet somehow McKinney's enthusiasm for swarming intelligence seemed greatly diminished. It wasn't academic anymore. How long until the weaver drones started appearing elsewhere? She tried not to think about it.

Instead she kept walking. While wandering the edge of an orange grove, McKinney heard a familiar *caw* and turned to see one of Odin's ravens on a nearby fence post. It examined her curiously. She noticed it wasn't wearing the wire filament headset or transponder. "Hello, Muninn. How are you today?"

The raven spread its wings and puffed up the feathers around its head, *caw*ing and hopping along the fence wire.

She stood in front of Muninn and leaned on her hiking stick. "Where have you been?"

The raven cocked its head at her.

In a moment Huginn landed next to Muninn on a nearby fence post. "Hello, Huginn."

The birds both *caw*ed in response, but then the first one started preening the new arrival, as the second one emitted gentle *keek-keek* sounds. It was as though he were caressing her.

"I guess this is a holiday for you two, then? A little jaunt down to Mexico?"

McKinney decided to leave them alone and returned to her walk along the edge of the orchard. The ravens started to tag along, flying in bounds overhead, and then across the road into a nearby peach orchard. They were both walking around the branches and took great interest in a squirrel that was gathering up rotting peaches that had fallen. One of the ravens apparently decided to have some fun and tugged at a peach on a branch until it broke off and rolled down onto the ground—where the squirrel immediately descended upon it.

McKinney watched in fascination as the ravens let out more clicking noises and hopped around the branches with apparent delight. They seemed to be . . . feeding the squirrels for the fun of it.

Soon bored with their game, they flew off, heading toward a copse of trees in the distance. McKinney watched them go, only to see them circle back and *caw* at her loudly. Another dip of the wings, and they headed back toward the distant tree line. McKinney watched them go again, this time more closely. The birds were clearly communicating with each other as they flew. It was fascinating to watch.

Another glance down at the Argentine ants, and McKinney decided to take a break from swarming models. She slipped beneath the fence wire and headed across a pasture toward the copse of trees a couple of hundred meters away. She could see the ravens sitting on a tree branch there, until one of them descended, presumably to engage in more mischief.

She remembered when she'd first arrived at the Ancile base in Kansas City and started exploring the halls. Muninn had sounded the alarm. Now they seemed to have accepted her. It surprised her how good it made her feel.

She considered this as she headed into the trees along a narrow but well-worn path. The ravens *caw*ed about something ahead. McKinney wondered whether she was being foolish for heading down this path on her own, but the presence of the ravens was oddly comforting. They didn't sound alarmed. It was their normal voice.

Before long she came to the edge of a stream that flowed over rounded stones in clear ripples and reflected the trees above in still pools. Standing there on the bank, his back against a tree, was Odin.

He was grimly concentrating on the water, lost in thought. He finally looked up in alarm as she snapped a branch with her foot.

His surprise truly surprised McKinney. "I thought you had eyes everywhere. Your trusty companions seem to have failed you."

He frowned and looked up at the ravens on branches above. "Someone's apparently getting a little too used to you."

She walked up to him and looked out at the water. "This is nice. I didn't know this was here."

He nodded.

She noticed he held a mirror and scissors. "What are you up to?"

"Shaving the beard."

McKinney put on an exaggerated, shocked expression. "Really? That thing must have taken you ages to grow."

He nodded again.

"Doesn't look like you've made much progress. Hard to part with it?"

"I guess it is. But it was for a mission I spent too much time on."

She studied his face and walked up to him as he tried to look into the tiny handheld mirror.

He stopped for a moment. "What?"

She extended her hand, and when he hesitated, she took the scissors from him. "I can see better. You want it all off?"

He nodded.

She started clipping through his beard and realized there was some gray in the black hair. This close to him, she realized what a formidable man he was. His jaw solid.

His face was still stern.

"You okay?"

"They'll be sending assets after us eventually, and I don't want to attract them here. Which means we need to move on."

"To where?"

He seemed at a loss. "That's the problem. I'm trying to figure out a way back for you."

"What about you? You're still going after these people—aren't you?" She kept clipping, and now she was starting to see his real face for the first time.

"I have no choice."

"Have you uncovered anything about who's behind this?"

"That's the other problem, but it's my problem." He looked at her. "I'm sorry you're involved in this."

McKinney continued clipping. "You saved my life. You don't have to apologize to me."

He absorbed the comment silently.

She stepped back a step and gripped his jaw in her hand, turning his head side to side. His beard was quite short now—at shaving length. McKinney couldn't help but notice how handsome David Shaw was. It was the first time she'd really seen his full face. "You look a lot better without that beard."

She let go, and he checked her handiwork in the mirror, rubbing a hand along his jawline.

He knelt down to pull shaving cream and a folded straight razor from a kit in the bag at his feet. As he stood she extended her hand.

"Let me."

He eyed her warily and gestured to the straight razor. "You know how to use one of these?"

She nodded. "I used to date a swimmer."

He gave her an odd look.

"Don't ask."

He reluctantly relinquished the razor and took off his T-shirt to hang it over a tree branch. McKinney noticed scars crisscrossing his back and shoulders. What looked to be old wounds along his ribs, another one above his right shoulder blade. His lean, muscular frame flexed easily as he splashed his face with water.

He turned to face her, and she could see more scars along his chest, one leaving a hairless trail along his right pectoral muscle. He had almost no fat on him.

Odin noticed the look on her face and nodded toward the razor she held. "You gonna be safe with that? 'Cause I'm full up on scars already."

"I'll be fine. I didn't know you'd been so badly hurt before. Are all these combat wounds?"

He shrugged. "Comes with the territory if you stay long enough. I've been luckier than most."

She pointed to the nasty scar tracing along his chest. "What was this?"

He looked down. "Training accident in Texas. We were dropped into trees. I got impaled on a branch."

He saw the look on her face.

"Ah, you were expecting it was from a knife-wielding terrorist?"

She nodded. "I guess I did."

He applied some shaving cream to his hand from a can and started rubbing it along his jaw and face. "That's this one over here. . . ." He gestured to his side.

She laughed then got the razor ready, holding his jaw. "Don't make me laugh." She looked into his gray-blue eyes as she made the first swift swipe of the blade. He didn't flinch. "How can you go back now, David? Do you even know who you're going after yet?" Another sweep of the blade.

"I can't sit by and let someone build an army of autonomous killing machines. We all know how that ends."

"You're going to get yourself killed."

"Maybe, but at least I will have tried."

She was rapidly clearing away his beard. His face was even more attractive than she'd first thought. She studied him for a moment more.

Or maybe her view of him was improving.

She leaned close to scrape away the last of the beard along his chin, edging around the slight cleft. She looked at his lips and then up into his eyes. She was an inch away.

And then she lowered the razor and kissed him. Almost immediately he began kissing her back. She dropped the razor, and they were immediately locked in a passionate embrace.

McKinney felt his powerful arms as he pulled her close to him. It had been a long time since she'd been with a man, but now McKinney realized she'd been attracted to him from the start—but especially so now. As she ran her hands over him and smelled his scent, she saw the kindness in his eyes. How he was letting her in, and how much she wanted to be let in.

They made love on the edge of the stream, at the base of an ancient oak, and as she kissed the scars along his body, his calloused fingertips ran along the scar of her own wound.

He spoke softly in her ear as she felt him within her.

"I lied to you." He searched her eyes. "I'm glad you got caught up in this, Linda. . . ."

The ravens observed curiously, perched on the branches above them.

Hours later McKinney and Odin lay in the bed at the hacienda. Having made love again, she felt spent, and calm for the first time in many weeks. Odin was a considerate lover. She turned to face him in the low lamplight, her arm across his chest. McKinney ran her fingers along his cleanly shaved chin. He looked like a different man. No longer the Taliban warlord or the ZZ Top drummer. "My God, you're handsome."

"There were arguments about who was going to get to rescue you. I had to pull rank."

"Rescue me? I'm in more danger than ever now. Some rescue."

He grabbed her close and kissed her forehead. "We'll figure something out. We have to."

She rested her face on his chest. "You said something by the creek that I've been thinking about."

"What's that?"

"About autonomous killing machines. I hadn't thought about it until now, but if machines based on insect intelligence are widely used in warfare, it could remove evolutionary safeguards that have been in place for millions of years. Among the creatures on earth only certain species of ants engage in unrestrained slaughter."

"What about the Holocaust? Or Hiroshima?"

"But that came to an end. People didn't continue the killing. And they didn't kill everyone who surrendered. Mammals aren't predisposed to murdering their own species; they engage in a primordial fight-flight-posturing-or-submission process that naturally inhibits killing. But replacing that with an insect paradigm: That means killing without exception. It could begin a self-destructive pattern that circumvents millions of years of evolution—in particular the safeguard that prevents humans from engaging in unlimited intraspecies slaughter."

He sighed deeply. "That's why I have to go back."

"Why we have to go back."

He glanced down at her.

"There's no one who knows more about these things than me. You know it, and I know it. And it's not negotiable."

He let a slight grin crease his lips, but then he said nothing.

"Besides, you remember back in Kansas City you had all those experts searching for a pattern among the drone attack victims?"

"Expert Three and Expert Five."

"Yes. Back then we still thought the drone builders were outsiders, but now we know whoever's behind this is inside the defense complex—or at least they have access to all the same data your team did. Maybe more."

"I don't see how that gets us closer."

"The Web is a lot like the pheromonal matrix of an ant colony; popular messages get reinforced, less popular messages fade away. That creates a data trail that others can follow. That got me thinking about all this data being gathered on everyone—purchase records, calling patterns, social media, and e-mails, everything. What if the systems that these private security firms built to analyze that data—to keep us safe—actually did the opposite? What if whoever's doing this is using that data to select targets?"

Odin leaned up on his side, looking at her. He nodded slowly, pondering what she'd said. "Meaning maybe we shouldn't have been searching for patterns between the victims but instead on who was watching their data trail just before they died."

McKinney nodded. "That might lead you to whoever's behind this."

"But that means the surveillance complex. NSA, telecom, consumer data-tracking firms. All our access was cut off when they discovered my team's existence. . . ." His voice trailed off as something seemed to occur to him.

"What is it?"

He turned to her. "There's a man we need to see. A very bad man. . . ."

Eight or nine miles outside the town of Reynosa, Mexico, and close by the U.S. border, Mouse, McKinney, Odin, and his team members stood at the bottom of a finished mine shaft hundreds of feet belowground. It was a concrete-lined elevator room brightly lit by fluorescent lights. Yellow wire mesh surrounded the cargo elevator that had delivered them here. The ceiling was mounted with what appeared to be an overhead rail system for hauling cargo down a nearby corridor. The elevator operator pulled the doors closed with a thunderous rattle. Its electric motor kicked in with a whine, and it began to rise to the surface, leaving them behind.

Mouse, whose prosthetic legs were concealed beneath jeans, walked confidently past several tough-looking Mexican men carrying assault rifles. They were dressed unaccountably in suit coats, silk shirts, and slacks. They nodded to Mouse as he brought the team into the corridor beyond.

They'd driven several hours north from Kalitlen through cartel-controlled territory to arrive at an innocuous-looking maquiladora marked by signs as Scholl Manufacturing. Mouse had guided them past several layers of concealed doors and smuggler security to arrive here.

McKinney glanced around as they continued down the corridor to a locked gate a hundred meters away. The overhead rail extended the entire way. "I thought we were crossing the border."

"You are."

"But we're miles away from it."

"That's what makes this so reliable. Welcome to the safest tunnel into the U.S. Seven hundred feet belowground and sixteen miles long."

"My God, sixteen miles?"

"Don't worry, Professor, you won't be walking."

"Did the cartels build this?"

Odin took her by the arm to keep her moving. "Not important. What's important is that it's one of the most reliable routes into the U.S., and if someone were to smuggle something or someone truly dangerous into the country, this is the route they'd use." Odin nodded to the men around them. "These men would let Mouse know. They work for him."

"Mouse is running an illegal tunnel into the United States?"

"Better a tunnel we know about than one we don't. If you shut them all down, the cartels just dig new ones."

"The more I learn about the sausage-making that goes on, the less I want to know."

They'd arrived at the steel gate. Mouse pulled it open with a clang and ushered the team into a dark, ten-foot-diameter circular tunnel perpendicular to the corridor. The tunnel ended just a few yards to their right, but to the left echoes hinted at a vast emptiness. Rails extended off into the darkness, and a seven- or eight-foot-wide and thirty-foot-long bullet-shaped fiberglass railcar stood in front of them alongside a concrete platform. Aside from its lack of windows, it looked like a tiny commuter train.

Mouse opened a breaker box on the wall and started slamming switches. Section by section a control console on a raised platform came to life nearby with dozens of glowing buttons. This was clearly a sophisticated operation.

McKinney noticed power conduits extending along the walls. A gentle hum started to reverberate along the tunnel. And a moment later the railcar rose several inches.

She nodded to herself. "You're running an illegal maglev train into the United States."

Mouse was now poking at switches on the console. "The economics might not scrub for passenger trains, Professor, but they sure as hell do for Schedule One narcotics. Quiet too. No seismic disturbances for the good folks in McAllen, Texas."

Her technical curiosity was getting the better of her as the solid gray doors opened with a hiss, revealing a Spartan but serviceable passenger and cargo area. "How fast can it go?"

Mouse looked down his nose at her. "It can go nearly two hundred, but you'll be doing one-twenty. That should get you Stateside in about eight minutes."

McKinney couldn't help but be impressed. Any concern she had that they'd be climbing into concealed truck compartments to cross the border had disappeared.

Mouse unslung a light rucksack from his shoulder and opened it. He passed Odin what looked to be a stack of black passports in plastic bags. "Canadian—two for each of you in case your initial cover gets blown. Some credit cards too, but go easy on those. I can't guarantee the numbers are still active. Oh . . ." He reached into the backpack and revealed packets of twenty-dollar bills several inches thick. "Some operating cash." He zipped the backpack and handed it to Odin. "The guys at the other end will hook you up with a passenger van registered to a Toronto reality television production company—along with a couple video cameras that'll give you cover for action just about anywhere." He stopped to look at the team.

Odin, Foxy, and the rest of the team embraced him one at a time with slaps on the back.

Foxy looked saddest. "Mouse, man. We owe you. Again."

"You don't owe me. Just complete your mission, and earn your damn paycheck."

"Wish you were coming with us."

He laughed good-naturedly. "Fuck that. I got my own war to fight. Find the bad guys and get back safe—and keep the professor here out of trouble."

McKinney hugged Mouse too.

He studied her with his one eye. "You remember what I said."

She nodded. "I will. Give my best to Lalenia. Hopefully we'll see you both again."

He saluted as they all entered the railcar, and the doors closed behind them.

CHAPTER 25

Personae Management

L inda McKinney gazed across the street at a generic four-story stucco office building near Palm River in East Tampa, Florida. It was the type of building you could drive past for years without noticing. The rest of the neighborhood was dotted with liquor stores and check-cashing outlets. She was dressed in business slacks and a cotton blouse, with a leather handbag over her shoulder. Odin walked next to her in khakis and a green polo shirt with loafers. It was a balmy seventy degrees and sunny. They traversed the cracked, weed-encrusted sidewalk to enter a musty lobby with a faded NO SOLICITING sticker stuck to the window.

Odin perused the disheveled lobby directory and tapped the black-and-white push-on letters above "Zion Strategies" on the fourth floor. He led the way to a worn-looking elevator carved with messenger graffiti.

McKinney spoke after the doors closed with a loud thump. "Would we need this person if we hadn't lost Hoov?"

"Probably. Hoov had scruples."

"How do you know this guy?"

"Someone I worked with in the past. His specialty is data—getting it and misusing it."

She looked at the shabby elevator car. "Looks successful."

"Flies below the radar. That's why he's useful to us. Which reminds me: Don't believe anything he tells you. He has talents we need, but this man is a manipulative sociopath."

"Sounds like a great addition to the team."

The doors opened and Odin brought them down a mildewed hallway past cheap wood veneer doors with no-frills black plaques listing immigration attorneys and mail order companies. Soon they arrived at a door with no plaque at all, only a peephole and a massive dead-bolt lock. None of the neighboring office doors had either.

Odin examined the lock. "An old Medeco biaxial. I should be able to bump this." He reached into his pocket to produce a small leather case, which he flipped open to reveal an array of tools. He slipped a small brass key out, then took his small Maglite with the end wrapped in duct tape. "If anyone's coming, cough."

McKinney raised her eyebrows. "Are you really—?"

"Watch the hall." He worked so fast, she barely had time to see it. He slipped what looked like a simple filed-down key into the lock, pulled it out slightly, and then gave it a quick whack with the taped end of the Maglite. He then turned the dead bolt as though he had the correct key and entered the office. A glance inside, and he nodded for her to follow.

Before McKinney had time to debate breaking and entering, they were both walking into a low-end reception area without an actual receptionist, just an empty front desk piled with FedEx and UPS packages. She could hear people talking and hands clattering on computer keyboards as they moved down a central hallway. The hallway opened up to a modest cubicle farm with tinny Christian rock music playing on PC speakers somewhere.

". . . *my savior! Savior! Say-vii-ooorrr!*"

Odin walked with purpose, having put away the key and Maglite, and he headed toward the closed office door at the far end. McKinney couldn't help but catch the eye of one of the office workers, a twentyish white kid with piercings and dyed blue hair. She nodded to him and kept going. He immediately turned back to his keyboard, uncurious.

Before they reached the office door, a heavyset, middle-aged blond woman in jeans and a bright pink T-shirt for a charity 5K came around the corner holding a manila folder blooming with colorful Post-it flags. She slowed. "Can I help you?"

Odin shook his head. "He gave me a key. You his admin?"

"The office manager."

"Then, no, you can't help me." He kept walking straight to the closed door at the end of the hall. It opened up into a sizable corner office containing IKEA furniture, a flat-screen TV, and gaming consoles. The whole office was a mishmash of styles. There were thick folders piled everywhere and stuffed shelves lining the walls, overflowing with fat programming books—dozens of languages and methodologies, from Perl to Java to Hadoop, to pen-testing, and exploiting online games.

The occupant of the office sat in a brown leather chair, talking on the phone with his back to them as he faced downtown Tampa in the distance. His silver-toed cowboy boots rested up on a credenza. McKinney followed Odin inside, still with no clear idea how she should be acting.

Surprised that someone had entered his office, the man put his feet down and rotated his chair, still talking into the phone. ". . . aged accounts—at least a year. The older the better. And active posters." He frowned at the office manager, then at McKinney—and then his eyes went wide when he saw Odin. He spoke into the phone. "Hey, man. I gotta take this. Text me when you got 'em. Yeah."

He hung up and just stared.

Odin nodded. "How are things, Mordecai?"

His office manager frowned. "There's been some mistake. Mister James is—"

"Get out, Maggie." When she didn't hop to it, he shooed her out with ringed fingers. "Now! And close the door."

She nodded and obeyed, her face taut with humiliation.

McKinney kept her eyes on the man. He was in his mid-twenties, reasonably good-looking, but with the oily presence of a gold-chain salesman in a bad part of town. He wore a denim shirt with embroidery on the chest pockets. His fingers held several rings of similar design. Though he was still young, his hair was thinning, a situation he compensated for with Isaac Asimov–style muttonchop sideburns. He was still staring at Odin with utter incomprehension.

Odin dropped into one of the chairs in front of the desk. "No hello?"

"Thanks for using my real name, asshole. I see you got rid of that bin Laden beard of yours. I barely recognized you. Why the fuck are you here?"

Odin motioned for McKinney to take a seat next to him. "So what is it now—Ryan James? That's pretty bland for a guy like you." Odin gestured in their host's direction. "Professor, this used to be the far more interesting Mordecai Elijah Evans—a very talented member of a U.S. Cyber Command worm squad—part of the Joint Functional Component Command for Network Warfare. Mort here was their pet black-hat. On a short leash under the threat of—what was it again, Mort?—sixty-five years and a two-million-dollar fine?"

"I paid my debt to society."

"But not your debt to me."

"You don't— You'd better not be here for me, Odin. One phone call, and you go away. I have friends now. Powerful, official friends."

"I need your talents."

"I don't work for DOD anymore. I got my package, motherfucker. Legal pardon. A new life." He gestured to the office. "I'm a legitimate businessman."

Odin nodded appreciatively. "Yes, very lifelike."

Evans sneered back at the sarcasm with an intense nasal imitation of Odin's voice. "Mmm . . . vera lifelike. Fuck you. I'm not the same person I was back then."

"Not the same name maybe, but I don't think you've changed. You forget how much I know about you."

"Leave, or I make a call."

Odin spoke to McKinney, keeping his eyes on Evans. "Morty here sold zero-day exploits to international criminal gangs—helped advanced technology escape to parts unknown. What we're dealing with right now might be because of him."

"I got my deal. They need people like me, Odin. It's that simple.

Door kickers like you are replaceable—or should I say disposable? I am not." He frowned. "How did you get in, anyway?"

"I kicked the door in."

"Look, this is all moot. You can't twist my arm anymore. I'm part of the system now. The system wants you to leave." He swept his arm dramatically to point at the door. "So leave."

"I need information. You're going to help me get it."

Evans just laughed. "Are you deaf? I've got powerful allies, and I don't work for you." He put his hand over the multiline phone system on his desk. "One more word, and I make the call."

Odin leaned forward and produced a black automatic pistol from the waistband at the small of his back. He held it up for Evans to clearly see. McKinney noticed a short exposed barrel with threads at the end of its blocky body. The words *USP Tactical* were engraved in letters large enough to read on its side.

Evans just frowned at it. "What, are you kidding me?"

Odin produced a metal cylinder from his pocket and proceeded to screw it onto the end of the barrel.

Evans laughed. "I feel insulted by this posturing."

McKinney grabbed Odin's shoulder. "What the hell are you doing?"

Odin finished screwing on the suppressor. "I'm doing what's necessary, Professor. I assure you, there's no other means to secure Mordecai's cooperation."

"But you're making me party to a— I don't think we need this person so badly that we need to resort to this."

"Listen to the lady, Odin."

Odin shook his head but kept looking at Evans. "Mort, would you cooperate under any circumstances other than the threat of physical force?"

Evans chuckled and ruefully shook his head. "You know, I'm going to have to say no to that—in fact, I'm going to say no to physical force as well." He picked up the handset of his desk phone. "If I disappeared—all these witnesses. Too many cameras. They'd track you down. It would be suicide to lay a finger on me."

Odin chambered a round. "Good thing I don't give a shit."

"Well, you care about your team. The man can get to them to get to you."

"My team's all dead. Betrayed by someone inside the system. The same system you now belong to, apparently."

Evans's smile started to fade.

"And if you check around, I think you'll find they're already hunting for me. Killing you would have no effect whatsoever on my afternoon, much less my life."

McKinney could see the change in Evans's face—the first time he'd shown any regard whatsoever for Odin. She watched, feeling bad for being a party to threatening this man she'd never met, and tried not to react to Odin's lie.

Evans had gone pale. "Who's your pretty friend, Odin?" Evans grinned weakly.

"You call her 'Professor.'"

Evans extended his hand. "Good to meet you, Professor."

McKinney nodded and shook his clammy hand.

Evans didn't let go immediately but instead studied her hand. "Not an operator." He pointed toward Odin but spoke to McKinney. "See that callus on Odin's gun hand? You get that firing fifty thousand rounds a year. The training acclimates you to gunfire. And the screams of innocents."

Odin still held the pistol aimed toward the drop ceiling.

Evans kept a wary eye on Odin. "Professor, do you have any idea how many people he's killed?"

McKinney couldn't help but glance with concern at Odin.

"You remember that shopkeeper in Dushanbe, Odin? How he pleaded for his life, and you just double-tapped him in front of his kid. So glad I could help you locate him. Makes me proud to be an American."

Odin remained emotionless. "If you were so disturbed, why'd you take his cigarettes?"

"Because they were French cigarettes." Evans was starting to perspire. "In your experience, Professor, what usually happens to witnesses when heartless guys like this get what they want? See, I think they kill witnesses to cover their tracks. That's what I think."

McKinney cast an impatient look at Odin and motioned for him to put the gun down. "Mr. Evans, we just need information. If you help us, I promise you that I won't let Odin harm you."

Evans laughed. "Oh, you won't let him harm me. I'd like to see that. What sort of information?"

McKinney cast Odin another look and kept the floor. "Communications records."

He looked back and forth between them, and then let out an exasperated sigh. "Okay, we're doing this the hard way: What sort of communication records?"

McKinney hesitated. "We need access to historical data—we want to find out who in the intelligence sector might have been searching for drone attack victims just before they were killed."

Evans cast an incredulous look at Odin. "Is she for real?"

Odin nodded.

Evans turned back to McKinney. "Ah. Right. Let me just hook you up. . . ."

"Mr. Evans—"

"No, let me just confirm this: You want to eavesdrop on the eavesdroppers—have I got that right? Which pretty much means you need root access to whatever the NSA developed Project ThinThread into, not to mention AT&T's Aurora database—quite possibly the biggest data store on earth."

McKinney held up her hands. "Look, I know that—"

"No problem. I figure we can knock this out in a few minutes."

Odin interjected. "Mort, this is no joke. My mission is to identify whoever's behind the drone attacks—and when we got close, somebody inside the system sent drones after us."

Evans just rubbed his temples and closed his eyes. "I'm not hearing this."

"Someone in the establishment might be behind the drones. I need to find out who."

"Fuck! Why the hell did you come down here? Goddammit, man! I finally have my life together."

Odin leveled the pistol at Evans. "I guess we're through, then. . . ."

Evans raised his hands to hold him off. "And if by some miracle I manage to do this? What then—you kill me and dump me in the Everglades?"

"Is there anything in my past behavior that leads you to believe I would kill for no reason? You know damn well that shopkeeper in Dushanbe was a bomb maker. That he strapped bombs to kids."

They sat staring at each other for several moments, Evans breathing heavily.

"There are big issues on the line—not just national defense, but the future of the human race, and I'm convinced you can point us in the right direction. Someone has hijacked at least part of the national security apparatus, and I think it's related to the multibillion-dollar autonomous drone bill being fast-tracked through Congress. How do we find out who?"

Evans looked horrified. "Oh, man! You've got to be shitting me. These are not people I want to tangle with."

Odin raised the gun again. "I'm going to make you do the right thing, even if it kills you."

McKinney nudged it aside. "He's going to help us."

"This is why you shouldn't get involved in the underworld, Mort. What's to stop me from letting them know you helped us, even if you haven't? I could just pick up your phone and speak over the line in my voice. That should do it." Odin reached for the receiver.

"Don't!" Evans slid the phone away. "What you're asking is hopeless, but I'll see what I can do. But we can't do it here. I need access to real equipment."

McKinney glanced around the huge condo with its tall windows and wide view of the bay. It was a penthouse unit in a quasi-Mediterranean twenty-story tower on Bayshore Boulevard. The condo was new and looked relatively unlived in—there was no clutter or dirty dishes. It was coherently, if a bit enthusiastically, decorated. There was an L-shaped sectional sofa on a zebra carpet, wide expanses of wood floor, a full bar, mirrors, brushed steel lamps, urns, bold modernist paintings that said nothing, but loudly, as well as petrified blowfish and other bric-a-brac on shelving units that McKinney couldn't quite map to the urban cowboy who presumably owned it.

Once he'd conceded defeat, Evans didn't put up much fuss about being hijacked by Odin. He seemed resigned to his fate. McKinney had followed Evans's Jaguar in her domestic rental car, watching as he chatted constantly at Odin sitting in the passenger seat. Now Evans seemed almost jovial, humming to himself as he fixed a drink at the bar just off the living area.

"Want anything, Professor?"

She shook her head.

"I make a mean mai tai."

"I said no. Thanks."

"Suit yourself. You know, you're pretty cute, in a tomboyish sort of way. What kind of chick joins CIA, anyway?"

"I'm not CIA. Let's just stick to business, Mr. Evans." She joined Odin, who stood at the glass wall overlooking the glittering water of the bay. "Do you really think this goombah can get us access to anything?"

Odin remained poker-faced. "No, but he can get us to the people who can. I'm just waiting for him to make his move."

This surprised her. She glanced over her shoulder.

Evans worked a silver martini shaker, then tapped the top on the edge of the bar, deftly pulling the halves apart. He poured through a strainer into a chilled martini glass.

Odin spoke while facing the window. "You've gone up in the world, Mordecai. How much did this place set you back?"

"A million five—only half a million more than it's worth now, which actually passes for real estate acumen in Florida nowadays. But I don't give a shit. Zion's doing booming business." He took a sip and let out a satisfied "Aaaahhh."

"Interesting that your company has no website—given your mad technical skills." Odin turned to him. "What does Zion Group do exactly?"

"We work under contract to public relations firms. Boring stuff, but it pays well."

Odin just stared at him. "I'm not going to ask twice."

"Jesus, Odin. Chill out, man. I just didn't want to bore your hot little friend here."

"Cut that shit out right now. The professor's smarter than you. Now tell me what Zion's a front for."

Evans held up his hands. "It's not a front for anything. We—"

Odin gripped the edge of a mango-wood shelving unit dotted with vases and small sculptures.

"Oh. Come on, Odin—"

He tipped it over and it crashed across the floor, shattering the edge of a glass coffee table.

"What the hell, man? I paid somebody to buy that."

Odin stepped over the wreckage toward the bar. "When I ask you a question, I want a prompt, thorough, and accurate response."

"What about elicitation? You're supposed to start with elicitation, for fuck's sake."

"I don't have time to pussyfoot around with you. You're a scumbag. You've always been a scumbag, and you'll always be a scumbag. What's Zion's real business?"

Evans was looking at his wrecked living room. "Dammit." He focused on Odin. "Fine. We do personae management. A gorilla like you wouldn't understand."

"Try me."

Evans searched for the words. "We harness social media for multinational clients—help push brands."

"Do you do intelligence work? DOD influence operations?"

Evans shrugged. "How the hell should I know?"

"Who were the 'official' friends you mentioned back at the office—the ones who supposedly have your back?"

"I don't know. I have a number to call if there are problems. I've never had a reason to use it."

Odin studied him. "So let me parse this into something I know Mordecai would be involved in. Let's see. . . . You game social media to make it lie to the world. Does that about sum it up?"

"It's a bit more sophisticated than that, and it requires engineering skill. They're called *sock puppets*. We create armies of artificial online personas—user accounts that espouse views certain interested parties want espoused. We flood forums, online comment sections, social media. It requires good software to manage it all—to automate the messaging while maintaining uniqueness, and to keep all the fictional personalities and causes straight. I took the logic from my bot-herding software—from the gold-farming operation in China."

"Where do you get your contracts?"

"I told you: public relations firms—or at least their secret 'whisper marketing' subsidiaries. In the old days they used armies of paid shills to sing the praises of products and causes online, but human beings are unreliable. We're more cost-effective. You want a million 'people' to say the same thing online, on a certain day, at a certain hour? I'm your man."

"Political work?"

"Sure. We have political clients. Beltway lobbying firms—but they're all public relations subsidiaries of big parents. They use scores of front companies."

McKinney looked to Odin to register her disgust. "They're undermining the democracy of the Internet is what they're doing."

"Oh, please. Look, we're using our technical savvy to promote a point of view. That's not illegal. And we've created some pretty popular personas— puppets with hundreds of thousands of followers. I've got actual goddamned fans for some of my personas."

"How many people in your organization?"

"It's way bigger than what you saw. I'm not a nobody, Odin. We manage operatives all around the world." Evans smiled at the thought. "I remember getting a thrill penetrating government networks, but this . . . hell. Nothing like the thrill of influencing events. It's amazing what a few people and a little money can accomplish online. Our puppets have turned whole elections. Especially when the oppo-research people give us something to go public with. And then our puppets up-vote the shit out of it, even if it's no big deal. We can create public outrage from almost nothing."

McKinney gestured to Evans. "How can you be proud of this? What you're doing is creating false consensus. A 'popular' movement that doesn't exist."

"The term is *astroturfing*, and, yes, it's quite a challenge."

Odin nudged McKinney back as she started getting angry. "Focus on the mission, Professor."

Evans chuckled as he sipped his mai tai. "Is she really upset?"

"People need to know what these guys are doing."

"Pfffftttt! Give me a break. Everyone knows. Why do you think they all want a piece of it? Detecting and neutralizing opposition or promoting your agenda—that's what social media's for."

"The purpose was to get around media gatekeepers."

He waved her off. "Yeah, and look how that turned out. Everyone on the Internet is talking about television and everyone on television is talking about the Internet. The whole damned thing is a self-licking ice cream cone, and you're blaming me? The big boys have taken over. They're fencing the Net off. Hell, even the CIA has a social media desk with hip young intelligence analysts 'monitoring the threat/opportunity profile' and reporting back in 140-character bursts of TWITINT."

Odin stepped between them. "Who are these PR firms that hire you?"

"Big. Owned by D.C. law firms. Powerful. Jacked into *everything*—all the data moving through society. Cell phone geolocation. Purchase records. E-mail, IM, social networks. They're mining it all in real time to find opposition to their clients' interests. To spot trouble and opportunities. If someone's talking about something they're interested in—they know about it. And they can change the public conversation if necessary, modify public perceptions—rewrite reality in real time. It's impressive. They could make Mother Teresa into the devil and Adolf Hitler into Saint Francis of Assisi if they wanted to."

McKinney stared at him with utter contempt.

He started making another drink. "Don't hate the playa, Professor. Hate the game. At least I'm not a bottom-feeder like the data cosmeticians and trash consultants—monitoring celebrity effluent to tell a consistent 'brand story.' Everything the public sees is managed. If there's a valuable brand to protect—whether it's a person or a dish soap—these fuckers are out there protecting it, shaping the narrative. I mean . . . who the hell follows dish soap on Twitter? How does anyone believe that shit's real?"

Just then McKinney noticed one of Odin's ravens alight upon the balcony railing beyond the glass. It looked agitated, *cawing* silently beyond the double-insulated panes and hopping along the metal railing in alarm.

Odin stopped cold, and then turned to Evans. "You never disappoint, do you?"

Evans looked puzzled. "What do you mean?"

Odin pulled the pistol again. "You sent out a distress signal."

"What are you talking about?"

Odin grabbed him by the collar and pulled him completely over the bar, sending barstools scattering as Evans landed on the floor with a thud. "When did you make the call, Morty? When!" Odin ground his knee into the back of the guy's neck, pinning his face to the wooden floor.

"Ahhh! Fuck! I didn't! Odin!"

McKinney shouted, "Odin, for godsakes—"

"Who did you call, Morty?"

After a moment of gasping, Evans held up a hand in submission. "My handler. Back at the office—when you broke in. I own the building. I get an alert when my floor button is pressed. I recognized you on the elevator camera—beard or no beard. For chrissake, Odin, we spent a year and a half in the asshole of the world—you think you're not burned into my memory? I should have taken the jail time."

Odin cast a see-I-told-you-so look at McKinney, then slammed Evans into the floor again. "You're about to find out why that was stupid."

McKinney could see that the raven had flown off. "Enough! Whatever it is, it's going to be here momentarily."

Odin got up and pulled Evans to his feet. "Where's your escape route?" He reached around behind the bar and opened drawers until he came up with a nickel-plated Colt .45. "I see you didn't have the balls to try and cap us yourself. Who are they sending?"

He nodded at the gun. "That's for personal protection."

Odin checked to see that it was loaded and set the safety. He handed it to McKinney. "Here. If he tries anything, shoot him."

McKinney took the gun but shook her head. "I'm not killing anyone."

"Do you know how to use a pistol?"

She nodded. "Yes, I had a boyfriend who was a cop. He taught—"

"Christ, how many guys have you dated?"

"Oh, you're going to turn this into a double-standard debate now?"

He held up his hands. "Forget it."

Evans looked at them both. "What's the deal with you two? Are you actually a couple?"

Odin grabbed Evans by the shoulder again. "Back exit. Where is it?"

"What do you mean, back exit? What am I, Pablo Escobar? It's a Florida condo. Look, I can make a call. I can. I promise. I'll call off the hit. I swear."

Odin was looking around for anything useful. "You don't seem to understand, Morty. They're not going to reward you for turning us in. You know too much now."

"Oh, come on."

McKinney stepped between them. "How long do you think we've got?"

Odin paced. "Special Operations Command is here in Tampa. These people might have anticipated I'd go there looking for help—which is why I avoided it. But it also means they probably have assets close by."

Just then Evans's eyes grew wide as shadows appeared around the window. "What the hell is that?"

McKinney and Odin turned to see a swarm of black dots—like a flock of birds approaching the tall windows.

Evans pointed. "What the fuck is that?"

"It's the future, Morty. And I don't think it cares what side you're on." He glanced at McKinney. "Do you recognize your algorithm, Professor?"

She studied their behavior as the cloud kept growing outside. "I don't know yet."

Evans watched the swarm gathering. "You're shitting me! That's what you do? Design swarms of robot birds?"

Suddenly one of the fluttering bots outside bumped against the window glass and exploded with the force of a shotgun shell—blasting the safety glass apart into a million beads that collapsed and spread across the floor, creating a six-foot-wide, twelve-foot-tall opening. A fresh breeze and the buzzing sound of ten thousand beating mechanical plastic wings filled the living room. The creatures spilled through the opening and into the room, blocking the path to the front door.

Evans shouted, "This way!" and motioned for them to follow. He headed down an adjacent hallway, deeper into the cavernous condo, as the swarm continued to pour through the opening. Evans raced down a wood-floored hallway, past expensive-looking but sterile artwork and closed doors. "What the hell are those things?"

Odin pushed McKinney ahead of him as he took rear guard. "They're a swarming weapon."

"No kidding—"

"Don't let them near you. They're flying handguns. They'll try to get right on top of you. If they corner you, you're dead."

"What the hell have you done to me! I finally had a good situation!"

McKinney pounded Evans in the shoulder as they reached the end of the hallway. "You did this to yourself, Mr. Evans. You were trying to have us killed."

Evans was struggling with a key ring to get a locked door open. Oddly it had a keyed dead bolt even though it looked to be an internal door.

"Heads up!" Odin aimed his HK pistol and fired at a swarm of bot birds surging into the far end of the hallway. With the suppressor off, the shots should have been deafeningly loud, but McKinney's adrenaline was pumping her heart so fast, she didn't even hear it. Several bots shattered without exploding and dropped in pieces to the floor—and only then exploded like a shotgun blast. But the swarm itself continued unaffected.

Evans was still struggling with the door keys.

"Dammit, Morty, get that door open!"

"I'm trying!"

"Try harder! Linda! Shoot!"

She raised the .45 and used the two-hand grip her ex had taught her. Squeezed the trigger. "Dammit!" She flicked off the safety, and squeezed off several booming shots. It had been a long time since she'd fired a pistol, and she had no idea if she was hitting anything.

The swarm was already halfway down the hall—the droning buzz getting louder.

"Got it!" Evans unlocked the door and pushed inside. McKinney and Odin followed—Odin last, firing off several last shots. Evans slammed the door as he crossed inside what appeared to be a computer lab. It was a server room lined with rack-mounted servers and a dozen large flat-panel monitors above two separate desks. The place was littered with DVDs, technical white papers, and colorful *hentai* posters involving seminude Japanese schoolgirls and tentacled monsters.

McKinney took the briefest of moments to be disgusted. "God, you're sick!"

Evans flicked the dead bolt. "We've got more pressing problems than my prurient tastes."

Odin examined the dead-end room. "Dammit, Morty. You trapped us!"

Evans was scurrying about, clattering at keyboards. "Not true. I just need to clear some machines and grab some gear before we bug out."

"Bug out where?" Odin looked around at the racks lining the walls of the small room. An explosion like a shotgun blast tore through the door, ripping an inch-wide hole in the wood laminate. Odin raised his gun but didn't fire. "They're breaking in! Evans, you stupid—"

"Would you give me a moment?" He was still clattering on keyboards.

McKinney could see he appeared to be launching a wipe sequence, and several screens started scrolling progress on a shell script.

Another last punch on an ENTER key and Evans grabbed a laptop bag hung over a chair-back. "Ready to roll!"

"Roll where, asshole?"

There were several popping explosions at the door, and now two foot-wide holes splintered the wood. Odin fired several shots at bot-birds that tried to flutter through.

Evans grabbed McKinney's shoulder and pulled her to a computer rack. He pulled back on it, and it swung away from the wall on a hinge, revealing a narrow corridor.

McKinney smiled in relief and turned to shout at Odin. "Odin! This way!"

Odin emptied his HK's clip at the door, blasting apart several more of the artificial birds, but they blasted several more holes in the door as well. He turned and gave Evans an irritated look before diving into the breach on McKinney's heels. "Why the hell didn't you say something?"

"Because I knew you'd force me to leave before I was ready." Evans stopped in the corridor opening. There were already lone bot-birds fluttering around the server room. Evans pulled a round olive-drab canister from a bracket on the wall and pulled a metal pin from it.

McKinney shouted, "What the hell are you doing? Let's get out of here!"

"Gotta clean up, or I'm going to have some legal issues later on. . . ." He tossed the now smoking canister into the server room, and a blinding white glow began to expand, followed by a wave of broiling heat. *Slam.* The secret door shut behind them, Evans raced ahead, leading the way. The blinding light showed through a previously unseen gap at the base of the secret door. A furnacelike roar came to their ears.

They raced down the narrow secret corridor, single file, until they reached another hatchway. Evans turned to them and held up a finger for silence.

He whispered, "We hang a left at the laundry room, and that's the maid's door. There's a fire stairwell across the hall."

Odin nodded. "Pablo Escobar . . ."

"I was keeping my options open, dammit."

McKinney and Odin nodded.

Evans pushed through and proceeded left. They were close on his heels. McKinney cast a glance at the place and realized this guy really did have a hell of condo. There was no swarm here, and in a moment they reached the service entrance. He unbolted it and ducked his head out. A quick wave, and they headed across and down the building corridor to the fire exit. The moment Evans hit the push bar, the fire alarm sounded. They ran down the stairwell, the fire-rated door slamming behind them.

Odin shouted, "There'll be fire and police here soon."

Evans nodded. "Good thing. Some asshole started a fire back there." He rounded the next stair flight with the others close on his heels. "You really fucked me this time, Odin! What the hell am I going to do now?"

"Help us stop these things."

"Oh, goddammit. You'd like that, wouldn't you?"

"You've got no choice now. Whoever is behind this has access to intelligence and surveillance systems. You and I both know what those systems are capable of. They'll find you no matter where you go."

"Goddammit!" Evans cast a sharp look back at Odin but kept running downstairs. "I don't appreciate being rewarded for being loyal by having a hive of robot hornets sent to kill me."

"Give me a name, Mort."

"Oh, don't worry. I'll give you more than a name. I'll give you a whole live person. . . ."

CHAPTER 26

The Puppet Master

Reston, Virginia, was a prosperous town—although it wasn't really a town. It was officially a "census-designated place" with "government-like municipal services" provided by a nonprofit association. The Dulles Toll Road ran straight through Reston's center and was lined with brand-new ten- and twenty-story office towers bearing clever logos that screamed high tech and whispered defense. There were German sedans in the parking lots. Scores of upscale eateries along with the usual midscale chain fried-everything theme restaurants for the junior engineers. There were plenty of trees and parks. Planned development was the norm here.

There were American flags too, of course, fluttering on vehicle fenders, corporate campuses, and public areas just as they had after 9/11. But there was a sense of purpose here as well; "stopping the evildoers" was what they did in the defense corridor. Half these companies hadn't existed before 2001. Now the military couldn't find its soldiers without them. National security was the town's main industry. And business was booming.

In college if anyone had told Henry Clarke he would be doing top-secret work, he would have laughed in their face. He was going to be the next social media wunderkind. In a way he was—except that he could never tell anyone. Now here he was, putting in another late night managing cyber battalions in far-flung time zones from a suburban tech defense park.

It was past one in the morning, and as he clicked across the quiet building lobby from the parking elevators, the RFID tag in his badge identified him to the armed security people at the front desk before he arrived. He didn't recognize this crew, but then, security people were always rotating. And the security system told the guards everything they needed to know about him.

"Evening, Mr. Clarke."

Clarke nodded as he passed the buff Latino and his female colleague in navy blazers.

"Should I turn on the lights for twenty-two?"

"Don't bother. I like the darkness."

Clarke nodded to them as the elevator arrived, and he tapped the button for the top floor. In a few moments he was moving through the lobby of his company's full-floor office. The full floor wasn't necessary, but then, they had lots of subtenants who didn't want nameplates and addresses of their own. It was hard to say what any of them did, but none were here at the moment. The place was deserted.

Although it was originally Marta's idea, Clarke had started to enjoy coming in to the office in the wee hours. It was relaxing not having his phone constantly ringing. Instead he was issuing most of the messages without having to deal with real-time responses.

He drew a key card out of his pocket and unlocked his office door with a muted *bleep-bleep*. Tossing his leather satchel onto the sofa, he moved across the large corner office in the dim emergency lighting. There along the far wall was his favorite piece of art—a slab of cut blue-green glass six feet wide, four feet tall, and one inch thick on a three-foot-tall granite pedestal. Projected into the heart of the glass by an ingenious arrangement of blue, white, and red lasers and spinning mirrors was a map of the world, onto which was projected the current "mood" of every continent as derived from word forms flowing through the public Internet—data from Web search queries, blogs, social media entries, Wikipedia edits, news articles, and on and on. Tag clouds of the ten most common words and phrases flowing through the veins of the Net filled the boundaries of each continent. Positive words such as *hope* and *great* were depicted in blue, neutral words in white, and negative words in red. Even as he watched, large red letters for *attack* seemed to encompass half of North America. He could spend hours watching the mood of the world shift and spread like a lava lamp of news. When the Japanese earthquake and tsunami occurred, he had seen the red data race across the globe faster than the actual shock waves.

The artful device had cost him two hundred and ninety thousand dollars, but he would have paid double. With it, the moment anything happened in the world, he knew. It was his personal crystal ball. Nothing could surprise him as long as he gazed into its depths.

"A fascinating piece," a voice spoke from behind him.

Clarke spun in alarm toward a darkened corner where his reading chair stood.

"I saw something like it in Germany. Except it wasn't so beautiful."

"What the hell? Who are you? How did you get in here?" Clarke started edging toward his desk and his phone.

"Looking for this?" The man tossed Clarke's desk phone into the center of the room, where it clattered to a stop. A tail of severed cord trailed from it. "Don't reach for your cell phone either. You wouldn't live to dial."

"What are you doing in here? Do you have any idea how serious . . ." Clarke was still backing up as an intimidating man with cold blue-gray eyes emerged into a shaft of light. The intruder was dressed in a white plastic smock with rubber gloves and plastic booties. A six-inch killing knife held firmly in one gloved hand. "Oh, God."

"Surely you knew there would be consequences for what you're doing?"

Clarke looked around and considered shouting for help.

"Go ahead. No one can hear. I imagine that's the whole point of this place."

Clarke bumped into the edge of his desk. "I don't know who you're working for, but I can pay you more."

"I'm not here for money. What I want is information."

"I'll tell you everything I know. No problem."

"Your firm is part of a private intelligence-gathering operation. One designed to detect and neutralize opposition to your clients' enterprises. Correct?"

Clarke struggled to find words. It was a familiar-sounding process but with an entirely different emphasis. "Wait, wait. We gather information from legal sources. We market ideas. We predict likely scenarios—what we do is simple business intelligence."

The man stared. "You're a propagandist, Mr. Clarke, and personally, I don't give a shit how you rationalize it in the wee hours of the night. What I want to know is who hired you to push autonomous drones."

Clarke was at a loss. "Is that what this is about?"

"Who hired you?"

"Surely you—"

"We could breach your network, examine your banking transactions, trace payments to and from offshore shell companies—but frankly, fuck that. I don't have the patience. It's three times now that some asshole has tried to kill me with a drone strike, and I'm ready to start sending back severed heads. And unless you tell me something I don't already know, I'm gonna start with yours."

"Oh, God." Clarke started to hyperventilate. "You think I have something to do with the drone attacks? Hold it, hold it. I've got nothing—nothing—to do with those attacks. We were hired by M and R to help mold public opinion in support of the drone appropriation. That's all I know. That's it—"

"Who at M and R?"

"I could give you names, but they're just lawyers. They're all just lawyers. I'm telling you, they're all half out of their minds with fear that they're going to be the next one hit by a missile—they're sending their kids to suburban schools like this is the London Blitz or something. We were paid to sell drones to the public, but frankly it makes sense—we're under attack. Why wouldn't we want to launch drones in our own defense as quickly as possible?"

The man moved closer, rolling the knife in his palm with frightening skill. "Time's up."

"Wait! Wait!" Clarke held up his hands defensively. "Rita Morehouse. Jack Allenby, Aaron Nichols, uh, Uma Verazzi."

"Those are your handlers at M and R?"

Clarke nodded, suddenly sweating and trembling. "Yes. Please don't kill me. I promise I won't warn them. I swear it."

"Well, you're not someone I'd want watching my back. I didn't even have to cut you." The man deftly grabbed Clarke's silk tie and, with a single frictionless motion, cut it clean away, leaving an orphaned double-Windsor.

Clarke recoiled, trembling and clenching his eyes shut as he held up his hands defensively. "Please! I promise you. I swear it."

After a few moments he opened his eyes warily, but the man appeared to be gone. Clarke lowered his arms to see his office door open and himself alone. He let out a deep sigh, just now realizing he'd forgotten to breathe. He leaned back against his desk and tried to collect his thoughts.

The first thing he did was edge toward his office door. He then leapt forward and closed, then locked it. He peered through the glass at an angle to see if anyone was outside. The man seemed to be gone.

Clarke reached into his jacket and produced his iPhone. A moment later he was listening. Even though it was one in the morning, it only took one ring to pick up. It never occurred to him to wonder why. "Marta! Some SAD-SOG asshole just threatened me at knifepoint in my own goddamned office."

"*He said he was SOG?*"

Clarke took a deep, calming breath. "No, but he sure as hell knew who we are. He said he'd been attacked three times by drones, and he was coming for somebody's head. He was definitely black ops and wanted the names of my contacts at M and R."

"*Who did you give up?*"

"Some mergers-and-acquisitions people. The first names that came to mind. . . ."

In a panel van half a mile away, Mordecai Evans, Linda McKinney, and Foxy sat listening to the conversation as they watched the voice patterns on a laptop monitor. The voice of Mr. Clarke was filled with anxiety.

"... I need protection, Marta. This guy walked in here like it was a public restroom. This wasn't some amateur. I don't know how he got past security."

"Calm down, Henry. If they wanted you dead, you'd be dead."

Evans was busy clattering at a laptop linked to an almost Soviet-looking stack of ruggedized radio receivers dotted with antennas. "I've got her IMEI and IMSI. Looks like a company phone—no name—but I place her near the Georgetown waterfront. Stationary, so she's probably at home. I'll use the control link to direction-find her when we're close."

Clarke's voice pleaded in the background. "... this is no joke, he literally cut the tie off my neck."

"It will be handled. Just go home. Get some rest."

McKinney watched Evans working.

Evans answered a question she was only thinking. "Multichannel digital receiver."

"I didn't know it was this easy to intercept cell phone conversations."

"Well, it is. It's called meaconing." He pointed. "Wireless phone systems consist of base stations spread around town. When you turn on your phone it searches for the base station with the strongest signal and establishes a control link—down which it sends information about the phone's identity. The first thing I do is jam the target phone's existing control link. That forces it to scan for a new base station—which I mimic by providing a stronger signal. Basically I become his cell tower, and that gives me a control link to his phone. I can then listen in and see the identities of any phone he communicates with. The control link is completely separate from the connection that people use to talk on the phone. That means I can remotely program a target phone to turn on even if it's off. I can activate the microphone when he's not on a call—use it as a bugging device. And lots of other things. Even if they're using civilian encryption, it won't help. Most encryption is done at the base station . . . and of course, I'm now his base station."

"Is this what you did for Odin overseas?"

He nodded. "Yeah, it's great for mapping the structures of fluid organizations like criminal gangs, knowing who's important to whom. Dropping bombs on people."

"I'm starting to realize that."

The rear door to the van opened, and Odin, Smokey, and Ripper entered—the latter two wearing security guard blazers.

Evans scowled at Odin. "I thought you said your whole team was dead?"

"I said what was necessary to get your cooperation."

"Asshole . . ."

Odin nodded to the screens as he closed the doors behind him. "Who'd he call first?"

Evan gritted his teeth for a moment. "Looks like a Beltway bandit. He wanted protection. She told him to strap on a pair."

Odin tossed the stub of a lavender silk tie into McKinney's lap. "Get us moving."

Marta's city address was an ultramodern penthouse overlooking the Potomac, just west of the Watergate. It had set the firm back five million, but it was essential to have a base of operations suitable for entertaining, close to the Kennedy Center, the waterfront restaurants, and other cultural landmarks. There was an expansive terrace area overlooking the Francis Scott Key Bridge—a terrace with built-in catering facilities and space enough for a hundred cocktail party guests. At night the view was beautiful, but she seldom noticed it—especially tonight.

Instead Marta sat alone at the head of a postmodern cherrywood table in her massive formal dining room, flanked by granite tile and glass walls and valuable modern art, idly perusing the latest foreign policy best seller—penned by a policy wonk she knew. Just another heavy business card. She took a sip from a full glass of very good Cabernet.

Before her hall clock sounded two A.M. she was startled by a hoarse *caw* and looked up to see a large black raven ominously perched atop the chair-back at the far end of her dining table, twenty feet away. She calmly closed the book and waited.

A few moments later a handsome, athletic man in a gas company uniform, helmet, and climbing harness stepped partway around the corner. He had cold steel-blue eyes and the self-assured gait of a special operator.

"I've been expecting you."

The man registered not the slightest hint of surprise. At a gesture from him the bird flew off, across the living room and out her open sliding glass door.

"Do you normally leave your doors unlocked and your alarms deactivated?"

"I didn't want you to break anything. I'm having a party tomorrow night."

"And your security detail?"

"Sent away for the same reason. I'm not foolish enough to resist the U.S. military." She appraised the man before her. "You'll have to forgive Henry. He's a bit naïve and self-impressed. But then, that's what the young are. The moment he called me, I knew to expect your visit."

The man said nothing.

"What can I do for our friends in The Activity?"

With his other hand he produced an insectlike robot the size of a toaster oven from around the corner and tossed it into the center of her dining room table. It left several nasty indentations on the rosewood before it clattered to a stop, facing her like a dead black spider.

She grimaced. "Ah, drones."

"Autonomous drones."

"And because we're promoting autonomous drones on Capitol Hill, you think we have something to do with these attacks against the United States."

"The drone strikes here are just the beginning. I'm more concerned about swarms of kill-decision drones overturning thousands of years of military doctrine and rules of conduct. That's a lot of hard-won experience to throw away without any debate."

"Well, we advise everyone from African dictators to country-western recording artists, to supermarkets—and, yes, aerospace. But we have nothing to hide from you."

"You're going to tell me who's running the project."

Marta pushed the book away. "You of all people should know these things are compartmentalized. Even if our side was somehow behind this, why would I know? And why would I know who knows? Tell me, Mr. . . . ."

"You call me Odin."

"Mr. Odin—you don't seem like someone who needs to be told what to do. In truth, despite the fact that everyone wants you to stop, you're still searching for the people behind these attacks."

He just stared, unreadable.

"That's because an expert knows what needs to be done. That's why they're an expert. I'm a public relations expert. My clients include aerospace interests, and I know that drones are the future. Dozens of nations plan on using drones to shift the balance of geopolitical power—to undo U.S. aerial and naval supremacy at a bargain price. We need to win that struggle. Are we behind the attacks? How the hell should I know? And, frankly, it doesn't interest me."

"You have no idea what this will unleash."

"And if we don't do it, everyone else will."

"Clarke and his people were manipulating social media. You were the one giving him access to raw telecom, geolocation, and Internet data—telling him who and what to oppose. How do you get access to that data? Are you NSA?"

She gave a tight smile. "It works the other way around, Mr. Odin. The NSA gets their data from us. A little-known fact got lost in the uproar about warrantless wiretapping: It wasn't the NSA that did the tapping. The work was outsourced to experienced companies that had already tapped most of the world's fiberoptic grid for other governments—some not so nice. Privately held companies the public's never heard of. Those companies have three thousand clients in a hundred and fifty countries—and one of those clients is the NSA. Do you get my meaning?"

"Did it ever occur to you that all this surveillance and data tracking has actually put the country in danger, instead of protecting it? It's being used to target drone attacks."

"That's a use I hadn't heard of. Although, this is the problem with a surveillance state; once you build it, it always grows. Do you realize how many industries use this data? How many people are busy building the systems to gather and analyze it? How much economic activity that's generating? Ah, but then, you've seen the valuations of social media companies and mobile start-ups. That list will continue to grow, and it will create inertia that resists any attempt to tear the surveillance system down. You're fighting against the tide of progress, Mr. Odin. It's not a matter of stopping me. I'm nothing. And there is no one person or group driving this. It's progress. You can't stop progress."

"This isn't progress. It's regression. We've been here before. Consolidation of power is as old as history. Power in the hands of very few. That's fundamentally at odds with democracy."

"I should think you'd be happy to have machines fight your wars for you."

"Whose wars? Who's to say who controls an autonomous drone? They can build their army in secret and fight wars anonymously, using surveillance data as the targeting mechanism. By that measure, America is more vulnerable to drones than just about any society on the planet. We're essentially giving an ant-level intelligence policing authority over us."

Marta took a sip of wine. "Well, I can hardly prevent that. And as you'll learn, there really isn't a central authority. There are only . . . interests." She raised her eyebrows. "Is there anything else I can do for my friends in The Activity, Mr. Odin?"

He stared at her, again unreadable. Marta usually prided herself on her ability to read people. This man was like a stone obelisk. His training, probably.

The man pulled an index card from somewhere with a close-in magician's dexterity. He approached Marta and left the card in front of her as he collected the carcass of the shattered drone.

"If this surveillance system can find anything, then you're going to make it work for me."

She shook her head. "I can't use it to find who's behind these drone attacks, Mr. Odin. I thought I made clear that there is no single entity resp—"

He put the card into her hand. "Read it. I want raw intercept data on anyone who's been dealing with that precise combination of chemicals over the past six months."

Marta sighed and read the words printed neatly on the index card.

She sounded the words out slowly. "Perfluoromethylhexane . . . dimethyl-cyclohexa . . ." She looked up. "What are these?"

"You have three hours to get the data. The where, the when, the who." He nodded at the card. "Have your people send it to the FTP share on the card. We hijacked it, so don't bother attacking the owner. If you don't comply or try to double-cross me, I'll take it as a declaration of war from you personally."

Marta held up her hands in acquiescence. "As I said, I'm always happy to help The Activity, Mr. Odin. And if this data pull will get you to move along, I'll be happy to accommodate you." Marta again lifted her wine-glass. "You do realize, though, that whoever is doing this might not be so happy to see you?"

Odin cast a parting glance at her as he carried his dead drone toward the exit. "You have three hours."

Marta watched him go before studying the list again in more detail—and taking out her cell phone.

CHAPTER 27

Proof-of-Concept

Linda McKinney watched an alien world through the slit of her all-encompassing black *niqab*. The restrictive garment felt like armor—disguising her. After all, Gaddani, Pakistan, was a place she'd never thought she'd be. About thirty miles north of Karachi, it was the third largest shipbreaking yard in the world. An operation conducted almost entirely without the aid of heavy machinery.

As she watched, a rusted freighter three hundred feet long steamed at full speed toward the wide beach. The vessel rode high in the water, its load line twenty feet above the waves, and its interior frame evident in the grid of worn, dented metal plates that showed its age. The tops of the propellers chopped the water into froth as the freighter pushed toward a wide beach littered with derelict ships, winches, rusting scrap metal, and dilapidated worker housing. Sparks and the hiss of a hundred blowtorches cutting through steel extended into the distance. Scores of men waited on the beach to receive the new freighter, their own blowtorches at the ready.

The ship plowed into the sand with an echoing, deep *boom* and groans of fatigued metal—like an office building running aground. In a moment it lurched to a halt. Even as the engines shut down, the men moved in to secure it with winches and chains.

McKinney glanced over at Odin and Foxy, who sat on the bench across from her in the back of a canvas-covered Bedford truck. They both wore shalwar kameez with black *shemagh* headscarves covering most of their faces. They held stubby AKS-74U carbines across their laps. The idea of people carrying around unregistered automatic weapons in public was something she never got used to, but then she knew Pakistan was a restive place. "How far does this scrapyard go?"

Odin swept his hand northward. "Five miles or more."

She gazed out at small hills of cut-up, rusted inch-thick steel. Lines of men were carrying newly cut metal plates up their slopes in a way so reminiscent of leaf-cutter ants it was uncanny. "I can see why you thought it was strange that large chemical shipments would be made here."

Odin nodded as he unfolded a printed map. "They go through a lot of acetylene and other volatile gases, so the chemical shipments wouldn't attract much attention from locals." He gazed out at the hills of scrap metal around them. "Plus, this place is busy enough and big enough to conceal a drone project. Welding wouldn't attract any attention. And it's a twenty-four-hour operation."

McKinney warily scanned the hazy sky. "Can you trust your contact?"

Foxy and Odin nodded confidently. Odin added, "He's not a company asset. We've known Azeem for years. Syrian. Ex–suicide bomber."

McKinney's look showed that had done nothing to ease her mind.

Odin shrugged. "He got disenchanted after he found out how much corruption there was. Wherever there's fighting, criminals capitalize on the chaos. They thrive in lawless environments. A lot of faithful teenage jihadists arriving here found themselves in rough company—heavily armed men more interested in moving heroin than defeating the infidel. We rescued Azeem from a criminal gang. He'd lost a lot of his idealism. He stuck around to rescue other idealists from their clutches and send them back home. That wasn't popular with my high command, but it opened up channels of communication."

The truck's diesel engine rattled in low gear as they navigated a tangled warren of dirt roads bustling with workers walking to and from their shifts, vendors hawking food, or phone cards, or cheap electronics. The carcasses of rusting cargo ships being cut to pieces loomed over the flat, dry landscape. It all seemed so dirty and industrial—not what she imagined Pakistan would look like. It made her realize that life goes on wherever you happen to be. She could see the tired faces of Pashtun workers treading along the roadside, goggles up on their foreheads, and tools over their shoulders. Some squatted in front of shacks, heating up tiny pots of tea with blowtorches. Not many of them had beards—a measure of practicality amid a daily shower of sparks. She could see just how hard these men worked, and she did not doubt that they supported families in distant villages. Life was a struggle.

McKinney heard Smokey's voice in her radio earpiece. *"We're arriving at Mantoori Industries. I see Azeem at the gate with two other men— both armed. He's giving the all-clear signal."*

Odin nodded and examined the Rover video tablet to see a raven's-eye view from Huginn and Muninn, who were covering them from overhead. "I don't see anything suspicious in the work yard. It looks abandoned. Keep weapons at the ready, and let's go in." Odin looked up at McKinney. "The presence of women here is unusual, Professor, but I need your expertise. So please don't speak or look any of these men in the eye. Basically, act like you don't exist. You and I will confer in private, like man and wife."

McKinney winced.

"We're undercover. Goes with the territory."

The engine of the truck slowed, and soon the Bedford truck turned to drive through a battered rolling gate painted in bright colors. The truck came to a stop. Odin and Foxy immediately opened the tailgate and leapt down, weapons held casually but at the ready.

Several Pashtun men, also in shalwar kameez, approached, weapons slung over their shoulders. A young, neatly groomed Arab man in his late twenties flashed a bright white smile and straight teeth. "Odin . . ." The two men shook hands and kissed each other on the cheek.

Odin nodded, *"As-salaam alaikum, Azeem. Kayf haalak?"*

Azeem nodded. "Fine, praise God. We should speak English. My friends here do not know it."

Odin gestured to his own companions. "You remember Foxy."

"Of course, my friend. . . ." They also exchanged handshakes and cheek kisses.

Ripper, Mooch, and Smokey emerged from the front cab. Ripper was likewise covered head-to-toe, but in a light blue burka. At least McKinney had company in this indignity. Azeem shook hands with the men but completely ignored the two women.

Odin was already studying the wide scrapyard, littered with rusting pieces of steel and derelict equipment. "How long has it been abandoned?"

"The security guard says the landlord is owed rent for two months now, but the tenant is gone. They paid cash."

One of Azeem's companions, a Pashtun man in his fifties, was speaking in what McKinney assumed was Pashto to an elderly man with a timeworn AK-47 slung over his back. Azeem listened intently to their conversation.

"He says the men who came here wore black—their faces always concealed with shemagh. Much like you, and they spoke through translators."

Odin exchanged looks with Foxy. "Does he know what nationality they were? Were they tall? Short?"

Azeem shook his head. "The workers in neighboring plots stayed away because they thought they were either extremists or a drug gang. You must understand, the workers here are of the lowest social rank. They want no trouble. So they kept their distance." He gestured to the rusting hulk on the beach behind the place. "That's why no one's touched the salvage ship left behind. They're afraid these men will return." Azeem listened again to the old man talking. "He says container trucks made deliveries at all hours, and these people did not observe Salah—or any of the Five Pillars."

McKinney had noticed that Odin was listening to the old man himself, and she suspected he didn't need Azeem's translation.

Odin studied the cinder-block warehouse in front of them. "You've checked the place out?"

Azeem nodded. "Whatever they did here was very strange, Odin. It doesn't look like any drug-processing lab I've seen. The old man says they cut ship steel but only at night."

"Wait here, Azeem." Odin nodded to his team as he moved toward the warehouse.

McKinney followed, surreptitiously producing the jury-rigged chemical detection device Tegu had made for them in Mexico. She unfolded the severed drone antenna that had been connected to the old voltmeter housing and powered up the LED display.

As they walked into a wide, almost empty warehouse, perhaps two hundred feet on a side, the faint peppery aroma of oleoresin capsicum immediately came to her. The entire group exchanged looks.

"That smells familiar."

"Colony pheromone." The detection wand in McKinney's hand started displaying parts per billion of perfluorocarbons as well—the odorless, colorless taggant chemicals that did not occur in nature.

McKinney showed Odin the red LED readout. "It lit up the minute we entered."

Foxy moved to the nearest wall, where empty plastic barrels were piled haphazardly. "Hey! Look here." He brought his face near to it but then turned away. "Empty barrels of 'anger juice.' From the looks of it. And probably some of the other chemicals too."

Odin was moving toward a forty-foot orange storage container sitting with its doors open at the far wall. McKinney walked alongside him, checking the readout occasionally. Odin readied his carbine and motioned for Smokey and Mooch to approach from other angles.

Odin peered weapon-first into the opening of the container.

Foxy called out. "What's in it?"

"Empty metal racks." Odin stepped inside, examining what looked to be built-in metal shelving. They looked like purpose-built storage racks, with odd dimensions and metal rollers built in.

McKinney scanned the container with the wand, getting only middling readings on her meter. "Not much residue here. Do you think these racks were made for drones?"

"Hard to say." Odin noticed something and moved to the container wall. He slung his weapon and grabbed what looked to be a sliding panel with handles built into the side of the container. With some effort he slid it down to open a five-foot-wide, two-foot-tall hatch. He was now staring at Foxy, who approached across the warehouse floor.

"Hidden panel."

Odin nodded as he examined the edge of one rack. "Doesn't look like this one was finished."

"Maybe they left in a hurry."

McKinney was already walking toward the far wall, watching the chemical readings going up again. "Hey! It increases in this direction. . . ."

Odin and the others followed her, weapons ready. "Stay alert, people." He made a circling motion in the air with his hand, and the team spread out in a skirmish line. They were moving toward a metal overhead door that faced the beach. The door was closed.

As they reached it, Foxy noticed a cracked tan fiberglass mold about ten feet long leaning against the wall nearby. The mold had a wing-shaped depression in it. He tipped it over with the barrel of his gun, and it rolled back and forth for a while on its rounded aerodynamic shape.

"Carbon fiber mold?"

Odin studied it while McKinney scanned with the detector. She looked up. "That's not where my readings are coming from."

"Let's get this door open. Move clear." Odin watched as the team took up positions to either side of the loading bay door, and then he pressed a worn button mounted on the wall. With a hum and a rattle the metal door started to ascend. The din of distant blowtorch cutting and diesel winches came to their ears as fresh air blew into the warehouse. Looming a hundred meters away was the rear half of a rusted cargo freighter, standing five stories tall in the water, its near end closed off by corrugated interior bulkheads.

The team moved out onto the debris-strewn beach, weapons ready, and taking different paths around piles of detritus. Inch-thick pieces of rusted steel were everywhere, cut cleanly into squares.

Even with the breeze, McKinney was suddenly getting a hundred and fifty parts per billion of perfluorocarbon—nearly three times what

she was getting inside the warehouse. "It's going up dramatically now. . . ."
She ignored the constricting black bag she was wearing and focused on
the detector as she walked on sandals across the beach toward the grounded
freighter. "It's coming from the ship."

Foxy pointed down as they moved across the hard-packed sand.
"Strange tracks here, boss." He nudged a booted foot at what appeared to
be striation patterns pounded deeply into the sand.

"Professor, let us take point." Odin edged ahead of McKinney as he
climbed a toppled section of hull as a ramp to get onto the keel of the
broken ship. The others were close behind, staring into a dark maw that
led into the darkness of the one remaining hold.

McKinney ran her hand along the inch-thick steel edge of the hull. A
clean, straight cut. "Doesn't look like someone did this by hand." She
gestured to the ruler-straight cuts, and then out to the men spraying
sparks in the distance as they cut the hulls. Those silhouettes looked far
more irregular.

"What do you think, boss?" Foxy inspected the edges. "Ship-cutting
drones?"

Odin looked back at them, shining his Maglite into the darkness
from the edge of the doorway. "I don't want us all in the hold at once.
Bullets will ricochet off this steel like tennis balls. You guys follow when
I give the all-clear." Odin stuck the duct-taped end of the Maglite into his
mouth and moved into the opening.

McKinney watched him go. "Be careful."

He mumbled something around the flashlight in his mouth, and then
disappeared into the blackness.

The rest of the team raised their weapons, watching his light beam
scan about in what, judging from the echoing, was a cavernous space.

After a tense minute or so they heard a shout. "Clear! Get in here!"

The team exchanged looks and hurried into the darkness. Foxy and
Mooch turned on Maglites of their own. McKinney followed on their
heels, and soon she was at the bottom of a huge cargo hold that was partially illuminated by bright shafts of light coming in from a series of holes
cut farther up in the hull and the deck overhead. It was easily over a

hundred feet to the top, with chains hanging down and water dripping into pools on the rusted steel floor, but the cut patterns in the walls were just as symmetrical as those on the hull outside.

McKinney glanced at the reading on the detector. It was now up to a thousand parts per billion. "Good Lord. Judging from the pheromone readings in here, we've entered the colony itself."

"You mean what was the colony."

McKinney looked up to see the team assembled around some sort of broken machine the size of a dog lying on its back on the floor. She walked up to them. "What is it?"

Odin and Foxy stepped aside to reveal what looked to be a metal armature—obviously not a complete machine, but the base of one. "Broken. Looks like it has magnetic feet."

"Careful."

Odin pointed. "Disassembled—the top's been taken off. There's no motor. No circuit boards."

McKinney leaned close and pulled off her veil to get a better look. The device looked like the articulated legs of a weaver ant on a central frame—with what appeared to be magnetic pads for feet. The upper portion of the machine was missing. She tried to raise it and was surprised it lifted off the metal—and it was lighter than she expected.

Odin examined the pads of the feet, tracing wires that led up the frame. "Electromagnets. They could switch off the magnets on each foot to provide traction and leverage for movement." He flexed the leg and found it springlike, with plastic rods rooted in place like tendons. "I've seen this before. Electroactive polymers. They contract like muscle tissue when subjected to electrical current. No moving parts needed."

McKinney's hands came up greasy. She wiped them on her black robe, then ran her hands along four aluminum canisters similar to the pheromone dispensers on the quadracopter drones they had encountered in Colorado—only, these containers were liter-sized. "Look. A similar configuration of four pheromone dispensers."

"But five times larger." He gave her a look of recognition for her earlier prediction.

She waved the detector over them, and above one it went up into the tens of thousands of parts per billion. "The mother lode. We should take these with us."

"Leave the pepper pheromone behind. They're angry enough already."

"We should take everything." She started unscrewing the canisters from the frame. "Why would they bother with this? A ship-based drone colony. I don't see how these would be better than what we've already seen."

Foxy nodded back behind them. "There was that wing section back there. You think these things fly?"

"A flying ship-cutter." Odin kicked the device over with his boot. "We're not seeing the whole picture." He stared up at the cuts made in the side of the hull—square holes. "Shipbreaking drones."

McKinney stood. "But why bother with that? Why not simply swarms of drones with bombs or missiles?"

Odin shook his head. "I don't know. But I do know that swarms of steel-cutting drones could play hell with shipping, radio towers, railroads, and bridges. Someone is building an integrated autonomous war machine, with varying types of drones that can work in concert with each other. Each with a specialized job to do."

McKinney nodded. "Like the polymorphism that ants exhibit."

"Right. We need to stop them before that integrated system is complete. We know that a few thousand barrels of those precursor chemicals were shipped here, and now they're gone—along with just about everything else that was here. And it looks like they loaded it all into shipping containers. Foxy, ask Azeem if he still has a contact in customs in Karachi."

Foxy nodded.

"Pack up those canisters. We need to find out where those containers went."

CHAPTER 28

Brood Chamber

Linda McKinney stood at the bow of the surging workboat as humid tropical air rushed past her. She was happy to be back in Western business casual clothing. Alongside her Odin gazed through binoculars at a row of massive blue loading cranes running in a line that extended halfway across the horizon. The land ahead was essentially a concrete island edged by massive pilings and a black-and-yellow warning strip. The scale of the Chiwan Container Port boggled the mind. Onshore workers looked like specks moving among the multicolored shipping containers that rose like a Lego mountain range as far as the eye could see. Monstrous container ships rested up against the island's geometric flanks, while high-speed cranes thirty stories tall loaded them like children stacking blocks.

A young Chinese man in a hard hat, rumpled shirt, and slacks stood some ways behind them, chain-smoking near the wheelhouse of the boat. He was looking a little sick as Evans lectured him about something in Chinese—how to avoid seasickness, possibly.

McKinney shouted in the wind to Odin. "Evans knows Chinese?"

"He had business here back in the day."

"Your other friend doesn't look like a sailor. Who is he?"

Odin spoke while still scanning the horizon. "Shipping agent. Old smuggling contact. We used to help his father avoid tariffs in exchange for letting us know if certain materials were moving in their ships." He lowered the binoculars. "We scratch each other's backs for paperwork-free favors."

"What does he think we're looking for?"

"Radiological material bound for the U.S."

"Nuclear bombs."

"Dirty bombs."

McKinney unzipped a backpack on her shoulder that contained the pheromone canisters from Gaddani as well as the jury-rigged detector. She lifted the detector up so Odin could see. "You think he'll notice this isn't a Geiger counter?"

"Wun isn't a technical guy. He's a shipping agent. It's his connections I need, not his grasp of nuclear physics." Odin turned to the wheelhouse and motioned to the left.

The pilot nodded and started turning the wheel.

Odin called out, "Wun! Hey, Wun!"

The Chinese man looked up.

Odin gestured to the docks, and Wun nodded, heading up into the boat's wheelhouse.

Before long they were cruising along the concrete coast. It was a wall twenty feet high with stone pilings every ten yards or so, faced with thick rubber stanchions laced with chains. There was no apparent way to get up to the level of the container yard. But as she looked ahead, McKinney could see a smaller dock at water level linked to the island by gangways leading up. Several men in shirtsleeves, ties, and hard hats were waiting there, waving.

Before long the engine of the workboat roared into reverse, kicking up turbulent brown water, and the pilot brought the boat skillfully to a stop inches from the dock. The waiting men were fiftyish Han Chinese, with moles and jowls, smiling and nodding as the Americans came ashore. Apparently they didn't know a word of English, because the lead one merely extended visitor badges and gestured for them to clip them to their lapels. Another handed them hard hats and motioned for them to follow him up the aluminum gangway. Evans went first, then Odin, and McKinney followed, looping her arms through both backpack straps to be certain it didn't fall into the water.

She glanced around and spoke sotto voce to Odin as they walked in single file up the ramp. "What if the authorities show up?"

"These are the authorities. Unofficial arrangements are a national sport in China."

When they got to the level of the shipping yard, McKinney got a full appreciation for just how vast the place was. Interlocking flagstones stretched away in two directions to a vanishing point. The yard was a hive of activity: Vehicles and people rushed to and fro, signaling as they guided crane clamps down onto the containers, and truck tractors roared around with and without loads.

Their hosts had a white compact car with a driver ready for them. The Chinese writing on the side was a mystery, but it had a circular logo identical to one on the massive cranes looming above them. McKinney and Evans took the backseat, while Odin got in on the passenger side, nodding good-bye to Wun—who waved enthusiastically.

The driver was a grim-faced, rail-thin man who could have been anywhere from thirty to fifty years of age. He looked more Vietnamese or Laotian than Chinese.

Odin looked in the rearview mirror. "Evans, tell him to just drive around from lane to lane. Let's open all the windows."

Odin and McKinney started rolling window handles, while Evans leaned forward and tapped the driver on the shoulder.

"*Dài wǒmen qù měi yīxíng. Wǒmen xiǎng zǐxì de kàn yīxià huòguì chǎng.*"

The driver nodded and got them in motion, racing around despite all the truck traffic.

Evans made a steering wheel motion with his hands. "Hey, pal. Let's not get us killed, okay?" He pointed. "*Nǐ kāichē xiàng gè fēngzi!*"

The man laughed but didn't change his speed.

McKinney held the pheromone sensor up to the cross-breeze. "If there's any perfluorocarbon here, even in low concentrations, this should find it."

The driver brought them for miles along narrow lanes dangerous with trucks racing around blind corners. McKinney wondered if the copious diesel fumes would ruin their sampling, but on they went for the better part of an hour. The team was weary by the time the car emerged at the end of the container yard to a stretch of open pavement extending several hundred yards along the sea. The damp outlines where containers had been were evident in neat rows on the stone.

As the driver turned the car to circle back, the LED counter on the detector started racing upward from zero to several hundred parts per billion.

"Whoa! Wait a second."

Odin motioned to the driver. "Stop!"

The car stopped.

The LED leveled off at three hundred twelve. Odin gestured back to the open stretch of pavement. "Go back. Over there." He pointed.

The driver shifted into reverse, turned around, and then headed out into the open area. Almost immediately McKinney watched the detector readout race up past seven hundred.

"It's getting stronger."

Indeed, McKinney could already smell the familiar peppery scent. "That's with nothing physical left behind. Whatever was here must have been bigger than what was in Gaddani."

They were driving along the empty dockside now. Odin looked to her. "They must have just loaded it. If we find out where that shipment was going, we might be able to intercept it. Jot down those bay numbers, Mort. And tell the driver to bring us to the shipping office."

Fifteen minutes later they were standing in a tiny cubicle in a grungy office that smelled of cigarettes and cheap aftershave. They were crowded around Wun's dusty computer screen, looking at a map of the vast container yard with thousands of little squares moving on it.

Wun changed some dates on the edge of the screen, and the pattern changed.

Odin pointed. "They were in Bays three thirty-six through five fifty-two."

Wun spoke with a thick accent. "Container IDs?"

"No container IDs, Wun. Just give a printout of all the containers that went on that ship—and the name of the ship. That's all we need."

"Probably more than one ship." Wun swept his hand across the yard map. "Big area." He clicked through a few command menus, and then snorted. "Ah . . . big ship too."

"Big ship—you mean they all went on one ship?"

Wun nodded. "Fourteen thousand two hundred forty-two container." He held up his index finger. "One ship. *Ebba Maersk*—biggest ship there is." A printer somewhere started spitting out paper.

McKinney leaned in. "The *Ebba Maersk*. That's the name of the ship?"

Wun nodded. "Big, big ship. Half kilometer long." He then scrolled through the list of containers in the manifest, shaking his head. "Different companies, same product and same weight. Machine tools. Six thousand two hundred three container machine tools."

McKinney was puzzled.

Odin pointed at the description line: *Machine Tools*. "Kind of unusual to have so many of one thing from different companies, isn't it?"

He nodded. "Never see before."

Odin narrowed his eyes. "Where's the ship heading?"

Wun ran his finger along the screen, then stopped on one line. "Singapore."

"You have Internet access?"

Wun rolled his eyes and gave Odin a dirty look.

"Okay, fine, Wun. Can I use this for a second?"

Wun pushed back and Odin leaned in to open a Web browser. He quickly typed into the URL line as McKinney and Evans watched.

She leaned in again. "What are you looking for?"

"Commercial marine traffic is carefully tracked. Retailers and other clients need to gauge arrival times."

Evan pushed in as well. "Ah, cool, what do you use?"

"Marinetraffic.com."

Odin entered the name *Ebba Maersk* in the ship name box, then clicked SEARCH. Moments later a Google map appeared showing a line of waypoints leading away from Hong Kong and forging out into the center of the South China Sea.

Odin stared at the screen without moving for several moments.

McKinney watched him. "What's wrong?"

"The route." He stood up, looking straight into McKinney's eyes.

She stared back. "You think all those containers are carrying ship-cutting drones."

"Eighty racks per container. Six thousand two hundred containers. What is that?"

Evans answered with a nervous laugh. "That's nearly half a million drones, Odin."

"Okay, so, what if they don't all contain drones? What if some contain fuel or pheromone chemicals, weapons—whatever; that could still leave a hundred thousand or more ship-cutters."

"But what would they be cutting? The *Ebba Maersk*?"

Odin shook his head. "It didn't make sense until I saw this." He pointed at the map. "Heading through the South China Sea." Odin opened another browser window and Googled the words *U.S. aircraft carriers South China Sea.*

Wun threw up his hands. "Why you search on my computer, asshole?"

Moments later the search results came up and Odin clicked on the first link from a recent article on the BBC News website. It was headlined, U.S. AND VIETNAM STAGE JOINT NAVAL EXERCISES.

Odin stood up. "USS *George Washington* carrier strike group out of Yokosuka. They've been operating here for a while. Joint naval exercises with Vietnam and the Philippines just south of the Paracel Islands. It's a geopolitical chess game with the Chinese."

"But why would China attack a U.S. carrier? It would start a war."

Wun looked up at her, both shocked and offended.

Odin paused, grabbed the thick stack of printouts from the printer, and then nodded to Wun. "Thanks a lot, Wun. We'll find our own way back to the dock. Give my best to your dad, okay?" He pulled McKinney away and started heading to the exit.

Evans was close behind. "Hey, later, Wun. Good luck with the smuggling."

Wun looked after them suspiciously.

Odin spoke softly as they headed down a box-lined hallway. "I'm certain the Chinese wouldn't attack a U.S. carrier group—but with drones no one would be able to tell who attacked it. Let's face it: We don't know either."

"But why would someone want to precipitate a crisis?"

"You remember the Cold War? Lots of unquestioned defense spending. Don't underestimate the tensions around global shipping lanes and energy, Professor. China is facing what they call the 'Malacca Dilemma.' Over three-quarters of their oil imports go through the Straits of Malacca—then up through the South China Sea. That gateway is currently dominated by U.S. naval power in the form of carrier strike groups. Which means we theoretically have a knife against their jugular—just like they do against ours. But if someone disrupts that balance . . ."

"You're not suggesting there'd be war?"

"No. There'd be no definite proof who the enemy is. But it might rewrite the rule book on war. What if those thousands of containers were all weaver drone nests, Professor? Do you remember the openings on the containers we saw in Gaddani? What if that container ship is one big interconnected colony, six thousand nests strong—marked with their pheromonal scent?"

"The dock reeked of it."

"Some were probably leaking."

McKinney imagined the same type of drone they had seen in Gaddani—a flying ship-cutter, swarming by the thousands with the same aggressiveness they'd experienced in Colorado. "They would destroy anything that got near their colony ship—no extra programming necessary."

Evans eased up alongside. "Then why didn't they go ape on the workers here? Or attack the ship's crew?"

"Maybe they're dormant."

Odin reacted to the suggestion. "They could activate when they crossed a GPS waypoint. Or via radio signal." He pointed at the map printout. "How close would something have to get to the ship to get attacked?"

McKinney shrugged. "It depends on the tolerance variable set in the model. The designer could make it anything. A hundred feet or a hundred miles."

Odin examined the printout of the container ship's course through the South China Sea. "Once it's out in open water . . ." He traced the path of the ship toward the Paracel Islands. "The picket ships and combat air patrol for a carrier group scout out to two hundred miles. But a commercial container ship like the *Ebba Maersk* won't raise any alarms. That means it could get in close, and the swarm would overwhelm the *George Washington*'s defenses. If it manages to sink that carrier, there'd be no way to positively attribute the attack to anyone. America couldn't strike back, and the rest of our carriers would be just as vulnerable. Our whole naval doctrine would be obsolete. An international arms race for swarming drones would follow."

McKinney grimaced. "Making war the province of autonomous machines."

He looked up. "We need to stop that ship."

Evans shrugged. "Easy. Call the navy. One antiship missile and BOOM—problem solved."

"We're going to need more evidence to convince someone to blow up a Danish-flagged ship, Mort. There are people on it."

"If this drone colony wakes up, then the crew's dead anyway—"

McKinney held a hand up to interrupt Evans but looked at Odin. "Evans is right about one thing: Warn the navy, tell them what we've discovered. Or get in touch with the *Ebba Maersk* by radio and have them turn around."

Odin shook his head. "My crypto codes are blown. I can't even get in contact with my own command. And I'd just sound like a lunatic to the *Maersk* people."

"What about the Chinese?"

"I don't think they'll be too eager to sink the largest container ship in the world without provocation. If they're not behind this, we'll wind up getting shot as spies, and if they are, then we'll wind up getting shot as spies."

"Can you call someone you know—someone high up in the Pentagon?"

Odin was still shaking his head. "That's not how things work. You saw that vocaloid, and besides almost no one knows who we are; that's the whole point of compartmentalizing The Activity. We function because very few people in Washington know us. The colonel was my contact, and they can apparently intercept my communications with him."

The three of them pushed through the shipping office door and out into the bustling container yard, only to be confronted by a score of grim-faced Chinese men in fairly good suits arrayed in a semicircle at a distance of thirty feet. They wore sunglasses and radio earphones. Several were holding MP5 submachine guns, raised skyward. Behind them, beyond the door they had just exited, McKinney could see several more men appearing in the reception area of the office.

They were surrounded.

Evans got deathly pale and unusually quiet.

One of the Asian men motioned for them to put their hands in the air. "If you please, Mr. Odin."

McKinney turned to Odin. He nodded encouragingly but without much conviction. She felt her heart sink. She wasn't used to seeing him caught off guard.

Several men rushed over to them, patting them down as a white, unmarked panel van rolled up nearby. Even more armed men in suits got out. One of the men grabbed the paper printouts of the *Ebba Maersk* from Odin. Another grabbed the backpack from McKinney.

She felt fear rushing through her again. Were these Chinese government agents? She, Odin, and Evans were, after all, in the country illegally. But the quality of the men's suits began to put doubts in her head. Corrupt officials, gangsters—there was really very little difference.

The men roughly and very intimately frisked her, while another man pulled her hands behind her back and secured them with plastic zip-ties.

They then marched all three of their prisoners to the panel van and pushed them inside.

Evans was looking more angry by the minute. "This is why I fucking hate you, Odin. I had a life, man." He closed his eyes in a hard squint as if having difficulty coping with his anxiety.

Odin shook his head, muttering. "Zollo . . . zollo . . . zollo."

"Don't even pull that bullshit with me right now."

They were all lying on the corrugated metal floor of the van with several men standing over them holding small black submachine guns. The van accelerated, sending the prisoners sliding. One of the guards kicked Evans.

"Ow!"

McKinney rolled over to look at Odin. "Odin. Who are these people?"

"Ānjìng!" One of the other guards stomped on McKinney with his expensive dress shoes. The effect was less than he'd probably intended, but she kept quiet.

Odin just stared ahead, unreadable. She'd never seen him like that, which worried her more than anything else.

They didn't drive long—just a few minutes. Given the size of the container yard, McKinney felt fairly certain that they couldn't have left the premises in that time. Sure enough, when the van stopped and the guards opened the rear doors to drag them out, she could see that they were in the vast, empty section of the container yard where the weaver drone shipment had departed. There was nothing but empty pavement and silent shipping cranes for hundreds of meters in every direction—and the water of the Pearl River Delta close at hand. There were fewer men now—but still about a dozen. And they were all armed. McKinney, Odin, and Evans each had two men haul them by the elbows toward the water's edge. McKinney felt her adrenaline spiking. This used to be an alien sensation—facing imminent death—but she was starting to become familiar with it.

The men stopped at the dock's edge and pulled McKinney and the others upright with their backs to the water. From this perspective McKinney could now see a sleek, midnight blue Sikorsky S-76 helicopter parked not too far away in the vast empty space, its idle blades drooping. The chopper was facing nose-away from them, and one of the suited Asian men approached it holding McKinney's backpack. He rapped on the fuselage, then handed the backpack to someone inside.

In a moment a suited Caucasian man stepped out of the chopper and approached with a casual confidence. Well before he reached them McKinney recognized him.

It was Ritter—the man who had pretended to be a Homeland Security agent all the way back in Kansas City. McKinney glanced over at Odin, but he seemed to be in his own world. That truly frightened her.

Ritter stopped ten feet away and nodded to Odin. "You got off with a warning as a professional courtesy, David. A warning you ignored." Ritter nodded to the lead Asian man. "Get this over with."

Odin spoke calmly, seemingly to himself. "White. Two through five. Red. One-two."

"Apologies, but I'll need DNA evidence."

McKinney felt her heart race as three of the Asian men produced long, sharp-looking stilettos and walked toward them.

Evans shouted, "Oh, God! No! No! Wait!"

McKinney was speechless, mouthing silent words.

A howling sound came in on the breeze—and a *thwack* as a fist-sized hole blasted through the nearest man's chest. The men to either side of her shouted, dropping her. She pitched forward onto the cement.

Odin shouted as he tumbled next to her. "Stay down, Professor!"

There were shouts in Chinese and she could see expensive shoes scrambling every direction across the pavement, and a thick rivulet of blood oozing toward her. Now there were short bursts of machine gun fire, followed by several more incoming high-pitched whines and *thwacks*. Screams. Men shouting, *"Bié kāi qiāng! Wǒmen tóuxiáng!"*

McKinney craned her neck to look up and saw several suited men dead on the ground at the center of blood spatter trails. Other men groaned with terrible wounds; still others were kneeling, hands in the air, as Odin shouted at them, *"Bǎ wǔqì rēngle fǒuzé wǒmen jiù kāi qiāngle!"*

Odin turned and shouted at Ritter, who was fleeing toward the chopper. "Stop, Ritter! You'll be dead before you reach it!"

Ritter was still a good hundred feet from the Sikorsky and something ricocheted off the pavement between him and the aircraft. He slid to a stop, his hands raised to the surrounding world. He turned around to face Odin, a look of considerable concern on his face. "It was the mission, David. Nothing personal."

"You always were a goddamned snowball. Even back in OTC. Did you even read the terrain? You really think I'd enter a place without over-watch? Without an exit plan?" Odin raised his bound hands behind his back as far as he could, and then brought them sharply down against his spine. The PlastiCuffs snapped, freeing his hands. Odin leaned down to pick up one of the fallen stilettos as he looked to McKinney and Evans. "Get up."

McKinney struggled to her knees, by which time Odin had reached her. He cut her bonds, then moved to free Evans—who looked shaky on his feet.

"Jesus Christ, Odin. I fucking hate working with you."

Odin grabbed one of the fallen MP5 submachine guns. He motioned for McKinney and Evans to follow him as he walked toward Ritter, who still had his hands raised, peering into the distance.

"Where are they? In the crane tower?"

Odin kept the gun trained as he frisked Ritter with his free hand. "Further."

Ritter eyed the wooded hills in the distance. "They're very good."

"They're the best." Odin frowned, having come up empty. "You surprise me."

Ritter looked feckless. "It seemed unnecessary. David, this accomplishes nothing."

Odin pushed Ritter along. "Is your pilot armed?"

"He's just a pilot. He doesn't even know why we're here."

"Move." He turned. "Evans!"

Evans was examining a wet spot in the crotch of his pants. "Yeah, what, asshole?"

"Grab a gun and meet us in the chopper."

Evans sighed, still obviously angry, but trudged back to a nearby dead man. "*Wánliǎo . . .*"

Ritter opened the chopper door, and the pilot looked up from his logbook. Apparently gunshots hadn't alarmed him. He was a clean-cut Caucasian with a military bearing and buzz cut blond hair.

Odin pointed the gun. "Don't be stupid, and you'll live. We're going to Xiaonan Shan trailhead, right on the hilltop, there." Odin nodded toward the forested hill overlooking the container yard, about a mile away. "There's a park on the summit. Land in the grass."

The pilot nodded grimly. "I have a wife and a young—"

Ritter just laughed. "That's funny."

"No one's killing anyone as long as you do what you're told."

Odin and McKinney got into the back of the nicely appointed commuter chopper. There was carpeting, wood trim, and a plush leather bench with four seats, along with two swiveling captain chairs, in addition to the two pilot positions. McKinney, Evans, and Odin slid into the bench seat, while Odin nodded for Ritter to sit in one of the captain chairs, where he was in the same line of sight as the pilot. McKinney noticed her backpack on the floor nearby. She opened it to find the pheromone detector and canisters of perfluorocarbon still inside.

The engines started to whine to life.

"Whistleblowers never get rewarded, David. They get punished."

The engines gained speed while they exchanged stares. They soon lifted off, rising over the vast container yard.

Ritter gestured to it. "That's the modern world down there. Automated. Why should war be any different?"

"Because war can destroy us."

Ritter sighed. "It's going to happen. They need to invalidate the traditional military. They need to show that it's obsolete—and that requires a demonstration. You know that."

McKinney narrowed her eyes at him. "Who the hell are you?"

He ignored her. "Listen to me, David. We shouldn't be fighting. Men like you will always have a place."

"I already have a place."

The chopper was rising toward a lush hilltop festooned with banners covered in Chinese script. The summit had a circular road with a swath of grass. It was the only obvious landing zone, so the pilot brought them down, causing a couple of park visitors to flee for cover from the wind.

Moments after they touched down, several people with long, black nylon bags slung over their backs rushed to the chopper. As the doors opened, McKinney smiled at the sight of Foxy, Ripper, Smokey, and Mooch. Over the sound of the idling rotors Odin shouted to the pilot, "Out!"

The man looked incredulous until he saw Foxy and Ripper with .45 tactical pistols at the pilot's and copilot's doors. He unbuckled and quietly exited the chopper while Mooch and Smokey climbed in back, unslinging their rifles. They also appeared to have small nylon enclosures for the ravens—each bird behind a screen mesh. They passed these inside. In a few moments Foxy had taken the pilot seat and Ripper the copilot's. They pulled on headphones as they did.

Foxy raised the throttle and the big chopper lifted off smoothly from the top of the hill. "Man, I love Sikorskys. This is the way to travel."

Ripper spoke in her headset, looking back at Odin. "Where we headed?"

Odin picked up the map of the *Ebba Maersk* from the printout sitting nearby and handed it to her. "South. Out to sea."

She examined the map. "We won't have the range to get out there and back again."

Odin just stared. "I know."

 **CHAPTER 29**

Improvise

Ritter contorted his body and pounded his feet into the wall panel. "Goddammit, David! What you're doing is insane! You can't stop this. You're too late."

Odin stared at the ocean passing below. He was now in the copilot's seat, headset on, examining his map of the South China Sea. "You'd better hope we can stop it."

"You're the reason they activated it early. It's already too late. What you're doing is pointless." Ritter nodded toward the instruments. "We've only got a four-hundred-mile range. We won't have enough fuel to get back to land."

"We'll be landing on the *Ebba Maersk*."

"No! You won't. Goddammit, that's what I've been . . . you won't be landing on the ship. What sense does it make to throw all our lives away?"

Odin turned slowly in his seat to face Ritter, as did McKinney and Evans.

Foxy spoke into his pilot headset. "That doesn't sound good."

Odin nodded toward Ritter. "What are you saying?"

"I'm saying, if we approach that ship, we will die. Anything that approaches that ship in the next seventy-two hours will die."

"Do you know how to stop it?"

"There is no way to stop it. That's the whole point. They take care of it."

"Who's behind this, Ritter?"

"I don't know! My job was to make you stop looking. But if you turn around, I'll help you find out who's in charge. I swear it. Just turn the chopper around."

Odin turned forward again. "Sure you will."

Ritter's face contorted, and he started kicking the wall panel again. "Goddammit, turn around!"

"What's that ahead?" Foxy pointed at a wisp of black smoke on the horizon.

Odin nodded. "Make for it." He turned back to the others. "Get ready."

"If you get too close, they'll knock us out of the sky."

Evans stared at Ritter, the man's panic starting to rub off on him. "Maybe we should listen to him, Odin."

"Mission's not done yet, Mordecai."

Evans sighed. "Fuck . . ."

The smoke on the horizon grew rapidly into a black plume, and then to a smoking ship wallowing on the waves.

Foxy brought them in low and fast as they passed over a two-hundred-foot-long fishing trawler crawling with what looked like black vampire bats the size of surfboards. The nets were torn apart on the booms, and the wheelhouse was engulfed in flames. There were burn holes in the steel hull. Bodies and debris floated in the water all around it. The ship was clearly sinking, its bow almost in the waves.

The black-winged drones swarmed over the surface of the vessel, showers of sparks flying up as they cut the ship apart even as it sank. Clouds of smaller drones hovered above them—and then rose to give chase to the passing helicopter.

"Heads up, heads up!"

Foxy leaned the chopper forward, increasing speed. "I'm on it."

The smaller drones fell back behind them.

McKinney stared at the carnage, trying to come to grips with what they were heading into.

Ritter just groaned. "I told you. And this is nothing. We need to turn back."

Odin nodded toward the horizon. "The colony ship must have left these behind."

McKinney tapped his shoulder. "They wouldn't know they're on a ship. It's just the nest to them. The model wouldn't make it easy for them to find their home ship if they couldn't see it."

"Then they're single-use. But I guess they have plenty of extras."

Evans was still looking back at the drones devouring the trawler. "I was standing on solid ground. I could have just gotten out with the pilot, but no . . ."

Odin looked at the map. "The *Ebba Maersk* came straight through here."

Ritter shouted, "I'm telling you, we need to turn back. It's too late to do anything about this!"

Odin drew a .45 tactical pistol and aimed it straight at Ritter's face. "You want to add something constructive, or do you want to go out the door right now?"

Ritter just stared at the gun barrel, then turned away sullenly toward the wall.

McKinney eyed Odin, but he stowed the pistol and turned back toward the front. "Professor, please think of a way to stop this Franken-stein monster of yours."

"It's not my Frankenstein monster—and I don't know. I'm . . . I'm thinking."

They traveled for another thirty minutes in deep existential silence, listening only to the white noise of the engines. Then Foxy pointed to the horizon again.

"More smoke ahead."

Odin nodded. "Two plumes this time."

Foxy glanced down at the fuel gauge. They had traveled about four hundred miles in two and a half hours, deep into the center of the South

China Sea. "Running low on fuel, boss. Probably not more than another thirty minutes' running time."

Odin nodded. "We saw the position of the ship. We're within range of it. Just keep going."

Ritter groaned in despair.

Soon they were roaring past two more vessels a mile apart, burning and adrift. One was a large pleasure yacht fully engulfed in flames on its way to burning to the waterline. The other was a rusted freighter, guttering plumes of black smoke from the stern, which just now rose up out of the water as the ship slipped beneath the waves—several drones still cutting into its keel with a brief shower of sparks and smoke.

Foxy grimaced. "Don't see any survivors in the water. Those hovering drones are probably the people killers."

Odin scanned the horizon with binoculars. He lowered them and pointed. "Up ahead. That's gotta be it. It's huge."

After a few minutes they could see the ship with the naked eye. It was a massive light blue container ship leaving a broad wake. It was easily two hundred feet wide, but they could see what looked to be a dark cloud swirling all around it. And then part of the cloud split away—heading in their direction.

McKinney put on her headphones. "My God. There are thousands of them—there's no way we're getting near that ship."

Ritter shouted, "I've been telling you. This is suicide!"

Odin turned to face McKinney. "The crew is probably dead and the ship on autopilot. If we can disable the rudder, we might be able to stop it from reaching the vicinity of the carrier strike group. That's about two hundred miles south of here."

Foxy veered the chopper to starboard, curving away from the *Ebba Maersk*—still only a blue smudge on the horizon. They were still about twenty miles from it at an altitude of five thousand feet, but the indistinct swarm was heading up toward them. "Those things aren't slow. Best not to stick around."

McKinney leaned forward to put a hand on Odin's shoulder. "We have no choice. If we don't leave their attack perimeter, they're going to knock us into the sea."

Odin stared straight ahead but then nodded. "Turn toward Paracel, Foxy. Maybe we can get some resources there."

"Wilco."

Odin was deep in thought while Foxy examined the GPS on the console. He pointed at the nav screen map. "With the fuel we have left, even Paracel is going to be dicey."

McKinney pointed far off to the right, westward. "Is that another ship?"

Odin raised the binoculars to the western horizon. He pondered what he was looking at, then lowered them. "A cargo ship. A big one, headed north—away from the *Maersk*." Odin pointed. "Make for it."

"Maybe we can use their radio to warn away other shipping or contact the navy."

Odin nodded.

It took several minutes for them to get into the vicinity of the second large ship. It had a sleek, aerodynamic design and was painted in bright orange and white. Despite its smooth shape, it was oddly tall and bulky for a cargo ship—shaped much like a passenger ship or high-speed ferry, but it had no windows along its side—just smooth white-and-orange-painted steel with the words *Wallenius Wilhelmsen* painted in two-story-tall letters.

Odin pointed down. "Car carrier. Bring us down."

"You want me to land on that?"

Odin examined it with the binoculars. "It's got a helipad right there in the center."

"Yeah, meant for something like a Bell or an MD 520. This is a god-damned Sikorsky."

Odin tapped the dash fuel gauge, which was already into the red. "We don't have a choice."

Foxy looked below again. "Oh, hell . . . aye, aye, skipper."

They descended toward the fast-moving ship. As they came up on it, several of the crew on deck waved—obviously thinking the chopper was just doing a flyby.

Foxy leaned down to examine the equipment-and-ventilator-shaft-studded deck. "Should I try to hail them on the radio first?"

Odin shook his head. "No. Signal an emergency with your landing lights and get this bird down, Foxy." Odin checked the safety on his stolen MP5 submachine gun, which he then slid into a satchel bag. He looked back to the others. "We are going to commandeer this vessel. Control must be established rapidly and with as little violence as possible."

"As little violence . . . ?" McKinney leaned forward. "My God, what are you doing?"

"Improvising. We're going to ram the *Ebba Maersk*, Professor. This vessel's clearly faster than that container ship."

The faces of the others registered varying degrees of shock.

Foxy chuckled. "All those years in counterterrorism, and here I am hijacking a ship."

Ritter stared in unbelieving amazement. "You can't be serious? That swarm is designed to kill ships. That's what they do."

"We'll see how long it takes them to do it." Odin turned around in his seat. "I know you'll try to warn the crew, Ritter. But in reality, you're gonna help us."

"The hell I am."

Odin gestured to Smokey with a choking motion. Smokey immediately grabbed Ritter from behind in a chokehold. The man kicked and clawed at Smokey, but he was no match for the muscular commando.

McKinney shouted, "David, what are you doing! This isn't right!"

"We're not killing anyone. Just making sure he doesn't mess up the plan."

Even now she could see Ritter's eyes rolling upward as Smokey's chokehold blacked him out. "Mooch."

Mooch had already opened his medical bag and was test-squirting a needle he'd prepared during the melee. "Roll up his sleeve."

Ripper quickly did so, and Mooch delivered the injection. "I don't know his health history, Odin, so this isn't a big dose. You've probably got twenty minutes or so until he wakes up."

"Good enough. If they ask, this is a medical emergency. He's an oil executive returning from an offshore platform." Odin tossed a container-yard hard hat into the backseat. "We think he had a stroke, and we need to see their ship's doctor. The doctor's cabin is usually close to the captain's quarters, and the captain's quarters are always next to any weapons."

Foxy frowned. "It's a commercial vessel, and this isn't the Indian Ocean. They probably won't have any weapons."

"Mooch, you can speak the most convincing medical bullshit—you play the role of personal aide. Ripper, you're his panicked wife."

Ripper started peeling off her tactical harness. "Haven't got a ring."

"Evans!"

Evans tried to conceal his ring-covered hands. "Goddammit, are you for real?"

"Cough up one of those pinky rings for Ripper, and put another one on our disabled husband here." Odin locked eyes with his team. "It's a modern car carrier, so we're probably looking at a crew of twenty to twenty-four people. We only need to gain control of the helm, engine room, and any weapons. Nonlethal force only. No knives—that means you, Ripper. No guns. Disable with hand-to-hand or lachrimatory agents only. Gear up."

They were stowing their rifle cases, shedding military gear, and concealing pistols beneath their shirts as Foxy brought the chopper down to within a hundred feet above the moving ship. Wind turbulence buffeted them about. McKinney just now realized how perilous landing on the ship would be. Her nervousness about the imminent hijacking and drones faded in importance as the chopper lurched, dropped, and yawed to the side.

Odin shook his head. "Jesus, Foxy, you still remember how to fly this thing?"

"That helipad wasn't meant for a chopper this size—and they're going full steam."

"Well, land this goddamned thing. We don't have the fuel to mess around."

Several crew members waved them away frantically as the large chopper continued its rapid descent, bucking against the turbulence.

McKinney felt her heart go into her throat as the Sikorsky quickly dropped half the distance to the helipad and slowed only ten feet or so off the deck. There was a bang as some part of the chopper hit a light mast or any of a number of objects crowding the helipad. Moments later the helicopter thumped down on the helipad, bounced slightly, and then finally came to a rest.

"Wow, you almost got part of the chopper onto the helipad."

Foxy was busy shutting off the engines, which began to wind down. "I deserve a goddamned medal for getting it on the ship with all that turbulence."

Odin noticed a half-dozen Caucasian men racing up a staircase toward the chopper, but they hesitated to be certain it had stopped moving. "Showtime, people." He opened the copilot door, rapidly followed by Mooch and Smokey carrying the unconscious Ritter from the larger passenger door. Everyone else piled out, sincerely relieved to have landed.

The lead ship crew member was a bearded, husky blond man in a neat khaki uniform and captain's hat. He didn't look at all happy as he noticed the unconscious Ritter being carried toward him. He shouted to be heard over chopper wash and decreasing turbofan engine noise. His English had a slight Nordic accent. "What's wrong with him?"

Odin leaned close, pointing to the stricken man. "Medical emergency. We think it's a stroke. Big oil executive. His wife ordered us to land."

"She could have gotten you all killed, not to mention my crew."

"Do you have a doctor on board?"

The captain nodded, still looking annoyed. "The second mate is a paramedic. Follow me." He turned to the other crew members. "Get that chopper tied down before it rolls off the pad. And deploy fire hoses."

The crewmen launched into action as Odin pulled McKinney along, following Smokey, Mooch, the inconsolable Ripper, and the ship's captain. Ripper shrieked, grabbing for Ritter's suit sleeve and blurting out exclamations in some language McKinney didn't recognize—possibly Dutch or German. It amazed her how quickly Ripper could transform herself.

In a few moments the captain brought them through a hatchway into the relative quiet and calm of the ship. As they moved down a stairwell, still more crewmen of various ethnicities—Asian, Caucasian, Latino, and Filipino—crowded the hall below and helped lower the unconscious Ritter down a narrow metal gangway.

They reached a pipe- and conduit-lined corridor below, and Foxy called after Odin, "You need us or should we wait, or . . . ?"

Odin gestured to Foxy, Evans, and now Smokey, who had fallen behind. "Is there somewhere where they can make a call to shore?"

The bearded captain called out to another, younger, clean-shaven blond man in a green jumpsuit. "Valentin, *ta dem till allrummet.*" The captain turned to Odin. "He'll take them."

Odin motioned for the remainder of his team to follow the younger seaman, and they continued carrying Ritter forward with the captain. After a few turns they arrived in a more comfortably appointed section, where the corridors were wider and better lit. There was even a room with a skylight, cabinets, and dining tables with chairs. This area was also painted in brighter colors and had wooden doors with names printed on them in English on black stenciled plaques.

A third Nordic man in a khaki uniform intercepted them. He was athletically built with dark hair, splotchy skin, and old acne scars.

The captain barked, "Jöran, they think he had a stroke."

The man became agitated. "*Varför fortsatte de inte till fastlandet?*"

"Just help them."

The second mate came alongside Mooch. "You should have kept going to the mainland. I don't have real medical facilities here."

The captain pushed forward. "The wife insisted they land. Jöran, please!" He motioned for them to follow toward a nearby open door.

Odin was already scanning the corridor, surreptitiously inserting his earplug radios. McKinney felt her anxiety build as she noticed there were only three crew members present: the captain, the second mate, and another crewman helping to carry Ritter.

Odin spoke softly. "Execute, execute, execute."

In an instant Ripper slipped a device from her sleeve into her palm and sprayed something in the second mate's face, dropping the man as he screamed. Mooch twisted the captain's arm back while he and Odin shoved him against the wall. Odin rapidly secured the man's wrists with zip-ties. By the time McKinney was able to look over to Ritter, she could see that Smokey had likewise subdued the crew member there with chemical spray. Both he and Ripper were zip-tying their prisoners, who were groaning pitiably.

Odin pulled the captain forward, as the bearded, barrel-chested Swede shouted, "You scum! *Du borde skämmas!* Taking advantage of our mercy—"

Odin produced the machine gun from his bag. He chambered a round. "Captain! What is your name?"

He stared daggers. "I am Birghir Jönsson, senior captain for W and W."

"Captain Jönsson, where is your weapons locker?"

"We don't have weapons on board this ship. We are civilized people."

Mooch nodded. "If it's a Swedish ship, I don't doubt him. Owners don't want the crew trying to resist pirates. They'd be outgunned."

The captain stared in rage toward his second mate, who was still coughing and gagging on the floor under Ripper's knee. "You're animals. . . ."

"He'll be fine in a few minutes. How many others aboard?"

The captain spoke through clenched teeth. "Twenty-two crew." McKinney noticed Odin listening to his earphone radio. "Okay . . . affirmative." Odin focused back on the Swede. "Captain, your helm and engine room are now under my control. No one has been hurt, and I don't want anyone hurt. Just order your crew to abandon ship."

He eyed Odin with growing rage. "You think you're going to just sail away with two thousand BMWs? You won't get far. I promise you that."

"We aren't planning on getting far."

Mooch raised his eyebrows. "Did he say two thousand BMWs?"

The captain was on a rant. "You'll have no way of unloading the cars from the ship before they track you down. You'll not reach land."

"Right on both counts." He pulled the bound captain toward his quarters and opened the door. "Get on the PA and order your crew to abandon ship. Time is a factor."

"You are an imbecile, if you think you can get away with this."

"The safest thing is for you and your crew to abandon ship. Without any hostages on board, the authorities can sweep down on us without innocent people getting hurt."

The captain just glared at him for several moments.

Odin leaned in toward him. "I saw that free-fall emergency boat. You and the crew get inside and launch. The sooner you evacuate, the sooner you can radio for help."

Jönsson narrowed his eyes. "There is something else going on here."

"Get on the PA, Captain."

"What are you planning on doing with my ship?"

"If I told you, you wouldn't believe me."

"I don't believe you now."

"Very well. This ship is about to be attacked by thousands of military drones that will kill everyone on board as they cut it to pieces."

The captain's face went slack.

"Now, you can either stick around for that or bail out now with your crew and call for help. Which is it?"

He was weighing the matter. "Are you the group causing the distress calls we've been hearing?"

"What distress calls?"

"An Indonesian freighter said they were under aerial attack. We haven't heard from them in the last twenty minutes. Search planes have been dispatched from the mainland."

"That's just going to wind up getting more people killed."

"Killed?"

"We passed that freighter just as it was going under. Did any of their broadcasts make sense to you, Captain?"

The captain struggled to find words, then finally settled for "No. They said dozens of small planes were attacking them."

"It's a new class of autonomous combat drone, Captain—ship-cutters. And they've gotten loose."

"You must be joking. Robot aircraft attacking ships?"

Odin grabbed the PA handset from the wall and shoved it in front of his face. "Get talking, Captain Jönsson. The longer you wait, the more likely it is that your entire crew will wind up dead."

"But we are under way at twenty knots."

Odin pounded the wall next to the man's head. "I'm finished negotiating with you. We both know damn well that boat can be launched while under way."

"It's not safe."

"*Safe* is a relative term. Inside an hour there will be ten thousand killer drones on top of us."

"Ten thousand?"

"Make the announcement—in English, please."

The captain sighed deeply, and then nodded as Odin keyed the PA handset. "Attention, crew. Attention, crew. This is Captain Jönsson. The *Tonsberg* has been boarded and hijacked by armed men. Do not panic, and do not resist them. All crew members are to move with urgency to the free-fall boat. This is your order to abandon ship. Repeat: Abandon ship with urgency and prepare to deploy while under way."

Odin nodded and hung the PA mic back on its hook. "Thank you."

They could already hear shouting and footsteps running over metal plating elsewhere above and below them. The ship started to lean to the left as it went into a steep turn.

The captain frowned. "Why are we turning?"

"Head for the lifeboat, Captain."

"Who is piloting my vessel?"

Two crewmen in blue coveralls came rushing out of a doorway and halted in surprise at the sight of Odin wielding the submachine gun.

The captain motioned to them. "Take Jöran and Pindal to the escape boat." On their uncertainty he added, "Now!"

Mooch was using wet wipes to wash away the mace from the faces of the stricken men. The two crewmen edged nervously alongside to take charge of them. "*Kommer du, Kapten?*"

"*Jag stannar med skeppet.*"

The crewmen looked grim-faced as they performed a capable fireman's carry and shouldered the men down the hall.

"Get going, Captain."

"I'm staying with my ship."

Odin raised the gun.

"My crew is leaving, and I cannot let you take charge of this vessel in an active shipping lane. You could cause a collision, an oil spill, or worse. You tell me where you need to go, and I will take you there."

Mooch was checking Ritter's pulse. "We could use the help, chief."

Odin shook his head. "He has no idea what we're headed into."

The captain looked down at Ritter. "Is that man really ill?"

Mooch put away his stethoscope. "He's been sedated. If you have any doubts that we're about to be attacked by drones, see how he acts when he wakes up."

"I am staying. If what you claim is true, then a skilled captain will be useful. And I know my ship."

Odin lowered the MP5. "I refuse to take responsibility for your decision. You were warned." He gestured for the captain to walk first. "Now lead us to the bridge."

Mooch called after Odin. "What about Ritter?"

"Secure him. We'll deal with him later."

McKinney followed Odin and the captain up several metal gangways, gaining height until they finally emerged in the center of a narrow but long control room running the entire width of the ship. It was lined, front, back, and sides, with tall, durable-looking windows fitted with vertical windshield wipers. The room was bordered at waist level with consoles populated by switches, phone handsets, radios, radar screens, and built-in computer displays. Behind that was another console with a ship's wheel and throttle controls, along with wide counters on which sat navigational charts and remote camera monitors for various sections of the ship.

The helm had a commanding view of the sea in every direction as well as down onto the ship's deck—a couple of hundred feet or so behind the control tower stood the Sikorsky helicopter, already lashed down on the small helipad. Beyond that McKinney could see the curving trail of the ship's wake as they made a one-hundred-and-eighty-degree turn to the south in pursuit of the *Ebba Maersk*.

Evans stood at the wheel of the ship, examining computer screens. He glanced up when they entered. "How's the hijacking going?"

"Don't touch anything." Odin nudged him aside.

"Foxy started the turn, and then took off with the crew. What's going on?"

"He's escorting them to the escape boat. The captain's staying."

Evans raised his eyebrows. "Really. Can I take his place in the life-boat?"

Odin shook his head. "Mission's not done yet, Mort."

The captain had already picked up large binoculars and was scanning the horizon while McKinney sat in a chair next to the navigational charts. The captain spoke while scanning the sea. "Who is your pilot?"

Odin was examining the radar and GPS navigation screens showing ship traffic in the area. "I am. I'm a licensed sea captain." He then moved alongside McKinney to examine the nav chart as well.

"Where are you heading?"

"In pursuit of the *Ebba Maersk.*" Odin pressed a finger into the navigational chart. "She's approximately thirty-three miles southwest of our position, doing roughly eighteen knots. What's the maximum speed of your ship, Captain?"

"We can do twenty-six in a favorable wind, but we'll burn twice the tonnage."

"Saving on fuel costs isn't high on my priority list." Odin moved to one of the ship's control monitors and started changing settings.

"What do you think you're doing?"

"Antiterrorism operators need to be able to pose as qualified airport and ship personnel, so we're cross-trained in the equipment. I'm programming an interception course. When we finish our turn, we go to full speed, heading one-six-eight."

A phone on the console rang. Odin grabbed it and listened for a moment. "Good. Get the team back here and let's plan this operation." He hung up. "Captain, your crew deployed the escape boat successfully. No injuries."

The Swede nodded grimly. "If your purpose was to catch up with the *Ebba Maersk*, why didn't you use your own helicopter?"

"Because the *Ebba Maersk* is infested with thousands of combat drones that will destroy anything that gets within twenty miles of it."

The *Tonsberg* was already completing its turn and leveling out.

The captain threw up his hands. "What you're saying is madness."

Odin traced his finger along the map, passing two red pins. "Those distress signals. Look, you marked their location on your own map. It's the same course the *Ebba Maersk* took." Odin lifted a handset from the console and passed it to the captain. "Here. Try to raise them on the radio. You won't be able to. The crew is either dead or in hiding."

The captain grabbed the radio and eyed Odin before keying the mic. "*Tonsberg* to container ship *Ebba Maersk*. *Tonsberg* to container ship *Ebba Maersk*. Do you copy?"

As the captain continued transmitting, Odin started making calculations on the relative movements of the two ships while McKinney watched closely. From his pencil markings she could see they weren't going to close the distance for a while.

"Will we catch it in time?"

He started to rerun his calculations. "I think we can."

In a few minutes Foxy, Mooch, Ripper, and Smokey entered, their pistols holstered. Foxy shrugged. "What's the plan?"

Everyone on the bridge gathered around, including the dour-looking captain, who had given up trying to raise the *Ebba Maersk*.

Odin gestured to the navigational chart as he spoke. "At twenty-six knots it will take us roughly three hours and fifty minutes to close with the *Ebba Maersk*. During that time she will travel another eighty-one and a half miles closer to Carrier Strike Group Five. That puts them within the radius of their CAP and picket ships—but only just."

Foxy nodded. "Hawkeye flights should spot the drones on radar."

Odin gestured to the nearby console. "Look at the swarm around the *Maersk* on the radar screen, Foxy. What's it look like to you?"

Foxy and the others turned to look at a nearby radar screen. "It looks like rain."

"Right. There are so many of them hovering around the ship, so close together, it looks like a squall line—like no aircraft any radar operator's seen before."

Foxy nodded. "Tricky bastards . . ."

"I estimate we'll be within the colony's attack radius for almost two hours before we catch up with the hive ship."

McKinney sucked in a breath. "Two hours?"

Foxy whistled. "That's a lot of time for them to go to town on us."

Odin nodded to McKinney. "The professor thinks there will be various morphologies of drones—and we saw that as we flew in. We can take some of this ship's firefighting gear—the oxygen masks, for instance—to conceal our chemical signature and faces. As for the ship . . . we'll just need to defend it as best we can until we reach our target."

No one looked particularly enthused about this plan.

The captain frowned. "But if what you're saying is true—that there are thousands of combat drones—what do you plan on doing when you catch up to the *Ebba Maersk*?"

Odin looked him straight in the eye. "We're going to ram it."

The look of horror on the man's face broke new ground. "This is insanity! Do you realize that the *Ebba Maersk* is one of the largest ships in the world? The environmental damage—not to mention . . . that's over a billion dollars' worth of shipping not including my cargo—not to mention the cargo on the *Ebba Maersk*."

"Yeah, I'm pretty certain they're insured, Captain."

Foxy was shaking his head. "This is one shitty plan, boss."

Ripper nodded agreement. "He's right."

The Swedish captain nodded vigorous agreement, his accent thicker than usual. "I am in agreement that this iz a shitty plan."

Foxy stabbed at the map. "How do we get clear? We sent the only damn lifeboat off with the crew. What happens when we ram this thing—we just hope we haven't sustained enough damage to sink ourselves? And what about the swarms of drones still flying around?"

McKinney was staring at her backpack, also shaking her head slowly. "You'll never get away even if this ship doesn't sink from the collision."

Odin stared at the navigation chart, obviously considering her words.

McKinney sighed. "But I have a better idea."

Everyone turned to her—Odin looking most relieved of all. "Good. Let's hear it, Professor."

"*Ichneumon eumerus.*" She unzipped the backpack. "It's a parasitic wasp that preys on ants. It does that by mimicking their pheromonal signature so it can get inside the nest without raising alarm."

Ripper frowned. "You mean it pretends to be one of them?"

Evans leaned in. "Don't the ants notice the wasp doesn't look like them?"

McKinney shook her head. "That's the thing. Ants don't process physical appearance—their pheromonal signature is all that matters. That's how they know their colony mates." She removed the two metal canisters of perfluorocarbon from the backpack and placed them on the table. "I propose we do the same thing with the helicopter."

From the expressions on their faces it appeared that minds had just been blown.

Ripper turned to Odin. "Is she fucking serious? Fly right into the middle of thousands of killer drones and do what?"

Odin was pondering it, nodding to himself. "Turn the ship."

"Are you kidding me?"

Foxy was the first to recover. "That is *fucking hard core.*"

Mooch shook his head. "But you have no idea whether this will work. And if you're wrong . . ."

"We know they run on my software model—and that software model is looking for a match on a pheromonal signature variable. If there's a match, no attack signal is generated. This is how they identify each other. I'm willing to bet my life on it."

Odin looked up. "You don't have to be one of those who go, Professor."

"The hell I don't. It will take some experimentation to get it right, and no one knows their behavior patterns better than me. Besides, what they're trying to do with my work might wind up driving humanity to a new form of warfare. I can't just stand by and let that happen."

Odin nodded to her with respect. "Understood."

Ripper was looking from one to the other. "Odin, are we really doing this?"

Odin took a deep breath. "No. The professor and I are doing this. You and the rest of the team are staying here. Except . . ."

Foxy nodded. "You need someone to fly the chopper." He turned to face McKinney. "Count me in. It should be an interesting trip. So how do we work this pheromone with the chopper?"

McKinney was studying the canister. She tapped the nozzle at the top. "When I saw this on the complete drone we had in Mexico it was smaller, but the perfluorocarbon nozzle was aimed at the body of the drone itself—to mark it. We'll need to fasten a rig aimed at the chopper fuselage. One that we can manually operate to depress the nozzle and spray the chopper as often as necessary to get the drones to view us as one of their own."

Odin accepted one of the liter-sized metal canisters from her. "How long will this last us?"

She shrugged. "I don't know, but they can't have to recharge too often or it would be impractical. Maybe we can find their supply somewhere on board?"

"We can't rely on that. We're just going to have to get this done as soon as possible. Figure we take firefighting gear from the *Tonsberg* here— oxygen masks to conceal our breath signature and faces. That'll give us an hour of air."

Foxy considered it. "As long as they don't attack us, an hour should be enough time to fly thirty miles or so, land on the ship, get to the bridge, and steer it off course. Helicopter fuel might be a problem, though." Foxy turned to the captain. "Do you have any Jet-A on board? Any aircraft in storage below?"

The captain shook his head. "No. Just automobiles, buses, heavy construction equipment, railroad cars, forklifts."

"Great." He turned back to Odin. "We probably have enough to reach the *Maersk* at thirty miles, but we won't have enough to get back."

"As long as we can get there and turn the ship, we'll deal with the rest."

Foxy frowned. "Why not just kill the ship's engine?"

"Because it's in the middle of a shipping channel."

"If we had explosives, we could scuttle her."

"Well, we don't have explosives."

"We could improvise shaped charges with wine bottles, some ball bearings, oil—"

"No, look here. . . ." Odin was studying the chart again. He jabbed a finger at a line to the east of them. "Tancred Shoal." He nodded to himself. "That's just off the shipping lane—another twenty miles. This chart shows exposed rocks. We can run her aground."

"That's better than just sinking her?"

"Yes. Ritter said these things only have a seventy-two-hour operating life. Whoever's behind this will try to conceal the fact that this ever happened. And we all know how deep inside our systems they are. If we sink the ship or let them tow it away, they'll just rebuild and relaunch. But if we run the *Ebba Maersk* aground on the Tancred Shoals, it'll take salvage crews months to clean up. A big public demise for the world's biggest container ship in hotly contested waters—highly visible with lots of evidence left behind. That's something the world won't be able to ignore. The physical evidence of thousands of swarming ship-killer drones will show that this isn't just some terror group. It might force international investigations."

McKinney studied the chart along with Foxy. "So we run it aground. How do we get away?"

"The *Ebba Maersk* has an escape boat too. Assuming the crew didn't have a chance to launch it, we cover ourselves in colony pheromone and head for the escape pod just before we run aground on the shoals."

The ship's captain was just shaking his head in confusion. "What the hell is everyone talking about—parasitic wasps and ants? What does this have to do with drones?"

Evans waved him off, looking considerably calmer than he'd been. "Believe me, ignorance is bliss." He looked to Odin, McKinney, and Foxy. "Well, it's big of you to take one for the team, guys. Best of luck."

Ripper was studying the pheromone canister. "Don't get too excited, Mort. We still need to chart a course to ram the *Ebba Maersk*."

"But they're going to—"

Odin turned to her. "Why, Ripper?"

"What if you fail, sir? This ship needs to already be on track to intercept, otherwise there won't be time to catch up." She jabbed a finger down onto the chart. "Which means this ship will be inside colony territory before we can be positive you've succeeded—at which point we can break off and head for safety."

Evans's eyes went wide. "For how long?"

Odin studied the map. "Probably fifteen minutes to a half hour."

"It beats two hours plus."

Odin nodded, then turned to the others. "She's right. Any objections?"

Evans raised his hand. No one else moved.

"So that means we all have jobs to do. Let's get moving, people. We're leaving within the hour."

CHAPTER 30

The Swarm

Linda McKinney watched Odin gently playing catch with Huginn and Muninn on the deck of the *Tonsberg*, near the Sikorsky helicopter. She knew he was saying his good-byes, since it seemed likely they would not return.

He looked over to her, and McKinney came alongside and tossed a pellet of food to Muninn. The raven caught it without difficulty.

"We'll be back."

He was stone-faced. "I hope you're right about this, Professor."

Foxy was finishing up the twin pheromone canister rig on the nose of the chopper. A wrench clattered to the metal deck and he stood. "Well, this is what we've got."

McKinney and Odin turned to see that the twin metal canisters had been clamped into place with fire extinguisher brackets bolted below the chopper's nose. The nozzles of both were aimed straight at the fuselage, and a braided copper wire ran through a hole drilled in the windscreen.

Foxy ran his finger along the copper wire. "Pull on this and it directly depresses the nozzle valves." He gave it the barest tug, and a cloud of pheromone vapor sprayed the chopper, leaving a wet spot two feet in diameter. "Voilà. What do you think?"

Odin examined the assembly and tugged forcefully at it, trying to shake the canister loose. He looked up at McKinney.

She nodded. "Simple's good. How do we detach it for the run to the ship's bridge?"

Foxy leaned in and threw the clamp lever, popping the canister bracket loose. "That easy. Then we depress the valve by hand."

"Let me see that. . . ." McKinney extended her hand and took the canister from him. "We need to dose ourselves too—for when we land." She pressed her finger down on the nozzle and sprayed herself with the odorless, colorless perfluorocarbon. It nonetheless felt moist and cool as she could feel it evaporating slowly. She handed the canister to Odin.

"How long does the coverage last?"

She shook her head. "I don't know. So watch how they behave toward you. If they start getting aggressive, you need another dose."

Foxy sprayed himself as well, and then reclamped the canister into place on the nose of the chopper.

Just then they heard the deep growl of a powerful engine, and they turned to see a new silver Bentley sedan drive up a ramp from the lower deck, leap the apex, and screech to a sliding halt in front of them. Steel deck plating crudely welded across all its windows marred the beautiful car, with burn marks at the connection points lending the appearance of smeared mascara. There were small view ports in the steel plates. After a moment the passenger door opened with difficulty, and Evans got out. Beyond him Smokey was behind the wheel.

"What do you think? The Mulsanne armored edition. Some billionaire in Hong Kong will be very disappointed with our mods."

"Can't say much for the styling."

Evans thumbed in the direction of the ramp. "There's six more wrapped in plastic down there. Buses, tractors, earth movers. And there's gonna be a BMW shortage in Beijing if this ship goes down."

Odin placed Huginn and Muninn in the folding cage and handed them to Smokey. "Keep them safe."

"Will do, chief."

"Where's Ripper?"

Smokey gestured down the ramp. "Welding armor plate onto trucks. Figure if we stay mobile, they'll have a hard time swarming us, and there's running room on the ramps down there. We might be able to crush them against walls, and whatnot."

Odin nodded, examining the weapons arrayed across the car's backseat. "Is that all we've got?"

Smokey nodded. "Pistols too. But three .338 rifles. A couple MP5s, and an HK416. A few hundred rounds and some frag grenades, some thermite." Smokey leaned forward. "You're not taking any weapons?"

Odin shook his head. "Where we're going, if we need to start shooting, we're dead already. Better that you have them to hold off an attack."

Smokey handed him an HK tactical pistol. "Take a pistol at least— you might need to shoot off a lock or something."

"Or something." Odin grabbed it and slid it into a leg holster.

The sound of a heavy diesel engine roared belowdecks, and in a moment a large front-end loader rolled onto the main deck with Ripper behind the wheel and Mooch sitting in the shovel. There were steel plates welded around the cab on this too. Mooch hopped out as it came to a halt. The engine cut off moments later.

"Should be able to stomp a few of the fuckers with that."

Foxy shouted, looking at his watch, "Time to kill drones, people!"

The team moved into a circle but did not touch or say good-bye. They simply stood looking from one to another. McKinney was slightly off-balance trying to understand this close-knit team's unspoken ritual, but they seemed to just be regarding each other. Evans also watched from the car door.

After a few moments Odin broke the silence. "You all know the stakes and what's expected of us. We will meet on the other side." With that he snapped a sharp salute, and the others returned it. They nodded to McKinney and immediately resumed their duties.

Foxy started flicking switches in the Sikorsky, and the engines began to whine to life. Odin opened the copilot door. "Time to go!"

Evans shrugged to McKinney and shouted over the noise, "Good luck, Professor."

She turned and entered the chopper as Evans watched. McKinney barely had her seat belt on by the time the Sikorksy lifted off and edged out over the ocean. She looked down to see the captain standing on the top of the control tower, simply watching them leave.

Odin handed her a set of headphones, and the moment she put them on, she could hear Foxy speaking.

". . . fuel to get there. We're gonna keep this straight and simple." He pointed. "Look, you can see the *Ebba Maersk* already."

McKinney craned her head and could indeed see a smudge on the horizon if she didn't look directly at it. "Foxy, fly low to the water. That's what they seem to be doing, and it might help contain pheromone dispersal."

Foxy nodded and brought them down alarmingly low—within twenty or thirty feet of the water's surface.

"Jesus! Not that low."

"I got it, Professor."

Odin turned back to her. "ETA about ten minutes." He extended the copper nozzle wire to her. "You're the best person to control this."

McKinney nodded and took the line.

Odin then spoke into the radio. "Safari-One-Six actual, crossing Lima Delta, out."

"TOC copies. Happy hunting."

He then pointed to a firefighter's oxygen mask and supply tank sitting on one of the captain seats. "Put it on, and we'll do an equipment check."

McKinney started prepping the gear, and the process considerably calmed her nerves. She knew enough about herself that when frightening events were afoot, she preferred to be actively doing something. Listening to Odin's instructions on the oxygen rig served that purpose. She tried to lock eyes with him, but he was all business—focused on the mission. She decided that came from experience and tried to put everything else out of her mind too.

They were coming up on the huge container ship all too fast for her liking. And soon they could see drones flying about in ones and twos, running forage patterns—with denser clouds closer in.

Odin raised binoculars, then shouted, "Incoming! Professor. Dose us. Oxygen masks on."

She tugged on the wire to release pheromone, then lowered her oxygen mask and turned on air.

Odin looked side to side as they skimmed over the ocean surface. "We've got six . . . hell, we've got several dozen headed this way with a lot more behind that." He lowered the binoculars. "How are we doing on pheromone?"

"We'll find out in a moment. Let me know if they get aggressive, and I'll increase the spray." McKinney tried not to get crazy with the application of pheromone. She imagined the size of an ant if its mandibular gland were the size of the canister outside. Then tried to remind herself how small an amount they could detect. Nonetheless, her first blasts from the nozzle felt excessive.

As she looked up from the canister, her heart raced. Flying in alongside them now were a dozen flat black flying wings only about five feet wide, with loud but small turbofan engines. These were clearly not ship-cutters because they didn't have legs or a welding torch nose—instead they seemed to have automatic rifles or similar weapons bolted under their wings. They looked cheap. Poorly made. Some were damaged, but they still functioned enough to fly.

Judging from the motion of their engine nozzles, they seemed to be able to rotate them to increase their maneuverability. They were flying in close to the chopper—mere feet from the window—almost bumping into the Sikorsky, skirting under it.

Foxy swerved and cursed. "Goddammit! They're going to take out our rotors if they crowd us too close."

A drone bumped into their fuselage.

But just as soon as they appeared, they dispersed. The chopper was suddenly flying in open air again, just off the water. Drones now occasionally crossed their path, but it was the more random activity of a hive running foraging patterns. McKinney let out a relieved breath and pulled the cord to apply pheromone again.

Odin and Foxy glanced back at her. "Looks like you were right, Professor."

"It was more than a hunch. These things operate on algorithmic principles." She nodded. "Now let's hope we don't run out of pheromone or oxygen before we get this done."

Odin keyed the radio. "TOC, this is Safari-One-Six actual."

"*Go ahead, Safari-One-Six.*"

"Looks like the pheromone ruse works. We are flying into the swarm and toward the ship right now. Will keep you apprised. Out."

"*Goddamn, that's good news, chief. Out.*"

Just a few miles ahead they could see the broad stern of the *Ebba Maersk*. McKinney swallowed hard at the swirling crowd of aircraft and the now discernible vuvuzela-like whine that came to them even through their own engine noise.

"My God, look at it . . . there are thousands of them."

Foxy shook his head. "I don't know how I'm going to be able to get close enough to land without hitting a dozen of those things. Look how packed in they are."

Odin motioned with his hand. "Get up higher. Try to come in from overhead." He glanced to the side. "Hey! Getting some aggressive approaches at three o'clock. Professor, give us another dose."

McKinney pulled on the nozzle.

Nonetheless a drone slammed into the side of the helicopter, cracking the side window and knocking their trim off before Foxy could recover.

"Jesus!"

McKinney watched the damaged drone spin apart and crash into the sea. No other drones seemed to be following its lead. She pulled several more times on the nozzle to coat their fuselage, just to be sure. Clear droplets traced along the glass.

Looking ahead, she could see they were now rising above the stern of the massive container ship. The water churned from the huge propellers as the ship steamed southward. The control tower in the distance rose like a massive T square near the center of the ship, probably twenty stories above the water—in the center of thousands of blue, gray, orange, and silver shipping containers that rose almost to the level of the control tower itself.

Unlike other shipping containers McKinney had seen, many of these had open panels in their sides and tops from which drones were entering and leaving the nests. She could see the turbofan drones tilting their engines down and hovering in for a landing, the air wavering with hot exhaust. But there were thousands of drones of still smaller size. She thought she could make out clouds of black quadracopter drones as well, not unlike the ones they'd faced in Colorado—but bigger, lawn mower–sized, with smoke coming off them as their two-stroke gasoline engines added to a deafening droning sound. It seemed to set the fillings in her teeth vibrating.

"God, would you listen to that?"

Foxy was bringing them into the cloud, angling for a landing. "Will these things make room for me, Professor?"

McKinney leaned forward to look. "If we collide they'll back away . . . after trying to exchange data via their sensilla."

There was a loud thump as a drone bumped into them from behind.

"Goddammit! We're running on vapors. There's no time for finesse. We gotta land."

Looking below, it seemed like the ship was the molting ground of some vast flock of birds. Tens of thousands of drones covered every available surface—others seemed to be crawling around. McKinney released more pheromone and looked on with amazement at the complex and terrifying manifestation of her work. In some sick way it almost gave her satisfaction to see her model working—but she quickly rebuked herself.

Another drone bumped into them, and there was a loud bang as pieces of something sheared away and fell out of sight along with the drone. McKinney hoped none of those pieces belonged to the Sikorsky, but moments later the chopper started vibrating. An empty water bottle rattled in a cup holder at her elbow. The vibration quickly increased. Several red lights and alarms went off on the console up front.

Odin looked up through the overhead view ports. "We're leaking something up there, and it isn't pheromone."

Dark fluid sprayed across the glass.

Foxy was checking indicators and struggling with the yoke. "Gotta land . . . gotta land."

Another bump, followed by yet another bang, as a drone edged into them.

"I don't see a way to clear a path without running into them. We've got some damage to a rotor blade already—maybe more than one."

McKinney scanned the vast expanse of containers below them but didn't see any helipad or unoccupied spot. They were now flying into a cloud of smaller drones, and the impacts were coming fast as popcorn popping. The chopper lurched, and a lawn mower–sized quadracopter bristling with antennas bumped right into the window next to her before it disappeared below them.

Foxy was wrestling with the controls. Alarms were wailing and lights flashing on the console. "We're going down. This might be unpleasant."

McKinney tugged on the pheromone cord. "Don't land nose-first, if you can help it. We need to preserve the canister."

He laughed ruefully as they started to spin. "We might be landing in a way that solves all our problems." He struggled to stop the spin, working the foot pedals, handle, and yoke frantically. "Tail rotor's going."

They continued to spin as they descended, and the collisions with drones only increased. There were several loud bangs.

"Prepare for impact! Prepare for impact!"

The chopper rotated, then slowed, then finally tilted rearward. McKinney could see them descending toward the top of a pile of drone-covered containers. Fifty feet. Thirty feet. Then ten feet.

They hit hard, tail first, but the landing surface gave way beneath them. The deafening whine of the drone engines all around them masked even the sound of the crash, and the crumpling of corrugated steel containers. The chopper collapsed partly into a container with its nose facing upward. The blades shattered with a loud snapping sound.

The impact knocked the wind out of her and caused her to lean on the pheromone cord. She struggled to release it, and then fought against gravity as the chopper rolled sideways. Then the copter mostly righted itself again before coming to a rest.

McKinney heard Odin's voice in the headphones beyond all the howling drone engines.

"Everyone all right?"

McKinney patted her body and checked the area around her for punctures or crash damage, but eventually she nodded. "Bruised, but I'm good. Foxy, okay?"

Foxy nodded as he was switching off the engines and the fuel pumps. "Fine. Turns out we should be happy we only had fuel vapors left. Otherwise I think we'd be on fire."

Odin spoke into his headset radio. "TOC, this is Safari-One-Six actual. We've landed on the mother ship. Chopper disabled, but crew okay. Moving on foot to objective. Maintain your present course until you get confirmation we've succeeded. Out."

"Copy that, Safari-One-Six."

Odin pointed at the intact canister bracket still affixed to the nose outside. "Grab the canisters and let's move." With one last glance at his companions he opened the copilot's door and climbed up onto the storage container roof. Foxy did so on the other side, racing forward to unclamp the canister. Odin turned to grab McKinney's hand and haul her up out of his door, since the rear doors seemed to be blocked by the walls of a shipping container.

In a moment they all stood atop a twenty-story-tall block of containers amid the deafening engine roar, with numberless drones flying, perching, and crawling about them. It was a vast field of seething machines. The bright Pacific sun was partly shrouded by a cloud of drones as well.

Foxy sprayed himself, McKinney, and Odin with pheromone, then looked out on the mass of drones in every direction. He shouted, "Well, that is something you don't see every day."

Four hundred feet ahead, across a series of container blocks separated by narrow chasms, loomed the white conning tower and the wide windows of the ship's bridge. The radar masts there were still rotating, but no human was in sight. There were scorch marks here and there on the metal and all the windows in the control tower were either shattered or missing, twisted windshield wipers dangling.

"We'll need to jump the gaps. It's a long way down, so be careful. C'mon." Odin nodded for them to follow, gingerly stepping over the wing of a dormant ship-cutting drone. McKinney could see its antennas and optic sensors moving to and fro. It was fascinating in a macabre way. Someone had actually breathed life into her work. Another foot-long ant-like crawling drone walked across the back of the much larger ship-cutter— on its way somewhere else. It looked like a small crawling wire-cutter. Then she realized there were dozens of the little things wandering around between the bigger drones.

"Professor! This isn't a goddamned field trip!" Odin tugged her away, and they moved across the seething field of machines to the tower.

Foxy pointed. "Heads up . . ."

McKinney and Odin looked up to see several drones racing back to the colony, microjet engines roaring. They created a visible commotion as they flew through the cloud. Soon a trail of other drones started following them.

And then McKinney saw the collective intelligence of the swarm, as the information, transmitted via pheromone and simple algorithms, manifested itself like a wave. Thousands of drones started taking to the air, leaking upward like liquid into the sky, following their agitated brethren— billowing outward in the direction from which the scouts had come—to the north. Back toward the *Tonsberg*, which was only just now visible on the horizon. The added roar of thousands of drones taking flight caused them all to crouch down and wince.

Odin leaned in and shouted into the headset radio. "TOC, this is Safari-One-Six actual. Heads up! You have incoming. Repeat: incoming. ETA ten minutes. Do you copy?"

There was a pause, and then Smokey's voice came over the radio. *"Copy that. How many we looking at?"*

McKinney watched the numberless horde rising into the sky.

"The skies will be dark with them. Just hang on as long as you can, and we'll get the colony ship diverted soon."

"Copy that. We'll keep 'em busy."

Smokey keyed off the mic and looked across the hood of the Bentley at Evans, who was pouring another glass of white wine from a bottle with

Swedish writing on the label. They stood on the weather deck, the wind from the ship's twenty-six knots flowing over them.

Evans nodded and looked to the south. He spoke in a dramatic, gravelly voice. "The forces of Mordor gather for the attack."

"Go easy on that shit, man. We might wind up in the water in a few hours."

"All the more reason . . ." He emptied his glass and poured another.

Ritter groaned in the backseat of a blue BMW M5 sedan parked next to the Bentley.

Evans looked down at him in annoyance. "How do you like your drones now, asshole?"

Nearby, at the railing, the captain scanned the horizon with his large binoculars.

"I can't believe what I am seeing." He lowered the binoculars. "They are coming. Perhaps six thousand meters out."

"Now you know why we wanted you to evac." Smokey grabbed an MP5 submachine gun from the car hood and strapped on a combat harness.

Close by, Ripper opened the cab door of her armored yellow front-loader and stowed an HK416 rifle next to the seat.

Evans tossed the wineglass into the wind and took a deep pull directly from the wine bottle.

Smokey grabbed the bottle from him and tossed it overboard as well. "Battle stations, Morty."

"Oh, nice! Litterbug."

Mooch raced out onto the deck from the crew quarters. "Radar shows a cloud inbound. We need to get to battle stations."

"We know." Ripper pointed to the horizon.

Mooch put a hand on the captain's shoulder. "So, the captain, Evans, and Ritter will stay in the engine room. It's safer there, and they can control the ship as well as direct us to hull breeches, fires, or anything else by radio."

The captain eyed Ritter, sitting handcuffed in the backseat of the BMW. "Who is this man?"

"He works for the people who built the drones—and he might be able to help us find out who they are. So keep him safe."

Smokey produced the key and unlocked Ritter's handcuffs. The man barely responded. "Morty! Go with the captain." He pulled a now staggering Evans over to the BMW's passenger seat and pushed him in as the captain started the turbocharged engine.

The Swede looked grim. "And what if everything goes wrong?"

"You mean we start to sink? We rally up in the ship's galley. That'll be our Alamo. They won't be taking prisoners." Smokey gave him a thumbs-up. "Stay in touch by radio, Captain." Smokey pounded the roof, and the BMW took off down the ramp, screeching through the garage levels.

Mooch, Ripper, and Smokey then stood side by side at the ship's railing watching the dark, writhing cloud coming toward them from the south, like bad weather.

Ripper checked the action on her pistol. "I don't know about you guys, but I am really starting to hate these fucking drones."

Smokey headed back toward the Bentley. "Best we can do is keep them too busy chasing us to cut up the ship. Deck three is the least crowded, so use that for speed. And for godsakes, Ripper, don't run that shovel into the hull walls below the waterline."

They ran for their vehicles even as the black cloud grew.

Smokey revved the Bentley. With tires screeching, he fishtailed down the loading ramp into the depths of the ship as the howling of a thousand small jet- and two-stroke engines became a deafening clamor—and the bodies of the drones blotted out the sun.

Evans sat unsteadily on a desk chair in front of several computer monitors in the spotless engine control room. He'd expected a dark and noisy place, but there were several sections to the ship's engine room—the engine itself was the size of a semitruck and occupied a cavernous three-story-tall space crisscrossed by piping, but there were also several smaller auxiliary engines that were idle, banks of large generators, cooling water and fuel pumps, fuel filtration systems, oil and fuel ports. The place was massive.

The captain and Ritter came back into the control room. "You shouldn't have drank so much. You're going to be useless."

Suddenly there was an explosion somewhere, and the deck vibrated.

Evans sat up straight as alarms went off on the control board. "What the hell was that?"

A klaxon sounded and red fire strobes started flashing.

The captain shoved the wheeled chair aside and starting clicking through screens. In a moment he brought up a surveillance camera on one of the monitors. It showed a downward view of the starboard hull near the bow of the ship. As they watched, several small aircraft raced into the frame and "landed" on the hull near the waterline in a shower of sparks, leaving long scars in the orange paint. Even as the first ones came to a stop, a dozen more were already screeching to land next to them—like leeches.

The captain watched, utterly confused.

Evans searched fruitlessly for cigarettes. "They've got electromagnetic landing gear, Captain. They'll stick to your hull like fucking barnacles. And that's when the fun really begins."

"Madness. Absolute madness!"

Ritter watched, shaking his head.

On-screen the first arrivals were already sending a shower of sparks into the passing waves as their steel-cutting torches kicked in. Their wing acted as a cowling to cover them as they worked, and they began cutting downward below the waves.

"My God! They'll gut us like a fish."

"That's the general idea." Evans was still patting his empty pockets for cigarettes.

Suddenly all three men looked up to trace a scraping sound as it passed fast along the hull wall opposite them. It was quickly followed by several more beyond the steel.

The captain clicked through still more control screens. "We have a double hull. It will take them some time to cut through." He grabbed the radio. "There are numerous drones cutting into the hull below the water-line, and there's a fire on deck one. Port side, compartment three."

The sound of gunfire and screeching rubber came in over the radio, along with Smokey's voice. *"We've got our hands full at the moment, Captain!"*

McKinney stepped carefully around scurrying wire-cutter drones, and then leapt the eight feet over a ten-story chasm to the last container block separating them from the control tower, which now loomed right above them. She landed next to Odin and Foxy, who caught hold of her to prevent her from tripping on still more winged drones and the hovering, lawn mower–sized quadracopter drones roving about.

They could barely hear each other above the mind-numbing noise of thousands of small engines. She watched as several of the quadracopter drones rubbed past each other, their sensilla antennas brushing together—an exchange of information.

Odin sprayed her and Foxy with more pheromone and leaned in to her ear, shouting, "These quadracopter drones seem to be more aggressive. Unless we keep spraying, they start following us."

McKinney watched one doing just that. "Those look like larger versions of the human-hunters we faced in Colorado." She noticed the twin gun barrels bolted into the frame. "These gas masks might not be helping us much. We're still exhaling. It probably requires a lot of pheromone to overcome the aggression score we're receiving from our other chemical signatures."

Odin motioned for them to keep moving. "Then let's speed up."

McKinney and Foxy followed toward the edge of the container field over the backs of winged drones.

Odin keyed his radio and shouted, "TOC, this is Safari-One-Six actual. What's your status?"

There was a pause, and then the sound of engines roaring and staccato gunfire came in over the radio. *"Our status is that they're cutting up the ship like we're not even on it. We're too busy dealing with the hunter-killers to do anything about the hull-cutters. Fire suppression systems kicked in, and the hull's penetrated in two places. So far the pumps are keeping up."* More gunfire. *"How about you? Over."*

Odin looked out to the horizon at the indistinct outline of a ship in the distance. "We need ten more minutes. What's your current position?"

"About sixteen miles north-northwest of you."

"If you think the ship can't make the distance to the *Maersk*, abort and head out of the colony's territory."

"So far we're holding up. But I copy that. Out."

They reached the end of the container field and looked at the bridge tower across a thirty-foot-wide chasm. McKinney peered over the edge at an eight-story drop to the ship's deck and a tangle of machinery.

Odin pointed and shouted over the din of the drone engines, "Crew didn't get a chance to abandon ship."

McKinney followed his gaze toward the ship's bright orange free-fall escape boat. It was suspended, angled downward in its launch chute on the starboard side. The boat was easily forty feet long and fully enclosed.

Foxy nodded. "Bad for them, good for us. But we're going to have to climb down. This gap is too big to jump, and we don't have ropes."

Odin started lowering himself over the side. "The containers have enough cross-braces and handholds for a free climb." He looked up. "You okay with this, Professor?"

McKinney was already lowering herself down, searching for a leg hold. "I've done my share of rock climbing in the field. Let's do it."

All three of them started the long climb down, keeping close together and receiving frequent sprays from the pheromone canister. It was already more than two-thirds empty. It took them a good five minutes to descend to deck level.

When they hopped onto the deck, Odin led them toward a watertight door at the base of the massive white-painted steel bridge tower.

Foxy grabbed his arm and pointed to the escape boat a hundred feet to their right. "I'll get it ready for launch while you redirect the ship."

"What about the pheromone?"

"That escape boat should be nearly airtight. I'll probably be safe in there. Just give me another dose for the run over to it."

Odin glanced at McKinney. "Is he making sense?"

She nodded. "We'll go through less pheromone, and if the boat's watertight and he's quiet, he should be okay."

Odin nodded to Foxy. "Do it."

"I'll be ready to launch when you head down."

McKinney sprayed him a double dose and watched him race off toward the starboard side.

Odin pulled her along, and in a moment they undid the latch on a waterproof door and entered the stairwell of the tower. McKinney pulled the door closed behind them with a clang. Almost immediately the deafening noise of the drones dropped to a tolerable level.

"God, that sound is from hell." She gazed up the stairwell.

"There's an elevator, but I don't think we should risk it." Odin smeared partially dried blood with the toe of his boot. The trail of blood led into the elevator lobby. He drew his pistol and motioned for her to follow him up the stairs.

Since they were both physically fit, they made quick work of the eight-story climb, and could now hear the penetrating hum of the drone engines return, along with a salt-laden breeze. Odin climbed the last stretch of stairs warily, with McKinney close behind. They emerged near the center of the ship's bridge and could see the entire place was spattered with blood, broken glass, and bullet holes. A dozen small quadracopter drones and an even greater number of wire-cutter drones moved in and out of the control room through the blasted-out windows. A twenty-mile-an-hour wind was blowing through it, sending loose papers flying.

Odin led her up to the central console, but half the computer screens here were shot out. There were literally hundreds of bullet holes peppering the walls and equipment. "Goddammit. . . ."

They stepped around the console to find a dead crewman on the floor. McKinney caught her breath at the sight of his mangled body. He'd been shot so many times in the face and upper torso that most of that portion was spattering the walls and floor around him, along with a five-foot-diameter pool of half-dried blood. What humanized him to her in a disturbing way was the man's Felix the Cat wristwatch and bright green sneakers.

McKinney ducked down as one of the smaller quadracopters hovered toward them. She sprayed her and Odin with pheromone again, her fear coming back.

Odin spoke into the intrateam radio. "Foxy, the nav computer screen's been shot out. Half the bridge controls are fucked. I'm going to redirect the ship manually."

"*Got it. Escape boat's ready to go when you are.*"

"I'll be here awhile. I need to make sure we'll hit those rocks."

"*Standing by.*"

Odin stood up and started tapping buttons to disengage the autopilot. Chimes sounded. Then Odin moved to the ship's surprisingly small rudder wheel. Closely watching the ship's compass, he started spinning it to port. Slowly the ship began to lean slightly to the right as its massive length turned left, toward the east.

McKinney came up alongside him, looking down the length of the massive ship, covered and alive with the colony of drones.

He looked at her. "Take the pheromone capsule and get to the escape boat."

"I'm not going anywhere."

He regarded her and shook his head. Then he grabbed the MBITR radio. "TOC, this is Safari-One-Six actual. We have successfully redirected the *Ebba Maersk*. Abort your attack run. Repeat. Abort your attack run."

"**Hallelujah!** Hey, Mooch, Ripper, you hear that?" Smokey brought the powerful Bentley slaloming down a ramp and screeching around a pillar, while several of the lawn mower–sized quadracopters hovered down the ramp after him, opening up with machine guns as he passed. Seven or eight more drones were already on this deck, and their streaming bullets raked across lines of plastic-covered BMWs strapped in tight rows and pinged off the steel plating covering his windows and doors. "Goddammit!"

He keyed the radio. "You hear that, Captain Jönsson? Turn us to the mainland!"

There was a pause, and the captain's voice came in. "*We've got two feet of water in the engine room. We're taking on water in three compartments. There are fires on four decks!*"

Smokey cringed as he passed a garage compartment with dozens of sedans fully engulfed in flames—smoke billowing up through the powerful vents and fire sprinklers engaged. "Will the damned thing stay afloat?"

A pause. "*It'll stay afloat.*"

"Then turn the damned boat!"

Smokey screeched around a corner, smashing a drone against the wall and smearing it to pieces in a shower of sparks. But then something caught under his wheel and the Bentley veered sharply and flipped onto its side as it slid down a ramp onto the heavy equipment deck.

"Dammit!" Smokey held on as the car rolled and landed against another pillar at the base of the ramp. It finally came to a stop, and already bullets were raking its sides. He keyed the radio. "Ripper! Mooch! I need help. I'm rolled!" He tried to kick the top door open, but the deck ceiling was too low with the car on its side to open the door.

Ripper's voice came in. "*Coming.*"

Smokey tried to shrink his body to as small a silhouette as possible as hovering drones riddled the Bentley with gunfire. He grabbed the key and turned the engine off. Then he aimed his MP5 through a narrow view port in the steel, raking a quadracopter drone.

He heard a large engine headed his way and moved to the other side just in time to see the bucket of the front loader lowering and smashing into the side of his car, spinning it free of the ramp and sliding it across the decking on its roof before raising the bucket and flipping it right-side up. Inside he went sprawling against the door.

Smokey crawled back toward the front seat, shouting into his radio, "Goddamn you, Ripper!"

"*You all right?*"

"Yeah." He watched the front loader smash its bucket down on top of a quadracopter drone firing at her, crushing it against the floor.

"Die, fucker! Die!"

"You're a sick lady, Ripper."

Evans followed the captain up a narrow flight of steel stairs and gazed back behind them at rising, bubbling seawater amid thick pipes and machinery below. Adrenaline had by now made him almost completely sober.

The captain grabbed his sleeve, practically dragging him up the steps. "We need to seal this compartment. Where the hell is that other man?"

"He locked himself in the generator room."

The captain stopped and pointed back down. "Go get him! I need to manage the bilge pumps to make sure we don't capsize." He shoved Evans. "Do it!"

The captain raced ahead and through the watertight door. Looking down again, Evans realized he could now see actual underwater cutting torches in the dark bubbling water. "Oh, no way . . ."

Suddenly Ritter scrambled through a side door some distance below. He was shouting, "Which way is out of this goddamned place!"

Evans nodded and started racing up the stairs. Ritter took off in his direction, mounting the steps as well.

Once he got to the watertight door, Evans turned to see the ocean surging upward now.

Ritter shouted, "No! Don't close the door!"

Evans grimaced. "Nothing personal, asshole. Just business." He slammed it shut and locked it down with the turn bolts. The metal was so thick he could barely hear the screams on the other side.

McKinney and Odin remained on the bridge of the *Ebba Mærsk* for nearly twenty minutes. The pheromone canister was getting low, but up ahead was the unmistakable outline of waves crashing against rocks. It stretched in a line across a third of the near horizon.

Odin had been manually adjusting the wheel back and forth for the entire run.

"Are we close enough to jump ship?"

"Just a bit more—we've come this far. We need to be sure. How we doing on pheromone?"

She shook the canister. "Not much. Maybe an inch left on the bottom, but at our consumption rate that should be plenty."

The quadracopter drones were even then starting to investigate their human breath again. McKinney depressed the nozzle to spray another dose on them.

But nothing came out.

She shook it and tried the nozzle several more times.

He noticed her efforts. "What's wrong?"

"Propellant. There's no more damned propellant."

They exchanged deadly serious looks and looked out at the thousands and thousands of drones around them. McKinney could see a quadracopter edging up over the windowsill of the control room, headed straight toward them.

Odin aimed the pistol and shot once, knocking it out of the air where it disappeared below the window. "Dammit!"

They could both see jagged rocks foaming in waves several kilometers ahead. He picked up a pair of range-finding binoculars in a holder on the console. He focused them on the rocks. "Two and a half kilometers. We just need to stay alive for about four more minutes."

McKinney pointed as a dozen quadracopter drones in two sizes started gathering around the bridge. She turned back the way they had come, to see that direction being closed off by twice as many more.

Odin grabbed the canister and threw it onto the console. "Stand back!" He aimed the pistol obliquely at the metal and fired several shots in succession, finally causing the canister to rattle across the floor.

McKinney grabbed it, only to find the dents hadn't penetrated.

Odin leaned down next to her. "Lean it against the wall."

McKinney carefully placed it and glanced around to see now six or seven dozen quadracopter drones gathering around the control tower. "Odin!"

He was busy aiming at the nozzle tip of the canister. He fired a shot that sent it rolling across the floor again. He scrambled after it, only to pick it up and find the nozzle pinched completely closed. He swung it around, trying to drain anything out of it. But nothing came.

He pointed at her backpack. "Anything at all?"

She unzipped it to show the detector—which showed fairly high levels of perfluorocarbon—and the metal canister of oleoresin capsicum. "This just induces the attack signal." She glanced around them as the quadracopters closed in. "And there's about to be plenty of that around here already."

He took it from her, then keyed the radio. "Foxy. If you don't hear from us in two minutes, launch the boat."

There was a pause of static, then: *"Fuck you. I'm not going anywhere."*

"Foxy, listen to me."

"You're breaking up."

He sighed and looked to McKinney.

They couldn't help but notice the solid wall of drones closing in around them. Their path to the stairwell was already blocked.

McKinney moved toward him, watching the drones move in.

Odin held her. They stood with their faces just an inch apart. The horrendous sound of the drone engines still hummed deafeningly all around them. A glance forward and she could see the rocks looming larger. "We did it. We stopped them—for now, at least."

Odin nodded and kissed her.

McKinney felt tears welling up as he kissed them away. "I wanted a chance to know you, David."

He nodded. "Then know this about me." Odin hefted the canister of capsicum. "I don't *ever* give up."

He kissed her quickly, then turned and smashed the nozzle end of the capsicum canister against the console, breaking off the tip. With the full canister under pressure it started hissing madly.

"What the hell are you doing? That'll enrage them!"

"I'm counting on it." He turned and hurled the canister out the window on the opposite side of the ship from the rescue boat. The canister tumbled end over end, falling ten stories into the canyons of the shipping containers below—gathering a swarm of drones in its wake, even as it fell.

The unprecedented concentration must have been like a beacon, because the power of the attack signal spread quickly and the entire host around the ship's bridge plunged down after it, creating a dense, mad crowd that jostled each other in pursuit.

Odin grabbed her by the arm. "Run like hell!"

McKinney smiled in surprise even as he pulled her along. Odin shot two small lingering drones out of the air near the stairwell and motioned for her to take the lead as he covered their rear. As they descended the stairs, McKinney could see through the portholes as hundreds of drones streamed past outside the bridge tower in pursuit of the canister. McKinney couldn't wipe the grin off her face as she circled down the stairwell. "Very clever, mammal!"

"Just keep moving."

At deck level they pushed through the watertight door and sprinted across the crimson-painted deck. The roar of drone engines coming from the far side of the control tower had risen to a crescendo by now. The air there was black with drones. They dashed across the decking and up to the sealed door of the rescue boat. There was a round porthole above the door near the words 38 *Persons*. Odin undid the latch and opened the door to reveal Foxy staring at him from the pilot's seat.

"You're such a drama queen. . . ."

Odin helped McKinney inside. "Careful, it's steep." He held her hand as she climbed in.

She had never seen such a boat. The seats were heavily padded and facing backward like a theme park ride. Only Foxy's seat faced forward, looking through what appeared to be a reinforced pilot's window. Otherwise there was only one other forward-facing window to let light in. The thing resembled a big orange torpedo angled downward at forty-five degrees.

Odin glanced toward the bow of the ship, and then ducked inside, slamming the hatch shut and throwing the bolts.

Foxy peered through the narrow side window. "If I'm not mistaken, those are rocks up ahead. Get seated, people!"

McKinney was already strapping herself in as Odin climbed into a seat across the aisle from her. He raced through the fasteners, and then shouted, "Hit it, Foxy!"

Foxy pounded a release button, and they dropped in free fall for a second or two before plunging into the sea, fully submerging. The impact knocked the wind out of her. The rescue boat rolled and bobbed like a cork and finally surfaced, as the roar of drones and something even deeper came to them.

Then she heard a water jet engine kick to life and saw Foxy push the throttle lever forward. "I don't give us much chance of outrunning them."

Odin unbuckled from his seat. "I do. They're otherwise occupied."

McKinney unbuckled as well and joined him to look out the narrow porthole above the rear entry door. She held her breath as the massive container ship, swarming with drones, thundered past behind them—a wall of blue steel the size of a shopping mall.

She craned her neck to look ahead, toward rocks rising ten meters out of the sea in a swirl of crashing waves.

And then the bow of the ship crumpled and ripped apart as it steamed full speed over itself along the line of jagged rocks. The water reverberated with the horrendous shrieking of metal, but the momentum of two hundred thousand tons of ship and cargo going twenty miles an hour just kept it plunging forward, rippling the bowline and spilling thousands and thousands of forty-foot shipping containers into the sea and over the shoals.

The cloud of drones dispersed, while many were caught in the collapsing towers of containers. The ship was already grounded up to its center tower when it started to break in half, flames erupting as the crash continued for nearly a minute more before the wreckage finally came to a stop.

The whole time Foxy roared away at full speed from the scene, increasing their view of the wreck.

The stern of the ship settled back against the shallows, and the bow remained buried under a ridgeline of multicolored shipping containers crawling with thousands of agitated and completely disorganized drones—some now flying around on fire. Billowing clouds of black smoke climbed into the sky, marking the spot.

McKinney nodded to herself. "Looks like colony cohesion has collapsed. That's not precisely how it works in the real world. I'll have to look at the model."

Odin just glared at her. "The hell you will. . . ."

CHAPTER 31

Reap the Whirlwind

Henry Clarke stood in front of his Reston, Virginia, office looking up at a crescent of ghostly white moon in the daytime sky of early spring. He'd never noticed that this place was actually beautiful.

A powerful V-8 engine rolled up somewhere behind him, followed by a few taps on a horn. He kept gazing at the woods just beyond the business park. How far did they go? Funny that he'd never wondered about that.

The whine of an electric window rolling down came to his ears, and he heard a familiar woman's voice shout, "Get in the car, Henry. We've got a disaster on our hands."

Clarke turned to see Marta peering out from the rear passenger seat of a black Cadillac Escalade. Steamlike emissions trailed from the tailpipe as the driver stood by, idling. Clarke walked toward the SUV as Marta's fingers drummed impatiently on the window frame.

She didn't look happy. "Why haven't you been returning messages? You're not even carrying your phone. I've been trying to find you all morning."

Clarke just stood silently at her window.

"What the hell is going on with you?" She grabbed her sunglasses from her purse and put them on with exaggerated irritation. "Get in the car!"

Clarke shook his head and looked around the parking lot. "I'm not coming."

She frowned and leaned forward. "Get in the damned car. I can't believe you aren't already scrambling to deal with this."

He gave her a blank look that must have spoken volumes.

She looked horrified. "Are you telling me you have no idea what's just happened?"

He shrugged. "I sure don't. And you know what? It's kind of nice not to know what's going on."

"I hope you're not still freaking out over your midnight visitor."

"He could just as easily have killed me, Marta. And what would have happened to him? Nothing. You and I both know it."

"Probably, but that's not the way it—"

"I had no idea I was signing on for that. I'm not a soldier."

"This is how the world works. Power comes at a price. Maybe now you'll realize there are one or two things I can still teach you."

He shook his head. "I've learned everything I want to know already. This isn't fun anymore. I need to get busy finding out what I want from life."

"Get in the damned car."

Clarke shook his head again. "I'm not getting in the car, Marta."

"This isn't a request." She pulled off her sunglasses again, her eyes boring into him. "There's a news story about to break in media outlets we have no control over. We've got to get out in front of this—disarm the opposition before our support in the House and Senate crumbles. There are hundreds of billions of dollars at stake, Henry. We need a full-court press, and it's going to take all of our resources to contain the damage. So get your ass in the car."

Clarke looked into her hazel eyes. He could see the unhappiness there. He'd never realized that before. It seemed a dismal prospect to think that this was all he could aspire to. "I'm done."

"You're done when I say you're done. There is the slight technical detail that you have a contract."

Clarke could smell her fear. "My company has a contract with your company. Remember, you didn't think enough of me at first to require my personal involvement. All you've got over me is a three-year noncompete clause." Clarke laughed ruefully. "And I won't be remaining in the profession."

Her eyes narrowed at him. "If you leave now, in the middle of this crisis, we will blackball you. You don't want to know what we can do to marginalize you, to discredit you—oh, but then again, maybe you do know."

He couldn't help but grin as he looked at her with something amounting to pity. "Who acts like this, Marta?" Clarke started walking along the horseshoe drive.

The black SUV rolled alongside him, keeping up. "You're like a mental patient."

He laughed, feeling lighter and happier with every step. "You know, I actually feel more sane than I've ever felt."

Her cell phone started warbling. "Last chance, Henry. If you don't get in this car immediately, you'll regret it."

At that he doubled his walking pace. It really was a beautiful spring day. He heard the electric window whine closed behind him, as the SUV's engine thrummed. It accelerated past him, the blacked-out windows sparing him her disdainful look.

Clarke smiled to himself—as though a huge weight had been lifted from his shoulders. He'd been dreading that conversation, and now it was over.

He watched her SUV halt at the entrance to the business park, signaling a right turn, heading to the centers of power.

Let them fight over it. He was done.

Suddenly a dark object streaked in silently from above—moving so fast he could barely perceive it. It impacted the black Escalade, waiting at the intersection, instantly detonating into a shock wave that sent metal parts, glass, hurtling into the air, followed quickly by a rolling fireball and a deafening BOOM that broke windows in the nearest office building. Car alarms started wailing all over the parking lot.

"Jesus!" Clarke was frozen in place on the sidewalk, watching the roiling flames as they consumed the twisted remains of Marta's SUV. People abandoned nearby cars and ran for safety. Others came out of nearby office lobbies to watch the vehicle burn. As spectators began to gather, Clarke pushed through them, passing dozens of people holding up their smartphones as they tried to take video of the wreckage.

CHAPTER 32

Prodigal Son

Professor Linda McKinney descended the folding steps of an un-marked Gulfstream V jet on the military side of Standiford Field in Louisville, Kentucky. It was early afternoon and a bright spring day, though a tad breezy. Cumulonimbus clouds dotted the sky like floating mountains. She closed her eyes and breathed in the fresh air. She was actually home—or at least where her parents had settled after her father retired.

She turned to see Odin in khaki slacks and a button-down blue shirt carrying a rucksack as he descended the steps behind her. A hard-faced Special Forces colonel stood waiting for them at the bottom of the steps. She recognized him from the video screen in Colorado—only this time he was real.

He extended his hand to Odin and gripped it firmly. "Congratulations, Master Sergeant. I knew if anyone could wreck their system, it would be you." He grimaced. "But did you really have to use a ship filled with BMWs to stop these things? That was quite a bill."

"I had to improvise, Colonel."

Odin stood alongside McKinney as the colonel nodded to her in turn. "Remember the terms of your debriefing, Professor. Until we locate the people behind this plot, you're still in danger. Are you sure you want to do this?"

She nodded. "I need to."

He nodded back. "Very well. Odin here will accompany you." He extended his thick, scarred hand to her. "Professor McKinney, the United States is grateful for your service."

She accepted his crushing grip.

"We might have reason to call on your expertise in the future. I hope you'll be willing to help us."

McKinney raised her eyebrows.

Odin stepped forward. "We can talk about that later, Colonel." They moved away across the tarmac.

The colonel called after him. "Take your time, Master Sergeant. Take all the time you need."

With that the colonel climbed into the jet, and a uniformed crewman pulled up the steps behind him, closing the door. The plane's engines whined to life as McKinney and Odin walked to a nearby hangar and a waiting civilian passenger van. It all seemed surreal as she looked around her. So normal.

After a few minutes of travel in silence, the van stopped near a public terminal. They disembarked, and Odin led them through a restricted access door, where two customs officials in uniform with IDs on lanyards waited for them.

Both men were in their fifties. One was pear-shaped and balding, with an extra chin; the other was thin and fit with a clean-cut appearance, despite his graying hair. He smiled to them both.

"Welcome back to the United States, Mr. Shaw. Ms. McKinney." He handed them both new, unstamped American passports. "You two have a nice day."

McKinney opened the passport, relieved to see her familiar, terrible photo. To have her identity back.

The other man entered a code on a keypad that unlocked a nearby steel door. He opened it to reveal a stairwell that led up.

Odin nodded to them both, and he and McKinney headed upstairs to a push door marked with warning signs that it must remain locked at all times. They pushed through and found themselves on the other side of the customs station and in the public air terminal among aircraft gates. Travelers walked past them.

People crowded around the many flat-screen televisions bolted at intervals along the length of the terminal. Cable news was on, and as they walked past, McKinney could see video images of a massive, smoking wreck viewed from the air—a colossal ship burning on shoals in the South China Sea.

McKinney slowed and craned her neck to look up at the screen along with fellow passengers.

The news anchor narrated the video. ". . . *felt the scope and sophistication of the plot presents a grave threat to UN member states. In the wake of the discovery both China and the U.S. have expressed support for an international robot arms control agreement to establish an international legal framework on the proliferation and use of lethally autonomous robots.*"

McKinney turned to Odin. She knew he could feel her gaze on him. A smile creased her lips.

"It's not over, you know." He nodded at the screen. "We set them back a year, maybe two."

"I'll take it." McKinney tugged at his arm and started them walking again. "It'll buy us civilians some time to sort things out. To let the law catch up with technology."

He shrugged. "We'll see about that. . . ."

Odin drove the rental car through suburban Shelbyville, past horse farms and orderly neighborhoods with lush trees and lawns. McKinney was deep in thought. "I guess this is the part where we try to figure out what's going on between us."

He grimaced. "You know how committed I am to my work. And I know how committed you are to yours."

She nodded, filled with conflicting emotions. Then she noticed that he was pulling into a park not quite in her father's neighborhood. "Where are we going? I thought we agreed you're taking me straight to my father's."

He pulled in to a parking space and shut off the engine. Then he faced her. "I said I was taking you to your father." He nodded through the windshield.

McKinney looked ahead to see her father sitting alone on a bench not far away, staring at ducks on a small pond. He stared expressionless, unmoving. "Oh, my God. Dad . . ."

She exited the car and walked across the grass behind him, feeling the tears on her face. But then she thought better of it, stopping to wipe them away as she collected herself.

Her father looked thinner. His bushy hair had become whiter.

After a moment she came up behind him. It took everything she had not to well up with emotion. "Dad . . ."

He turned on the bench, and the moment he saw her, the face she had so missed returned. His expression slowly turned to a tight smile, and he stood, walking toward her, accelerating as he came. "My little girl . . ." Then he wrapped his arms around her in a crushing embrace, and she began to cry along with him.

"I'd thought I lost you." He started to shudder with sobs, holding her even tighter.

She hugged him back. "No. I'm right here. I'm right here."

"What happened to you? Are you okay?"

"I'm fine. The State Department helped me get back, but I can't stay."

He leaned back to look at her, puzzled. "But why? And why didn't they contact us? Why didn't you call from . . . I don't understand."

"I'll explain later." McKinney pivoted to see Odin watching from near the car. He nodded to her.

"Hey!" McKinney pulled away to look her father in the eye. "There's someone I want you to meet."

He held her chin, still smiling at her. "I can't believe it's really you. I can't believe you're here, safe."

McKinney shouted and waved at Odin. "Get over here, you coward!"

Odin appeared to sigh impatiently, but he got out and approached them.

McKinney turned to her father. "Dad, this is the man who saved my life."

Her father turned to face Odin and his extended hand, but her father's expression changed, and he launched past it to hug Odin tightly. "My God, thank you. Thank you for bringing my girl back to us."

McKinney could see the emotions coursing through Odin as her father gripped him.

Her father held tight, slapping Odin on the back. "Thank you."

Odin nodded. "You're welcome, Mr. McKinney."

Her father pulled away to look Odin in the face. He extended his hand. "What's your name, son?"

McKinney shook her head. "Dad, he can't—"

Odin shook her father's hand. "David Shaw, sir."

McKinney gave him a stunned look.

"David. It's an honor to meet you. I don't know how I can ever thank you for bringing her back."

"There's no need, sir."

"I have to hear all about it." Her father motioned for them to start walking along the path, and he leaned toward Odin as he hooked his daughter's elbow. "What on earth happened back in Africa? I hired investigators, and—"

"In a moment, Dad. I need you to do something for me first."

"Anything, honey. Anything at all." He was smiling.

"Can you loan me your phone for a second?"

"Oh, to call your brothers? Of course. My God, they're going to be so, so happy. . . ." He reached into his jacket pocket and passed her his phone.

McKinney took it, cocked her arm back, and threw it into the very center of the nearby pond, sending the ducks into flight.

Her father looked at her, and then to the pond, in utter confusion. "What on earth did you do that for?"

She looped her arms under her father's and Odin's elbows and started them along the path. "Let's just call it a precaution." McKinney grinned as her father still looked back, puzzled.

They passed under a tree branch on which two ravens perched. The birds fluffed up their feathers and let out a loud *caw* as they closely watched the humans below.

Further Reading

You can learn more about the technologies and themes explored in *Kill Decision* by visiting www.daniel-suarez.com or through the following books:

Adventures Among Ants by Mark W. Moffett (University of California Press)

Ant Colony Optimization and Swarm Intelligence by Marco Dorigo, Luca Maria Gambardella, Mauro Birattari, Christian Blum, et al. (Springer-Verlag)

Blank Spots on the Map: The Dark Geography of the Pentagon's Secret World by Trevor Paglen (Dutton)

Inside Delta Force by Eric L. Haney (Delacorte Press)

Killer Elite by Michael Smith (St. Martin's Griffin)

The Master Switch by Tim Wu (Knopf)

Masters of Chaos: The Secret History of the Special Forces by Linda Robinson (PublicAffairs)

Mind of the Raven by Bernd Heinrich (Ecco)

On Killing: The Psychological Cost of Learning to Kill in War and Society by Lt. Col. Dave Grossman (Little, Brown)

Roughneck Nine-One by Frank Antenori and Hans Halberstadt (St. Martin's Griffin)

The Super-Organism by Bert Hölldobler and E. O. Wilson (W.W. Norton)

Swarm Intelligence by James Kennedy and Russell C. Eberhart (Morgan Kaufmann)

Tactics of the Crescent Moon by H. John Poole (Posterity Press)

Top Secret America: The Rise of the New American Security State by Dana Priest and William M. Arkin (Little, Brown)

The Watchers: The Rise of America's Surveillance State by Shane Harris (Penguin Press)

What Technology Wants by Kevin Kelly (Viking)

Wired for War: The Robotics Revolution and Conflict in the 21st Century by P. W. Singer (Penguin Press)

The Wrong War: Grit, Strategy, and the Way Out of Afghanistan by Bing West (Random House)

Acknowledgments

It would have been impossible to complete this book without the gracious assistance of many people. Thanks to John Robb at Global Guerrillas for sharing his extensive knowledge of all things military and otherwise. Thanks also to Chris Paget for providing an up-close view of what was possible in a DIY airborne-hacking platform. Thanks as well to rock-climbing (and atomic clock) expert Eric Burt for helping me learn the ropes. Likewise, my continued gratitude to Christopher Pearson.

Sincere thanks to Frank Antenori, William M. Arkin, Mauro Birattari, Christian Blum, Marco Dorigo, Russell C. Eberhart, Dalton Fury, Lt. Col. Dave Grossman, Hans Halberstadt, Eric L. Haney, Bernd Heinrich, Bert Hölldobler, Kevin Kelly, James Kennedy, Mark W. Moffett, Trevor Paglen, H. John Poole, Dana Priest, Linda Robinson, P. W. Singer, Michael Smith, Bing West, E. O. Wilson, and Tim Wu—scholars all, whose published works greatly enriched this story.

I'd also like to thank Viviana Pendrill, Trenton Broughton, and Christoffer Kuja-Halkola for assistance with Spanish, Mandarin, and Swedish dialogue (respectively).

As always, my thanks to Adam Winston and Don Lamoreaux for last-minute notes. Likewise to my literary agent, Rafe Sagalyn, and the entire team at Sagalyn Literary. Also a huge thanks to my editor, Ben Sevier, at Dutton for seeing the potential in this topic and this story.

And most importantly: heartfelt thanks to my wife, Michelle, for her counsel, friendship, and affection. This journey would be no fun without her.

About the Author

DANIEL SUAREZ is the author of the national bestseller *Daemon* and *Freedom*™, and is an independent systems consultant to Fortune 1000 companies. He has designed and developed software for the defense, finance, and entertainment industries. He has also been an invited speaker at the headquarters of Microsoft, Google, Amazon, and The Long Now Foundation. Suarez lives in Los Angeles.